A SAVAGE FEUD

HEATHER ATKINSON

B

Boldwood

First published in Great Britain in 2023 by Boldwood Books Ltd.

A CIP catalogue record for this book is available from the British Library.

Paperback ISBN 978-1-80415-202-7

Large Print ISBN 978-1-80415-200-3

Hardback ISBN 978-1-80415-201-0

Ebook ISBN 978-1-80415-204-1

Kindle ISBN 978-1-80415-203-4

Audio CD ISBN 978-1-80415-195-2

MP3 CD ISBN 978-1-80415-196-9

Digital audio download ISBN 978-1-80415-197-6

Boldwood Books Ltd
23 Bowerdean Street
London SW6 3TN
www.boldwoodbooks.com

1

Dean parked his four-year-old silver Vauxhall Insignia at the kerb and switched off the engine. He turned to study the mansion, gazing at it through the open gates and up the drive to the grand red sandstone building, which was situated in the west end of Glasgow.

'What do you think?' he said.

'It's pretentious,' replied Carly. 'It's even got a fountain.'

'From what I've heard, the person who lives in it is pretentious too.'

'Judging by this house he must be loaded, so how come he's into the Tallan family for fifty grand?'

'He's probably a tinpot millionaire. All show, no substance. He doesn't own the house, he rents it. That fancy Porsche on the drive is most likely on tick.'

'What's his name?'

'Victor Wellington.'

'Sounds like a twat.'

'Aye,' chuckled Dean.

Carly turned to face him and smiled. 'Let's get it done then.'

Dean smiled back at her. He thought she was the most beautiful woman he'd ever seen, as well as the smartest and toughest. It had been six months since he, his brother and father had moved to Haghill to help Carly and her sisters when they'd had trouble with another local family. He'd shared a kiss with her and confessed his feelings but she'd told him she needed time to get over her ex, a little scrote called Cole Alexander. He had hoped they would be together by now, but she hadn't mentioned anything happening between them since and he was starting to lose hope. On the bright side, she hadn't dated any other men, despite plenty of them sniffing around. Sometimes he wondered if them not getting together would be for the best. After all, they were cousins, their fathers were brothers, but he loved Carly far too much to allow that to get in the way and his feelings for her only grew by the day.

They got out of the car and wandered up the drive to the front door. They were dressed smartly, Dean in a sharp light grey suit and Carly in black trousers, high-heeled boots and cropped black jacket. Her long light brown hair was tied back into a high ponytail. Dean thought she looked strong and business-like.

Carly knocked and the front door was pulled open by a short, stocky man with a terrible dark brown toupee perched atop his round head. In one hand he held a mugful of coffee.

'What do you want?' he demanded.

'We've been sent by the Tallans,' replied Dean politely. 'It's time to pay up.'

The man looked them up and down, his gaze lingering longer on Carly. 'Rod and Neil are sending wee lassies to do their dirty work now, are they?'

'It would be preferable if we discussed this inside,' said Carly, ignoring the stupid comment.

'Fine, come in then,' he replied, appearing amused by the whole thing.

As he wandered back into the house, casually sipping his coffee, Dean and Carly glanced at each other. They weren't used to this reaction. They were working as debt collectors for the Tallan family and usually the people they visited were on their knees, begging and pleading.

Still, they stepped inside, Dean closing the door behind them.

'Something isn't right,' whispered Carly.

'I agree,' replied Dean. 'Stay alert.'

They followed Victor down the long, ornate hallway, the marble floor gleaming, an enormous chandelier hanging over their heads. They entered a large, elegant lounge that was the essence of minimalism, all the furniture white. The thick carpet was a light cream colour, giving the eyes some slight relief.

Victor stood in the middle of the lounge.

'Where's the money?' Dean demanded of him.

'I've got it,' replied Victor casually.

'Good. If you could hand it over then we can get out of your hair,' said Dean, eyes slipping to the terrible toupee.

Victor took his time replying, sipping his coffee and swallowing it before smiling smugly. 'You're no' getting it.'

'Excuse me?' said Dean, a little nonplussed but doing a good job of hiding it.

'I said you're no' getting it. I've decided to keep it.'

'The Tallans won't like that.'

'The Tallans can go fuck themselves.'

'That's not a very wise thing to say.'

'They can't be the hard men they make themselves out to be if they're sending in weans to do their dirty work.'

'You shouldn't judge by appearances.'

'Aye, I'm sure you're big and tough when you're battering

fifteen-year-olds for their pocket money but me and my pals are a different matter.'

'Pals?'

'Come on in, boys,' called Victor.

A door behind him opened and in walked three large, aggressive-looking men.

'Where did this bunch of orangutans come from?' said Carly.

Their lack of fear puzzled Victor but he quickly shook it off. 'I wouldn't call them that,' he said. 'You'll only make them angrier. They're pissed off that you're trying to take my money from me.'

'Money you borrowed,' Dean told him. 'And so far, you've no' paid back a penny.'

'And I don't intend to. Now, you can either leave in one piece or my pals here will rip your limbs off. Your choice.'

'You're no' gonnae be smart and just pay up?'

'The smart thing would be for you two to get lost while your kneecaps still work.'

Dean looked to Carly. 'You take the one on the left and I'll deal with the other two,' he said under his breath.

'Nae bother,' she replied.

The wink she gave him sent tingles racing down Dean's spine. In fact, he almost forgot about the three violent men in the room.

They turned back to face their aggressors. The three men stepped forward, flexing their muscles while a smug Victor retreated into a corner, out of harm's way, that insufferable smirk still plastered to his face.

While Dean ran at two of the men, Carly produced a small baton from inside her jacket and smashed it into the face of the third man when he stomped up to her. He dropped to his knees, eyes wide with shock. He was sent crashing sideways to the floor when Dean hurled one of his friends into him and they fell in a tangled heap.

Victor could only watch in horror as his third and final man received a kick to the chin from Dean that sent him staggering backwards into the fireplace, which fortunately wasn't lit. As Dean grabbed the man by the front of the shirt and pulled him towards him while drawing back his fist, Victor realised he'd made a huge error and ran for the door at the back of the room that led into the kitchen.

'I've got him,' said Carly.

As Victor reached the back door, she drew a taser from her jacket pocket, aimed and pressed the button. The two barbed electrodes embedded themselves in his back. Victor dropped to the floor, landing on his side, jumping and jerking, face screwed up with pain. All he could do was stare up at Carly, who glared down at him pitilessly.

'You're a really stupid man,' she told him while yanking the electrodes free from his back. 'You do know that, don't you? The Tallans don't employ us for no reason.'

Dean joined her in the kitchen. 'Where's the money?' he demanded.

Victor opened his mouth to reply but all that came out was a weak groan. At least his body had stopped twitching.

'If you cannae tell us, then you can show us.'

Dean dragged him to his feet by the back of his shirt. Victor's toupee slipped sideways off his head and landed on the floor, revealing his shiny, bald pate, making Carly chuckle.

'Where is it?' Dean asked him, easily bearing his weight with one hand.

Victor attempted to speak again but he just groaned, drool dripping from one side of his mouth and running down his chin.

'Your taser's really done him in.' Dean grinned at Carly.

'Serves him right,' she replied.

'I don't think he'd keep the cash in here. Let's try the lounge.

Are we getting warmer, Victor?' he said as he dragged him out of the kitchen.

This time, Victor managed to nod. The three men were still lying on the floor, in pain.

Dean marched Victor out of the lounge and into the hall. 'Which way?'

Victor raised a shaky hand and pointed to a door further down the hall. Dean marched him to it and shoved it open to reveal a study.

'Safe,' Victor managed to breathe.

They all looked to the silver door with the dial set into the wall behind the grand oak desk.

He was manoeuvred towards the safe before being dumped on the floor before it.

'Keep an eye on the others,' Dean told Carly.

She nodded, loaded a fresh gas cartridge into the taser and repacked the electrodes before leaving the room.

Dean was a menacing shadow looming over Victor as he opened the safe with weak, shaky hands. He struggled pulling the door open, so Dean did it for him to reveal an enormous pile of cash inside.

'Jesus, Victor,' he said. 'There's way more than fifty grand here. Why didn't you just hand it over?'

Victor's response was another groan accompanied by more drool.

'You're an idiot,' commented Dean as he began taking out stacks of cash.

He looked around for something to put them in and spotted a carrier bag on the desk. He snatched it up and realised there was something inside. With a smile, Dean pulled a curly blonde toupee out of the bag.

'Here you go, pal,' he said, dumping it on Victor's head, the price tag sticking up out of the top of it.

After stuffing the money into the bag, Dean closed the safe and got to his feet.

'Good news,' he told Victor, who remained limp on the floor. 'You've paid off your debt to the Tallans. Well done,' he added sardonically.

He was alarmed by a crash from the direction of the lounge and he raced out of the office, down the hall and into the room to find Carly wrestling for the taser with the man he'd thrown.

'Carly,' he cried, rushing to help her.

He needn't have worried. She kicked the man in the knee, causing him to stumble forward before bringing her own knee up under his chin, snapping back his head. Carly tore the taser from the man's hand, pointed it at him and pressed the trigger. The barbs struck him in the abdomen and his body spasmed before he fell.

'Let's get out of here,' said Dean when the man's two friends began hauling themselves to their feet.

As they raced out of the room, the other two men made chase. Dean snatched up a vase of flowers from the hallway table and threw it to the floor where it smashed, spattering water across the shiny marble floor. The two men slipped in it, their trainers making a squeaking sound as they frantically attempted to remain upright before landing heavily on their backs.

Dean and Carly were laughing as they ran out of the front door and down the drive. They hopped into the car, Dean handing Carly the bagful of money so he could drive.

'That has to be my favourite job we've done for the Tallans so far,' said Carly as they set off. 'The way Victor's wig fell off was hilarious.'

'And those orangutans slipping in the water,' he said, smiling.

'That was a great idea of yours. How much did Victor cough up?'

'The whole fifty grand. His safe was stuffed full of cash, so maybe he's no' such a tinpot millionaire after all.'

'Hmm.' She frowned.

'What is it?'

'If he has so much ready cash, why borrow off the Tallans?'

'Some people are just greedy.'

'Or there's more going on than we know. We've been doing this job for six months now and everyone we've visited for the Tallans has paid up no problem because they've been shit scared. None of them lived in posh drums like that.'

'Whatever's going on, it's none of our business. We did what we needed to do. Job done.'

'It won't be that simple if we've just done over someone dangerous.'

'Dangerous? That wee fanny in the wig?'

'We really have no idea who he is.'

Dean considered her words before replying, 'We'll see what David says when he asks how the collection went.' David was their point of contact for the Tallans. Carly and Dean rarely had anything to do with Neil and Rod directly, who were in charge of the family.

'He won't give anything away,' replied Carly. 'David has a face like a brick. I'd hate to play poker with him.'

'It's worth a try. We'll mention it to my da' too. He's in the know.'

Carly just nodded, thinking it was the only thing they could do and hoping she was letting her imagination run away with her. Life had been pretty peaceful for the last six months, the only worry her father's health. He had Parkinson's disease and every month his condition seemed to degenerate. Just the thought of losing him turned her cold.

Dean glanced sideways at Carly when she suddenly fell silent. From the pained look in her eyes, he knew she was thinking about her father. It surprised him how well he understood her. He'd spent the majority of his twenty-three years on this planet being baffled by women but Carly he could read in an instant. He got her but she got him too.

2

Dean drove them to a gym in Springburn, a district in Glasgow that was run by the Tallan family who also owned the gym. The pretty blonde receptionist gave Dean a smile and a coy wave. When he waved back, she giggled and twisted a curl of hair around her finger.

Dean and Carly walked inside the large, modern building to find their contact, David, talking in the gym's café with a man with a large forehead and knuckles covered in thick black hair. David looked like a typical ned in his tracksuit and baseball cap but he was extremely intelligent. He was also quiet, thoughtful and respectful, even to those he didn't like. David was always polite and never dismissive, even though Carly and Dean were at least ten years younger than he was.

'Office,' was all David said to them.

They nodded and headed straight there without a word, passing floor-to-ceiling windows through which they could see people working out. They walked into the sparse office that contained only a desk, a couple of chairs and a filing cabinet. Five minutes later, David entered.

'How did it go?' he asked.

'We got the money,' said Dean, holding the carrier bag out to him.

'But from your expression I can see there was some trouble,' said David, opening the bag and peering inside.

Dean had enormous respect for this man. He didn't miss a trick. 'We did. Victor had three men with him, but they were nae bother.'

'Glad to hear it,' said David as he produced the money from the bag, placed it on the desk and sat down to count it.

Neither Dean nor Carly took offence as this was part of the routine.

David frowned into the bottom of the bag. 'Why is there hair in here?'

'Victor was keeping one of his wigs in it.'

David cracked a rare smile. 'He always was a vain bastard. What he's never understood is that he looks even more repulsive with the wigs.'

'This one was a curly blond one. He looked a proper fanny in it.'

'I can imagine,' said David, turning his attention back to the money, indicating the conversation was at an end.

That was another thing Dean liked about him – he didn't talk much.

The two cousins waited in patient silence for David to finish counting.

'Fifty thousand exactly,' he eventually announced. 'Exemplary work as always. Rod and Neil will be pleased.'

'We were surprised Victor put up a fight,' said Carly, keen for more information. 'He was really confident we wouldn't be getting a penny. I've never known anyone to challenge the Tallan brothers before.'

David's narrow gaze studied her curiously. It seemed he'd

worked out she was fishing for information. 'If you have a question, Carly, just ask.'

'Why did he think he was strong enough to go up against them?' she replied, undeterred. 'Dean said he had more than enough money to cover the debt.'

'Victor's always been greedy and greedy people don't like settling their debts.'

'He was very confident that Rod and Neil weren't a threat to him. Is Victor in with someone nasty who may come after us for what we did to him?'

The thought appeared to amuse David. 'No. He's nothing more than an unpleasant wee tick with a gambling problem. This cash was no doubt a rare lucky win for him at the casino and he couldnae bear to part with it. He saw you were young and thought you would be easy targets, an assumption you no doubt made him regret?'

Carly and Dean nodded.

'Good. And that's all there is to it. No insidious plot, I'm afraid.'

'That's disappointing,' said Carly with a cheerful smile to hide her embarrassment at being caught out.

David didn't reply. Instead, he delved into one of the desk drawers and produced two large wads of notes bundled up in elastic bands. 'Payment,' he said, dumping them on the desk.

Carly and Dean took them without a word and slipped them into their jacket pockets.

'Good work. We'll be in touch soon.'

The two of them nodded and left. The man with the hairy knuckles was hanging about in reception and regarded them curiously as they passed. With his pot belly, large yellow teeth and nicotine-stained fingers, he didn't look like the type to frequent a gym. Dean nodded at him but the man didn't return the gesture. However, his gaze was curious rather than hostile.

'So it seems there's nothing to worry about,' Carly told Dean once they were back in the car. 'Victor just didn't want to pay up.'

'You sound sceptical about that explanation,' said Dean, pulling on his seat belt.

'Because I am. I'm sure more's going on than we know. The way that gorilla with the hairy hands looked at us as we left was weird too.'

'He was probably just wondering who we are. A lot of people are curious about what the Tallans and their associates get up to.'

'Maybe.'

'You look edgy.'

'I just hate feeling that other people know what's really going on and our family's stuck in the middle, clueless.'

'We're the lower orders, so we'll never know more than the higher-ups.'

'I don't like being called the lower orders.' She frowned at him.

Dean smiled, amused. 'But that's what we are.'

'We won't always be,' she said determinedly.

'We can but hope.'

'How can you sound so casual about all this?' she said as Dean started the car. 'We could be caught in the middle of something nasty.'

'Or David might have been right and we're not.'

'He was hiding something, I'm sure of it.'

'What makes you so certain?'

'Women's intuition and don't you dare laugh,' she said, narrowing her eyes at him.

'I wouldn't dream of it. My da' might know something.'

Carly nodded. There was little else they could do.

* * *

Eddie was standing at the door, ready to greet Carly and Dean with a big smile as they entered the flat Carly shared with her sisters and father, hands resting on his pendulous beer belly.

'How did it go?' he asked them. 'I hope you got the cash?'

'We did,' replied Dean. 'All of it.'

'Good, well done,' he replied, patting his son and then his niece on the shoulder.

They entered the kitchen, which was the heart of the flat now that the living room had been turned into a bedroom.

The three of them took a seat at the kitchen table with Harry, the elder of Eddie's two sons and Jane, Carly's older sister. Harry and Jane also worked together as debt collectors for the Tallans. Harry was big, blond and muscular, like his younger brother, and Jane was tall and lithe, just like Carly. However, while Carly had long light brown hair, Jane had cropped hers short.

'How's Da' been?' was Carly's first question.

'Great,' said Jane. 'I made him Thai green curry and he ate the lot.'

'That's great news.'

'He's fast asleep now, so it's safe to talk.'

'That's good because there's something we need to discuss. A weird thing happened this morning.'

After explaining the situation and David's response to it, they all sat back in thoughtful silence.

'I've heard of Victor Wellington,' said Eddie, who was the first to break the silence. 'Wee prick in a wig?'

'That's him,' said Dean.

'He must have paid those gorillas to attack you. He doesnae have any muscle of his own.'

'What is he involved with?'

'Nothing dodgy really. He's a degenerate gambler, which is why he keeps getting into debt, but he's also an astute businessman with his own successful property development company. He could be one of the richest men in the city if he could get his addictions under control. He's a coke head as well as a gambling addict.'

'Oh,' said Carly.

'You look disappointed, hen.' Eddie smiled.

'I just thought there was more going on than David was saying, especially when Victor thought he could get away with not paying the Tallans.'

'If there is I cannae see how. But he must know they'd have his kneecaps broken for not paying up or that they might torch that wanky Porsche of his.'

'They wouldn't kill him then?'

'What's the point in that? A deid man cannae cough up. I reckon he got caught up in his greed and put his cash before his health. That does happen a lot.'

'Aye, probably,' replied Carly, her voice full of doubt. 'Then why was that hairy guy staring at us at the gym?'

Eddie's eyes twinkled with amusement. 'You're a very pretty lassie and men like to look at pretty lassies.'

'It wasn't that sort of look. He was staring at Dean too.'

'Maybe he swings both ways?' chuckled Harry.

Carly rolled her eyes. 'It was like he was trying to figure out what we were doing there.'

'What's weird about that? Everyone knows David works for the Tallans. He might have been trying to work out how you two fit into the operation.'

'That was probably it,' said Dean.

'Don't look so serious,' Eddie told his niece when she frowned. 'It's all fine. Don't start seeing conspiracies where there aren't any.'

'I'm still not convinced of that. Something about today felt all off.'

'We should listen to Carly,' interjected Jane when Eddie opened his mouth to reply.

'Don't tell me you think there's some big plot too?' Harry asked her.

'Why not? I certainly wouldn't put it past the Tallan brothers. They're as slippery as eels.'

'I'm not saying there's a conspiracy against us,' said Carly. 'But we could well get caught up in one and I think we should stay on our guard.'

'Sounds like a good idea,' said Jane.

Eddie looked to Dean. 'What do you think about all this?'

'Carly has a point,' he replied.

'Harry?' said Eddie.

'There's no harm in erring on the side of caution,' he replied.

Eddie rolled his eyes. 'Weans,' he sighed. 'All right, fine. We'll stay alert. Happy now?' he asked Carly.

'I feel a bit better,' she replied.

'Good. Well, we've nothing else to do today, so you can all sod off and do whatever disgusting things you get up to on your time off.'

There was the tinkle of a bell and Carly got to her feet. 'That's Da'. I'll go and see him.'

'I'll come with you,' replied Jane.

Eddie didn't speak until the two women had left the room.

'Right, you,' he said to Dean. 'Was there really something strange about what happened today or were you only agreeing with Carly because you're into her?'

'No, she's right. Victor's confidence that he could keep the money he'd borrowed was out of character because he did seem like a wee coward.'

'Maybe he'd heard something that convinced him the Tallans are done?' said Harry.

This comment gave Eddie cause for concern. 'I'll ask around, see what I can find out. Harry, can you gi'e me and your brother a minute?'

'No problem,' he replied. 'I need to nip to the shop anyway.'

Harry left, shutting the door as he went.

'I'm going to ask you a question, son,' began Eddie. 'And I want you to give me an honest answer – has anything ever happened between you and Carly while you've been out working together?'

'No,' replied Dean.

'Good. I know how you feel about that lassie but nothing can happen.'

'Why would it be so bad?'

'Because you're first cousins.'

'So what? It's legal.'

'But not accepted. People would look at you like you were a couple of freaks.'

'I don't care what anyone thinks.'

Eddie's look was disapproving. 'I had hoped your feelings for her would have faded but they're getting stronger. Maybe you should return to Clydebank?'

'No,' he retorted. 'I am not leaving my family. You want to send me back there alone while you all stay here?'

'I don't want to but I might have no choice.'

'I'm no' a wean any more, Da'. You cannae just send me away. I'm a man and I choose where I want to live.'

'Think about it – if you get together with Carly and it goes wrong, it'll tear this family in two and I'm no' losing my brother again, no' when I've just got him back. It would mess up everything for us just when we're finally making some serious money. This is our big chance and your hormones are no' gonnae ruin it.'

Dean sighed. 'Look, I understand your concerns but you don't need to worry. Carly told me a while ago that nothing can happen.'

'Oh,' said Eddie, looking happier. 'So she's no' into you then?'

'That wee tit Cole really hurt her. She's not interested in another relationship.'

'So that's why she turns down every man who comes sniffing round. Well, it's only a matter of time before she takes one up on their offer, she's a fantastic lassie. That's another reason why I don't want you getting with her – you'd only end up hurting her like you did every other girl you dated.'

'Not all of them,' he muttered.

'Aye, all of them because they're no' intellectual enough or they talk too much or their voice gets on your nerves. It always starts well then something happens and it goes down the pan.' Eddie sighed heavily. 'Surely you understand my fears?'

'Course I do but I've never felt like this before. I couldn't hurt her.'

'Find some other girl. It doesn't have to be anything serious but get your mind off Carly.'

'I wish I could. It's bloody torture,' Dean sighed, dragging his hands through his hair.

'Maybe I should team you up with Jane and send Harry out with Carly? I should have done that in the first place but Jane and Harry work so well together.'

'Me and Carly work well together too. We handled those men today no problem because we're totally in sync. If we hadn't been, it could easily have gone bad.'

Eddie nodded. 'All right, I'll do you a deal – you can carry on working with Carly as long as you get your mind off her and onto someone else.'

'You're actually telling me to find another woman?'

'Aye I am. There are loads of them out there who you aren't related to. Fall in love with one of them because if you don't then you won't work with Carly again.'

Dean scowled and folded his arms across his chest but they were forced to halt the conversation when Jane and Carly returned to the room.

'Da' wants a brew.' Carly smiled. 'Anyone else want one?'

'Aye, sounds good, hen,' said Eddie.

Carly opened the fridge and frowned. 'Bugger, we're out of milk.'

'I'll go and get some,' said Dean, getting to his feet. 'I could use some fresh air anyway,' he added with a scowl at his father.

'Thanks,' called Carly, missing the atmosphere between father and son.

Eddie was disheartened by the way she looked over her shoulder at Dean as he left and her eyes sparkled. It seemed his son was wrong when he'd said she wasn't interested in another relationship. He had to do something about the pair of them and fast before their feelings for each other destroyed the family.

3

Rose, Carly and Jane's younger sister, returned home from school later that afternoon looking tired and washed out. This was so at odds with her usual chirpy, exuberant personality that both her sisters were immediately concerned.

'Are you okay?' Jane asked her. 'You don't look well.'

'I had my maths exam today,' she muttered, slumping into a chair at the kitchen table. 'It went crap.' Sixteen-year-old Rose was taking her SQA exams at high school.

'Why? You're good at maths.'

'I forgot everything. It was like my brain froze. Exams are so shite. Every subject should just be coursework, like photography. Tamara's developed Tourette's with the pressure. She keeps shouting and swearing.'

'She did that anyway,' replied Jane wryly.

'Aye but she cannae control it now. She's been diagnosed by her doctor and everything,' Rose said, wide-eyed.

'I know it's hard but they'll soon be over. You've only got three exams left, is that right?'

Rose nodded miserably. 'Geography, English and Spanish. I can't wait until it's finished.'

'When they're over, we'll take you out for the day, wherever you want to go.'

'Great,' she said, looking more cheerful. 'Harry, Dean and Uncle Eddie too?'

'If you like.'

Rose's smile fell. 'What about Da'?'

'We can get Mary from next door to sit with him. Have a think about where you want to go.'

'Will do. It's my turn to make tea. What do you fancy?'

'I'll do that,' said Carly. 'You rest. You look knackered.'

'Cheers,' yawned Rose. 'I've got more revision to do. I also need a shower after how much I was sweating in that assembly hall.'

Rose left the room, looking miserable.

'Poor love,' said Jane. 'She'll be much better once her exams are finally out of the way; they've been stressing her out for months. It's wrong putting weans under so much pressure.'

'Aye it is. I remember it well. I threw up before each exam.'

'You still passed though and Rose will too.'

'We can but hope. The last thing we want is her getting into the business we're in. I still can't believe I'm a debt collector for a couple of gangsters. That is not how I saw my future.'

Concern filled Jane's eyes. 'Do you want out?'

'No. The weird thing is, I enjoy it.'

'The work, or spending so much time with Dean? Don't give me that haughty look. I know you have feelings for him. It's obvious every time you look at him.'

'No, it's not.'

'Maybe not to anyone else but I know you too well.'

Carly sighed. 'Aye, all right, I do, but I won't do anything about it.'

'Because he's your cousin?'

'Honestly, that doesn't bother me. I just don't want to get into another relationship, not after what Cole did to me. That bastard tore my heart out and I can't go through that again.'

'Understandable.'

'I've had enough of men. Maybe I'll go gay?'

'I think the best thing you can do is be on your own for a while.'

'That's the problem, I've been on my own for a year and a half,' said Carly miserably.

Jane's heart went out to her sister. She was lonely but too afraid of being hurt again. 'One day it will get better,' she said, thinking how lame the words sounded.

When they heard the bell in their father's room ringing, Carly got to her feet. 'I'll go.'

'Cheers, love,' replied Jane, watching her younger sister tramp out of the room looking as miserable as Rose had. After everything Cole had put Carly through, Jane thought it so cruel that she'd now fallen for a man she couldn't be with.

* * *

'All right, Da'?' Carly smiled as she entered her father's room. He used to be in the bedroom at the front, which had originally been the lounge, until Cole's brother Ross had lobbed a brick through the window. That had forced him to swap rooms with Jane and once the trouble with the Alexander family had been put to bed, he'd elected to stay in that room at the back of the flat.

Alec Savage had once been fierce and strong. Although he'd never strayed into criminal activity like his brother, nephews and daughters, he had once been a force to be reckoned with in Haghill. Standing at six foot three, he'd been a builder and a talented amateur rugby player. That only made the fact that he was now practically bedridden even harder for him to deal with. All the muscle and bulk was slowly wasting away, his face growing thinner and paler because he rarely left the flat any more.

'Sorry... to disturb you,' he breathed, having to take his time pronouncing the words because it was getting increasingly difficult for him to talk.

'You could never disturb me, Da'.' She smiled, perching on the edge of his bed. 'I love spending time with you.'

He attempted to smile but his face was even more mask-like than usual, another effect of the illness. But Carly could see the love and affection shining out of his eyes and that was enough for her.

'My book,' he mumbled, nodding at the table at the far side of the room.

'Nae bother,' she said, getting up to retrieve it. Carly pulled the table across the bed. It was the sort that was on wheels and was used in hospitals. She then set up the book stand and placed the book on it, open at the right page.

'Thanks, sweetheart,' he mumbled.

'You're welcome,' she said chirpily. Carly often wondered if her father had worked out what his daughters were really up to. They'd told him she and Jane were working as debt collectors but they'd made out it was legitimate work for a finance company, jobs they'd got thanks to a friend of Eddie's. If he didn't believe them then he hadn't said but he was not a stupid man. Perhaps he simply wasn't up to facing the truth? He already had enough to contend with on a daily basis.

'Keep an eye on Rose,' he told her. 'She's struggling. Exams.'

'I know. Don't worry, we'll make sure she's okay. We promised to take her out for the day after she's finished. That cheered her up.'

'Good idea.' Alec leaned back into his pillow, looking tired. 'You're not okay?'

'I'm fine. I always am.'

'No. Cole hurt you. Now you're always so sad.'

'He did hurt me, but I'm not always sad.'

'You are. I can see it.'

'Why would I be sad? Life's getting a lot easier and I love having all the family around.'

'There's more than that,' he said, reaching out to take her hand.

Carly decided not to say that she constantly worried about him and dreaded the day she would have to say goodbye forever. The thought of it was more than she could bear.

'No, really,' she said, forcing another smile. 'I'm good.'

'Life is short. Do whatever it takes to make you happy.'

Carly's thoughts immediately leapt to Dean. Had her father picked up on that? She dismissed the idea. He was just giving her a pep talk.

'I will, Da'. Don't worry.'

She sat with him while he watched one of his beloved cookery programmes before nodding off as the programme ended. Carly returned to the kitchen to find Jane in conference with Jennifer, her second-in-command of the Unbeatable Bitches, the girl gang she ran. Jane had given up the leadership when their father became ill but six months ago she'd taken it back from Emma, who was using the women to do the bidding of the Alexander family. Jennifer had fully supported Jane taking back control and had helped ensure the other women felt the same way. Jane hadn't encountered much resistance, Emma's few supporters having left with her. Jennifer was a pretty woman in her early twenties with long black hair. Her nose was pierced and she had piercings all the way up her left ear.

'Hi Carly,' lisped Jennifer, who was cradling a mug of tea. 'How's your da' doing?'

'Not so bad, thanks,' replied Carly, joining them at the kitchen table. 'He's asleep now. Why are you talking like that?'

Jennifer grinned and stuck out her tongue. Carly's stomach lurched at the sight of the silver barbell through it. She'd never been a fan of piercings, she didn't even have her ears pierced. The prospect of having a needle stabbed through a part of her anatomy never failed to make her feel queasy.

'Oh, nice,' she said uncertainly.

'I don't think you mean that,' said Jennifer with mischief in her eyes. 'You've gone pale.'

'It was just unexpected, that's all. Did it hurt?'

'Like a bastard. As soon as he put the needle in, blood spurted out of my tongue. It's a muscle you see, so it's no' like having your ears or nose done. You okay?' she added when Carly looked down at her hands.

'Aye, fine,' she replied before taking in a long deep breath to try and control her churning stomach. She'd watched Brian Alexander have his nails pulled out with pliers and not felt a thing, so she should be able to tolerate Jennifer's piercing.

'You're one hard bitch, Carly Savage. Don't tell me you've got a phobia of needles?'

Carly raised her head proudly. 'Naw, I don't. I can have jags no problem. It's just the thought of having a needle rammed into my tongue that I don't like.'

'Don't worry, no one's gonnae pin you down and stab your tongue.' Jennifer grinned while Jane smiled with amusement.

'They'd have a shock if they tried,' replied Carly.

'That's the spirit,' said Jennifer, slapping her on the shoulder.

Carly nodded. 'Are you in conference?' she asked the two women. 'I can leave if you are.'

'We had a bit of business to discuss but we've finished now,' replied Jane. 'You could sit in on every meeting if you joined us.'

'I appreciate the offer, but I've got enough on my plate as it is.'

'The offer's there if you change your mind but Jennifer will always be my lieutenant.'

'And that's the way it should be because she's a bloody good lieutenant.'

'Thanks,' said Jennifer chirpily.

'You're welcome, although I'm curious to know if you've had any bother from Emma?'

'No and that's what worries us,' replied Jane. 'We keep expecting her to try and take the leadership back but so far she hasn't bothered.'

'Because you beat the absolute shite out of her.'

'She's not the type to let that stop her.'

'I reckon she couldn't stand the humiliation of losing again,' said Jennifer. 'You knocked out some of her teeth and broke her nose,' she added with a smile at Jane. 'That's a lot for someone who's so into her looks to deal with.'

'I don't like it that she's been so quiet,' said Carly. 'The Alexanders have been too and it makes me nervous.'

'You need to stop worrying so much,' said Jane.

'We could go and give Emma a good kicking,' offered Jennifer. 'Just to make sure she stays quiet.'

'As much as I'd love to,' said Jane, 'we're better off not rocking the boat. Let's just keep an eye on her. I'm more worried about the Alexander family. They wanted what our family have too much to just let it go.'

Jennifer was aware the Savages were doing some work for the Tallans. After all, the Alexanders had blabbed that news all over Haghill but she didn't know what the work entailed. Neither would she ask. If Jane needed to tell her, she would.

'Maybe they're waiting for Ross to recover from having his balls nearly twisted off by Rose.' Jennifer laughed. 'Bloody hell, I'd have paid good money to watch her do that.'

'Maybe she'll treat you to a repeat performance,' smiled Jane.

'He's only just stopped walking with a limp. Serves him right after what he tried to do to Alec, the cowardly shite. Ross wouldn't have dared go near him if he'd been at full strength. Alec would have tied him up in a knot and thrown him into the Clyde.'

'Too right he would,' said Carly, proud of how strong her father had once been.

'Me and the girls can watch the Alexanders. Donna and Stacey live on the same street as Brian, Jessica and Cole and Leonie works down the road from Cole's garage.'

'And Lucy works at the nail bar Jessica goes to.'

'Between us, we can keep an eye on them all.'

'Ross is the one who needs watching the most. Dominic can't take a piss without his brothers' help, so he's not really a concern. The same goes for Brian. They're the weakest members of the family.' Brian was the Alexander patriarch who had lost all authority and was now treated as a lackey by his sons.

'I can keep an eye on Ross,' said Carly with a dark look.

'And that's all you're to do, for now,' Jane told her. 'You're not to approach him.'

'I know but I hate the bastard. He kidnapped me and Dean and then attacked Da'.'

'And he was made to pay. If he's any sense he'll think twice before going anywhere near our family again.'

'That's the problem, he doesn't have any sense.'

'Just keep your distance. We don't want to kick off another war.'

Carly nodded but already she was thinking about how much fun it would be to make Ross and Cole Alexander suffer all over again for their many sins.

4

The next morning as he drove himself and Carly to their next job, Dean wondered if he should mention what his father had said to him. If Carly knew he still had feelings for her, she might not want to work with him any more so he decided silence would be the wiser choice.

'Well, this is different to the last job,' said Carly as Dean parked outside a tatty terraced house in Govan. 'How much are they into the Tallans for?'

'Twenty grand,' replied Dean. 'A man called Spider.'

'Well Spider didn't borrow it to do up the house.'

'It's a drug debt. David said this lot are known for being nasty bastards, so we need to watch our backs in there.'

Dean and Carly steeled themselves for battle as they got out of the car and marched down the crooked, uneven path riddled with weeds to the dented, faded red door. As Dean knocked, they put on their most threatening expressions. The door was opened by a large, flabby man with a spider's web tattooed on top of his bald head, presumably the reason for his nickname.

'The Tallans sent us,' began Dean.

To their surprise, Spider held out a small grey backpack to him. 'There's the full twenty grand,' he said.

'Oh, right,' said Dean, taking it from him. He opened it carefully in case something nasty had been secreted inside but all he saw was wads of money.

Dean just nodded and slung the backpack over his shoulder. David had told them never to say thank you. The Tallans never thanked anyone for anything.

With that, he and Carly returned to the car. They paused to look back at the house and saw Spider was watching them curiously.

Dean and Carly got back into the car and Dean handed her the backpack.

'Did you get a weird vibe from Spider?' she asked him, resting the bag on her lap.

'Aye. Maybe he's just a weird guy? Anyone with a cobweb on the top of their head cannae be normal.'

'He's still watching us,' said Carly, glancing out of the window.

Dean turned to look and sure enough there was Spider staring intently at them. When he saw he was being watched, he stepped back inside the house and closed the door.

'Let's get out of here,' said Carly. 'I'm getting bad vibes.'

'Me too,' said Dean, starting the engine.

He set off faster than he should, eager to escape the area.

'I'll double check the bag, make sure nothing's been hidden inside,' said Carly.

She opened it up, tipping the money into her lap, which had been bundled into four neat piles of notes tied with elastic bands. After running her hands around the lining and flicking through the piles of notes, she replaced them in the bag, having found nothing. She then checked the one pocket on the outside of the bag but that was also empty.

'Maybe Uncle Eddie's right and I am getting paranoid?' she said.

'No, you're no',' replied Dean. 'I feel it too.'

He kept checking his rear-view mirror but no one seemed to be following them.

'The sooner we're back in Haghill the better,' commented Carly, who, for some reason, felt it safer to cling onto the bag.

'We'll soon be home.' Dean's eyes flicked back to the rear-view mirror at the sound of an engine. 'There's a motorbike behind us.'

Carly turned in her seat to look. 'He's keeping his distance. It's probably just someone out for a ride in the sunshine. Or I could be wrong,' she added when the bike suddenly accelerated towards them.

They were on a quiet residential road lined with houses. As it was midday on a Wednesday, everyone was either out at work or school so there was no one to see when the bike pulled up by the driver's side.

'Look out,' cried Carly when the pillion passenger on the back produced a crowbar from inside his leather jacket, face hidden by a helmet.

Dean leaned away from the window as it was smashed in. When the passenger attempted to grab the steering wheel, Dean punched him in the wrist. There was a crack and the man screamed with pain, the sound muffled by the helmet. Hastily he retracted his arm and the driver was forced to drop back when they saw a car coming in the opposite direction.

The car safely passed them and the bike pulled back out onto the driver's side.

'He can't do anything with his knackered arm,' said Carly. 'And the driver can't try because they'll crash.'

At the sound of a second engine, Dean looked to the passenger side of the car. He wrapped an arm around Carly and pulled her against him to shield her as the side window was smashed by the passenger on a second bike that they'd failed to notice.

Before either of them could react, the passenger had reached in and grabbed a handful of her hair, yanking her towards the window.

'Carly,' cried Dean.

He was powerless to act as he had to concentrate hard on keeping the car at equal speed with the bike otherwise the consequences for her didn't bear thinking about.

The passenger on the bike flipped up the lid of his helmet with his free hand.

'Give me the fucking bag,' he roared.

'Don't you bloody dare,' Carly told Dean when he moved to snatch it out of her lap. She gripped onto it tighter with one hand, her other hand frantically clawing at the man's fingers, which were tangled tightly in her hair but she couldn't reach the skin as they were encased in gloves.

'Give me the fucking bag,' bellowed the man again.

'Fuck you,' yelled Carly.

Furious that his demand wasn't being met, he pulled her harder out of the car, so her top half was entirely hanging out.

Panic threatened to overwhelm Carly like it never had before. The only thing that kept her from giving into it entirely was the feel of Dean's hand on her leg, pulling back. He would not let her fall.

The only weapon she could reach was her taser but she couldn't see to aim.

Dean groped under his seat for the tyre iron he kept there but he couldn't strike the man without hitting Carly. 'Here,' he said, placing it in her hand.

Carly had her back to her assailant, so she couldn't see him. It was also difficult for her to see clearly as her eyes had filled with tears of pain at having her hair pulled so hard. Taking a deep, determined breath, she gripped the tyre iron tightly and swung it back over her head. There was a grunt and she felt it connect with the helmet but the man's grip on her didn't loosen.

'His leg, Carly,' cried Dean. 'Get his leg.'

Carly swung the tyre iron downwards. It met the man's knee hard. He roared with pain and released her. Dean took Carly's hand and pulled her back inside the car. The passenger on the bike threw himself about with such force he overbalanced the bike and it veered from side to side before running into a small red car parked at the kerb. The second bike with its injured passenger dropped back, deciding to relinquish the chase.

'Are you okay?' Dean asked Carly, daring to take his eyes off the road to look at her.

'Aye, fine,' she said. 'Apart from an aching back. The bastard pulled out a few strands of hair too,' she added, running her fingers through it. 'Still, it could have been a lot worse.'

'I'll pull over.'

'No, keep going. We need to get this money to David.'

'Okay,' he said, putting his foot down. Wind blasted through the car, blowing Carly's long hair about her face as both the side windows had been smashed.

'Who the hell were they?' said Carly.

'Probably pals of Spider's,' growled Dean. 'I feel like going back there and beating the living shite out of him. He's another arsehole who probably thinks he can keep the cash. Either that or someone who thought they'd steal the money before we could get it to the Tallans.'

'Either way it's not good. It shows people aren't afraid of them any more.'

Dean's gaze turned to steel. 'Then we'll have to make them afraid.'

Tingles ran down Carly's spine. The first time she'd heard him talk like that it had disconcerted her, scared her even. Now it excited her.

'We need to pull over,' said Dean. 'The window on my side wasn't smashed cleanly and there are jaggy pieces sticking up. We don't want the polis pulling us over when we're carrying weapons and twenty grand in cash. I'll find somewhere quiet to stop.'

Dean only dared pull over down a quiet back street once he was sure they'd left the motorbikes far behind. He and Carly got out of the car and Dean used the tyre iron to knock out the remaining glass in his window.

'Thank God that didn't happen to my window or my back would have been shredded to bits,' commented Carly.

The thought made Dean's blood run cold. 'Thank God, indeed.' He replaced the tyre iron under the driver's seat and took her by the shoulders. 'Do you need a doctor?'

'No, I'm fine. I've just some bruises, that's all.'

'Good.' Unable to help himself, he pulled her into his arms and hugged her tight. He was delighted when she hugged him back, both needing the warmth and reassurance after what they'd just been through.

Carly raised her head and smiled up at him.

'You've got a tiny cut on your cheek,' said Dean, brushing the area just below the cut with the tip of his thumb.

'It must have been from the glass,' she replied, her eyes locking with his.

They held onto each other tighter. Dean's heart pounded and his blood surged as it felt like they were on the verge of another kiss...

There was the roar of a motorbike from somewhere close by and they jumped apart.

'Do you think that's them?' said Carly.

'Can't be,' replied Dean. 'Not with the injuries we gave their passengers.'

'They might be ruthless enough to throw the passengers off and continue the chase.'

'It sounds like only one bike, not two.'

To their relief, the sound of the engine faded away before vanishing altogether.

'I don't think it was them,' breathed Carly. 'We'd better get this money to David and then go home.' After what she'd just been through, the thought of home made her heart ache.

'Aye, you're right,' mumbled Dean, disappointed the moment between them had been broken by some arsehole on a bike.

* * *

Dean and Carly arrived at the gym feeling tired and spent. David was once again in the café, sitting at a table reading a newspaper.

As they approached, he folded up the newspaper, placed it on the table and frowned at them.

'You two don't look happy,' he commented.

'We're not,' replied Dean. 'We need to talk.'

David nodded, got to his feet and led them into the office.

'Well?' he said once they were ensconced together.

'Here's the money,' said Dean, dumping the backpack on the desk.

'All of it?'

'Aye but someone tried to take it off us.'

'Spider?'

'No. We don't know who they were. Four arseholes on motorbikes. They hit us a few minutes after we'd left Spider's house.'

'Judging by the fact that you still have the money, they failed?'

'I broke one of their wrists and Carly smacked another in the knee with a tyre iron.'

'Nasty,' commented David, raising his eyebrows. 'Well done.' He delved into his desk and produced two more rolls of notes. He tossed them one each before producing two more rolls and giving them those too. 'Call it danger money,' he told them.

'Cheers,' replied Dean.

'There are people out there who don't gi'e a shite about Rod's and Neil's reputations. Usually it's coke heads willing to do anything for a few quid. Rest assured, we will find them and make sure they can't hit you again.' He looked to Carly, whose gaze was hard. 'What is it this time?'

'Oh, nothing really. Just the thought that any arsehole on a bike can grab a chunk of my hair and attempt to drag me out of a moving car is a disturbing one.'

'If you don't like the danger then you're in the wrong game, sweetheart. You were warned it's a hazardous job. You can always quit and go and work in a fucking call centre.'

'I didn't say I want to quit,' she replied. 'I'm just pissed off.'

'I don't blame you. I would be too but if you've no' got the stamina for this job then you need to tell me now. You can leave with no hard feelings but the deeper you're in the harder it is to get out.'

'I don't want to leave,' she said, voice growing colder with each word. 'But I would like ten minutes with the wanker who nearly pulled my hair out.'

The corner of David's mouth lifted into a smile. 'That's the spirit. Now away you go. You don't have any collections for a few days so relax, spend your money and have fun. You both look like you could use some down time.'

Dean and Carly nodded and left. Once they'd gone, David left

the office, wandered down a back corridor and entered another
room used for meetings when the Tallans wanted privacy. There
waited Rod and Neil, sitting in chairs watching a monitor linked to a
hidden camera in the office. Neil was smoking a thick Cuban cigar.

'You heard all that?' David asked them, closing the door
behind him.

'Every word,' replied Neil before taking a drag on the cigar and
puffing out smoke rings.

'That Carly bird was pissed off.'

'If I'd been half-dragged out of a car by my hair, I'd be pissed off
too.'

'They've more than proved their worth. They put two of our
people in hospital.'

'How are they?'

'Charlie's got a fractured wrist and Pete's kneecap's broken.
They'll be out of commission for weeks. In Pete's case, perhaps
months.'

'It serves him right; he went too far. We never told him to try
and pull anyone out of a moving car. He always gets carried
away.'

'True. We wanted to test them, not kill them. But they brought
the cash back and they fought off their attackers, so we know we
can rely on them.'

'Carly's getting suspicious. She reckons it's weird Victor thought
he could challenge you and now she thinks Spider's done the same.
She doesn't know he was working for us.'

'Let her think what she likes, she cannae do anything.'

'Are you sure about that? She just broke one of our men's
knees.'

'At the end of the day, she's still young and inexperienced. What
about Dean? Is he suspicious too?'

'It's hard to tell. He plays his cards close to his chest. He's much harder to read. Carly hasn't mastered the art of controlling her emotions yet.'

'One day she will, I've no doubt.'

'They're taking a few days off and I think they need it.'

'Are you saying they cannae handle the stress?'

'No but it might help Carly unwind enough to pull the pole out of her arse.'

'Now that's something to consider.' Rod smiled, speaking for the first time.

'What is?' Neil frowned.

'Carly Savage's arse.'

Neil rolled his eyes. 'Can you please be serious? The Savages are working very nicely for us now but if they chose to, they could cause us a lot of trouble. They can never know the full extent of our operation.'

'That family are nothing more than a bunch of neds,' said Rod with a dismissive wave.

Neil's eyes glittered. 'Thank you, David. You may leave us now.'

He nodded and left.

Neil turned to his brother and blew a stream of smoke into his face, knowing it would annoy him. 'The Savages are far more than a pack of Burberry-wearing pricks. They won't be as easy to control as the majority who work for us.'

A wicked smile split Rod's face. 'There's only one member of that family I'm interested in controlling.'

'Let me guess, Carly? Will you please get your mind out of the gutter? That girl is as sharp as a tack and she's clocked on that something's wrong.'

'Relax. She'll never find out what. You worry too much, you always have. The Savages are proving to be very efficient. They've never failed on a collection yet and they're more than capable of handling difficult situations.'

'So capable they put two of our men in hospital.'

'Our people behaved like idiots and went overboard. They were supposed to have a go at them outside Spider's house, no' chase them through the streets on motorbikes like something out of *The Fast and the Furious*. What in the name of Christ were they thinking? They could have attracted the attention of the polis, so they deserve to have their knees and wrists broken.'

'Good point. Well, the Savages have more than proved themselves, so I think it's time to crank things up a notch. Our marks are all ripe and ready. Let's start the blackmail operation.'

'I agree. We've waited long enough. I'm going to that charity do on Saturday and I'm thinking of inviting Carly as my plus one. What?' he added when his brother sighed and shook his head.

'You're getting obsessed, that's what and I don't like it. Have you forgotten Sylvia Langton?'

'What about her?'

'You hounded her for months. I had to pay her a huge amount of cash to stop her from making a complaint to the polis.'

Rod's face creased with anger. 'You shouldn't have given the bitch a penny. You should have sent the boys over to break her fucking jaw.'

'Unlike you, I have a sense of right and wrong. That lassie was only twenty-four and she'd done nothing to deserve a beating. I wasnae gonnae hurt her because you'd got obsessed again.'

'It wasn't an obsession. I just wanted her.'

'And she didn't want you because you freaked her out. She liked you at first, until you went all bunny boiler on her. You've no one to blame but yourself and I'm buggered if I'm going through that hassle again with Carly Savage, who is capable of causing a lot more mayhem than Sylvia.'

'Fine, I won't invite her to the party,' sighed Rod, holding up his hands.

'Good and you don't ask her out on a date at all. You need to keep your mind on the job and off hot twenty-year-old hard bodies, okay? We're about to cut the biggest deal of our lives and I'll allow nothing to stand in the way, including your disgusting perversions.'

'I am not a pervert,' exclaimed Rod.

'We both know that's a lie. How many women have made complaints against you for going too far during sex?'

'All right, that's enough.' Rod glowered at him.

'You don't like it when people get too near the truth, do you? You've been the same since we were teenagers. I don't know where you get it from. Probably Maw. She's a sadistic bitch. Anyway, that's enough. Just as long as you stay away from Carly Savage.'

'I've got the message, for Christ's sake.'

'I'm glad you understand.' Neil extinguished the cigar in an ashtray, got to his feet and buttoned up his suit jacket. 'Right, I'm thinking lunch at that Michelin-starred restaurant on Kelvingrove Street, the one with the poncy name I can never remember.'

'I know the one you mean but we don't have reservations.'

'Never you mind about that. I'm well in with the owner and a table will always be made available for us.'

'Sounds good,' said Rod, also getting to his feet. 'I could use some culture and sophistication after sitting in this place for an hour surrounded by muscle heads.'

Neil smiled and nodded but inwardly he was troubled. The last thing he or his brother had expected was for Dean and Carly to not only beat their men but to put them in hospital. They'd fully expected their people to return with the bag of cash, having easily taken it from them. They'd selected to test that pair as they were the younger ones. It was always best to test the weakest links in the chain first but all they'd done was prove that those weak links were in fact incredibly strong. If those two were capable of such carnage, what could Jane and Harry do? Harry had more experience than his younger brother and Jane was the leader of a feared girl gang. Eddie he wasn't so worried about, despite his sly brain, because that man looked like he was one fry-up off a heart attack. It was the younger generation that concerned him. Perhaps Rod was right and he did worry too much? Anyone else would be delighted that their employees had proved to be so tough and resilient, especially in a world that seemed to be populated with morons, but he was wary of anyone he thought competent enough to take what he'd spent years building up.

'I know what you're thinking,' said Rod as the brothers left the gym by the back door, not wanting anyone to know they were there.

'And what's that, Mystic Meg?' snapped back Neil.

'You're wondering if we've made a mistake hiring the Savages.'

'How do you always do that?'

'Because I've known you all my life and I can read you like a book,' replied Rod with a satisfied smile. 'And I'm telling you to relax. The Savages might be good at battering people, but they don't have our experience.'

'Eddie does and that sod runs them like Fagan.'

'You mean that arsehole in Partick?'

'No, I mean the guy who runs the kiddy gang in *Oliver Twist*, you philistine.'

'He's a sly sod, I'll gi'e you that, but he's no' in our league, so take it easy. Getting all riled up is a sure-fire way to give something away. Stop worrying. Life's just fucking dandy.'

5

'Hmm,' said Eddie, reclining thoughtfully back in his chair at the kitchen table of the Savage home.

'Is that all you've got to say?' Dean demanded of his father. 'We were attacked and Carly was almost dragged out of a moving car, for Christ's sake.'

'Aye, I'm just thinking,' he murmured.

'Are you sure you don't need a hospital?' Jane asked her sister for the second time.

'I'm sure,' replied Carly. 'I'm just a bit bruised and a few strands of hair lighter than I was this morning.'

'At least it's not noticeable.'

'This is the danger of the business we're in,' said Eddie. 'People are bound to find out we're delivering big chunks of money and will try and take it from us.'

'That's what David said,' replied Dean.

'And he's right. His people will have gone through it many times before. I'm just so bloody proud of how you handled yourselves. I bet the sods who hit you are really regretting it now,' he chuckled.

'I still say the Tallans are up to something,' said Carly. 'They're keeping something from us.'

'And if they are it's none of our business. We do our jobs and keep our heads down. So far, we havenae had to deal with the blackmail side of the operation. They've kept us on the debt collecting but I know that will soon change. Neil's already hinted as much to me. They've spent months getting their targets to trust them enough to allow them to lure them into compromising situations and they have enough dirt on them to... to... fill in a big hole,' he ended lamely.

Harry snorted. 'I wouldnae bother with the analogies again, Da'. You're shite at them.'

'Whatever,' he snapped. 'Very soon we'll be brought deeper into their operation, so prepare yourselves.'

'We're prepared,' replied Harry flatly.

'Ah, the lairiness of youth.' Eddie smiled, clapping him on the shoulder. 'Things will get more difficult and you'll need to be on the ball. It'll be a lot more complicated than debt collecting.'

'I can handle it.' He casually shrugged.

'That remains to be seen.'

Harry narrowed his eyes at his father. 'You don't think I can?'

'Course I do. I just think you'll be in for a wee shock, that's all.'

'Well,' said Carly. 'I could use a drink after today. Anyone fancy going to the pub?'

'Aye, sounds good,' said Dean.

Eddie didn't want his son going to the pub alone with Carly where they could get even closer. Before he could think of a way to come between them, Harry and Jane said they wanted to go too.

'Enjoy yourselves,' a relieved Eddie told them. 'I'll sit with Alec and have a good gab.'

'Like a couple of fishwives,' said Jane with a fond smile.

'Aye. He gets all the local gossip from Mary next door and passes it onto me.'

The four cousins walked to The Horseshoe Bar which wasn't far from the Savage home. They entered to find Derek, the landlord, doing his usual dance behind the bar.

'Carly, doll,' he exclaimed. 'Thank Christ you're here. I know you don't work here any more but could you keep an eye on the bar for me while I go for a pish? Sharon's no' due to start for another hour.'

'No problem,' she replied. 'Away you go.'

'You're an angel, hen,' he said before shooting out from behind the bar and rushing off in the direction of the toilets.

Carly smiled as she took her place behind the bar. She had loved working here. Derek had even been talking about making her manager, until the Alexanders had forced her to quit by threatening to torch the place. Granted, she hadn't been earning the big money she was now but it had been legal and a lot less dangerous.

'What are you all having?' She beamed at her cousins and sister.

The two men ordered pints of lager and Jane a white wine.

'She's really enjoying herself,' Jane told her cousins as they watched Carly happily bustle about the bar.

'Do you think she wants to come back to work here?' replied Dean, concerned.

'No, not with the money she's making now.'

'But she looks so happy. She doesnae look like that debt collecting.'

Jane couldn't help but smile. Dean was worried about not

working with Carly any more. 'None of us look happy when we're debt collecting. It's not that sort of job.'

'I know, but look at her.'

'I see what you mean,' said Jane as Carly placed their drinks on the bar before them with a big grin. 'Glad to be back behind the bar again?' she asked her sister.

'Aye, it is pretty nice,' she replied. 'I have missed it.'

'Enough to come back?' said Dean, deciding to bite the bullet and ask. If she was going to leave debt collecting, then it would be better to find out now so he could prepare himself.

'No, I don't think so. Besides, Derek already gave my job to Sharon.'

'There are bar jobs at other places,' said Jane, to Dean's annoyance.

'I know but it wouldn't be the same. No, this game is behind me now.' Carly took the money Harry handed her and turned to the till.

'You can relax now,' Jane told Dean while picking up her glass of wine.

'I don't know what you mean,' he replied.

'Course not,' she said knowingly.

The three of them took a table while Carly continued to happily serve.

'Carly, doll,' slurred John, the elderly man who could usually be found propping up the end of the bar. 'Is that you back working here?'

'No, I'm just covering for Derek while he has a pish.'

'Old teabag bladder never changes,' he chuckled. 'Aww, it's a shame you're no' coming back, you've been missed.'

'I still come in as a customer.'

'Aye but it's no' the same. Your smile lit up the room. Sharon's smile is just scary, especially as she usually has bright red lipstick smeared all over her teeth,' he added with a shudder. 'It makes her look like she's just bitten someone.'

'That's Derek coming back,' she told John when the landlord returned to the bar area. 'So that's me done here. Cheer up, Sharon might decide to stop wearing lipstick.'

'I'm starting to think it's no' lipstick and she's really a vampire. She's moody enough.'

Carly was still smiling as she joined her sister and cousins at the table, taking the chair between Dean and Jane. 'What?' she asked when they all stared at her.

'Nothing,' said Jane. 'Let's have a drink and a laugh. We deserve it.'

'And we've no jobs on for a few days.' Harry grinned. 'So we can get pished.'

'I never get drunk,' said Dean.

Harry rolled his eyes. 'Jesus, you're an old biddy in a young man's body, always have been.'

'I bet you have some funny stories from when you both were younger?' said Carly.

Harry's eyes filled with mischief.

'Don't you dare.' Dean glowered at him.

Harry grinned and shrugged. 'Maybe later,' he told Carly.

As the drinks flowed, they all began to relax and enjoy themselves. The four of them got on well and had become good friends. Dean switched to orange juice after his second pint but the other three kept on drinking.

An hour later, the door opened and all three Alexander brothers strutted in – Ross, Dominic and Cole, the youngest brother and Carly's ex.

Instantly the tension returned to Carly, Jane and their cousins, their eyes narrowing as they prepared for a fight.

'Oy you lot,' Derek told the Alexanders. 'You're barred after what you did.'

Ross held up his hands, although his eyes danced with amusement. 'We're only here for a quiet drink.'

'Bollocks. You're here to cause trouble, that's all your family knows how to do. I cannae believe you've got the bloody nerve to even walk in here after you threatened to torch the place.' Derek turned redder with each word, so enraged was he about them having the temerity to enter his establishment.

The whole pub had gone silent, glaring at the Alexanders with a mixture of outrage, loathing and trepidation. The Savage family's reputation had increased tenfold since their war with the Alexanders while their rival's had sunk. However, everyone was still painfully aware that the three brothers were very capable of causing more carnage if they chose. But the Savages would have the loyalty of the people of Haghill, especially now Jane was once again running the Bitches. No one wanted to get on the wrong side of that lot.

Harry got to his feet, expression grim. 'You three had better piss off, while you still can.'

Carly, Dean and Jane rose too.

The three Alexander brothers knew they couldn't possibly stand up to the Savage brothers, as well as the two sisters and Derek, who would undoubtedly join in if they started anything.

'We didn't come here for a fight,' said Dominic, who was the most reasonable of the three. 'We just thought enough time had passed for us to come back. Water under the bridge and all that.'

'Get this into your thick skulls,' said Derek. 'You are never welcome here ever again. You're barred for life and that includes your maw and da' too. Got it?'

'I'm amazed you're back on your feet after wee Rose nearly twisted your tiny baws off.' John grinned at Ross.

When Ross's hands tightened into fists and he grunted with rage, Dominic clamped his hand down on his shoulder. 'Don't,' he whispered in his ear.

Ross nodded and took a deep breath to try and calm himself down, the titter of laughter that ran around the room infuriating him even more. There had been a day when none of these bastards would have dared laugh at him.

While this was going on, Cole's gaze connected with Carly's. She hadn't seen him since the night his family had attacked hers and he'd gone for her with a knife in the graveyard opposite her flat. He hadn't stabbed her; in fact, he'd kissed her before running off to escape the wrath of her cousins and he'd kept a low profile ever since. She'd only seen him or his brothers at a distance before now. At least she knew she'd got over what had happened between them – especially as all the desire she'd once held for him failed to affect her any more. Prison had changed him for the worse and he'd come out a cold, hard creature who had been more than happy to use her to further his own ends. The love she'd once felt for him was gone but neither did she hate him. His own mother had been responsible for grassing on him to the police, leading to him getting arrested and being sent to prison and Carly couldn't help but feel that he was a victim of his mother's greed and malice too. She had told him about Jessica's confession, which had been more of a proud boast than a shameful admission but he'd refused to believe his mother would do anything like that to him. Jessica had seen prison as the only way to separate her son from Carly, who had been having an unwanted positive influence on him and how Carly hated the bitch for it. Jessica Alexander had not been punished anywhere near enough for her sins but Carly had sworn that one day she would make her suffer for what she'd done.

'Fine, we're going,' muttered Ross, who was still struggling to contain his anger. 'But one day you'll regret this.' He looked to

Derek. 'You'll be begging us to come back. That lot won't stay on top for long,' he added, jabbing a digit at the Savages.

'Oh, fuck off, you prick,' Harry told him, spoiling for a fight.

To his disappointment, Dominic hustled Ross outside before he could launch himself at Harry, whose grin only enraged him even more.

Cole quietly followed his brothers outside, his gaze fixed on Carly. When he saw Dean glaring at him, he glared back, menace gathering around him. The two men only broke eye contact once Cole had gone out the door.

'Thank Christ for that,' said Derek, who was breathless with rage. 'I cannae believe their fucking cheek.'

'They're gone now and hopefully they won't come back,' said Jane while Dean went to the window to make sure the Alexanders had really left.

'They'd better not because next time I will get out my baseball bat and batter their fucking melons in,' he added.

All the customers returned to their conversations now the show was over and Derek had an invigorating shot of whisky to help him calm down.

'They've definitely gone,' said Dean, returning to the table. 'I saw them turn the corner at the end of the street.'

'And good riddance,' said Jane as they all retook their seats.

'Well, that's the sign then,' said Carly.

The other three frowned at her.

'What sign?' said Harry.

'The Alexanders are going to kick off again. I had the feeling they would; there's only so long that lot can remain quiet.' She'd expected to have her fears dismissed, but on the contrary, no one objected.

'I think you could be right,' said Dean. 'They came in here to test the water, not with us but with everyone else. If they know they don't have the back-up of the locals it will make it much harder to attack us. Since Jane took back the Bitches, they're on their own while we're stronger than ever.'

'We could hit them before they can hit us. After all, who's gonnae complain about it?' Harry looked to Jane and Carly. 'What do you think?'

'I don't know,' said Jane. 'I don't like the thought of maiming someone just because they walked into a pub. It doesn't seem right, somehow.'

'I agree,' said Carly. 'And before you say it, I'm no' getting sentimental over Cole. I just think there should be more provocation before attacking someone.'

'Maybe you're right,' said Dean. 'Especially now we're working for the Tallans.'

'Fine,' sighed Harry. 'I suppose that's the important thing right now,' he added, disappointed that he was being denied a scrap. His eyes lit up when two very attractive women entered the pub. 'Do excuse me,' he said, getting to his feet. 'I have some business to attend to. Come on, Dean.'

'Why?'

'Jeezo, have you gone blind? Look at those birds that have just come in. They're crackers.'

Dean turned in his chair to look. 'They're okay, I suppose.'

'Okay? They're gorgeous.'

'They're wearing too much make-up.' He cringed when one cackled with laughter at something her friend said. 'And annoying. I bet they only talk about celebrities and clothes.'

'That's very judgemental of you, but I'm no' interested in their conversation.'

'I'm shocked,' said Dean sarcastically.

'Well, I'll just have them all to myself then. See you later,' he said, picking up his pint and walking over to the women who were standing at the bar.

The women smiled and started purring at him and tossing their long hair over their shoulders. The Savage brothers were well known in Haghill and their reputations for fierceness and making money were just as highly regarded as their good looks.

'We won't be offended if you want to join your brother,' Jane told Dean.

'They're not my type.'

'You mean pretty with killer legs?' Jane cringed when one of them brayed with laughter again. 'I see your point.'

'Leave Harry to it. He's in his element.'

'Now he's gone,' Carly told Dean, 'you can tell us those embarrassing stories from your childhood.'

Dean smiled wickedly. Jane sighed as he and Carly began to eagerly chat, thick as thieves. He hadn't fooled her for a moment. Dean hadn't wanted to talk to those women because he only wanted Carly. Eddie had already spoken to Jane and Harry about Dean's feelings for Carly and said they needed to come up with a way to ensure they didn't get together. He'd asked her if Carly felt the same way about Dean but she said she didn't think so in the hope of getting her uncle to stop his schemes. His plans could cause damage he hadn't even dreamed of. Jane knew from experience that trying so hard to avoid a certain outcome could lead to you bringing about the thing you dreaded the most. But she understood Eddie's reasoning. Carly and Dean really seemed to have no idea of the damage a relationship between them could cause.

6

'Bloody lesbians, the pair of them,' muttered Harry miserably as he made his way home with his brother and cousins, disappointed the evening hadn't panned out as he'd hoped it would.

'No, they're not,' said Carly. 'They just took offence when you suggested a threesome.'

'I thought it's what they wanted,' he exclaimed.

'You'd only been talking to them for half an hour before you brought it up. You really have no idea about women, do you?'

Harry scowled at Dean when he chuckled. 'I think you'll find every woman I've been with has been extremely satisfied.'

'And how many of them stuck around after?' said Carly.

'I didn't want them to stick around, that's the point.'

'Classy,' she said sarcastically.

'I'm no' ready to be tied down. Well, not in the metaphorical sense anyway.'

'You're a dirty sod,' said Carly, playfully smacking him on the arm, making him grin. 'But one day the right woman will come along and she'll knock you off your feet.'

'No' me. I'm gonnae be single forever. I saw what our da' went through with our maw. She treated him like shite then broke his heart, ran off to Blackpool with some loser with a comb-over. That will never be me.'

'Was it bad?' said Jane. Her cousins had never really talked about their parents' divorce before, although Dean had opened up a bit about it to Carly.

'It was,' said Harry, expression turning serious. 'For a while, I didn't think Da' would ever recover but he did. He's too strong to let anyone break him.'

'Was she a good maw to you?'

Harry's eyes flickered. Clearly this was a painful subject for him. 'At first,' he replied. 'Until I turned twelve and Dean was ten. Then she became distant, like she couldnae be bothered any more, no' just with Da' but us too. I don't know what brought it on. I reckon she'd been feeling like that for a while and she couldnae hide it any more. She was tired of constantly putting on a show. She didn't want to be tied down with a husband and kids, she wanted to be free to do what she liked, she was sick of responsibility. The daft cow thought she was nineteen again. One day me and Dean came back from school and she wasn't there waiting for us, like she normally was. We thought she'd nipped out to the shop and would be back soon but by the time Da' came home from work she still hadnae returned. Da' was frantic, he was ready for calling the polis. Then we found the note. It had fallen off the windowsill where she'd left it. She wrote she felt stifled by us all and needed to leave to clear her head. Da' kept saying she'll be back soon, she just needs a wee break. Things get on top of us all sometimes and she'd done the sensible thing. He kept sticking up for her and telling us how great things would be when she came home. But I knew as soon as I read her note that she wasnae coming back. I remembered how she'd been the past few months. She was fed up with us. She didn't want us.'

The sadness in his eyes touched the sisters' hearts. Carly glanced at Dean and saw the same sadness reflected there, although his eyes also glittered with anger.

'We're better off without her,' said Dean. 'Any mother who can abandon her own weans isnae worth a second thought.'

'I quite agree,' said Carly. 'Kudos to Uncle Eddie for bringing you up alone. I know it can't have been easy for him.'

'How can you possibly know that?' exclaimed Harry. His eyes widened when he realised what he'd said. Carly and Jane's mother had died of cancer a few years ago, leaving Alec to raise the sisters alone. 'God, I'm sorry. I didnae think. Talking about my maw really fucks me up.'

'It's okay,' said Carly. 'You're upset. It's understandable.'

Harry forced a smile. 'Cheers. I'm a walloper sometimes.'

'Only sometimes?' said Dean, mischief dancing in his eyes.

It was the perfect thing to say and broke the awkward moment. They all laughed.

'No' as much as you, wee brother.' Harry grinned, wrapping an arm around his neck and attempting to bend him forward but Dean threw him off and the brothers began to playfully tussle.

'Shall we leave you two to it?' Jane asked them.

'We're just messing about,' said Harry, releasing his brother.

'We know and it's adorable,' she replied, making them both blush.

Carly frowned when she spied movement further down the street. 'Is that Cole?'

The merriment died instantly and the four of them turned to look where she indicated.

'Let's get the prick,' growled Harry, who was even more keen for a fight now he'd been turned down by the two women.

'Wait,' said Carly, grabbing his arm before he could run off.

'What?' he demanded.

'He's just standing there staring at us. He's no' done anything wrong.'

'Don't tell me you're still soft on the twat?'

'Course not but he might just be out for a walk.'

'What I want to know is where are Ross and Dominic?' said Jane.

'Da' and Rose,' breathed Carly.

The four of them looked at each other before breaking into a run, Cole watching them impassively. Rather than race toward where he stood, they detoured down a road to the left, which was the quickest route back to the Savage flat.

'We could be playing right into the Alexanders' hands by doing this,' said Harry as they ran.

'I know but we've no choice,' replied Jane.

They turned onto their street and could see nothing out of the ordinary. They all glanced uncertainly at the graveyard across the road from the flat. Even though it was only five o'clock in the afternoon, the cemetery was gloomy and could hide a multitude of attackers but no one rushed out to meet them.

Carly reached the front door first, but Dean grabbed her and pulled her back so he and his brother could charge inside first.

'Oy,' she exclaimed.

They raced into the kitchen to find Eddie and Rose sitting at the kitchen table eating pizza.

'Jesus, you scared the crap out of me,' exclaimed Eddie. 'I nearly choked on my pepperoni pizza with anchovies.'

'Anchovies?' said Harry. 'Urgh.'

'Is something wrong?' Rose asked them.

'Cole's hanging about a couple of streets away,' replied Jane. 'And we were worried he was coming here to cause trouble with his brothers. All three of them came into the pub earlier.'

'Did they kick off?' said Eddie.

'No. They said they were only in for a drink but they were up to something, I'm sure of it.'

'Why now, after six months?'

'Ross has probably only just recovered from having his baws twisted by our wee Rose,' said Harry proudly, patting his young cousin on the shoulder.

'And if he's no' careful he'll get them twisted again,' she announced, slapping her palm off the table.

'That's the spirit,' Eddie told her.

'Something strange is going on,' said Carly, thinking of everything that had happened on the last two debt collections, on top of this.

'You could be right,' replied Eddie but his look said not to discuss it in front of Rose.

'How's Da'?' said Carly.

'Fine. Mary's in with him having a good gab. She made him fresh pancakes and syrup and he pure lapped them up.'

'Great. Mary's a brilliant cook.'

'Aye she is. Those pancakes smelled like heaven but she wouldnae let me have any. She said they were only for Alec, so me and Rose decided to order pizza.'

'Did you order any for us?' said Dean.

'Naw. You weren't here. Anyway, I didnae think you ate pizza because you're always saying it's unhealthy.'

'I know but it smells great.'

'I'll order us some,' said Carly, picking up the phone.

Just a few months ago a luxury like ordering pizza would have been an impossible dream. Now, thanks to the work they were doing, they could order it any time they liked and she loved the freedom of finally being able to indulge all her whims.

After she'd finished her pizza, Rose disappeared into her bedroom to study, leaving the others to talk in peace.

'It's no coincidence the Alexanders come into the pub just as this weird stuff starts happening on our collections,' began Carly.

'But I just don't see what connection the Alexanders have with the Tallans,' said Harry before biting into a slice of his pepperoni and pineapple pizza, cheese dripping down his chin.

'Maybe there isn't a connection?' said Jane, who ate her chicken and mushroom pizza much more delicately. 'I know you don't trust coincidences, Carly, but they do happen sometimes.'

'Still,' said Dean. 'It's better to err on the side of caution.'

'I agree,' said Eddie. 'I'll speak to my contacts, see if they've heard anything. Jane, ask the Bitches.'

'Will do.'

'Weren't you going to speak to your contact in Bar-L?' Harry asked his father.

'I was, until the prick attacked another prisoner and got put in segregation but there's someone else I can talk to. There's nothing more we can do for the moment except stay vigilant. Those bastard Alexanders might have just decided it's time for some revenge.'

* * *

The next few days were quiet and the Savages returned to working for the Tallans, thinking perhaps the presence of the Alexanders in the pub had been a coincidence after all, especially when neither Eddie's nor Jane's contacts could confirm anything.

Carly however decided to still be very careful and she and Dean spent longer assessing the house of the next mark before going anywhere near it. They parked further down the street and casually walked by it, as though out for a stroll. It was a pleasant if rather dull detached redbrick house on a leafy residential avenue in Shawlands.

'It seems okay,' said Dean as they walked by, doing their best to make it look like they weren't staring at the house.

'But we've no idea who or what is waiting for us inside,' replied Carly.

'True but we have to go in.'

'Course we do. Don't get me wrong, I'm no' getting cold feet.'

They reached the end of the block, promptly turned around and headed back the way they'd come.

'We can't keep marching up and down the pavement,' said Dean. 'Some nosy neighbour will remember us. What are you doing?' he added when she took his hand.

'If anyone does see us, they'll just think we're a young couple in love out for a stroll.'

Dean hoped he wasn't blushing because his cheeks felt to be burning. He glanced at Carly, who looked relaxed about the fact that they were holding hands. Suddenly he felt very awkward and clumsy.

'Do your hands always sweat so much?' she asked him.

'No,' he quickly replied. 'It's just a warm day.'

'I suppose it is pretty mild for April.'

Dean was relieved his little lie had seemed to work. He didn't want her thinking he was naturally sweaty.

They walked past the target's house once more, giving it a sly look before returning to the car.

'What do you think?' he asked Carly.

'Let's get it over with,' she replied.

After ensuring she had her taser and baton safely nestled in her jacket, they wandered up the drive to the front door. Dean reached out to knock and hastily retracted his hand when there was the sound of savage barking on the other side of the door. Two enormous paws slammed against the glass panel in the middle of the door, which were attached to a huge Rottweiler.

There was the sound of shouting from inside the house and the barking stopped. The door was pulled open by a tall, athletic-looking man in his early thirties with spiky dark brown hair. Carly and Dean already knew his name was Mark Fowler and he was into the Tallans for seventeen grand. He had his hand on the dog's collar, the animal snarling aggressively at them.

'That's stopped you in your tracks, hasn't it, you bastards?' Mark told Dean and Carly. 'You try and take any money from me and Elizabeth will tear out your insides.'

'Who's Elizabeth?' said Dean.

'Who do you think? This massive Rottweiler, if you hadnae noticed her.'

His lips twitched. 'That monster's called Elizabeth?'

'Aye. After Elizabeth Bathory, the Blood Countess. Sixteenth century serial killer who bathed in the blood of virgins because she thought it kept her young. And that's what Elizabeth will do to you two if you don't bugger off.'

'Well, we're safe because neither of us are virgins,' said Carly belligerently.

'Just fuck off out of it,' shrieked Mark. 'Before I set her on you.'

In response to her master's raised voice, Elizabeth began barking again and straining to attack but Mark kept a firm grip on her collar.

Carly reached inside her jacket pocket, produced a carrier bag and dumped the contents on the doorstep.

The barking immediately stopped and Elizabeth started to devour the heap of sausages.

'Elizabeth, sic 'em,' Mark told his dog.

The dog ignored him and continued to eat.

'You treacherous bitch,' he exclaimed.

Dean grabbed him by the back of his shirt, propelled him down the corridor and into a room on the left. Carly followed and closed the door behind them so Elizabeth couldn't enter.

'We'd already been warned about your dog,' Dean told him. 'So we came prepared. Right. Where's the fucking money?'

'I haven't got all of it,' he muttered, much less mouthy now he didn't have his dog.

'How much do you have?'

'Eleven grand. But I can get the rest in a few days. I've been told about a horse that's a dead cert.'

'Have you any idea how many times we've heard that shite? Wake up, Mark. The dead cert never comes in. Mugs like you waste their money backing them and they lose it all, leaving themselves in an even worse spot. That's how you got into this mess with the Tallans in the first place. So do yourself a favour – don't bet on the dead cert, okay?'

'I suppose you're right but I've no other way of getting the remaining five grand.'

'The eleven grand should keep the Tallans happy for a wee while.'

'Thank God,' breathed Mark, pressing a hand to his chest.

'But we'll have to give you a bit of a battering.'

'What?' he cried. 'But... that's no' fair.'

'You knew what you were getting into when you borrowed the money. You're warned physical damage is the price for non-payment.'

'It's not non-payment. I've given you the lion's share.'

'So far we've no' seen a single note.'

'I can get it right now,' said Mark before rushing behind the couch.

Worried he was going for a weapon, Dean and Carly followed. Mark tore off the fabric at the rear of the couch, which was held on with Velcro to reveal a stack of money piled up inside. He began taking out the money and dumping it on the floor.

'There,' he said when he'd finished. 'Eleven grand exactly.'

'We can't take it outside like that,' Carly told him.

'A bag,' he shrieked. 'I'll get you a bag.'

He ran to the door but Carly got there first and stood before it.

'I wouldn't recommend trying to escape,' she told him.

'I'm not. I'm just getting you a bag.'

'Never mind,' said Dean, picking up a gym bag off the armchair and tipping the contents onto the floor.

'Hey, you cannae take that,' protested Mark. 'I need it.'

'There's a pair of socks and a vest in there. Use a carrier bag.'

As Dean began stuffing the money into the bag, panic filled Mark's eyes and he started to sweat. He turned to Carly. 'Let me out.'

'Not yet,' she replied.

'I have to get out, I cannae breathe.'

'You'll be fine.'

'I said let me out,' he growled, grabbing her by the shoulders.

Mark was sent to his knees by her fist in his stomach. She snapped out the baton and loomed over him.

'Do yourself a favour and stay down,' Carly told him.

Dean finished stacking the money in the gym bag and zipped it up. He and Carly looked down at the pathetic figure sobbing on the floor before looking at each other, both feeling a distinct lack of enthusiasm for what they had to do.

'Why don't you wait in the car?' Dean told Carly, not wanting to put her through it.

'No way am I leaving you on your own after what happened last time. We do every job together,' she replied.

Dean was touched. 'Okay. Let's get it over with. I'll do it, you keep an eye out.'

'I want to ask him a question first.'

Dean nodded.

Carly knelt before Mark. 'Why did you think you could challenge the Tallans?' she asked him.

'Ch... challenge?' he stammered. 'I didnae challenge anyone.'

'Aye ya did, at the front door, with Elizabeth. You're not so tough without your Rottweiler,' she added with a curl of the lip. 'Why did you think you could get away with that?'

'Because of what I heard.'

'What did you hear?'

'That the Tallans are finished. They're being taken over and when that happens everyone's debts will be wiped out. I wanted to keep my eleven grand.'

'Taken over by who?'

'Some family called the Alexanders in Haghill.'

Carly looked to Dean and saw her own astonishment reflected in his eyes.

'The Alexanders are a bunch of low-level losers,' she told Mark. 'How the hell would they manage to pull off such a coup?'

'I've nae idea. Like I said, this is just what I've heard.'

'Where did you get your information from?'

'Some guy called Eric Martin. He's a regular at my pub.'

'Which pub?'

Mark rhymed off an address and Dean nodded. 'I know the place,' he told Carly.

'Good.' She looked back at Mark. 'Your information is wrong. The Tallans are stronger than ever and you made a big mistake challenging them.'

With that, she walked over to the window and drew the curtains.

'What are you doing?' cried Mark, dragging himself to his feet.

'You know what we have to do,' Dean told him. 'We cannae let you get away with challenging our bosses. Jeezo,' he sighed when Mark buried his face in his hands and sobbed. He looked to Carly, who shrugged.

Just wanting to get out of there and knowing he couldn't leave until he'd delivered some sort of punishment, Dean punched Mark three times in the face before concentrating on his ribs and arms. He felt a rib crack and ensured he left plenty of bruising should the Tallans check up on his work. Even though he could have done so much worse, Dean still felt really shitty.

'It's time to go,' he said, picking up the bag. 'And don't even think of calling Eric to warn him we're on our way,' he told Mark. 'If you do, we'll come back here and put you in intensive care.'

Mark just nodded, too sore to speak.

Carly opened the door a crack and peered out. 'The dog's asleep.' She opened the door wider and stepped into the hallway. 'Let's go before she wakes up.'

They rushed to the front door, passing Elizabeth, who didn't even stir, enjoying a deep slumber after her feast.

No one was outside on the street and all seemed quiet, so Dean pulled the door closed behind them and they returned to the car, locking the doors after they'd got in. Carly shoved the gym bag full of money into the footwell.

'We'll drop off the money at the gym and then go and talk to Eric,' said Dean as they set off. 'We won't mention anything Mark said to David, we'll just act as though it was a normal collection.'

'Agreed,' replied Carly. 'I can't get over what he said about the Alexanders. There's no way they could beat the Tallans.'

'Unless they've teamed up with someone else, someone stronger.'

'Then why isn't their name being bandied about rather than the Alexanders? It doesn't make sense. Something is going down and we need to find out what and fast.'

7

They dropped off the cash with David, who didn't seem at all surprised that Mark had failed to pay the full amount. He was satisfied with the way they'd dealt with the situation and told them to go back in a week to collect the remainder. If Mark failed to pay up, they were to break his kneecaps. To Dean and Carly, David seemed relaxed and casual, not at all like a man whose bosses were on the verge of losing everything. They got back in the car and drove to the pub where they hoped to find Eric Martin.

It was a typical back street boozer, the exterior of the building pebble-dashed with mesh across the windows. Inside, it was low-ceilinged, gloomy and depressing. Middle-aged men sat around quietly chatting. Dean had told Carly that this place had a notorious reputation for violence, especially at the weekends. There were only two female customers. Both were in their fifties and they looked haggard and worn out with life. They wore fake fur coats and too much make-up and were sipping gin and tonics. They glowered at Carly as she passed their table. Carly shivered, hoping she didn't end up like them one day.

Dean had a quiet word with the landlord, who pointed to a big, beefy man in a leather jacket and blue jeans standing at the fruit machine. The man had a shaved head and a ginger five o'clock shadow.

Carly and Dean came up on either side of him.

''Scuse me, pal,' opened Dean.

Eric didn't reply, attention riveted to the machine.

'I take it you're Eric Martin?' continued Dean undaunted.

'What about it?' he replied without deigning to look at him.

'We need a word.'

Finally, Eric raised his head to regard them both. He looked from Dean to Carly and back again and smiled. 'Shouldn't you two be at school?'

Dean decided to ignore the stupid comment. 'We've just been to see your pal, Mark Fowler.'

Now they had Eric's attention. He rounded on Dean with a snarl. 'What the fuck did you do to him?'

'Let's just say he won't be going to the gym for a while.'

'Bastard,' he spat.

When he drew back his fist, Dean grabbed his arm and twisted it downwards. He held Eric there, so the right side of his body was pulled down.

'Don't make me embarrass you in front of your friends. We just want to talk.'

'Aye, all right,' he grimaced.

Eric gasped with relief when Dean released him, massaging his shoulder while looking around to see if anyone had witnessed his humiliation. A few people had but they hastily looked away.

'Do you want a pint, Eric?' Carly asked him.

That cheered him up. 'Aye, that would be great, thanks doll. I've got a real drouth on.'

'Why don't you two take a seat and I'll get the drinks in,' she said, smiling.

As Carly bustled up to the bar, Eric looked to Dean. 'Your wee girlfriend's got manners. You could learn a thing or two from her.'

'She's my cousin, no' my girlfriend.'

'If I were you, I wouldnae let that stop me. She's got a cracking arse.'

Dean rolled his eyes. 'Sit down.'

Eric grunted again but obeyed, still massaging his shoulder. 'Why did you hurt Mark?' he demanded the moment they'd sat down together at a quiet table in the corner.

'Because he failed to pay back all the money he owed the Tallans.'

Eric's eyes widened. 'You work for the Tallans?'

Dean nodded.

'Oh, shite. Look, I wasnae really gonnae hit you...'

'Forget about it, I already have. Mark said you told him the Tallans were finished and the Alexanders from Haghill were taking over.'

Eric turned bright red before all the colour drained from his face. 'He's lying.'

'No, he wasn't. The man's an abject coward and he only thought it safe to try and get his dog to attack us because, in his mind, the Tallans were a spent force, which is bollocks by the way. They're stronger than ever.'

'Have you told Rod and Neil what he said?' replied Eric awkwardly.

'No. So far, only me and my cousin know. If you want to keep it that way, then you'll tell us where you got your information from.'

'Some arsehole called Reggy Jones. He works for the Tallans.'

'Doing what?'

'He runs their gym.'

'The one on Clements Street?' said Dean. That was the same gym where they always met David.

'Aye, that's the one. He's been there for five years now and he's pretty close to David, who's the Tallans' top lieutenant. So, if anyone's in the know, it's him.'

'Did he say where he got his information from? Was it David himself or someone else?'

'He didnae say and I didnae ask. I've no' blabbed it about, I'm no' stupid. The Tallans will do anything to protect their reputations and I didnae want them coming after me for running my mouth off. The only person I've told is Mark because he's my pal and he was really feared about the consequences of no' having the full seventeen grand to hand over. I wish I'd kept it to myself now. He's really landed me in it.'

'Do you know the Alexanders in Haghill?'

'I'd never heard of them until Reggy mentioned them. Cheers, doll,' added Eric when Carly placed his pint of lager before him and took the chair beside Dean. She'd bought an orange juice for herself and her cousin, which she also placed on the table. Carly didn't interrupt, not wanting to make Eric clam up.

'Does your friend Reggy know the Alexanders?' Dean asked him.

'I assumed from the way he was talking he did.'

'The Alexanders are petty criminals. How would they be capable of taking anything from the Tallans?'

'Nae idea. Reggy was very hush-hush. He kept tapping the side of his nose and winking, like a proper prick. If Mark hadnae told me about his debt, I would have forgotten all about it.'

'Can Reggy be relied on to tell the truth?'

'In my experience, aye and no way would he talk against the Tallans if he wasnae sure of himself. He knows what they'd do to him if they found out.'

Eric couldn't tell them anything else useful and he kept giving

Carly lascivious glances, so Dean decided it was time for them to leave.

'This gets weirder and weirder,' said Carly once they were back in the car and they'd left the pub behind. 'I don't have a bloody clue what's going on.'

'Me neither and I'm reluctant to approach Reggy, especially at the gym.'

'Me too. I get the feeling it wouldn't go very well for us if the Tallans found out we'd been asking about them.'

'I think our best bet is to tell the rest of the family. Da's contacts might know something.'

Carly nodded. 'Let's head back to the flat.'

They arrived back to find everyone was out. Derek was sitting with Alec who was asleep, leaving his friend to watch the television in his bedroom.

When Carly and Dean returned, Derek crept out of Alec's room and quietly closed the door.

'Where is everyone?' Carly asked him.

'Harry and Jane are working, Rose is at school and Eddie's gone to the supermarket. I popped by for a visit and said I'd sit with Alec until someone came back. Jane said you wouldn't be long.'

'Thanks, Derek. That's really good of you.'

'It's the least I can do for one of my oldest pals. We had a good catch-up and watched a cookery programme. I enjoyed it. I'm thinking of serving food at the pub, so I've been inspired. It was pretty fancy nosh on that programme though. I'm no' sure my customers would like sous vide duck with pickled shiitake and date puree. Alec does like his pretentious cookery shows. If I served that shite to my customers, they'd lock me in the cludgie and set fire to the pub while waving their pitchforks and torches.'

'Are you saying your customers are unsophisticated?' Carly asked him with a smile.

'No. I'm saying they're a bunch of uncultured pigs who are only satisfied with food swimming in grease with a side order of baked beans.'

'Hey, we're your customers too,' she said, playfully slapping him on the arm.

'Aye, I know, hen. Don't worry, I'd get in a vat of chips for you lot.'

'Away with you, ya cheeky sod,' she laughed.

'I'd better get back to the pub. I've been gone a bit longer than I told Sharon and she'll give me one of her looks. I cannae stand it when she puckers those massive red lips of hers at me in disapproval. Makes me feel like a naughty wean.'

Carly and Dean watched Derek pull open the front door and stand frozen in the doorway when he saw the cemetery across the road. That place never failed to freak him out, even in broad daylight, a fact the Savages were well aware of.

'Something wrong?' said Carly knowingly.

'No,' replied Derek. 'I was just wondering if I left my phone in Alec's room.'

'It's sticking out of your back pocket.'

Derek reached around to the back of his jeans. 'Oh, aye. Right, well, I'd better be going then.'

He continued to hesitate on the doorstep, reluctant to step outside.

Derek physically jumped when an eerie laugh cackled in his ear.

'Jesus Christ, Dean, ya bastard,' he exclaimed, putting a hand to his heart.

'That was cruel, Dean,' said Carly while trying not to laugh.

'What?' he innocently replied. 'It was just a joke. There's no way Derek's scared of a wee graveyard.'

'I'm going before you give me a heart attack,' muttered Derek.

Dean grinned when he stepped outside and hesitated once again. When Derek glanced over his shoulder and saw they were watching him, he threw back his shoulders and confidently strode down the street, only slowing his pace once he'd got well past the graveyard.

'You're a mean bugger,' Carly told Dean as she closed the door.

'I couldn't help myself.' He grinned.

'I'll check on Da', make sure Derek's girly screams didn't wake him.'

She pushed open the door of her father's bedroom and saw he was still fast asleep, so she quietly closed it. 'He's out for the count,' she told Dean.

'What do we do now?' he replied. 'Just wait for the others to return?'

'I suppose.'

They looked at each other, both very conscious of the fact that they were alone together in the flat, for once.

Dean couldn't keep his feelings in any longer. He had to be true to himself. If he let her go, he would always regret it. His father's warnings instantly went out of his head. 'Carly, I...'

The front door opened and Carly and Dean took a step away from each other.

Jane stopped and frowned. 'Why are you two lurking in the hallway?'

'We're not lurking,' replied Carly. 'I've just checked on Da' to make sure he was still asleep after Derek screamed like a girl.'

'Why did he scream like a girl?' said Harry, who had followed Jane inside.

'He was getting spooked by the graveyard and I did a creepy laugh in his ear,' replied Dean.

Harry sniggered. 'Nice one.'

'How did your collection go?' Carly asked her sister.

'Fine, no problems. You?'

'We had another fanny who thought he could challenge the Tallans. He tried to set a Rottweiler called Elizabeth on us.'

'Elizabeth?' Harry laughed. 'Brilliant.'

'Why is it all your collections get challenged and not ours?' said Jane.

'That's what I'm starting to wonder,' replied Carly. 'Has your da' heard anything from his contacts?' she asked Harry.

'Not that I've heard. Where is he? He was here when we left.'

'Derek said he went to the supermarket.'

'Which means he's really in the pub,' commented Dean.

'I'll call him and get him to come back,' said Harry, producing his phone. 'We need another pow-wow.'

* * *

Eddie arrived at the flat half an hour later smelling of alcohol and cheap perfume.

'And what have you been up to?' Harry asked his father as he slumped into a chair at the kitchen table. 'Boozing it up while we were all out working?'

Eddie's look was haughty. 'Actually, I was talking to a contact of mine.'

'A contact who buys shitey perfume from the market?' he said sceptically.

'Hey, women can be contacts too. It's no' just men in the know. I didnae expect such a sexist comment from you, pal.'

'All right, all right. And what did the old tart have to say?'

'Candice is not an old tart. She's actually pretty classy. She raises her pinky when she drinks her pints of Guinness.'

'Wow, impressive,' his son sarcastically replied. 'Did she have any useful information?'

'Aye. You can unclog a drain with coffee grounds. You can use them as a degreaser too.'

'Jeezo, I meant information about the Alexanders and Tallans,' he exclaimed.

'Oh, them? No.'

'Great,' Harry sighed. 'Well, while you've been out drinking, Carly and Dean had more trouble at another collection.'

'Trouble?' said Eddie, looking to his younger son and niece.

Carly left it to Dean to explain.

'The Alexanders?' Eddie laughed when he'd finished. 'That's the stupidest thing I've ever heard. How could that bag of fannies ever hope to take on the Tallans? They'd be obliterated. Naw, either Reggy has got it wrong or he's deliberately stirring the shite.'

'Or maybe he knows something we don't?' said Carly.

She had expected her uncle to shoot down this statement, but instead his expression turned thoughtful.

'Or he could be spreading those rumours on behalf of the Tallans,' he said.

They all frowned at him.

Harry frowned. 'Why the hell would they want that?'

'Nae idea but it's possible. What would they have to gain from it?' He murmured this last question to himself as he attempted to puzzle it out.

'Nothing,' said Jane. 'They'd only make themselves look weak if everyone thinks the Alexanders can beat them.'

'Always let your enemy underestimate you,' replied Eddie. 'That's one of the first rules of this game.'

'If that is their plan then they've gone way beyond everyone underestimating them. They'll all think they've lost their minds.'

'A lot of people wouldn't even believe it,' said Harry. 'They'd just think it was the Alexanders telling lies to make themselves look the big men.'

'Maybe, maybe not,' replied Eddie. He looked to Carly. 'You know that family better than any of us. Is it possible the Alexanders started that rumour themselves?'

'I don't think so,' she replied. 'They're ambitious but not stupid. Well, not *that* stupid. They know the Tallans would find out and punish them. Not even Jessica would be willing to take that risk.'

'I reckon you're right.'

'It's strange how it's mine and Dean's collections people keep challenging. Only one person has done it to Harry and Jane.'

'And that's only because the person in question was aff his nut on crack at the time,' said Harry. 'He actually thought we were a pair of trolls who wanted to eat him.'

'I can see how he made that mistake in your case,' Dean told his brother.

'There's only one way to find out what's really going on,' said Carly. 'Speak to the Alexanders.'

'We cannae trust a word that comes out of their mouths,' said Harry.

'It's either that or ask David and we can't trust him to tell us what's going on either. Plus he won't like it that we're asking questions.'

'You're right,' Eddie told her. 'Speaking to the Alexanders is the best bet. The question is, which one?'

'Not Brian,' said Jane. 'He's kept on the periphery now. Jessica will just lie and Ross will want a scrap.'

'That leaves Cole and Dominic.'

'I could speak to Cole,' said Carly.

Dean opened his mouth to object but his dad got there first.

'Absolutely not,' said Eddie. 'No' after he chased you through a graveyard with a knife.'

'But he didn't hurt me, even though he could have done.' Carly decided against telling them about the kiss they'd shared. 'We have to ask one of them and I think he's the best bet.'

'Dominic can be weak when Ross isn't around,' said Jane, who wasn't happy either about her sister approaching Cole. 'He would probably tell us more.'

'I'm just thinking about what Jessica told me – she said Cole's the future of their family, the real leader. I got the sense that all the big decisions will be made by the two of them. He might know more than his brothers.'

'That's a good point, hen,' said Eddie. 'But I don't like the thought of you going to see him alone."

'Neither do I,' said Dean and Jane in unison.

'I'll approach him at the garage where he works.'

'He won't tell you anything,' said Harry. His eyes narrowed with malice. 'Unless you're gonnae torture it out of the bastard.'

'It's not what I had planned but you never know. Besides, he won't try anything at work.'

'All right, do it,' said Eddie.

'I'm no' sure this is a good idea, Da',' said Dean.

'It's the best we've got and the lassie can handle that prick.' He fixed Carly with a hard look. 'Just don't go falling for the walloper again, okay?'

'As if I'd ever do that after what he did,' she retorted. 'My feelings for Cole have completely gone.'

'Aye, good. Just make sure it stays that way.'

'Why wouldn't it?' demanded Carly.

'Because love is a sadistic bastard that suddenly sneaks up on you when you least expect it and when it does, it knocks you off your fucking feet, bringing back with it all that horrible pain.'

His niece's expression softened as she realised he was thinking of his own lost love. 'I won't let it, promise.'

'Good because I'd hate you to go through what I've had to suffer,' he said, eyes stormy.

Carly glanced at her cousins and saw they were looking away, embarrassed at this unusual outburst from their father.

'I appreciate that,' she gently replied, not knowing what else to say.

Eddie nodded once and took a deep breath, the cheerful smile returning to his face. 'Anyone fancy a pint?'

8

Cole sighed as he worked on the Ford Focus ST. This model had once been his dream car, especially as it was the sporty version, but now he wanted more. His mother had made him realise that he deserved the best and the nippy little Ford he'd imagined in his future had been replaced with a Porsche or a Tesla or maybe even a Lamborghini. Why shouldn't he drive a car like that? He was fucking entitled; he worked hard enough.

He straightened up and stretched, back aching after bending over the car for so long. Cole sighed again as he looked around the garage, which was little more than a junk yard. Only the clapped-out cars or the dodgy ones were ever brought here. He never got his hands on anything decent but he swore that one day he'd have a garage full of top-of-the-range motors. If his family's plans worked out, then that day wasn't very far off.

His attention was drawn by someone entering the garage. Cole watched with interest as Carly Savage walked in. He had to admit that she looked good. Since she'd started working for the Tallans she'd ditched her usual jeans, jumpers and trainers. Now she wore smart black trousers and shirts with a black jacket and boots. There was a new confidence and maturity about her that screamed here was a woman not to be messed with. It made him a little sad that she was so far from the Carly he'd loved.

The heads of his colleagues turned to watch her pass, but she paid them no attention.

'Hello Carly,' said Cole when she came to a halt before him.

She regarded him with her head tilted to one side before replying, 'Hello, Cole.'

Carly was concealing her thoughts and emotions so well it was impossible for him to read her, despite how close they'd once been. 'Can I help you?' he said.

'Aye, I'd like a quick word.' The way she said it indicated he had no choice in the matter.

'If you insist.' He called over to one of the other two mechanics, 'Davey, I'm taking my break.'

'Nae bother,' he replied.

'This way,' Cole told her.

Carly followed him into the office, which was a draughty Portakabin. The rickety desk was heaped with paperwork. Mugs containing dregs of cold tea were lined up on the windowsill to go mouldy.

'Sorry about the mess,' said Cole. 'Take a seat,' he added, indicating the ugly chair with the ripped orange seat.

'I'll stand if you don't mind,' she said, not wanting to touch anything in the filthy room.

'Oh, right,' he replied, deciding to do the same. 'What can I help you with then? What is it?' He frowned when she smiled knowingly.

'So polite when only recently you were chasing me through a graveyard with a knife.'

His gaze grew cold. 'And if you remember, I didn't stab you. In fact, I kissed you.'

If the memory meant anything to Carly, she didn't show it. Cole controlled his annoyance. She'd matured and he should show that he'd done the same.

'Your family's been really quiet since that happened,' she said, slowly walking around the small room, studying items as she passed them by. 'So we're curious why you've suddenly decided to start causing trouble now.'

'Trouble?' He frowned again. 'Are you talking about when we went into the pub?'

'That's part of it. Why were you there?'

'To get a drink,' he replied as though she were simple.

'You're lying.' She cocked her head to one side in a way that said she could see right into his soul. 'Or don't you know? Are your older brothers keeping you out of it because you're the baby of the family?'

The mocking in her tone annoyed him but he swallowed down his anger. However, he wasn't controlled enough to stop it from showing in his eyes. 'Now it's my turn to ask the questions – why are you here? You're worried about something, aren't you?'

'The only thing that worries me is your family being humiliated again. If you are planning something, I seriously recommend you think again.'

'What's happened to make you think me and my family are plotting against you? It can't just be that time me and my brothers went into the pub.'

'Why were you near my home the same night?'

'Aye.' He smirked. 'I saw the way you all ran off. Scared, were you?'

'Oh yes,' she replied flatly. 'Me, Jane and our mega hard cousins were all feared of you taking down all four of us on your own. We ran off because we were worried about Rose and Da'. So I repeat, what were you doing there?'

'Just taking a stroll,' he replied with a casual shrug. 'It's a free country. Your family might be dominant around here, for now, but that doesnae mean you can dictate where people go.'

'Not yet,' she replied with her own smirk.

Cole moved so he was standing right before her and gazed into her eyes. 'Aren't you going to tell me what's really going on? Is it not working out with the Tallans like you thought it would?'

'It's nothing to do with them.'

'You're lying to me again, Carly. There was a time when we had no secrets from each other.'

'That was before you went to prison and came out a different person. Your mother really did call the polis on you the night of the burglary. She admitted it to me herself. Why won't you believe me?'

'Because I know my maw would never do something like that. Stop trying to come between me and my family because it won't work. We're too tight. So, you're no' gonnae tell me what's going on then?'

'Nothing's going on,' she said coldly. 'How many times must I repeat myself?'

He reached out to touch her face but she slapped his hand away. Cole's laugh was mocking and he was satisfied when he finally saw anger flash in her eyes. Not such an ice princess after all.

'Do your family know you're here?' he asked her.

'Course they do.'

'They must be desperate if they'd send you into the lion's den alone.'

'Lion's den?' She laughed. 'I hate to break it to you, but three grease monkeys are hardly threatening.'

'Don't call me a fucking grease monkey,' he hissed. 'I'm far more than that.'

'Oh aye, I forgot. You're part of a pack of losers too.'

'You cheeky bitch,' he spat. 'You never used to be like this. It's your cousins, they're a bad influence, especially Dean.'

'Still jealous, are you? Pathetic. Go on,' she added when his hands balled into fists. 'Hit me. You can try anyway.'

He thrust his face into hers, so their lips were just inches apart.

'I know all about the taser and baton you carry,' he said. 'Don't think they'll help you here.'

'Three men on one woman. How tough,' she said sarcastically.

'You're hardly a damsel in distress, are you?'

'True. I'll batter the shite out of the lot of you.'

'I always did like your spirit. I hope your new life doesn't kill it.'

'Is that some sort of threat?'

He leaned in to whisper in her ear. 'You'll just have to wait and see.'

Carly took a step back from him. She had expected being so close to Cole would set her heart pounding but he no longer had the same effect on her and that was because he'd betrayed and used her. She'd never forget the way he'd looked at her when he'd set her up for his brothers to kidnap. If it hadn't been for Dean and Harry, they would have been successful. That pain had changed her feelings for him forever.

'I will find out what you're up to,' she told him. 'And when I do, me and my family will make you regret it.'

She turned on her heel and stalked to the door.

'I didn't say you could leave,' called Cole.

'I don't need your permission,' she called back before pulling open the door and exiting the office.

Carly came to a halt when she saw the door into the garage had been closed and the two mechanics were standing before it holding wrenches. Ross and Dominic were also with them.

She reached inside her jacket and pulled out the small baton she kept there. Unfortunately, she'd left the taser at home, not wanting to be caught walking the streets with it.

Carly's gaze was mocking as it settled on Ross, even though she was starting to feel a little nervous. 'I suppose it's understandable you've come mobhanded, especially after what my wee sister did to you.'

Ross glared at the younger of the two mechanics when he sniggered.

Cole casually exited the office behind her. 'We had the feeling that at least one of your lot would come calling,' he told Carly. 'Thinking they can throw their weight about because they work for the Tallans. So I told them to call my brothers if that ever happened,' he added, nodding at the mechanics.

'Oh, I see,' she retorted. 'They're your wee pets.'

'They work for us. They can see we're on the rise and your reign around here is only temporary.'

'How can they possibly think that after you were embarrassingly defeated only six months ago?'

Ross snatched up a piece of piping and slammed it against the wall. 'I'm gonnae break your jaw,' he thundered. 'That'll stop that big fucking mouth of yours.'

'Your threats don't scare me, especially after I saw you greetin' like a wean in A & E after having your tiny testicles twisted.'

Ross's eyes blazed with anger. 'That's it, you bitch.'

They all looked round when there was a thud on the other side of the closed garage door. There was another thud before it burst open and Jane, Jennifer and the rest of the Bitches marched inside carrying tyre irons, baseball bats and crowbars. The room wasn't big enough to accommodate them all, so half the Bitches waited outside, crowding in the doorway to watch the proceedings while the rest followed their leader inside.

The two mechanics put down the wrenches and took a few steps back, hoping the women wouldn't notice them.

'Need a hand, Carly?' Jane asked her.

'Aye, I do,' she replied. 'These cowardly shites were gonnae attack me.'

'I wouldn't expect anything less from these pathetic excuses for men,' replied Jane, lip curling with disgust.

'Who the hell do you think you're talking about?' demanded Dominic.

Jennifer slammed the crowbar she held against the wall beside him, making him jump.

'Shut the fuck up,' she bellowed at Dominic, pointing the crowbar at him.

The tension in the room grew as the men realised these women were perfectly capable of battering the hell out of them.

'You don't look so cocky all of a sudden,' Carly told Cole.

'I wouldn't say that,' he replied. 'I have something none of you do.'

He reached around the back of his jeans, drew a gun and aimed it at her.

Jane's face turned white when she saw a pistol being pointed at her sister's chest. 'Where the fuck did you get that?' she demanded of Cole.

'I've come a long way from the boy you used to know,' he replied, gaze and hand steady. 'I don't want to shoot you, Carly, but I will if anyone lays a hand on my brothers.'

'You dare and I will fucking kill you,' roared Jane, her cheeks flaming crimson with rage.

'Just calm yer jets, you,' Ross told her.

Jane rounded on him, looking so furious he took a step back.

'I'll fucking do you too,' she yelled at him.

'It's all right, Jane,' said Carly, her gaze locked on Cole. 'We're leaving now anyway. This meeting was very informative.'

Carly was satisfied when Cole's gaze flickered. Now he'd worry that he'd inadvertently given something away.

The men didn't interfere as the women backed out of the garage, Carly not daring to turn her back on Cole and his gun until she was outside on the pavement and the garage door had been closed behind them.

'Jesus, that was intense,' said Jennifer as the women hurried down the street in a pack.

'Where the hell did he get that gun from?' exclaimed Carly.

'That's something I'd like to know too,' growled Jane, jaw set. She'd never forget the sight of Cole pointing a gun at her sister and swore that one day she would make him suffer for it.

Sensing her tension, Carly gave her hand a gentle squeeze.

'Thanks, girls,' she called to the Bitches. 'I owe you all a drink.' She smiled when the women let up a cheer.

'That won't be a cheap round,' commented Jennifer. 'Hey, isn't that your hunky cousins at the top of the street?'

The women all looked to see Dean and Harry striding towards them.

'What are you doing here?' demanded Carly when they met in the middle of the street. 'You were supposed to wait back at the flat.'

'We couldnae just hang around doing nothing,' replied Harry. 'It was doing our nuts in.' He looked past his cousins to the Bitches. 'Hello, ladies,' he said, giving them his best smile.

Dean paid them no attention, solely concerned with Carly. 'What happened?'

'Cole pulled a gun on me.'

His entire body went rigid, hands snapping into fists, jaw tensing.

'I'll kill him,' he hissed.

'Don't,' exclaimed Carly when he moved to rush towards the garage. 'It's been dealt with.'

'How? I hope the twat's in a pine box.'

'No, of course not but he knows when to back off.'

'Pricks with guns never know when to back off.'

'If you charge in there, you'll only get shot.'

Jane thanked the Bitches for their support and sent them on their way.

'I can't believe that wee dick has a gun,' said Harry as the four of them continued their journey alone. 'Where did he get it from?'

'That's what I'd like to know,' said Carly. 'Maybe someone he met in prison with the right contacts on the outside?'

'Could be. We can look into that.'

'Was there anyone he was in prison with who could be out now and strong enough to challenge the Tallans?' said Jane.

'Hey, now that's an idea,' said Harry. He glanced at his brother, who nodded in agreement.

Dean was only just managing to keep his mind on the conversation because he was so furious about Cole pulling a gun on Carly. How could he do that to a woman he'd once professed to love?

'I've still got a couple of pals in Bar-L,' continued Harry. 'I'll see what I can find out.'

9

Rose had a couple of friends over and the nurses were with Alec, so they went back to the flat Dean was renting. When they'd first arrived in Haghill six months ago, Eddie had rented a house for himself and his sons, however Dean liked his own space, especially because he was neat and tidy and his brother and Eddie were slobs. His flat was on the ground floor of a large sandstone block and had recently been renovated with a brand-new kitchen. It was always spotless and the only things he owned apart from the essentials were clothes and books, both of which he loved. He'd filled the wardrobes in each of the two bedrooms with his clothes and the spare bedroom contained only an enormous bookcase, which was packed full. Harry liked to joke that it was fortunate he was on the ground floor otherwise his bookcase would have crashed through to the flat beneath with the weight.

Jane and Carly settled themselves on the couch while Harry and Dean went into the kitchen to get drinks and snacks.

'Are you okay?' Jane asked her sister.

'Fine.' She shrugged.

'It's okay not to be after having a gun pointed at you, especially by someone you used to be in love with.'

'I'm totally fine. I admit, it was a bit of a shock but I'm no' gonnae sit around crying about it if that's what you're worried about?'

Jane smiled with pride. Her sister was incredibly tough. She wasn't sure she could have been so calm about having a gun aimed at her.

'Although it does make me sad that he could do that to me after everything we shared.'

'He only cares about ambition and money. He's just like his bitch of a maw.'

'You and the girls were so impressive when you burst in. If Cole hadn't had his wee pea shooter, we would have smashed the shite out of the lot of them.'

'Too right we would, which shows how weak they are.'

'But it means we'll have to be extra careful in our dealings with the Alexanders in the future. If Cole's got a gun then guaranteed his brothers have too. Ross couldn't bear for his little brother to have one and not him.'

'That's a good point. Well, that makes this situation ten times more dangerous. Did you manage to get anything out of him?'

'He didn't admit to anything but he's definitely got a secret. He couldn't help having a good gloat.'

'Who was gloating?' said Harry as he and Dean entered the room with drinks of orange juice and a big bowl of tortilla chips.

'Cole, the wee rat,' replied Carly. 'The Alexanders are definitely up to something, although I couldn't confirm what. Sorry.'

'Don't you apologise, you did the best you could,' said Dean as he and Harry took a seat on the opposing couch.

'So what do we know?' said Jane. 'The Tallans are being challenged by a family as weak as the Alexanders and Cole suddenly has a gun. Why would he even feel the need to take that into work?'

'In case us lot came calling?' said Harry.

'That's a bit much, isn't it?' said Dean. 'You only take a gun into a fight when you expect your opponent to have one and he knows we don't.'

'Maybe he thought it necessary after we hammered his family?'

'Even so,' replied Jane. 'A gun is a bit much especially as it could get him years in prison. I know the last thing he wants is to go back to Bar-L, so carrying it is a huge risk for him.'

'I don't think that gun was meant for us,' said Carly. 'Cole just wanted me to know he had it.'

'Say you're right,' said Harry. 'Then who was it for?'

'Absolutely no idea.'

'He didnae gi'e you a clue when you were talking?'

'Nope. He just spent the time being smug and gloating. He also said the two blokes who work in the garage are now working for his family because they know the Alexanders are on the rise and our reign around here will only be temporary.'

'That confirms it,' said Harry. 'They're scheming. We need to find out what's going on.'

'How do we do that?'

'Well, we... we...' Harry sighed. 'I've nae idea.'

'We could get hold of one of those mechanics and make them tell us why they're supporting the Alexanders,' said Dean.

'That's one possibility,' replied Harry. 'But they will only have been told so much. Da's gone to speak to a couple of contacts. Let's see what he comes back with first.'

'His contacts told him nothing the last time,' commented Carly.

'I don't want to sit around waiting,' said Jane, shooting to her feet and pacing back and forth. 'I want to be doing something. It was my sister Cole pointed a gun at.'

'And she's my cousin,' Harry replied coolly. 'Don't get me wrong, I'm fucking raging about it but Da' may get some information we really need to know before we go steaming in and get shot.'

'You're right,' sighed Jane, raking her fingers through her hair. 'Sorry.'

'It's okay. Sit down and have some tortilla chips.'

Jane retook her seat, scooped up a handful of chips and began munching on them.

'I bought the new Jason Statham film, if anyone wants to watch it?' said Dean.

'For inspiration?' Carly grinned.

'Naw. He comes to us for lessons.' He smiled back.

'I can well believe it.'

The action film distracted them all from their worries and by the time it had finished, they were all in better spirits, the tortilla chips gone. Harry called his father, who was back home, so the four of them walked over there to see him. Dean's flat was a few minutes' walk from Eddie and Harry's house, as was the flat the sisters shared with their father. They wanted to be close so they could reach each other's homes quickly should the need arise.

'Urgh, Da',' exclaimed Harry when the four of them entered to find Eddie in the living room, his top half bare, scratching his pendulous belly.

Carly frowned at the scars on her uncle's stomach. They appeared to be far too haphazard to be surgical scars. Eddie caught her studying them and hastily pulled on his T-shirt.

'Well, it's your own fault for bursting in without knocking,' said Eddie indignantly.

'Why should I knock? I live here,' exclaimed Harry.

'Aye, well... the rest of them should,' he muttered.

'They're your family. Anyway, that's no' important. Carly went to speak to Cole and the wee turd pulled a gun on her.'

'What?' roared Eddie, making them all wince.

'Calm down, she's fine.'

'That's no' the point. Right lads, we're gonnae go and gi'e him a severe doin'.'

'No, you're not,' said Carly. 'We've already been through all that. The Alexanders are up to something and we want to know what. Did your contacts tell you anything useful?'

'Aye, actually. They did.'

Eddie indicated for them all to sit down on the couches, which they did, although Jane had to move the heap of newspapers from her seat and dump it on the floor first.

'I spoke to Winston Dodds,' began Eddie. 'You remember him, boys? He lived a few doors down from us in Clydebank before he moved to Cambuslang.'

'Aye, we remember him,' said Harry. 'He's so crooked he cannae even walk straight.'

'He's got a club foot, ya cheeky wee sod. And he's in the know. He's been working for some pretty heavy-duty dealers and he says strange things are happening. A couple of people connected to the local underworld have disappeared and Winston reckons they're in a shallow grave or have been put in an incinerator.'

'Why something so drastic?' said Dean. 'They could have got bored of their lives and left or done a runner to avoid a debt.'

'Because both of them were really nervous for a few days before they went missing. They thought they were being followed.'

'By who?'

'They didnae know but they were really jittery and these weren't a pair of wussies. They were proper hard men. Winston was certain someone got to them and did them in.'

'It doesn't mean it's anything to do with us,' said Dean.

'I don't like it when stuff happens at the same time. Even if it isn't related it gets everyone edgy and things get worse. No one trusts anyone and people start stabbing each other in the back.'

'Literally or metaphorically?' said Jane.

'Both. I'm going into Bar-L to speak to a pal of mine. I've got a visit booked with him tomorrow. He's in for three years for robbery. If there's anything worth knowing, then he'll know it. My other pal's still stuck in segregation, so he's no use.'

'How can your pal know anything being stuck in prison?' said Carly.

Eddie's smile was patronising, pleased he was able to dispense some wisdom. 'Prisons are full of interesting gossip. People are constantly coming in, bringing fresh news, and prisoners have little else to do other than gossip.'

'I see,' she muttered, not liking his tone but understanding her uncle meant no offence, it was just his way. She glanced at Dean, who was sitting beside her and his eyes twinkled with amusement.

'I cannae wait to hear what he has to say,' continued Eddie. 'Hopefully he can shed some light on the situation.'

'Good,' said Jane. 'Because if the Alexanders are arming them-selves then we need all the help we can get.'

* * *

After only two days off, Dean and Carly were unexpectedly called into the gym to meet with David.

'Neil and Rod have decided to step things up a little for you,' he opened once they'd joined him in the office to talk. 'You're moving onto the blackmail operation.'

'Are Jane and Harry moving onto it too?' said Carly.

'No, but they didn't just fight off four people on motorbikes.' He produced a mobile phone from his desk drawer and held it out to them. Dean took it from him.

'There's only one thing on that phone,' continued David. 'A video of the mark getting up to the thing we're gonnae blackmail him over. Watch it. You need to know what he's done if you're gonnae convince him to cough up.'

Dean brought up the video and held it out so Carly could see too. They found themselves looking at a flabby middle-aged man wearing only a studded black leather posing pouch and a black leather waistcoat. He was being led around the room by a chain wrapped around his testicles. The woman holding the other end of that chain was clearly a dominatrix in her incredibly high heels, tight black PVC miniskirt and black bra.

Dean winced. 'Jeezo.'

'I know,' said David. 'Makes your eyes water, doesn't it?'

'What the hell does he get out of that?'

'Nae idea but he bloody loves it. That man is Alan Harper, a renowned plastic surgeon. He's fucking loaded and you're gonnae demand ten grand from him.'

Dean and Carly both frowned. 'Is that all?' said the latter.

'For now. Start off low, he'll pay up just to get rid of you and think himself lucky. But each time you visit the price will go up by five grand.'

'For how long?'

David shrugged. 'We'll play that by ear. This is a new business to us, so we can't predict how it'll go yet. You're the litmus test.'

'And you're not going to use Eddie for your first litmus test?'

'Why should we?'

'Because he's older and more experienced.'

'Rod and Neil have their reasons for using you two, so take it as the compliment it is. Well, don't just stand there looking confused, get on with it. Alan's at home Tuesday mornings, so you'd better get there before he goes out.'

'What if he refuses to pay?' said Dean.

'Then change his mind.'

'How far should we go?'

'You can break some bones but don't get carried away. I trust you both to use your judgement. Besides, it won't be you two he's afraid of, it'll be that video. If he doesn't pay up then it'll be posted to social media and sent to all his colleagues as well as his wife and daughter.'

'How old is his daughter?' Carly frowned.

'Twenty-one. Don't panic, we wouldnae send it to a wean.'

Dean and Carly left, feeling a little blindsided by this turn of events.

10

Dean and Carly found themselves pulling up the drive of another mansion, only this one was newer and more modern. A white Audi SUV was parked outside.

Dean pressed the doorbell, which they heard tunefully peal through the house. No one answered and he was about to ring again when the door was opened by the man they'd seen in the video, only this time he was wearing a white shirt, sleeves rolled up to the elbows, and baggy beige cargo trousers. His feet were bare and his sandy-coloured hair was ruffled. He looked like he should be in a shack on the beach rather than in this grand home. In one hand he cradled a whisky glass that was filled to the brim with Scotch, ice cubes clinking against the sides. His eyes were bloodshot and there were dark shadows under them. It looked like he hadn't slept very well.

'Hello, Alan,' said Dean.

'Sorry, do I know you?' he politely enquired.

'Not yet.'

'I don't understand.'

'Can we come in? We've some business to discuss.'

Alan glanced from Dean to Carly and back again, uncertainty in his eyes. 'I've no idea who you are and I don't let strangers into my home.'

'We work for the Tallans.'

'Rod and Neil?' He smiled. 'Oh aye, how are they?'

'Very well, thank you. There's something they want you to see on this phone,' said Dean, producing the device David had given him from his inner jacket pocket.

'Oh, right,' he replied, puzzled by this turn of events. 'You'd better come in then, I suppose.'

They followed Alan inside and he closed the door behind them but he kept them in the hallway, not wanting to let them any further into his home.

'So, what's this about?' said Alan a little impatiently.

Without a word, Dean played the video and held out the phone for him to see. Alan's eyebrows shot up his head as he watched but he didn't speak.

'All right, I've seen enough,' he sighed after watching only ten seconds of it.

Dean nodded and slid the phone back inside his jacket, a little confused by Alan's reaction. He wasn't upset or angry. He didn't even seem embarrassed. They watched him drain the glass of whisky in a couple of gulps. It only struck them then that he was a little drunk.

'Why did you show me that?' muttered Alan. His tone indicated he already knew where this was going.

'Rod and Neil want ten grand so they won't send this video to your wife, children and colleagues.'

'Ten grand?' Alan chuckled. 'That's all?'

'Aye, so do the sensible thing and pay up.'

'But it won't just be ten grand, will it? I know what expensive tastes those bastards have. That's just the first payment. Then they'll send you back again and again and each time the price will get higher. Ten grand won't keep them in fancy dinners and suits for very long.'

'I can't say what will happen in the future.'

'Don't treat me like an idiot. I know what this is. I suppose I've only myself to blame; I knew what I was doing when I walked into that brothel but that's the only way I can get my rocks off because my wife refuses to do anything like that with me.'

Dean and Carly glanced at each other, both a little embarrassed by this admission.

'We'll wait here while you get the money,' said Dean, who just wanted to get out of there.

'I'm no' giving you a penny. You can tell Rod and Neil to go ahead and send that video to whoever they like. I don't care. I'm being sued for malpractice and my wife has left me. That's what I get for marrying a gold-digging tart, I suppose. I'm finished. Soon I won't have a pot to piss in.'

'Oh,' said Dean, who was totally unprepared for this eventuality.

'I need a top up,' muttered Alan, gazing into his empty glass. 'You can see yourselves out.'

'We were ordered not to leave without payment.'

'Get this into your skulls – I don't have the money. I suppose you have to do terrible things to me if I don't cough up?'

They both nodded solemnly.

'Fine,' he sighed as though it were all a nuisance. 'I do have something that I know Neil especially has been after for a while and can't get, despite all his cash. A bottle of whisky worth seven grand. Take it or leave it.'

'We'll take it,' said Dean.

'Good. Wait here.'

Alan disappeared through a door to the left and returned a few seconds later clutching the bottle.

'Here,' he said, thrusting it at Dean, who took it from him. 'Now go away and leave me to wallow in my misery.'

Dean looked questioningly at Carly, who nodded and they left quietly. Just before she closed the door behind them, Carly heard Alan start to cry.

'Poor sod,' she said as they returned to the car.

'Aye,' replied Dean. 'That made me feel really shitty, although we don't know why he's being sued for malpractice. He could have done something terrible.'

'True. Well, we'd better get back to David and break the bad news. He won't be happy.'

'Maybe the whisky will take the sting out of things,' said Dean, handing her the bottle so he could drive.

'We can but hope.' She studied the label. 'I've never heard of it but it looks old.'

'It's a good job he didn't give it to my da' because he would have drunk it before we could get it to David.'

'At least Alan didn't try to set a Rottweiler on us.'

'But he did refuse to pay.'

'Aye, but the circumstances are different, aren't they?' She frowned.

'Perhaps. He wasn't trying to challenge the Tallans, he just seemed too depressed to care about what happened to him but it is still another person who didn't pay up. David won't be happy that we didn't batter him but I don't care, it would have felt wrong.'

'It would,' sighed Carly. 'Alan has much more to worry about than us.'

* * *

David didn't take the fact that they failed to get a single pound out of Alan very well. Although he didn't shout, his demeanour grew so cold Carly began to get a little worried. She knew David was a dangerous man but she hadn't seen it for herself, until now.

'So,' he said in a quiet, low tone, voice full of restrained anger. 'Not only did you no' get a penny out of Alan but you didnae kick his heid in either?'

They both nodded.

'And you thought a bottle of fucking whisky was payment enough?' he added, nodding at the bottle that Carly had placed on the desk.

'Alan said Neil had been after that particular bottle for a long time,' said Dean. 'We thought that would be even better.'

'Well it's not,' he growled. 'You don't get it. This job was never about the money, it was about the start of a new operation and you two fucked it up.'

'With all due respect,' said Dean calmly and politely, 'what were we supposed to do? He said he didn't care if we made the video public.'

'It doesn't matter. I wouldnae have thought you two were suckers for a sob story, because that's what he gave you.'

'He said he's being done for malpractice,' said Carly. 'And I did a search on my phone on the way here. It's true. He's being sued for a botched facelift. He stretched his patient's skin so tightly it died.'

David's eyebrows shot up his forehead. 'You mean the skin on her face died?'

Carly nodded.

'Jeezo, I didnae know that could happen.'

'Neither did I and it's horrible.'

'And you think a bastard who kills the skin on women's faces deserves sympathy?' David glared at them before continuing. 'It seems I was wrong about you two. I thought you were more than up to this job but you're too fucking soft.'

Dean's eyes glittered at being called soft but he wisely kept his mouth shut.

'Maybe I'll try Harry and Jane on it instead? I've no doubt they would have hammered Alan, sob story or no'.'

Carly had the feeling he was right. Jane had always been more ruthless than her, it was how she was able to lead the Bitches, and Harry didn't care who he battered, just as long as he got some action.

'If you think it's the right thing to do,' said Dean.

The casual way he spoke annoyed David and his eyes narrowed. 'Fine, I will. You two are good debt collectors but you're fucking useless with anything more complicated. You'll never rise above where you are now while your brother and your sister will go far. Now fuck off out of my sight.'

They left without a word.

'I didn't like being spoken to like I was a naughty wean,' muttered Carly once they were outside. 'Who the fuck does he think he is?'

'Our boss,' replied Dean.

Carly didn't reply until they were back in the car. 'He's not our boss, Rod and Neil are. He's just a go-between.'

'After Rod and Neil, he's next in charge.'

'Whatever,' she retorted. 'What the fuck did he expect? We've never done anything like that before and he expects us to get it right the first time. Well, fine. We'll stick with the debt collecting and let Jane and Harry sort out that shower of shite. Why are you smiling?' she demanded. 'This isn't funny.'

'Sorry, I know. Don't let him get to you, he was just blowing off steam. To be honest, I'd be more than happy for him to hand the blackmail operation over to Harry and Jane and leave us doing what we do best.'

'But you heard him. We'll be stuck at the bottom forever.'

'No, we won't. He was just pissed off. Besides, he's right. We didn't follow the brief.'

'Because we didn't have the heart for it.'

'Which proves we're not right for that sort of work.'

'Maybe.' She sniffed, unwilling to concede that David had been right but unable to contest it either.

'The way I see it, we've got what we want. In my book, that's a good day. How about we grab something to eat? My treat.'

This drew from Carly a reluctant smile. 'Pasta?'

'If that's what the lady wants,' he said, starting the engine.

'Excellent,' she said, feeling happier already.

* * *

A delicious bowl of spaghetti bolognese and a glass of red wine perked Carly up no end. Dean had taken her to a nice little Italian in the west end of the city. They chatted and laughed while they ate and Carly almost managed to forget that she'd been told off.

'I don't want to go back to Haghill,' she said when they'd finished eating. 'Let's go somewhere else.'

'Like where?'

She was tempted to say Gleniffer Braes where they'd shared their first kiss but she didn't want him to think she was hinting at a repeat performance as she had no idea what he felt for her now.

'I don't know, anywhere,' she said instead. 'Somewhere peaceful we can forget about all the shite for a while.'

'We're not far from Kelvingrove Park. That's nice.'

'Okay,' she said.

After Dean had paid, they left the restaurant and drove to the park on the banks of the River Kelvin. They parked up and strolled along the river together. It was a sunny, mild day and there were other people out making the most of it, casually strolling along, talking and smiling.

'Is this peaceful enough for you?' Dean asked Carly.

'It's very nice,' she replied, feeling herself unwind.

They walked in silence for a few minutes, both of them appreciating not having to talk.

'Where do you think our family will be in five years' time?' Carly asked him.

'I really have no idea.'

'I often wonder that. Will we be in an even better position than we are now, or a worse one?'

'I wish I could see into the future but none of us can. All we can do is make the best decisions with the information we have at the time and hope it goes in our favour.'

'I'm worried that we buggered things up for the rest of the family today.'

'I don't think so. Our services are too valuable to the Tallans.'

'Let's hope Jane and Harry do a better job than we did.'

'They will, don't worry.'

'You seem very casual about all this.'

'What's the point in worrying? I can't control what's gonnae happen and I've noticed that things have a habit of working out.'

'I wish I could be as relaxed as you.'

'There is an art to it,' he replied with a devastating smile.

'Go on then.' She smiled back. 'Teach me the art.'

'It's just a matter of silencing that nagging wee voice at the back of your mind telling you that everything is turning to shite when it's not.'

'That's easier said than done. I've tried silencing that voice loads of times, especially when my da's had a bad day or when I didn't know how we were going to pay the bills.'

'But you always managed to pay the bills somehow, didn't you?'

'Aye, something always turned up.' Her sunny expression faded. 'But I know that one day my da' will never recover from a bad day.'

'But you still have time with him. You need to make the most of it.'

'I try but it's so hard sometimes knowing what's gonnae happen. I suppose that's why I got so mad at David today. There he was whining that his target didn't fall for his blackmail scheme, like the Tallans even need that ten grand, when so many families are struggling and suffering. It's pathetic.'

'The Tallans are greedy. They could be billionaires and it would never be enough for them.'

'They've traded their souls for money. Their greed makes them lesser.'

'That's deep,' said Dean with a thoughtful nod. 'Is this leading up to you saying you don't want to work for them?'

'I don't know. I couldn't face going back to how things were before, struggling for money, and I love working with you, Harry and Jane. We're a great team but I don't have it in me to blackmail people. I know that now.'

'And the debt collecting?'

'It's okay, but I certainly don't want to do it forever. Whatever happens, it's so important that our family sticks together.'

'Course we will. It's us against the world now.'

They smiled at each other coyly and Dean felt that intimacy blossoming between them again that he'd felt when they'd been alone at Carly's flat. They turned to face each other and were forced to immediately jump apart when two figures went flying between them on skateboards.

'Oy, watch it, you fucking fannies,' Dean yelled at them, furious about the moment being interrupted.

The two men – which was what they were, not kids – stopped, hopped off the skateboards and rounded on him.

'What the fuck did you say?' demanded one of them with long black hair down to his shoulders.

'You heard,' retorted Dean. 'What were you trying to do, run us down? And aren't you a bit old to be on a skateboard. What are you, thirty?'

'I'm twenty-four, you cheeky bastard.'

'Wow, that must have been a tough paper round, and twenty-four's still too old to be going about on a skateboard. Why don't you get a job?'

'That's fucking it,' snarled the man, snatching up his skateboard and wielding it menacingly. 'I'm gonnae dae you in.'

Dean lowered his head, like a bull about to charge. 'Try and you'll regret it, I promise you that.'

He was using that low, menacing tone that always made Carly tingle and warned his assailant of extreme danger. The long-haired man glanced at his friend.

'Let it go, Davey,' said his friend. 'It's no' worth it.'

'You'd better listen to your pal, Davey boy,' growled Dean. 'Before you get hurt.'

Davey suddenly looked unsure of himself and lowered the skateboard. 'Prick,' he told Dean before running away, skateboard tucked under one arm.

His friend followed, both of them glancing uncertainly back at them.

'You really scared the shite out of them,' Carly told Dean.

'Good. Davey saved himself from getting a skateboard in the face.'

Carly glanced at her watch. 'We've been gone a while. We'd better get back to Haghill or the others will start to worry.'

'Aye, okay,' he replied, disappointed that the intimate moment between them had been ruined by a pair of fuds on skateboards.

11

Dean and Carly were shocked when they returned to the latter's flat to find ten of the Bitches hanging about on the street outside.

'Oh, God,' said Carly as Dean parked the car at the kerb. 'Something's happened. I bet it's because we messed up that collection today.'

'Now we don't know that. It could be anything. Let's find out before jumping to conclusions.'

Carly took a deep, calming breath. 'Aye, you're right. I just can't bear the thought of my family getting hurt because of something I've done.'

Dean smiled. He loved how much she cared about others and always put them first. Every woman he'd dated in the past had been selfish and self-absorbed.

They got out of the car and hurried up to the flat.

'What's going on?' Carly asked Donna, a twenty-year-old woman with masses of curly brown hair.

'Dunno.' She shrugged. 'Jane called us and said to keep an eye out. She's expecting trouble but we've nae idea what.'

Dean and Carly rushed past them and inside.

'Jane,' called the latter the moment they were through the door. 'What's happening?'

Jane emerged from the direction of the kitchen. 'It's all right. Rose just saw Cole pass by the flat and look in through my bedroom window as he went. That was an hour ago and we've not seen him since, but I thought it wise to get some of the girls round to keep an eye out.'

'Have you seen any more of the Alexanders?'

'No, it was just Cole but I was taking no chances, especially with just me, Da' and Rose here. Harry and Uncle Eddie are out.'

'Come on, Carly,' said Dean. 'We'll take a look around.'

'Are you sure that's a good idea?' Jane called after them as they hurried to the door.

'It can't hurt to check,' Dean called back over his shoulder.

The two of them rushed out of the flat, through the throng of Bitches and up the street.

'We could be overreacting,' said Carly. 'Cole might have just been passing through.'

'The Alexanders have gone out of their way to avoid this part of Haghill for the last six months.'

'Cole probably got overconfident because of his little pea shooter,' said Carly bitterly.

'Maybe but it's better to err on the side of caution.'

'What if we do come across him and he's armed?'

'We'll play it by ear. I don't think he's stupid enough to shoot either of us in broad daylight in the middle of the street.'

'You're right, he's not.'

'Let's hope the polis catch him,' growled Dean. 'I'd like to see the wee bastard flung back into Bar-L.'

'That's his biggest fear now. I saw that much in his eyes six months ago whenever prison was mentioned. He could never go back.'

'Then he shouldnae go around pointing pistols at people. If he does that to you again, prison will be the least of his worries because I will bury the twat.'

Carly stopped and took Dean's hand, halting him in his tracks. 'You are not to kill anyone,' she said under her breath. Even though the street was deserted she couldn't trust that no one was listening.

'Don't stick up for him,' he retorted, annoyed.

'I am not sticking up for Cole, I'm trying to protect you. The last thing I want is for you to be sent to prison, especially for him.'

Dean's expression softened and he gave her hand a gentle squeeze. 'That won't happen.'

'It might if you kill someone.'

'I don't intend to kill anyone. I was just mouthing off because I'm so furious about what he's done to you. Breaking your heart and kidnapping you wasn't enough for him, he had to point a gun at you too.'

'If I got over it you can too,' said Carly, very conscious of the fact that he was still holding her hand.

'I want to make him hurt for what he did to you,' he replied, expression darkening.

'You don't need to. He'll probably end up doing it to himself,' she said sadly. 'I knew him before he turned into what he is now and it makes me so sad that that man is gone and is never coming back.'

Dean released her hand and looked away.

'What have I said?' Carly frowned.

'Nothing,' he replied. 'We just need to keep looking.'

'All right,' she said.

They continued walking down the street, Carly giving Dean puzzled sideways glances while he got lost in his own thoughts.

'You sure you're okay?' she asked him.

'Fine,' he replied in a tone that indicated he didn't want to talk.

Carly attempted to shrug off his sudden bad mood and act as though she didn't care but this change had upset her. Had it been something she'd said or was something else bothering him?

They wandered around the streets of Haghill in silence, only this wasn't the restful silence that often existed between them. It was awkward and made Carly not only uncomfortable but feel as though she'd offended him in some way, even if he wouldn't admit it.

After tramping the streets for a good half hour and seeing no sign of any member of the Alexander family, they returned to the flat. Dean hadn't spoken a single word.

'Are you going to tell me what's bothering you before we get back to the flat?' said Carly when they were just a minute's walk from her home.

'Nothing's bothering me,' he mumbled.

'That's shite and you know it.' Carly knew something was definitely wrong because he was avoiding making eye contact. 'So come on, spill.'

'I said nothing's wrong,' he retorted irritably. 'Just drop it, okay?'

With that he marched off down the street leaving Carly to follow him wondering what the hell was going on.

The Bitches were still out in force and stood aside to allow them to pass. They entered the kitchen to find Eddie and Harry had returned. Eddie was making a cup of tea and Harry was sprawled on the couch watching television, which he switched off when they entered.

'Anything?' said Jane, who was washing up, hands encased in yellow rubber gloves.

'Not a thing,' replied Carly.

'I think it's safe to send the Bitches home now,' said Eddie, turning to face them with a teaspoon in his hand. 'I don't think anything's gonnae kick off immediately, although tell them to stay alert.'

Jane nodded, pulled off the rubber gloves, dumped them on the unit and left the kitchen.

'That wee bastard Cole wants us riled up,' continued Eddie. 'He wants us on edge looking for trouble. That's the only reason he made his presence felt here earlier. Do not let him win,' he told his sons and niece sternly.

'Aye, all right, Da',' said Harry while Dean and Carly nodded.

'You two wantin' a brew?' said Eddie, looking from his niece to his younger son.

'Please,' replied Carly.

'No thanks,' muttered Dean. 'I'm going home.'

'I'm no' sure that's wise just yet,' said Eddie. 'Wait here until we're sure it's safe.'

Dean glowered at his father but did as he was told, petulantly flinging himself onto the couch beside his brother.

Eddie looked questioningly at Carly, who shrugged. 'Did your contact in Bar-L know anything?' she asked him.

'Naw, which isnae good.'

'Why?'

'Because it means whatever's going on is being kept very quiet, telling me it's big. And dangerous.'

'Well that's reassuring,' she sighed.

Eddie looked to his niece and frowned when he saw she was shifting awkwardly. 'All right, what's happened?'

'Our collection went a bit wrong today,' she began slowly.

'You didnae get attacked again, did you?' said her uncle as he put the kettle back on.

'No. David started us on the blackmail operation.'

Jane re-entered the room just as she said this and she stared at her sister in surprise, as did Eddie and Harry.

'Why did he put you two on it?' demanded Eddie before adding, 'Nae offence.'

'He was impressed with the way we handled things when we were attacked by those men on motorbikes. He showed us footage of the mark being led about by a dominatrix with a lead tied to his baws.'

'Who was the mark?'

'Some rich plastic surgeon but he said he couldn't pay up because he was being sued for malpractice. So he gave us a bottle of whisky Neil had been after. David was not impressed with us.'

'Why didn't you batter the sod for no' paying?'

'Because he wouldn't have cared. He'd lost his wife, job and reputation and he was soon to be bankrupt. He's being sued for malpractice after killing the skin on a woman's face during a botched facelift.'

'So what? You should still have done it.'

'You didn't see him, he was so pathetic, wasn't he Dean?'

'Suppose.' He shrugged, as though he were only half-listening.

Carly narrowed her eyes at him for his lack of support before turning back to her uncle.

'You knew this was coming, so how could you fail so badly?' said Eddie.

'That's a bit harsh, Da',' said Harry.

'I agree,' interjected Jane with a frown at her uncle, folding her arms across her chest.

'No, it's not.' He looked back at Carly, expression hard. 'You're no' working for Derek any more. If you mess up, the Tallans won't laugh it off and say, *never mind, you'll do better next time.* You fuck up in this game and it could be the last thing you ever do.'

Eddie looked truly angry. It was the first time Carly had ever seen it directed at her or one of his sons. His eyes flashed, the vein in the centre of his forehead popped out and it was as though his body was being inflated by his rage.

'David said he's handing the blackmail side of the operation over to Harry and Jane,' she told him, tilting back her head, refusing to show how disconcerted she was.

'That's fucking lucky for you two then because, had he so chose, David could have decided to get rid of the lot of us.'

'And why would he do that?' she said impatiently. 'It would serve no purpose and killing an entire family would bring a lot of unwanted attention on his bosses. He even said if I didn't have the stomach for the work I could leave with no hard feelings.'

'I didn't think you were stupid, Carly. Do you seriously think he'd allow that with what you know?'

'Well... yeah.'

'Course he won't, he'd see you deid first. Jesus Christ, you're gonnae have to wise up and fast,' he barked at her.

'Don't talk to her like that,' Jane told him.

'Aye,' said Harry. 'That's no' fair.'

'I made a promise to your da',' said Eddie, pointing from Carly to Jane. 'And I'm buggered if I'm gonnae break it but I cannae keep that promise alone. You have to help me, girls, and you can do that best by not being so bloody naïve.'

Carly recognised he was only so angry because he was afraid and her own anger at him dissipated. She glanced at her sister and saw she was thinking the same thing.

'Sorry,' said Carly sheepishly.

'Don't be sorry, just do better next time,' snapped Eddie. He sighed, planted his hands on his hips and shook his head. 'Maybe it's my fault? I haven't trained you well enough. You're only young and just starting out in this game while I've been in it for years.'

'No,' said Carly. 'I let my temper run away from me. I know something strange is going on and I was trying to wheedle it out of David. He didn't like that.'

'You must learn to curb that curiosity. Don't get me wrong, it's a good thing but don't let anyone else see it. That way, you'll find out more.'

Carly nodded thoughtfully. Wise words indeed.

'I'm sorry for shouting,' continued Eddie. 'But I'm so scared I've dragged you into something you cannae handle and now you can't get out.'

'You haven't; I can handle it. Today was sprung on me and Dean, we weren't expecting it and David told us next to nothing. We did our best.'

'Well it's time for a masterclass. All of you,' he told the room firmly. 'Don't whinge,' he told Harry when he groaned.

'Great,' muttered his son. 'Eddie Savage's School for Blackmailers. Sounds thrilling.'

'You'll be the first to get the cane if you keep up that attitude,' retorted his father. 'You and Jane could get called up at any moment to take over the blackmail operation and you will be ready. We're starting right now just in case David changes his mind and decides to gi'e you both another chance,' he added, looking from Dean to Carly.

'Is that likely?' said Carly.

'You never know and that's the first lesson – assume nothing and expect the unexpected.'

'Isn't that two lessons?' said Harry.

'Keep mouthing off at me, boy, and you'll get my foot right up your arse.'

Harry pouted at his father.

'You've all got time, I suppose?' added Eddie. 'None of you have got any embarrassing medical appointments booked or a hot date?'

'If we had, would it get us out of it?' said Harry.

'No.'

'Shame.' He sighed and got to his feet. 'Okay, professor, let's get on with it then.'

'Park your arses,' said Eddie, pointing at the kitchen table.

As they all took their places, Carly glanced at Dean, who still hadn't said a word and who was avoiding her gaze. What the hell had she done to bring this on?

The lecture Eddie gave them lasted a full two hours. He went over how to approach the mark, how to present the evidence they had against them and how to deal with them when they refused to cough up, which mainly involved violence.

'Threaten to go for their eyes,' said Eddie, his own orbs lighting up diabolically. 'They'll shite themselves if they think you're gonnae blind them.'

Carly wasn't comfortable making threats like that but she decided not to let her uncle know because she didn't want him getting on her case again. She looked to Jane and Harry, whose responsibility it would soon be and they both nodded. Somehow she didn't think they would have as big a problem with it as she and Dean had.

Just as Eddie was winding down his lecture, Harry's phone rang.

'It's David,' he said, glancing at the screen.

'Answer it,' replied Eddie.

'I was going to,' he muttered before putting the phone to his ear. 'All right?' he said casually. Harry listened before saying, 'I understand.'

'Well?' said Eddie when he'd hung up.

'David wants me and Jane to meet him at the gym in half an hour.'

'Did he say why?'

'Naw, but I think we can guess.'

'Did he mention us at all?' said Carly, pointing from herself to Dean.

'No.'

'I hope that's a good sign.'

'I guess we'll soon find out.' Harry looked to Jane. 'We'd better go.'

She nodded. 'See you later.'

'Bye,' said Carly.

Her gaze connected with her sister's and Carly wished she didn't have to go to that meeting because she knew what she would have to do.

'Remember everything I just told you,' Eddie called after them as they left.

'It's etched on our hearts,' called back Harry sarcastically.

'He's got a mouth on him has that one,' said Eddie but his eyes were filled with worry.

'They'll be fine,' Carly told him. 'You gave them some really good advice.'

'I wish I'd done the same with you two. What happened earlier was my fault, no' yours. I didnae train you right.'

'We did go soft on Alan. We knew it at the time but he just looked so pathetic.'

'You have to harden your heart in this business.'

'I won't lie, that's something I'm gonnae struggle with.'

'You had no problem watching Brian Alexander being tortured.'

'Because he deserved it.'

'You think someone who kills the skin on people's faces doesnae deserve a good kicking?'

'If I'd known that before we went in then I wouldn't have had a problem.'

'The people the Tallans have selected as targets in this black-mail operation aren't innocents, otherwise how could they be blackmailed? Anyway, there's something else I want to discuss with you. Have you two had a falling out or something?'

'That's what I'd like to know,' said Carly with a hard look Dean's way.

'Eh?' said Eddie.

'He's been really weird since we went out looking for Cole. He suddenly went all quiet and sulky and hasn't said a word since.'

'And you don't know why?'

'Nae idea. I know he's quiet but this is taking the piss.'

'He's always been like that, right from being wee. Always telling off me and Harry when we got too noisy.'

'I am here, you know,' said Dean. 'Don't talk about me like I'm not.'

'Oh, it speaks,' said Eddie, turning to his son. 'So go on then.'

'Go on then what?'

'Tell us why you've got a face like a slapped arse.'

'I haven't,' he mumbled.

'Aye ya dae.'

'I'm just pissed off that today didn't go well, okay?' he growled, willing his dad to let it drop.

Eddie was unconvinced but realised that whatever was wrong with his son was connected to Carly and he wouldn't want to discuss it in front of her. Fortunately at that moment, Alec rang his bell and Carly went to attend to him.

'She's gone now,' Eddie told his son. 'So you can tell me the truth. I won't stop asking until you tell me.'

'Fine,' grunted Dean. 'She started banging on about how sad it is Cole's no longer the man he used to be. I reckon she's still in love with him.'

'Course she's not.'

'You didn't hear her. I really think she is.'

'That lassie stopped loving Cole the moment he tried to abduct her but she will always miss who he was, that's only natural. Who the hell are you to tell her how to feel?'

Dean's expression softened. 'I'm being a prick, aren't I?'

'Aye. This is why I don't want you two getting together. Look what happened today and you're no' even a couple.'

'Don't start all that again.'

'I'm just giving you a wee reminder.'

'Well don't. I haven't forgotten.'

Both men were concerned when Carly entered the room looking stricken.

'What's wrong?' said Dean gently, his previous bad mood forgotten.

'It's Da',' she replied, swallowing down the lump in her throat.

Eddie leapt to his feet, eyes full of pain. 'Does he need an ambulance?'

'No, it's nothing like that. He needs the bathroom but he can't get there on his own, even with the Zimmer frame.'

'Oh hell,' sighed Eddie, knowing exactly what that meant. 'Come on, Dean. Your uncle needs help.'

'Aye, course,' he said, getting to his feet.

Carly stood aside to allow them to pass. Eddie patted her on the shoulder as he went. Dean hesitated by her and Carly was relieved that he was once again looking at her as he always had. He didn't say anything, he just gave her hand a gentle squeeze before following his father into Alec's bedroom.

Carly waited at the kitchen table for them to return, knowing her father wouldn't want her seeing him having to be helped to the toilet. What did this mean for things going forward? He would never allow her and her sisters to help him to the bathroom, he would find it far too humiliating. He had a commode in his room that he had never used because he loathed it. If he couldn't even make it to that on his own then would Eddie, Harry and Dean have to move in here and she and her sisters move out? The thought of not living with her father was a painful one. The prospect of him going into a home was even worse.

Eddie and Dean returned ten minutes later.

'How is he?' said Carly anxiously.

'He's fine; we settled him back into bed,' replied her uncle. 'You know your da', tough as old boots.'

Carly was quick to spot the sadness in his eyes. 'He's getting worse and soon everything will change.'

'It was just a one-off, that's all.'

'It's not, I just know it. What if you and Dean hadn't been here? No way could I have got him to the toilet on my own.'

'Then he would have used the commode instead. He only didn't because he knew we were here to help.'

'He hates the commode.'

'But he will use it if the only alternative is being parted from his girls.' He rested his hand on her arm. 'You're no' losing him yet, hen. I promise you that. We'll do whatever it takes to keep him at home for as long as possible. I'll sleep on the bloody couch so I can be around to help if needs be but he is staying in his home, okay?'

Carly's eyes filled with tears but she didn't wipe them away, knowing her uncle wouldn't see them as a weakness because he felt exactly the same way. 'I don't want Rose knowing about this, not with all the pressure she's under with her exams.'

'Of course. We'll shoulder the burden so she doesn't have to.'

A tear spilled down Carly's cheek. 'I'm so glad you're here,' she told them.

'And we always will be. Don't you worry about that.'

'Course we will,' said Dean. 'We're going nowhere.'

'You've no idea how much that means to me,' she replied, wiping her eyes on the backs of her hands.

Dean was ashamed about his previous sulk. Carly already had so much going on and he was getting angry with her for such a petty reason. He swore he would never get angry with her ever again.

12

Jane and Harry returned to the flat nearly three hours later. They both looked so sombre Carly was afraid they'd stuffed up their latest collection as she and Dean had, until Harry broke into a grin.

'It went like a dream,' he said.

'Thank God for that,' breathed Carly.

'David sent us to this flash penthouse. The guy we were there to blackmail was having an affair with his twenty-three-year-old personal trainer. To be honest, I felt like battering him for his lack of imagination. He started crying when we threatened to tell his wife and he paid up no problem. David was really pleased.'

'To be fair,' said Jane. 'Our mark didn't try to object; he was too scared when the Tallans' name was mentioned.'

'It won't be the last time you pay him a visit,' said Eddie. 'Now he's coughed up once you'll have to keep going back until he's nothing left.' He studied Jane and Harry carefully as he spoke, searching for a wince but neither of them reacted. 'Good work,' he told them.

'Thanks,' said Jane while casting an apologetic look at Carly and Dean.

'It's fine.' Carly smiled. 'Honestly. You two are obviously better at it than us, which I'm rather glad about. It means we can stick to debt collecting.'

'Good,' said Eddie. 'Then everything's worked out for the best. You're all happy and the Tallans will be happy too.'

They all looked at Dean when his phone rang.

'I don't like that timing,' said Carly.

'Me neither,' said Dean, studying his phone screen. 'And it says number withheld.'

'You'd better answer it,' said Eddie.

Dean nodded and put the phone to his ear. 'Hello?' He listened before replying. 'Okay, we'll...' He frowned at the screen. 'He hung up. That was Neil Tallan. He wants to talk to us,' he added, looking to Carly. 'We've to go straight to the pub they own.'

'Shite,' she sighed, raking her fingers through her long hair.

'We'll come with you,' said Harry, pointing from himself to Jane.

'You won't help their cause by going along to hold their hands,' said Eddie. 'After today's mess up they need to look strong and capable and they cannae dae that taking along their big brother and sister.'

'You're right,' Carly told her uncle.

'Aye, I am. They're no' gonnae dae anything to you in a pub. You'll be fine. Now away you go. You don't want to piss them off even more by being late.'

Dean and Carly nodded and got to their feet.

'Are you sure about this?' Jane asked Eddie, her eyes bright with worry. 'Perhaps we should be nearby, just in case?'

'No,' said Eddie. 'You won't be doing them any favours, trust me.'

'We'll be fine,' Carly told her sister. 'Don't worry.'

But Jane's eyes were heavy with worry.

'We'll call you as soon as we're out of the meeting,' said Dean before he and Carly left together, leaving the rest of the family behind. They all looked anxious, even Eddie, despite his reassuring words.

* * *

Carly was relieved that Dean was being his normal self with her again, especially as they were going into this meeting, because it was vital they were united.

'I'm not looking forward to this,' said Carly as Dean parked further down the street, as there were no free spaces outside the pub.

'Me neither but we've no choice. And it's like Da' said – they can't do anything to us inside a pub.'

'Are you sure about that? The worst thing will be if we walk in there and find it empty, just plastic sheeting down on the floor.'

'That won't happen. The Tallans aren't idiots.'

'What if they're the ones who've been making people disappear?'

'If the Tallans were responsible for making those men disappear then they're no' stupid enough to call us to lure us out because they must know we've told the rest of the family that we were coming here.'

'That's a good point. Oh, well, we'd better go in.'

'Suppose,' he muttered, as reluctant as she was.

They got out of the car and strode purposefully down the street together, looking strong and confident, although inside they were both jittery.

To their relief, the pub was busy and bustling, people either propping up the bar to chat and drink or sitting at the tables to eat. The delicious aromas made Carly's stomach rumble and only then did she realise she'd missed her dinner with everything going on.

David was waiting for them at the back of the room. He gave them a stern nod, indicating for them to follow before vanishing through the door at the rear of the room.

'He still looks pissed off with us,' said Carly.

Dean nodded but didn't reply and they crossed the room, no one paying them the slightest bit of attention, before going through the door David had disappeared through. He was waiting for them on the other side and gave them another hard look before continuing on his way down the corridor.

David opened the door to the same meeting room where they'd met Neil and Rod for the first time, to find the brothers seated at the head of the table, looking very stern.

Carly didn't like the way Rod's eyes bored into her, but she forced herself not to show it.

'Thank you, David,' said Neil. 'You may leave us.'

He nodded and left the room, closing the door behind him.

'Take a seat you two,' said Neil, gesturing to the chairs at the opposite end of the table.

Carly and Dean sat and regarded the brothers expectantly.

'We heard about the fuck up with Alan Harper,' said Rod.

'Sorry about that,' replied Dean.

'Sorry doesnae cut it.' He scowled. 'You were given a job to do and you bollocksed it up.'

'Although I must say,' interjected Neil. 'I was very pleased with that bottle of whisky.'

'But you weren't sent to get a bottle of whisky,' Rod told them. 'You were supposed to pick up ten grand, so that money is going to come out of your own pockets.'

Carly opened her mouth to tell them that wasn't fair but she caught Dean's gaze and decided against it.

'Any objections?' said Neil with a raised eyebrow.

'No,' she muttered while Dean shook his head.

'You're paid well, so it shouldn't be a problem if you've been wise with your cash. Anyway, from now on you will stick to debt collecting while Jane and Harry tackle the other side of our operation. They were very efficient today, unlike you two,' he added with a severe look that made Carly feel like she was back at school getting told off by the headmaster. It annoyed her.

'Maybe if we'd been given some warning or even a little advice then things would have gone better,' she retorted.

Dean shot her a look to be quiet but she ignored it.

'What did you say?' said Neil, screwing up his face with annoyance.

'David just sprung it on us knowing full well we'd done nothing like it before in our lives and he expected it to go perfectly, which is completely unreasonable.'

'Carly,' Dean hissed at her when Neil's face turned puce with anger.

'Who the fuck are you to talk to us like that?' demanded Neil.

'I don't mean any disrespect...'

'It doesn't fucking sound like it.'

'...but it has to be said. We went into that situation totally unprepared. Fortunately, the worst that happened was that you got a very expensive bottle of whisky.'

'No' that expensive. I've got one worth forty grand.'

'But it could have gone a lot worse.'

Neil looked from Carly to his brother, who merely appeared amused, and back again.

'Is that the end of your grand speech?' Neil demanded of her.

'That's it but you have to remember that I'm only twenty and Dean's twenty-three. Dean has some experience but this is my first time working in this industry.'

'Industry,' chuckled Rod.

'So mistakes will be made; we are only human after all but we do pick things up quickly and we learn from our mistakes.'

'You're saying you want another shot at it?' said Neil.

'No, that's not—'

But Neil spoke over her. 'It sounds like it to me. Fine, Little Miss Gobby, have it your own way. You're going for a second try and, so help you God, if you don't come back with the full amount in cash then both of you had better prepare yourselves to spend some considerable time in intensive care.'

Carly decided not to speak again. She clearly hadn't helped so far.

'David will give you your instructions and if you've any questions, then ask him,' yelled Neil, thumping his fist off the table. 'Now fuck off out of my sight both of you.'

Dean got to his feet. 'Thank you,' he told them politely before looking to Carly and jabbing a finger at the door.

She nodded and rose, looking sheepish. As she left with Dean, she could feel Rod's eyes boring into her back.

'Well that was very entertaining,' laughed Rod when they'd gone.

'Entertaining?' spluttered Neil. 'What a cheeky bitch. That lassie's got a gob on her the size of the Clyde Tunnel and she's fucking lucky she's walking out of here in one piece.'

'Oh, please,' said Rod, waving a dismissive hand. 'There's no way you would have laid a finger on either of them with all the customers in the pub and you know it. Don't you admire her courage? No' even David would have dared speak to us like that.'

'Because he knows his fucking place. That mouthy wee coo has a lot to learn.'

'Of course she does. Like she said, she's only twenty. If we employ people that age, then we have to make allowances for the recklessness of youth. Don't you remember how we were at the same age?'

'Aye, but... that's no' the point,' Neil barked. 'I will not be spoken to like that, especially in my own pub.'

'I admired her. That took a lot of courage. Her big, muscular cousin wasnae gonnae say a word.'

'Because he's got more sense.'

'You should be glad we're employing someone with such backbone. Don't forget, this is the same woman who managed to break our man's kneecap while she was being pulled backwards out of a moving car by her hair.'

Neil sighed and nodded. 'Aye, which is why the lassie walked out of here with her kneecaps intact. But I mean it – they fuck up again and they will pay the consequences. This isn't a school we're running, it's a business and we cannae afford any more mistakes.'

'Fair enough. They won't let us down.'

Neil narrowed his eyes at his brother. 'The only reason you're being so calm about it all is because you fancy her. If she'd been a man, you would have broken her jaw.'

'Perhaps. I'd love to see her naked.'

'You're no' to touch her. Working with that family is going to be complicated enough without bringing your penis into the equation.' Neil grimaced. 'There's an image I didn't need.'

'Relax, I've already said I won't act on it. But I can admire her from afar.'

'Just as long as all you're doing is looking.'

Rod smiled again, thinking how funny it was that his brother had let Carly Savage get to him so much when very few people could.

13

David was waiting for Carly and Dean outside the door.

'Well?' he asked them.

'We've to try again,' said Dean.

'I am surprised, or maybe not. This way.'

They followed him into a room further down the hall that turned out to be the pub office. Carly threw Dean an apologetic look, which he returned with a hard look of his own.

David threw himself into the chair behind the desk but didn't invite them to sit.

'I'm guessing if you fuck up this job there will be consequences?' he asked them.

They both nodded.

'Then you'd better get this right because I'm sure Neil and Rod will come up with a very special punishment just for you two if you fail again.'

'We won't,' said Carly with much more confidence than she felt.

David's look was doubtful. He handed Dean another phone. 'Melanie Jones,' he told them. 'Or at least, that's the name she's using now. Her real name is Megan Joinson. A thirty-seven-year-old

English woman living in a big posh house with her rich husband and two weans. What her family doesn't know is that she was released from Bronzefield Women's Prison in Surrey seven years ago. She spent nine years inside for trying to castrate her lover. It's also thought that she murdered an ex-boyfriend but nothing was ever proved. She might do a lot for charity and run a girls' basketball team now but she's a very dangerous woman, so don't underestimate her. She'll go to great lengths to keep her secret.'

'What sort of lengths?' said Carly.

'I guess that's something you're going to find out,' he replied with a smug smile. 'You'll have to be on your toes. Tackle her tomorrow morning. The weans will be in school and the husband at work.'

'How much are we asking her for?' said Dean.

'Twenty grand or all the evidence about her disreputable past goes to her husband as well as all the major newspapers.' He looked to Carly. 'And if she gi'es you any sob story, just think of the poor bastard she left with his dick hanging off after she went at it with a bread knife. That phone contains all the information you need. We were going to give this job to Harry and Jane. Don't make us regret it.'

Neither of them replied and they left looking miserable as they wended their way through the busy pub.

'Go on, say it,' Carly told Dean once they were back in the car.

'Say what?' he replied. 'How you should have kept your mouth shut and now we've got to tackle a possible murderer and try and get twenty grand out of her?'

'Aye, I know but Neil was being a pompous git.'

'He's entitled to be because he's the boss.'

'And how he revels in it. His brother didn't say much, he just sat there looking like he found the whole thing funny.'

'Luckily for us,' said Dean, eyes flashing.

'You're pissed off at me, aren't you?'

'Yes.'

This reply hurt her feelings and she winced. 'Well, I'm not apologising. I was only sticking up for us, which is more than you did. You just sat there silently.'

Dean sighed inwardly. So much for his promise not to get angry at her again. 'Because it was the right thing to do. Don't you remember my da' telling us only this afternoon to say nothing if we're unsure of our ground? Well, we were standing on quicksand back there.'

'We were sat down, not standing,' she muttered petulantly.

Dean turned in his seat to face her. 'You've got to remember who these people are. They're dangerous, Carly, and mouthing off at them could get you badly hurt, or worse.'

She narrowed her eyes at him. 'You're scared of them.'

'I am not scared,' he retorted.

'Aye ya are, that's why you sat there all timid like a wee mouse.'

'Unlike you, I know when to keep my mouth shut,' he barked at her.

'And sometimes speaking up is the right thing to do,' she yelled back.

'You're right, it is, but you need to choose your battles and not have a go at a couple of very dangerous men.'

Carly's eyes narrowed and she gritted her jaw. She flung herself back in her seat and folded her arms across her chest. Dean was rather enjoying her anger. Her cheeks were red, her eyes were bright with wrath and she was breathing hard. She looked furious and sexy. It was then he became conscious of the fact that David was standing outside the pub watching them. He decided not to mention it to Carly in case she got out of the car and gave David a gob full.

'Your problem is that you're incapable of admitting when you're wrong,' he said as he started the engine.

'No, I'm not,' exclaimed Carly. 'I've done it lots of times. Just ask my sisters.'

'I will,' he replied, steering the car into traffic.

'God, you sound childish.'

'Me? I'm not the one who just had a big tantrum in front of two gangsters.'

'They wouldn't be impressed if they heard you calling them gangsters. They think they're businessmen.'

'Well, they cannae hear me but they heard you loud and clear.'

Carly was about to shout back at him but restrained herself. It would only make him smirk even more, so she turned her attention to the window for the rest of the journey, refusing to look at him.

When they returned to the flat, she got out of the car without a word, slammed the door shut and stalked up to the front door.

Dean followed her inside where the family anxiously awaited. Relief filled all their eyes when they saw they were unharmed.

'Well?' said Eddie.

'Carly gave the Tallan brothers a proper telling off,' said Dean.

She rounded on him. 'You grassing git.'

'Please tell me you didn't, Carly?' Eddie sighed, massaging the bridge of his nose.

'I didn't tell them off,' she said testily. 'I just defended us.'

'Defended from what?'

'Neil got all up himself and had a proper go at us. I told him it was David's fault for not giving us proper instructions.'

'Christ,' he exclaimed. 'Are you trying to gi'e me a heart attack?'

'Look, it's all fine,' she said wearily. 'They've given us another chance.'

'You'd better pull it off this time because if you don't... God, the consequences don't bear thinking about.'

'We'll do it, don't worry.'

'Don't worry? Are you serious?' he yelled.

'Uncle Eddie,' said Jane. 'You'll wake Da' and he can't know about this.'

'Aye, sorry, hen,' he replied, simmering down. Eddie pointed at Carly. 'You have to gain control of your mouth and fast. Your actions today didnae just affect you, but Dean too. Did you even think of him when you got on your high horse?'

Carly felt ashamed because she hadn't.

'I guess that look says it all,' muttered Eddie. On the bright side, he couldn't help thinking this incident might put his son off her.

There was the sound of the front door opening and Rose's voice called, 'Only me.'

Eddie hissed at Carly, 'This isn't over.'

'I had the feeling you'd say that,' she sighed moments before Rose entered the room looking tired and pale.

'How did the exam go?' Jane asked her.

'Shite. I thought I was good at Spanish but I'm sure half the stuff I put down was wrong.'

'Don't be so hard on yourself, sweetheart,' said Eddie. 'I'm still struggling with English. I couldnae cope with a foreign language.'

Rose managed a weak smile for him. 'Something else happened at school today,' she continued. 'Something you should all know about.'

They regarded her with concern.

'If someone's been bullying you then we'll go and sort out the wee shite,' said Harry.

'It's nothing like that and if they tried, I'd punch them right in the face.'

'Good for you,' he said, smiling.

This smile cheered her up a little. 'Amber Stewart is in my Geography class. She's the daughter of one of the mechanics who work with Cole. She told me she heard her da' discussing with his brothers how to attack our family. Amber's really nice and sweet and she was worried for us, so she decided to tell me.'

'Did she say how they were going to attack us?' said Eddie.

'No. All she heard was that they wouldn't come here, not after what happened to the Alexander brothers when they tried that the last time.'

'They don't want to get their baws twisted by you.' Harry winked at her, making her blush.

'Who are the Stewart brothers?' said Dean. 'Are they anything to worry about?'

'They're a bunch of dicks,' said Jane. 'There's four of them and two of them are well over forty.'

'What's wrong with that?' demanded Eddie.

'Please let me finish. Two are over forty and both have arthritis in their backs and knees. One even uses a walking stick.'

'Well, they shouldnae pose us any problems,' he replied with a satisfied smile.

'Let's go and batter them before they try,' said Harry, already marching to the door.

'Just hold your horses,' said Eddie, halting him in his tracks. 'All we've got is the word of a sixteen-year-old lassie.'

'Amber isn't a liar,' announced Rose, eyes flashing. 'She's really nice and sweet.'

'I'm no' saying she is, darlin',' replied Eddie with an indulgent smile. 'I'm just saying her brothers might have let her overhear all that on purpose to get us to do something stupid.'

'That's true,' said Dean. 'Bursting in and battering them could be playing right into their hands.'

'Aye, all right,' sighed Harry, who was getting fed up with continually being denied the fight he wanted. 'What do we do then?'

'Right now,' replied Eddie. 'Gathering intelligence is our main goal and we do nothing stupid and over the top that could draw unwanted attention to us from the polis.' He glanced at Rose, indicating he was saying no more in front of her.

'Shall I go to my room?' she asked, catching the look.

'No need, hen, we're done talking.'

'Shall I make you something to eat?' Jane asked her. 'You look like you could use it.'

'I'm not very hungry,' replied Rose.

'You skipped breakfast because you were so nervous about your exams and that's not good.'

'A growing lassie needs her food,' Eddie told Rose.

'Okay, I'll have something.' Her eyes lit up. 'Do we have any pizza?'

'If you're no' careful you'll turn into a pizza, you've eaten so much of it lately.'

Rose giggled.

'There's some lasagne left,' Jane told her. 'I could warm that up?'

'Yes please,' she said so sweetly they all smiled.

While Jane cooked, Dean put the kettle on and Eddie and Harry turned their attention to the television. Carly slunk out of the room, intending to seek the sanctuary of her bedroom. She felt like such an idiot now her anger her worn off. Her uncle was right, she should never have spoken to the Tallans like that, although she didn't think Rod was that angry about it because he'd looked like he'd found the whole thing amusing. She had been reckless and allowed her emotions to get the better of her. Anything could have happened to them because of her weakness. She wouldn't be able to bear it if Dean was hurt because of her big mouth.

Deciding to check on her father before heading into her bedroom, she gently pushed open his door and peered inside. To her surprise, he was awake, gazing out of the window. Had he heard anything of their discussion?

He turned his head to see who his visitor was and smiled. 'Hi, sweetheart.'

Just that smile made her feel infinitely better. She stepped into the room and closed the door behind her.

'Hi Da'. How are you feeling?'

'Oh, fine,' he replied, which was now his stock reply. 'I...' He paused to swallow. 'Heard shouting.'

'It wasn't shouting. Just Uncle Eddie being his usual noisy self.'

Alec studied her and Carly saw something of the powerful man he'd once been in his eyes. He didn't believe her.

'Sounded serious,' he said.

'It really was nothing, he was just telling Harry off for being mouthy.'

Carly forced every muscle in her body to relax as her father scrutinised her closely, searching for any sign that she was lying to him. It pained her to have to lie to her own father.

'Okay,' he said, relaxing and sinking back into the pillow.

Carly smiled, hoping she didn't look as relieved as she felt. She knew she hadn't fooled him, he just lacked the strength to press her. Besides, it would be much better for him not to know of their troubles because he was unable to help and that would frustrate him no end.

Alec held out his shaking hand to Carly and she took it.

'Promise me,' he began before pausing to swallow. 'Put me in a home.'

'But Da', you are home,' she replied, wilfully misunderstanding him.

'I don't want to be... a burden.'

Carly swallowed down the lump in her throat. 'You could never be that.'

'I'm getting worse. Put me in a home soon. Then you'll be free. Don't cry,' he added gently when the tears started to roll down her face.

'I know you're only thinking of us,' she told him. 'But it would hurt us much more to put you in a home.'

'And it hurts me that I'm taking away not only your youth but your sisters' too.'

'You're the only one who thinks that. We need you here, we couldn't bear to lose you.'

'I cannae get to the toilet on my own now.' He once again had to pause and pressed the handkerchief to his mouth with his shaking hand. 'I won't let you help me with that. It's too humiliating.'

'We've been talking about that and perhaps Uncle Eddie and Harry could move in?'

'Which means two of you have to move out and that's no' fair. You and your sisters need to stick together. Rose especially needs you and Jane.'

'Rose is tougher than you think.'

'But still just a child. I would... put myself in a home before I allowed my girls to be split up.'

Alec sank back into the pillows, pressing the handkerchief over his mouth as he took a moment to recover from this speech. Carly anxiously watched as he attempted to swallow several times to clear the excess saliva and failed. Just as she was becoming concerned, he managed it and they both sighed with relief. Only then did she reply.

'We wouldn't be far. We'd only be at the house Uncle Eddie's renting.'

'No. I need to go into a home soon. I'm going to tell the nurses when they come tomorrow.'

'I don't want you to leave, Da',' she breathed, fresh tears sliding down her face.

'I don't want to go either but I have to, for myself as well as my beautiful girls.' Alec raised a trembling hand to touch her face.

Carly hugged him, burying her face in his shoulder as she cried. When she was younger, he'd been so big and strong. Hugging him had made her feel so safe. No one could hurt her or her sisters while he was around. Now he felt shrunken and wasted and it broke her heart.

What a crappy day she was having. She'd fallen out with Dean, argued with her uncle, got on the wrong side of a pair of gangsters and now her father had said he wanted to go into a care home. How could it possibly get any worse?

Carly raised her head when there was a knock at the front door. She listened to the sound of footsteps as a member of her family left the kitchen and went to answer it. When she heard raised voices, she leapt to her feet.

Opening the door, she peered into the corridor to see an enormous black man lifting her uncle off the floor.

'What the hell?' she exclaimed.

'What is it?' murmured Alec before clamping his handkerchief to his mouth.

'Just someone here to see Uncle Eddie,' she told him while throwing him a reassuring smile. 'Back in a minute.'

'Carly...' he began.

But she exited the room and closed the door.

14

'Dean, Harry,' yelled Carly before rushing towards the umbrella stand in the hallway where they kept a baseball bat. She snatched it up and drew it back over her shoulder. 'Let him go before I break your fucking legs,' she yelled at the intruder.

'Woah, who's this wee firecracker, Eddie?' said the man while releasing him.

'It's okay, Carly, hen,' her uncle told her. 'This is my pal, Peanut.'

'Peanut?' she said, lowering the bat.

'Aye, I'm allergic to them,' said Peanut with an enormous smile.

'You got a nickname from an allergy? It's lucky you're no' allergic to spotted dick.'

Peanut burst out laughing and clapped Eddie on the shoulder with one enormous hand, nearly knocking him off his feet. 'I like her. Who is she?'

'This is my niece,' said Eddie. 'My brother's daughter.'

'Aww, that's nice. Do you want a lollipop, sweetheart?' he asked her in a voice reserved for the very young. 'I think I've got one here.'

She narrowed her eyes. 'Do you want a baseball bat in the mouth?'

'Carly,' exclaimed Eddie. 'That's no' very nice.'

'I'm twenty years old, no' five.'

'You're never too old for a lollipop,' said Peanut, unwrapping a red one. 'I'm forty-three and I love them. I've always got one on me if you change your mind,' he told her.

'Thanks,' she said flatly, unable to repress a smile when he grinned at her.

Peanut couldn't be called handsome, not in the way Dean and Harry were handsome, but he certainly had charm and a larger-than-life personality. He was huge standing at six foot three with broad shoulders and a slight gut. There was a lump on the bridge of his nose, which looked like it had been broken in the past and he had cauliflower ears, but his teeth were perfect and his dark liquid eyes large and expressive, and the overall effect was rather pleasing. Clearly the man was a boxer, especially with the calluses on his knuckles.

The others had rushed into the hallway when Carly had yelled but Dean and Harry's reactions to the visitor had reassured Jane and Rose that he meant no harm.

'Peanut.' Harry grinned. 'Great to see you.'

'You too, Harry, boy.' He smiled back.

Harry gave him a hug with lots of manly backslapping, as did Dean.

'What's that noise?' said Peanut when he heard the tinkle of a bell.

'That's Da',' said Carly. 'I'll let him know everything's okay.'

'I'll tell you later,' Eddie whispered to his friend when he regarded him questioningly.

Carly poked her head into her father's room. 'Don't worry, Da', it's just a friend of Uncle Eddie. He's called Peanut.'

'Peanut?' He smiled. 'Great. I'd like to say hi to him later. Not now. Too tired,' he said, eyes growing heavy. 'I'll just sleep.'

'Okay,' she replied before leaving quietly.

'So these are the Savage sisters I've heard so much about, are they?' Peanut grinned at them.

'You have?' said Rose.

'Aye, your uncle's told me all about you. He's so proud of you three, as well as his boys,' he hastened to assure Dean and Harry. He looked back at Rose. 'You must be the wee baw twister?'

'I am,' she said proudly.

'Remind me never to get on the wrong side of you,' he added, making her giggle.

Peanut's big presence was warm, friendly and he obviously had a great sense of humour. He was just what their family needed and her father's approval of him reassured Carly that he could be trusted.

'Let's no' hover in the hallway,' said Eddie. 'Do you want a brew, Peanut?'

'I thought you'd never ask,' he said.

'What's your real name, Peanut?' Rose asked him.

'Boris.' He grimaced. 'Which is why I prefer Peanut.'

'I would too.'

'Cheeky,' he said, grinning, making her smile. 'This is a pretty cool flat. I love the graveyard across the road.'

'You're the only one,' said Jane.

'It's much better than the slaughterhouse I have to look at from my window. I can see straight into the slaughterhouse floor and saw some of the staff beating the poor pigs with golf clubs. It's why I got the flat so cheap.'

'What?' exclaimed Rose, stricken.

'Aye,' he said, eyes flickering. 'I waited for the bastards to come out of work and gave them a taste of their own medicine with my own golf club. They won't be doing it again.'

'You really need to move,' said Harry.

'You're telling me. Well, now Eddie's made me that business proposition, I'm looking for somewhere in Haghill. Ah,' he added awkwardly when they all looked to Eddie blankly. 'I can see he hasnae mentioned that yet.'

'No, he hasn't,' said Harry.

'Let's sit down and discuss it,' said Eddie, gesturing to the table.

'I can leave if you want to talk in private,' replied Peanut.

'No need,' said Harry, clapping him on the shoulder. 'You're always welcome.'

'Great,' he said, the smile returning. He seated himself at the table and nodded approvingly. 'Feels more like a conference table than a dining table. I'm guessing you have all your business discussions here.'

'Aye we dae,' said Eddie. He looked to Rose. 'Sorry, doll.'

'No, it's okay,' she sighed. 'I'll eat my dinner in my bedroom.'

They didn't speak until Rose had left, carrying her plate.

'So she's not in on any of this then?' said Peanut.

'No,' retorted Jane. 'She's going to university and keeping on the right side of the law.'

'I don't blame you for wanting to keep her out of it. It's the right move to make.'

Jane relaxed and nodded.

'So, you're the leader of the Unbeatable Bitches? Awesome name by the way.'

'I am and thanks.'

'You're making a reputation for yourself. I've heard people talking about you all over the city.'

'Really?' She frowned.

'Aye. There's no' many girl gangs around here and yours is definitely at the top of the tree.'

Even Jane, who was always in control of her emotions, was unable to resist a proud smile.

'And what's this business proposition you've come up with?' said Dean, looking from his father to Peanut.

'Peanut's here as a sort of bodyguard,' replied Eddie.

'You mean a babysitter, don't you?'

'No, no' like that.' He sighed when his sons scowled at him. 'All right, maybe a wee bit.'

'We're no weans any more, Da',' said Harry. 'We can look after ourselves.'

'Listen, there are a lot of people out for us at the moment – the Alexanders, now these Stewart fannies with the arthritis. Plus people in our game have started disappearing. A man Peanut and me have known for years vanished just yesterday. Things are getting dangerous and I want someone watching your backs.'

'How is Peanut supposed to watch both of us?'

'No' just you two but Carly, Jane and Rose as well.'

'You're a big man, Peanut,' Carly told him. 'But how can you watch all five of us?'

'He will remain here at Haghill watching over those of you who are here,' said Eddie. 'Everyone who's disappeared has gone missing from their own turf. Here is where the danger lies.'

'No one's gonnae make us disappear,' said Harry with a dismissive wave.

'Aye they're not and I'm gonnae make damn sure of it. Peanut is here to stay and you will cooperate with him. Carly, I'm looking at you.'

'Are you the rebel then?' Peanut asked her.

'I have my moments,' she smiled.

'Good for you. Just don't make my job difficult, okay?'

'I'll do my best.'

'I think you're gonnae keep me on my toes.'

'Aye she will,' said Eddie. 'If she's happy enough giving the Tallan brothers a telling off she won't think twice about you.'

Peanut's deep, pleasant chuckle rolled around the room. 'Did you really do that, Carly?'

'I did,' she said, tilting back her head proudly. 'Neil was being pompous, so I set him straight.'

'I would have loved to see that. Did he turn purple?'

'Aye. Bright purple.'

'Nice one,' he laughed. 'He always does that when he's angry.'

'You know the Tallans?'

'I've done some work for them in the past, mainly body-guarding.'

'You're a boxer?'

'Was. I got out of the game ten years ago. I thought it time to give the young blood a chance. I was professional but all the blows I'd taken over the years were doing me no favours. I didnae want to drop dead of a cerebral haemorrhage like a pal of mine.'

'Oh, I'm sorry to hear that.'

'It gave me a big wake-up call.' He forced a smile. 'But that won't stop me from battering the hell out of anyone who tries to lay a finger on any of you.'

'Glad to hear it.' Eddie smiled, patting his shoulder. 'I've found you a place to stay while you're here. It's the flat above Dean's. The auld biddy who was living in it got too old to manage the stairs, so she moved to a nice wee bungalow in Giffnock.'

'Great,' said Peanut. 'I've got some stuff in the car, so I can move in straight away. I'll go back for the rest of my things in a few days. It'll be nice no' to have to listen to the screams of the pigs.'

'They scream?' said Carly.

'Aye, poor wee souls. I cannae even look at a piece of bacon any more.'

'We're glad you're here, Peanut,' said Eddie quickly, who didn't want to be put off his daily fry-up.

'Me too. The last couple of years have been a bit miserable. It's good to have a purpose again.' He regarded the cousins one by one. 'And no trying to gi'e me the run around. I know every trick in the book.'

Carly smiled, wondering if she could come up with some new tricks of her own.

* * *

'What do you think of Peanut?' Jane asked Carly once their uncle and cousins had left to help their friend settle into his new home and Rose was in the bath.

'I like him,' she replied. 'He's friendly but I've no doubt he could be lethal if he needed to be.'

'That's the impression I got. It could be useful having him around, especially with all the weird stuff that's been happening lately. What do you fancy for tea?' added Jane, getting to her feet and opening the fridge.

'Leave that for now. There's something I need to discuss with you.'

Jane turned to face her. 'It's Da', isn't it?'

'How did you know?'

'He told you he wants to go into a home.'

Carly nodded.

'He told me the same thing.'

'What are we going to do?'

'We have to comply with his wishes.'

Rebellion filled Carly's eyes. 'No.'

'He has no control over his body any more. The least we can do is allow him to have control over his own future.'

'He'll be much happier here with us.'

'And you think he'll still be happy having to suffer the humiliation of his own daughters helping him to the toilet?'

Carly sighed and bit her lip.

'I don't want him to go either and neither will Rose; it will break all our hearts but we knew this day would come.'

'Uncle Eddie said he and Harry could move in here and we can take their house.'

'And what about Rose? There's only two bedrooms at their house, meaning she'd have to stay here and it would upset her being separated from us, especially at a time when she needs so much support.'

A tear slid down Carly's cheek and dripped onto her hand. 'We wait until after her exams to tell her. She can't take that upset too.'

'Agreed.' Jane crouched beside the chair her sister was sitting on. 'We have to gi'e Da' the dignity he wants. It's all he has left.'

Carly shook her head. 'He has us too.'

'And he doesn't want our last memories of him to be us dragging him to the toilet. We're doing this for him, no' us.'

'I know,' murmured Carly, wiping away her tears. 'At least now we can afford to send him somewhere really nice.'

'Exactly. He'll get the very best care and I know Uncle Eddie will contribute too. He's already told me about the home he wants to go into and it's only a fifteen-minute drive away.'

Tears welled in Jane's eyes and the two sisters hugged, quietly crying so Rose wouldn't hear.

15

'I get the feeling we're about to tackle the biggest psychopath we've ever met,' Carly told Dean as he pulled onto the drive of the Jones home the next morning. The house was another large, detached residence, only this one was brand new, its paintwork bright white in the morning sunshine.

'Me too. This should be fun,' he said wryly as he got out of the car.

Carly followed Dean up to the front door. He pressed the bell and chimes pealed through the house. The door was opened by a tall, athletic-looking woman wearing only bright orange yoga pants and an electric pink sports bra. Her long blonde hair was pulled back into a high ponytail. She was extremely attractive, even more so than on the image David had shown them. Megan, or rather Melanie, looked very different to the glowering mugshots they'd seen of her online while doing their research. She'd dropped a couple of dress sizes, grown her jaw-length hair and sported contact lenses instead of thick black-framed glasses.

'Hello.' Melanie smiled, homing in on Dean immediately.

'Melanie Jones?' he asked her, forcing himself not to look at her smooth, exposed stomach.

'Yes?'

'Your husband told us to come round; we're interested in buying the BMW you have for sale.'

'Oh, yes. It's a lovely car but I got the brand-new model, so I don't need it any more,' she said in a strong cockney accent. 'Come through to the garage and I'll show you what I've got,' she added with a wink at Dean.

He smiled back at her, the smile dropping when he caught Carly's scowl.

They followed Melanie inside the flash house, the sound of Carly's boots echoing off the polished floor.

'Nice place you've got here,' said Dean.

'Thanks,' said Melanie, throwing him a flirtatious smile over her shoulder.

'We couldnae have a house like this; the weans would demolish it in ten seconds flat. There'd be toys and jam all over this nice floor.' This was Dean's way of steering the conversation to the children to ensure they were all definitely at school. He and Carly had watched Melanie drive them to school that morning but her car had blacked-out windows, so they'd been unable to confirm that they'd both been inside.

'Not my two,' she replied. 'They wouldn't dare. All toys are confined to their bedrooms and are put away the moment they've finished playing with them.'

Carly got the feeling that Melanie's children didn't smile much. 'I love weans,' she said. 'Yours are very quiet. I've not heard a peep from them.'

'That's because they're at school,' said Melanie as though she were simple, earning herself a scowl from Carly.

She led them through the immaculate house, pausing to collect the car keys from a drawer in the kitchen before heading through a side door into the garage where there were two BMWs, one black and one white.

'The white one's the one for sale,' said Melanie.

'It's very nice,' replied Dean, walking around it thoughtfully.

'Only thirty-two thousand miles on the clock, serviced every year. It's a cracking car but I don't like a motor older than three years. I'll open the bonnet for you.'

Melanie unlocked the car then purposefully bent right over as she reached inside to pull the lever, giving Dean a prime view of her backside. He glanced at Carly, who was scowling at that taut, round bottom.

Melanie eventually straightened up and smiled at Dean. 'Would you mind opening it? I don't want to damage my nails,' she said, holding up her hands to reveal light pink talons.

'Aye, no problem.'

'Thanks,' she purred.

Dean popped the catch, lifted the bonnet and propped it up.

'So strong,' said Melanie.

Carly was getting seriously pissed off. The silly cow hadn't even looked her way yet. Although she and Dean weren't really boyfriend and girlfriend, Melanie thought they were and she didn't give a shit. Carly's hand slipped inside her jacket pocket to the taser, tempted to let rip on the bitch. Dean spotted the movement and shook his head at her.

'As you can see,' said Melanie, once again addressing Dean. 'The engine is in perfect condition. I admit, I know nothing about them myself but I'm sure you do, you seem so clever.'

Carly rolled her eyes. The woman was nearly double his age. It was pathetic.

'Actually, I don't know much,' said Dean. 'But it does look clean.'

'It's a very fast car too. Lots of thrust,' said Melanie suggestively.

'Is it manual or automatic, Megan?' said Carly.

For the first time, Melanie looked at her.

'What did you say?' she demanded.

'I asked if it was manual or automatic,' replied Carly.

'You called me a name,' said Melanie, chest heaving. 'What name did you call me?'

'Melanie. Sorry, did I get it wrong?'

'I...' She took a deep, calming breath. 'No, that's my name. Sorry, I must have misheard. It's a manual.'

'Oh, I prefer automatics.'

Melanie's lips thinned into a line. 'Sorry,' she said insincerely before looking to Dean, her smile returning. 'So, what do you think?'

'I don't like the colour,' said Carly, wanting to annoy her. 'White's a bit tacky and it gets dirty really quickly.'

'Tacky?' exclaimed Melanie. 'I can assure you I have exquisite taste and white is the most fashionable car colour right now.'

'Then why did you get a black one?'

'Because I got a new jacket and it matches it.'

'You bought a new car to coordinate with a coat?' said Carly incredulously.

'Some of us have that luxury.'

'Sounds like a waste to me.'

'I suppose some of us just have better taste.'

'Says the woman in bright orange yoga pants.'

'Look,' snapped Melanie, her temper starting to slip out of her control. 'Do you want the car or not?'

'No, we don't, not in that crap colour, Megan.'

Melanie was so incensed about this slur that she almost missed the real meaning in that sentence. 'I knew it, you did call me Megan the first time.'

'Aye, I did. Do you ever see the poor bastard whose cock you mangled?'

'Get the fuck out of my house right now,' screeched Melanie, jabbing a pink talon at her. 'Before I make you regret coming here.'

'We'll leave, when you've given us twenty grand not to tell everyone what we know about your past.'

Melanie's eyes widened so much Carly expected them to fall out of her head.

'You know nothing,' she spat at her.

'We know that not only did you try to castrate your ex but that you're suspected of murdering another boyfriend. You've done well so far to keep that secret but then again you do look very different to your mugshots. You were a bit of a munter back then, weren't you, Megan?' She chuckled.

Melanie hissed, lips drawing back over her teeth.

'By the look of the place, twenty grand is nothing to you,' continued Carly. 'So just hand it over nice and quietly and we'll be on our way. If you don't, then your little secret will be all over social media by dinnertime. We'll also make sure to tell the newspapers all about it too. You'll have journalists camping on your doorstep for weeks; they love stories like that. But don't worry, I'm sure they'll take some really flattering photos of you in those hideous leggings.'

There was a screech and Carly ducked when Melanie attempted to punch her. She found she was enjoying this assignment. She loathed the woman, who was so far from the pathetic Alan Harper that she knew she'd feel no guilt about taking money from her.

'Don't embarrass yourself,' said Carly. 'It would be best if you just coughed up.'

'And have you two coming back again and again like an unwanted fungus? No fucking way. You made a mistake coming here.'

Melanie snatched up a hammer that hung from a nail on the wall and attempted to strike Carly with it.

'Woah,' exclaimed Carly, leaping backwards.

'There you go again winding people up,' Dean told his cousin. 'When will you learn?'

The end of this sentence was almost drowned out by Melanie's wild shriek as she lashed out with the hammer again, making Carly duck.

'She deserved it,' said Carly.

Carly was forced to throw herself backwards when Melanie attempted to strike her again, eyes wild.

'I'll kill you both,' she screamed.

Carly snatched up a black box containing a drill and used it to block the hammer when Melanie attempted to hit her again. She kicked Melanie in the stomach, sending her staggering backwards a few paces. Melanie quickly recovered herself, raised the hammer even higher and charged at her. Carly's fist met her face and put her on her backside.

'Thank Christ she's shut up,' said Dean. 'All that screeching was really getting on my nerves.'

'Aww, bless,' said Carly sarcastically. 'You're not the one she came at with a hammer. You just stood there and let me deal with it.'

'Because once again you brought it on yourself. You have to learn to control your mouth.'

'Don't start,' said Carly, snatching the hammer from Melanie's hand before she had time to recover her senses.

When Melanie tried to leap to her feet, Carly's foot on her chest kept her pinned to the floor, making her writhe and spit like a snake. Melanie attempted to claw at Carly's leg but was unable to break through her skinny jeans and one of Melanie's pink talons snapped.

'You bitch,' she shrieked. 'Look what you've done to my nail.'

'You did it to your own nail, you silly cow and if you don't shut your face I'll snap off the rest of them.'

Melanie realised Carly was capable and very willing to carry through this threat, so she went silent, but she glared up at her while breathing furiously.

'That's better,' said Carly. 'Now, you're gonnae pay us the twenty grand and you know what will happen if you don't.'

'I don't have that sort of cash lying around.'

'Bollocks. You keep a lot of cash in the safe in your bedroom.'

'How the fuck do you know about my safe?' demanded Melanie.

'We have our ways. Now, I'm going to move my foot. If you try to attack either of us my friend will throw you through the windscreen of your brand-new – if rather boring – BMW. That will fuck up your face very nicely, so be sensible and give us the money.'

Carly removed her foot from Melanie's chest and took a couple of steps back as she dragged herself to her feet, sweating and breathing hard, her eyes filled with a venomous hate.

'Well don't stand there glaring at us,' Carly told her. 'Go and get the cash.'

Melanie opened her mouth to yell something back at her, thought better of it, turned on her heel and stalked out of the garage and back into the house. Dean and Carly hastened to follow.

'Let's hope she doesn't go for the butcher's knife,' Carly whispered to Dean as they walked through the kitchen.

But Melanie didn't make a grab for any sort of weapon and headed straight upstairs. Carly didn't like this sudden obedience.

They entered a huge, sumptuous bedroom full of eggshell-blue, crushed-velvet and light greys. Carly decided that Melanie did actually have good taste. It was a beautiful room and made her want to lie down and rest on the enormous bed. When she finally had her own place, she would decorate her bedroom just like this.

Melanie took down a large painting of an abstract seascape to reveal a safe cut into the wall.

'Hold that,' she told Dean as she thrust the picture at him. 'And don't drop it. It's an original and very expensive.'

Dean obediently held the painting while Melanie turned to the safe and began twiddling the knob. There was a click and the door popped open. Inside were stacks of cash. Carly breathed a sigh of relief. She'd been half afraid that the information David had sent them was wrong. At least this time they wouldn't fail to deliver.

Her relief was short-lived when Melanie took a gun out of the safe and pointed it at them, a malicious smile on her face.

'You've made a big mistake,' she told them. 'I will allow nothing to ruin my new life. I've finally got everything I want – the big house, the money, the cars...'

'I noticed you didn't mention your loving husband or weans,' said Dean.

Melanie scowled at him. 'You remind me of my ex. He couldn't help but talk back too. Well, I soon shut his mouth.'

'Is this the boyfriend whose cock you cut off or the one everyone thinks you murdered?'

'The second one.' She took aim at his chest. 'Seeing how I'm going to kill you anyway, I may as well tell you – I killed that twat too. I shoved him off the top of that cliff when we were taking a walk but he was such a stupid, clumsy bastard nothing could be proved.' Melanie took a deep breath and grinned maniacally, destroying her good looks. 'God, it feels good to finally get that off my chest. Right, it's time for you two to go.'

'And how do you propose to get two dead bodies out of here without anyone noticing?' Dean calmly asked her. 'You won't even be able to shift my body alone. Plus, you'll never get our blood out of your carpet.'

Carly gaped at him. How could he sound so calm when a lunatic was pointing a gun at them? This was much scarier than when Cole had done it because Melanie looked to be rapidly losing control of herself.

'My husband's gone away for a few days for work and the kids know never to come in here,' replied Melanie. 'That gives me plenty of time to get rid of you both. I'll probably cut you up in the bath, put you in bin bags and dump you in the Clyde. No one will trace your disappearance back to me because I'm willing to bet no one knows you're here.'

'That's where you're wrong,' he replied. 'We're working on behalf of the Tallan family. They're very dangerous gangsters who will want to know what happened to their employees and they'll come round here and torture you until they get it out of you.'

'Nice try. Now stay still,' she said, pointing the gun at his head. 'It's such a shame I have to do this because you are very easy on the eyes.'

'No,' cried Carly.

Melanie swung the gun round on her and she went still.

'Maybe I'll kill you first instead?' Melanie told her. 'You're a lot more annoying.' She looked to Dean. 'Aren't you going to plead for your girlfriend's life?'

He shrugged. 'Why should I? She's no' my girlfriend, she's only my cousin and we were estranged for years.'

Carly regarded him with outrage but didn't speak.

'So that was all crap about your kids then?' demanded Melanie.

'Aye.'

'You pair of bastards. I'm going to enjoy killing you.'

Carly tensed, wondering if she should just sod it and attack the woman. No way was she going to stand there and allow her to shoot without even trying to save her own life. Dean looked relaxed and casual, so she couldn't rely on him to lift a finger, just like he hadn't in the garage.

'You're killing no one with that gun,' Dean told Melanie.

'Don't think I don't know how to use it,' she told him. 'I've had lessons.'

'No, you haven't. If you had, you'd know it was a starter's pistol.'

'Liar.'

'I know my weapons and that is a starter's pistol. The only thing you're gonnae do with that is start a race.'

Carly wasn't sure if he was lying or not and from the expression on Melanie's face neither was she.

'Also, the sound it will make will probably draw the attention of all your neighbours,' he added. 'Where did you get it from anyway?'

'I told my husband I wanted one for protection, so he got me this,' she added, frowning at the weapon. Melanie shook her head. 'No, you're just lying to try and save your own skin. My husband has always given me everything I've ever wanted. Now, hold still so I don't make too much of a mess,' she added, taking aim at Dean.

She squeezed the trigger and nothing happened. Her eyes widened when Dean knocked the weapon from her hand and it went sailing across the room. Melanie tilted back her head and released a screech before charging at Dean, who grabbed her by the throat and shoved her up against the wall.

'Get the money,' he told Carly while he kept Melanie pinned there.

Carly nodded and rushed to the safe. She took out four wads of cash worth five grand each and looked around for something to put them in. She spotted the Gucci holdall and decided that would do.

'Don't you dare touch that bag,' snarled Melanie.

'It's very nice.' Carly smiled. 'I think I'll keep it.'

'You fucking bitch,' spat Melanie. 'That cost sixteen hundred quid.' She grimaced when Dean tightened his grip on her neck, forcing her to go still.

'More fool you,' said Carly. She stuffed the cash into the bag, zipped it up and got to her feet. 'It was nice doing business with you.'

'I will kill you both,' rasped Melanie, straining against Dean's grip.

He released her and she dropped to the floor. Her talons dug into the carpet, tearing at it.

Dean and Carly looked down at her with disdain before leaving, the Gucci bag dangling from Carly's hand.

'I will kill you,' Melanie screamed after them.

The pair of them were laughing as they got back into the car.

'Well, that was fun.' Carly grinned, cradling the bag on her knee.

'Aye, but it could so easily have gone wrong,' replied Dean. 'That gun might have been real.'

'But it wasn't because her husband was too sensible to give her a real one.'

'And you wound up another dangerous person.'

'Because she was stupid and annoying.'

'And a murderer. You seriously need to stop mouthing off at people.'

'I'm getting sick of being told I've got a big mouth.'

'You didn't used to. It's something that's developed recently. Is it because you're earning good money or because you're paid to scare people for a living?'

'Are you trying to say that I'm getting up myself?'

'No, but I am saying that you've changed.'

'Only because I feel more confident. Why is that such a bad thing?'

'It's not, usually, but it's making you reckless, so you need to get it under control. We could have been shot today.'

'That wasn't because of my mouth. The moment Melanie found out we were there to blackmail her she started plotting to murder us and she probably won't be the only one. Others will try.'

'Winding these people up will only make it worse. Just remain quiet and polite and things will go much more smoothly. It's a job and like any job you have to put on a front. Don't look at me like that, Carly. I'm only saying this because I don't want you to get hurt.'

'Actually, it sounds like you're getting sick of me,' she said, turning in her seat to face him, eyes flashing.

'I could never get sick of you.'

He spoke so gently Carly's anger immediately evaporated and they gazed into each other's eyes.

Movement out of the window caught Carly's attention and her eyes widened.

'Start the engine,' she told him.

'Why?'

'Because Melanie's coming out of the house with a huge knife.'

Dean turned to see Melanie in her tight yoga pants and sports bra storming down the driveway with a butcher's knife clutched in one hand and her eyes alight with a scary mania.

He started the engine and Melanie broke into a run, racing after the car as it sped down the drive.

'Bastards,' they heard her scream.

Carly clung onto the door as Dean whipped the steering wheel around, so the car was pointing in the right direction, and stomped on the accelerator. She turned in her seat to keep Melanie in view, watching as she came to a halt in the middle of the road, a spot of brightly coloured, Lycra-clad chaos in this quiet suburb. A man walking his dog saw her standing in the middle of the road screaming and waving the knife around. He snatched up his poodle and hurried back the way he'd come.

16

'Twenty grand,' said Carly, placing the bag on David's desk. Keeping Dean's advice in mind, she kept the smug grin off her face and attempted to look serious and contrite.

David gave her a hard stare before unzipping the bag and pulling out the money. He took his time counting it, testing Carly's patience. She maintained her equilibrium even though she knew he was purposefully being slow to annoy her.

'Twenty grand exactly,' he said when he'd finally finished counting it. 'Nice bag too.'

'Melanie wasn't impressed that we took it.'

'I'll bet. It would have cost her a chunk of money. How was she?'

'Violent and psychotic.'

'Did she attack you?'

'She tried but we dealt with her easily enough. She did run after the car with a knife when we were leaving. When she couldn't catch us she stood there screaming in the middle of the street like a total psycho. And she admitted that she pushed her ex-boyfriend off a cliff.'

'Really? That's very interesting information.'

'She's completely mental and I feel sorry for her husband and weans.'

'From what you've said, I don't think it's worth sending you back there. If she draws that much attention to herself then she could draw the polis's attention too.'

'So sending us there was a test?'

'Aye. Congratulations, you passed, but don't go getting complacent. You've proved you can do the job. I knew she would be a tough assignment. Your next job will be a standard debt collection. I'll let you know when the next blackmail job will be.'

He handed them money before dismissing them.

'Carly,' he added.

She stopped at the door and turned to face him. 'Yes?'

He tossed her the Gucci bag, which she caught.

'Keep it,' he told her. 'Call it a bonus for finding some self-control.'

She nodded in acknowledgement.

'You both still owe the Tallans ten grand each. Don't forget that. Give me the payment by Friday.'

'Will do,' said Dean before they both left.

'Have you got the ten grand?' Carly asked Dean.

'Just about, although it will pretty much wipe me out. You?'

'I'm a grand short.'

'Even with the money you've just been paid?'

'Aye.'

'You could sell that bag,' he said, indicating the Gucci bag she held.

Carly had never considered herself materialistic before but the thought of parting with the gorgeous bag was more than she could bear. 'Piss off,' she told him.

'Second hand you could probably get a grand for it, maybe more.'

'This is the nicest thing I've ever owned and I don't want to give it up.'

'Would you rather have that bag or be stuck in intensive care?'

Carly sighed. 'Fine, I'll sell the bloody thing.'

'You'll easily be able to afford a brand-new one with the money you're making.'

'I could never spend that much money on myself. I'd hate myself for it and every time I looked at the bag, I'd just feel guilty. This way, I get the bag without the guilt.'

'It's no' worth it,' he said gently. 'Think how your da' and sisters would feel if anything happened to you all because of a bag.'

'You're right, I know.' She looked down at the holdall sadly. 'It was nice while it lasted.'

'One day that guilt will go and you'll enjoy spending money on yourself.'

'No, it won't. It's been with me too long and is deep in my bones. I'll never enjoy spending money on myself but maybe that's not such a bad thing? I'll never get into debt.'

'True,' he replied, although he thought it a little sad that she couldn't enjoy the money she worked so hard for.

As they walked outside to the car, Dean suddenly whirled around, startling Carly.

'What's wrong?' she asked him, turning to look in the direction he was staring.

'It feels like someone's watching us.'

Carly didn't have the same feeling but she trusted Dean's instincts. On the surface, everything looked normal, cars passing them by, people walking on the pavement, no one paying them any attention.

'It's probably Melanie,' she said. 'I wouldn't be surprised if she'd tracked us down and is hiding behind a tree with a huge carving knife, waiting to take back her bag.'

'I don't think so,' he murmured.

'Let's get back in the car.'

After taking one last look, Dean headed back to the car, Carly following. He unlocked it with the fob.

'Wait,' he said when she moved to open the door.

Carly watched as he flung open the rear driver's side door and peered inside. He then did the same with the front door before checking the boot.

'All clear,' he told her.

'What did you expect, assassins waiting for us inside?'

'I just thought it wise to double check, especially after what Da' told us about those men who disappeared.'

Carly stared at him in surprise as he got into the car. After taking an uneasy look around, she got in too and Dean locked the doors.

'You think we could be next?' she asked him.

'No, I'm probably being paranoid but like I said, it's wise to take precautions.'

'Great, I'm creeped out now.'

'I could be wrong. I mean, why would anyone bother stalking us?'

'They might if the Tallans are behind those disappearances. We have pissed them off recently.'

'I'm not convinced they're the ones responsible. It doesnae feel right. Let's get back to Haghill.'

'Yes please,' said Carly. She stared out of the window as they set off, looking out for any lurking stalkers but she saw no one.

* * *

Jane peered down the street. It was just after midnight and, for once, all was quiet. The recent mild weather had just broken and the rain had poured down relentlessly from eight o'clock that evening, driving everyone indoors. It had eased off half an hour ago and was now a chilly, miserable drizzle.

The garage where Cole worked was closed for the night, the wet pavement reflecting the glow of the streetlight.

'There's a camera,' Jane whispered to Jennifer, nodding up at the device mounted to the wall above the door into the garage.

'Not a problem,' she lisped back. 'I came prepared.'

Jennifer produced an extendable baton from inside her jacket, clambered on top of a wheelie bin and used the baton to push the camera upwards, so it was facing the sky.

'Nice one,' said Jane as she nimbly jumped down.

'It's all clear now.'

Jane nodded and glanced back over her shoulder at the three women standing behind her. She'd brought only her most trusted women for this job.

While the other women kept watch, Jane hastily picked the lock on the door. When they'd been here when Carly had come to speak to Cole, she'd had the opportunity to confirm that there was no alarm. No one bothered stealing the old bangers this garage dealt in.

She had the door open in under twenty seconds. The five women slipped inside and Jennifer closed the door behind them. From under their coats, they produced baseball bats and golf clubs.

'Go to town, ladies,' Jane told them with a dark smile.

They got stuck in with glee while Jane turned her attention to the office door. That too was locked but she had it open in no time and stalked inside. She homed in on the paperwork, which she gathered up and stuffed into the carrier bag she'd brought with her. From the workshop came the sounds of smashing glass accompanied by laughing. The girls were enjoying themselves.

'Are you after something specific?' said Jennifer, who had followed Jane in.

'Anything that will fuck up the Alexanders and Stewarts.'

'I wonder if they keep any cash here?'

'Take it if you find it.'

Jennifer began rummaging around while Jane opened cupboards and drawers, hoping to find something that could tell them what the Alexanders were up to. She wondered if Cole kept his gun here but there was no sign of it. There wasn't even a laptop, there was only the paperwork. Hopefully there would be more in it than just log books for clapped-out cars.

After ten minutes of searching in the office and blatant vandalism in the garage, Jane decided it was time to leave and they snuck out, Jane closing the door and locking it behind them. They vanished down the darkened street without anyone seeing them.

* * *

'You look like you didn't sleep well,' Rose told Carly with concern when she wandered into the kitchen the following morning, yawning and running a hand through her hair.

'I didn't,' she replied, sinking into one of the chairs at the table.

'Is anything wrong?'

Carly noticed the anxiety in her sister's eyes and smiled. 'No, nothing. It was just one of those nights.'

'I've had a few of those recently.'

'Just hang in there, the exams are nearly over.'

Rose sighed. 'I know.' She was ready for the day in her school uniform, long light brown hair held back off her face in a high ponytail.

'Is anyone giving you a lift into school?'

'Harry said he would.'

'Good. It's English today, isn't it?'

'Aye. I don't mind English, so hopefully it should go well.' Rose hesitated before adding, 'I noticed that Da' hasn't been using his Zimmer frame like he used to and he seems to be spending even more time in bed.'

'He's just been a bit tired lately, that's all.'

Rose's eyes were wide and sad and she was burning to ask for more information but she was under so much pressure and knew she couldn't take any more, so she decided to let it drop and just believe her sister.

'Looks like I'm not the only one who didn't sleep well,' said Carly when Jane wandered in still in her dark purple pyjamas. 'Eight o'clock and you're not dressed yet,' she added. 'You're not ill, are you?'

'No, I just had a rough night,' she replied, picking up the kettle and carrying it to the sink to fill it.

'Must be something going round,' said Rose. 'Carly didn't sleep very well either.'

'Why not?' Jane asked Carly.

'No reason in particular, just one of those nights. What about you?'

'Same.'

Carly gave her a scrutinising look. Something was going on but she didn't want to ask in front of Rose.

Harry stopped by half an hour later to collect Rose and once she'd gone, Carly said to Jane, 'So what's really going on? Why do you look so tired?'

'I was up most of the night going through some paperwork.'

'What paperwork?'

'The stuff I stole from the garage where Cole works.'

Carly's eyes widened. 'What?'

'Me and four of the girls broke in last night, vandalised all the vehicles and I took every slip of paper I could find, hoping it could tell me something.'

'Christ, Jane, that's a bit extreme, isn't it?'

'Someone had to do something. I don't agree with Uncle Eddie that we have to watch and wait. In the meantime, anything could happen.'

'I hope to God no one saw you.'

'They didn't. We know what we're doing.'

'The Alexanders will blame us for it.'

'Probably, but they'd blame us if lightning had struck the place. It would have been worth it if I'd found something in those papers but so far, nothing.'

'Are there still more to go through?'

Jane nodded.

'Then I'll help you with the rest.'

'Thanks. So why did you sleep badly? And remember you won't be able to fob me off like you did Rose.'

'It's nothing much really. When me and Dean left the gym after dropping the money off with David yesterday, Dean thought someone was watching us.'

Jane sat up straighter with interest, recalling what her uncle had said about those people who'd disappeared thinking they were being followed. 'And were they?'

'Not that we could see but he was pretty positive.'

'Did you feel like anyone was watching you?'

'I didn't notice anything until Dean mentioned it but then I thought they might be.'

'We need to keep an eye out, especially with these recent disappearances. We should have a sit down and discuss security.'

'Sounds like a good idea, especially as we'll probably have the Alexanders round here causing trouble again.'

Jane bit her lip, wondering if she'd made a big mistake.

'I'll get Da' his breakfast,' said Carly, getting to her feet.

Half an hour after Carly had ensured her father had eaten and she'd brushed his hair for him, Eddie stalked into the flat with both his sons. He found his nieces tidying up after breakfast.

Their uncle's angry look told them everything they needed to know.

'What the hell did you go and do that for?' he demanded of Jane, keeping his voice low so Alec wouldn't overhear.

She turned to face him, expression cold. 'I wasn't going to let Cole get away with pointing a gun at Carly.'

'You're right, the wee toad needs punishing, but it needed to be done in a smarter way. Four cars were smashed up, that means insurance companies are gonnae get involved with their nosy bastard investigators, which means the polis will get involved too.'

'Those motors were probably nicked.'

'No, they weren't. They were in for legitimate repairs.'

'Even better. That will trash the Stewart family's reputation.'

'I've heard Cole is furious. He's already pointed a gun at Carly. What do you think he'll do now?'

Jane's eyes flashed with anger. 'Someone has to do something. His family's got guns, they're plotting to attack us with the Stewarts and what was your plan? Sit around doing nothing.'

'Jesus, you're as stubborn as she is,' said Eddie, pointing at Carly. 'I wasnae doing nothing, I was waiting for my contacts to get back to me with information that we needed before rushing in and doing something stupid. This is the sort of thing I'd expect from Harry and Carly but I thought I could rely on you of all people to keep their head. It seems the only one with any sort of control over themselves is Dean. The Alexanders haven't got all fucking cocky for no reason,' he continued. 'They've made a deal with a powerful family.'

'Not the McVays?' said Jane, eyes widening.

'No.'

Both she and Carly breathed a sigh of relief. The McVays were the top family in the whole of Scotland. Their leader was called Toni and she enjoyed plucking out the eyeballs of those who displeased her and keeping them in glasses cases. They had international contacts and were capable of wiping out all of Haghill should they so choose.

'I don't know who it is,' continued Eddie. 'The Alexanders have called in a relative from England. From Yorkshire.'

Harry laughed. 'A bunch of sheep shagging farmers.'

'No, Harry, no' a bunch of farmers,' said Eddie, voice heavy with restrained anger. 'It's a cousin of Jessica's called Jack. He was released from Wakefield Prison seven months ago. You must have heard of that prison, it's famous. They call it Monster Mansion. It holds the worst of the worst.'

'What was he in for?' said Carly.

'Attempted murder. He's just spent ten years in one of the worst prisons among the most infamous criminals in the country.'

'If he's been stuck inside for ten years then he'll be completely out of touch and he'll have no contacts up here,' said Jane.

'He's a violent lunatic who was a terror before he went in and time in that shitehole among the murderers and sex offenders will not have improved that. He's capable of causing us a hell of a lot of trouble and you just trashed the garage where his second cousin works,' he told her.

'I never heard mention of any family in England.' Carly frowned. 'I take it this Jack is English and he didn't just serve time in prison down there?'

'His parents moved to Yorkshire from Glesga when he was five years old. From what I've heard, Jack's da' was a convicted paedo, which is why Jessica never spoke about them. Both her aunt and uncle have died and Jack has no one else, so she said he could stay with her when he was released. No doubt that shrewd bitch spotted what an asset he could be to her family and decided to recruit him. She's no' offered him a home out of the goodness of her heart.'

'Because she doesn't have a heart.'

'Exactly, hen. Now we have to try and figure out how a man we don't know will come at us for attacking Cole's garage.'

'He might not do anything,' said Jane. 'Just because he's staying in Haghill doesn't mean he wants to get caught up in all his family's shite.'

'That will be Jessica's price for giving him a roof over his head,' said Carly.

'I've no doubt you're right,' Eddie told her. He fixed Jane with a hard stare. 'And that's why it's always wise to learn everything you can before making a move.'

Jane held up her hands. 'All right, I admit I was probably a bit hasty but there are still some of the papers I stole to go through. They might be useful yet.'

'Let's hope, although if they were anything important we would have had the entire Alexander clan around here by now demanding them back.'

That thought had already occurred to Jane and the fact that they hadn't seen a single Alexander told her they were worthless but she was determined to study every single sheet of paper, just in case.

'What's our next move then, Da'?' said Harry, hoping it involved them giving someone a kicking.

'We keep our heads down for a bit,' replied Eddie, to his eldest son's disappointment. 'Let that incident at the garage blow over with the polis. Don't tut,' he barked.

'Sorry,' replied Harry. 'But I don't like waiting around.'

'None of us do but blame your cousins for that,' said Eddie bad-temperedly, waving a hand at Carly and then Jane. 'One of them gets a pair of gangsters riled up and the other goes around breaking into garages.'

Harry didn't mention that he thought that was better than sitting around doing nothing.

'Where's Peanut?' said Carly. 'Da' said he wanted a catch-up with him.'

'We had a few bevvies last night to celebrate his moving to Haghill but he cannae take the pace like he used to,' replied Eddie.

'You mean he's hungover?'

'Aye.'

'Great. If the Alexanders do decide to do something today, then our security will be tucked up in bed with a headache.'

'Don't you worry about Peanut, he'll be fine. It might be best if Harry and Dean stayed here again, just for a wee bit.'

Eddie was so consumed with his thoughts that he missed the way Carly and Dean glanced at each other. But Jane didn't.

'Is that really necessary?' said Jane. 'It'll tip Da' and Rose off that something's going on and they've got enough on their plates without worrying about this fresh mess.'

'Aye, you're right and you three girls can handle most things sent your way.' Eddie wasn't keen on the prospect of Carly and Dean sharing close quarters either.

'If Jack does turn up, Rose will just twist his baws off.' Harry grinned.

'Probably,' said Eddie, smiling. 'That lassie is a wee terror. Okay, for now we'll see how things go and we'll keep an eye on Jack Alexander. From what I've heard, he enjoys a good drink. We'll go to the pub tonight and hopefully something will happen to point us in the right direction.'

'Great.' Harry grinned.

'No' you. You'll stay here and keep an eye on Alec and Rose.'

His smile fell.

17

Eddie had thought tonight would be a good time to introduce Peanut to the local community, so he decided to take his friend to the pub along with Carly and Jane and leave Dean and Harry with Alec and Rose.

Peanut, being a large, charming man, naturally drew a lot of attention from the local ladies. Derek pouted behind the bar as Brenda and her two friends – who were normally his cheerleaders – fawned all over the newcomer.

'Don't look so down,' Carly told him. 'It gives you a break from them.'

'Maybe I don't want a break,' he muttered.

'Are you finally going to bite the bullet and ask Brenda out on a date?'

'I don't want to go that far. If I do, she'll think we're married and I am no' going through all that again.'

'But you like your wee fan club.'

'Aye,' he sighed.

'Peanut's just a novelty. It'll soon wear off.'

'I cannae believe I've been rejected for someone called Peanut.

What is it with your family bringing in these big, handsome sods into my pub? Who else are you related to? Gerard Butler? Sean Connery?'

'Sean Connery's dead, so you don't need to worry about him.'

'I may as well be too for all the attention I'm getting,' he said, glancing sideways at Brenda when she shrieked with laughter at something Peanut said.

'They'll soon flock back to you, I've no doubt,' said Carly before picking up the tray of drinks she'd ordered and carrying it over to the table where Jane and Eddie waited.

'Cheers, hen,' said Eddie when she placed his pint of lager before him.

Carly handed Jane her glass of white wine before taking a seat with her half a lager.

'Peanut always did enjoy being the centre of attention,' said Eddie.

'Derek's not happy that the ladies are ignoring him,' replied Carly.

'He'll get over it. The guy owns a pub, so he won't be short of attention for long.'

It was just a normal night in the pub, no strangers making any dramatic entrances or members of the Alexander family causing trouble. Carly was disappointed. She wanted to get the confrontation with Jack Alexander over with but it seemed it wouldn't be that night.

The three of them stayed until eleven o'clock, when they decided it was time to go home. Peanut had said he would stay on, enjoying the company of Brenda and her friends too much to relinquish it just yet.

Just as the Savages were pulling on their coats, the door opened and in walked a man who rivalled Peanut in size and breadth. His black hair was streaked with grey at the temples. His cheeks were grazed with dark stubble and his eyes were black and hard. He wore blue jeans, a black leather jacket and a black shirt underneath. He was also extremely handsome.

'For God's sake,' sighed Derek.

Brenda and her friends turned their attention off Peanut and onto the newcomer, tossing back their hair and sticking out their chests.

'Stop that, for God's sake,' one auld woman told them. 'You're too old to shove your bits into people's faces like that.'

'I don't mind it,' commented Peanut with his most charming smile but he was ignored in preference of the newcomer.

'And who are you?' Brenda purred up at the man.

He regarded her with disinterest before turning to look at the Savage family.

'Jack Alexander, I presume?' said Eddie.

Eager whispers rolled around the room. Everyone had by now heard all about this man. Eddie had made sure of it.

'What of it?' said Jack, whose body instantly swelled with aggression.

'I can see the resemblance. You've got the same vicious look as the rest of your family.'

'And you all look like dead meat,' he replied in a strong Yorkshire accent. His voice was very deep and dripped menace. His dark, piercing gaze flicked between Jane and Carly. 'Which one of you two is Cole's ex?'

'What's that got to do with you?' said Eddie.

'I want to know and it will be easy enough for me to find out, so you may as well tell me.'

'I am,' said Carly steadily.

Slowly he looked her up and down. 'Very nice.'

'I don't want or need your approval.'

'Don't look at my niece like that, you fucking perv,' Eddie told him.

'It was a long ten years inside just among men,' he said, allowing his gaze to linger on her.

'Don't,' said Jane, grabbing her uncle's arm when he moved to charge at Jack. 'He's doing it on purpose; he wants you to attack him. Don't let him win.'

'Aye, you're right,' he said, taking in a deep, calming breath.

'He wouldn't win,' said Peanut stalking over to Jack, the two men of equal height.

Jack's lips curled into a malevolent smile as he quickly assessed him. 'So you're the ex-boxer I've heard so much about. You took a lot of punishment in the ring. I'm willing to bet one good hard hit to the temple and you'll be down and out. Permanently.'

Peanut sniggered. 'And you're like a pantomime villain. All you need is a black cloak and a goatee beard to complete the look.'

Jack's eyes flashed with anger when there were a few laughs. 'I'm not interested in you. You're just some lackey brought in by Eddie to protect his delicate little nieces.'

'Delicate?' Eddie laughed. 'If that's what you think then you're in for a shock.'

'Hey, you,' Derek told Jack. 'If you're no' here for a drink then you can piss aff. All your family does when they come in here is cause trouble and I'm no' having it.'

Jack turned to face him and Derek felt sweat break out on his back. He was a tough man, used to throwing out rough customers and he'd never once felt intimidated by anyone. Until now. It was all in Jack's freaky, black-eyed stare that was completely and utterly pitiless.

'I'm not here for a drink,' Jack told him. 'I'm here to meet the people standing in my family's way, so shut the fuck up,' he said, yelling the last few words in his face.

Usually after being spoken to like that, Derek would be leaping over the bar with his baseball bat ready to batter the offender but he just remained quiet. To salvage some of his pride, he glared at Jack but, to his shame, that was the best he could muster.

Jack sneered at him before turning back to face the Savages. 'Where are those sons of yours?' he asked Eddie. 'Oh, I see.' He smirked when they failed to reply. 'They're keeping an eye on your little sister and your dad, aren't they? Jess told me all about Alec; he used to be the big man around here. Now he can't even wipe his own arse. Fucking pathetic.'

'Don't you dare talk about him like that,' yelled Carly.

'Take it easy,' Jane told her, grabbing hold of her arm before she could charge at Jack.

'At least someone's got some guts around here,' said Jack. He tilted his head to study her. 'I wonder what they'd look like spilled all over the floor.'

Jane's eyes flashed and she opened her mouth to yell at him but Eddie got there first.

'That's what you did to your victim, isn't it Jack? You slashed him across the stomach and his intestines fell out.'

Brenda and her friends grimaced with disgust and hastily backed away from Jack, who didn't even notice, his attention riveted on Eddie.

'You tried to kill him but you failed,' continued Eddie. 'And that's what you went to prison for – being a failure. You're the pathetic one. Go on, big man,' goaded Eddie when it appeared Jack was going to charge at him. 'Attack me, then you'll get sent back to prison with the rest of the monsters.'

Jack took a deep breath and forced himself to relax. 'I know what you're trying to do and it won't work. There's no way I'd give you the satisfaction. Besides, I only came here to size up the competition.' His smile was derisive. 'I must say, I find it lacking.'

'Coming from the man who must have been the laughing stock of Wakefield Prison.'

'Most of the other prisoners were only big and brave when they were attacking kids or women. I was the one who scared the monsters,' he added, dropping his voice to a harsh whisper.

A chill ran down Carly's spine. It wasn't so much what Jack said but the way he said it.

'You're no' in prison now,' said Eddie. 'Here, there are no rules.'

'Just the way I like it.' Jack smiled.

'And in our *who can sound the most macho competition*,' said Jane. 'I call it a draw. No matter how many bad men you scared in prison, Jack, you're outnumbered, so I suggest you get lost. If you know what's good for you, you'll go back to Yorkshire. You're no' wanted around here and you're on the losing side.'

Knowing filled Jack's eyes. 'It's funny how confident ignorance can make you.' He smiled at the rest of the room, the gesture full of malice.

With that, Jack strolled towards the door, purposefully taking his time. Silence filled the room as everyone watched him go.

'What a creepy bastard,' said the old woman who'd chastised Brenda, the moment the door had banged shut behind Jack.

'Aye,' said Derek. 'The man's a freak.'

'Is that right what you said?' John slurred at Eddie. 'Did he cut someone's belly open and their insides poked out?'

Eddie nodded.

John's eyes widened and he turned and threw up all over the floor, splattering Brenda's shoes.

'I just bought these yesterday,' she screeched before proceeding to bash him over the head with her handbag.

'I don't know why you're moaning,' Derek told her. 'I'm the one who has to clean it up.'

'Jack's just like the rest of the Alexander family,' said Pauline, one of Brenda's friends. 'All bark and no bite.'

'The man was locked up in Monster Mansion for slicing someone's belly open,' retorted Derek. 'That sounds like someone with bite to me.'

'He was looking at you in a strange way, Carly,' Brenda told her. 'I'd watch myself if I were you.'

'You're not helping, Brenda,' Derek snapped at her. 'Carly's got enough on her plate without you making things worse.'

'I was only warning her because Jack was looking at her like a bear looks at a honey pot.'

'I think it's best if we left,' Carly told Jane and Eddie when Derek and Brenda continued to bicker, the rest of the customers looking on in amusement.

They left with their uncle, the door closing behind them blocking out the sound of arguing. Once outside on the darkened street, they looked up and down the road but saw no one.

'It wouldnae surprise me if Creepy Jack was lurking somewhere in the shadows, waiting for us,' said Eddie.

'Is that what we're calling him now?' Jane smiled. 'Creepy Jack?'

'I think it's pretty appropriate. It would be a good idea if my boys stayed over at your flat tonight, just in case.'

'But that will leave you all on your own,' said Jane.

'I'll be fine.'

'No, I don't think that's right. Harry can stay with us and Dean can stay with you. We don't want to take any chances.'

'Okay, sounds reasonable,' said Eddie. 'Let's get home and off the street.'

* * *

Carly woke up the next morning to find Harry lying face down on the couch, out for the count and drooling. She thought that if anyone had attacked them last night, he wouldn't have heard a thing.

Jane walked in and smiled. 'Our alert guard dog.'

Carly smiled wickedly. 'Let's shave his head.'

'That wouldn't wake him up either.'

'I can hear you, you know,' Harry mumbled into the pillow.

'You can't be comfortable lying in that big drool patch,' said Carly.

He raised his head and rubbed his eyes while yawning. Harry was bare-chested and Carly was unable to prevent herself from looking. It had been eighteen months since she'd last been with a man and she was really starting to feel it. Maybe she should forget about Dean and find someone else? It couldn't go anywhere with him, the family wouldn't tolerate it and everyone would just think it incestuous. She'd turned down a couple of men who she'd rather liked because of her feelings for Dean. It was time to move on and find someone else.

She was roused from her reverie by Jane when she realised she was speaking to her.

'Are you all right?'

'Aye, fine,' replied Carly. 'Brew?'

'Please. Are you and Dean on a collection today?'

'We are.'

'Be careful, won't you?'

'We will be. Hopefully this one will be an ordinary collection and no one will try to challenge us. Actually, scratch that. It would just be nice not to be attacked by a murdering bitch with a carving knife. There's been no takers for that Gucci bag either.'

'The one you're selling to raise the money for the Tallans?'

'Aye.'

'Keep the bag. I'll give you the grand.'

'I don't want to borrow money off you.'

'Don't be silly. I know you love the bag and you'll never buy one for yourself because of your guilt complex.'

'Well,' said Carly, who was loathe to part with the bag. 'I could have it paid back quick enough.'

'Course you could.' Jane rolled her eyes when Carly still hesitated. 'Will you please spoil yourself for the first time in your life?'

'Okay.' She smiled. 'I will.'

'Thank God for that. I'll go and get the cash.'

'Thanks, Jane.'

'You're welcome,' she replied before leaving the room.

Harry had sat up and was only wearing his pyjama bottoms, so Carly turned her attention to making the tea. Why did her cousins have to be so hot?

'I think it's unfair of the Tallans making you cough up ten grand each,' he told her.

'Me and you both,' she replied. 'Just when I'd finally got some savings behind me it's wiped out by two men who ten grand is nothing to.'

'They enjoy having control over other people. That's as big of a drug to them as the money.'

'I hope none of us end up like them – soulless.'

'It's the risk of being in this game. You have to keep giving away pieces of yourself.'

18

Dean picked up Carly half an hour later and they drove to their next collection, at a swanky interior design shop. The woman who greeted them with a cheerful smile had a mass of curly black hair. Her make-up was immaculate, her white blouse pure silk and grey pencil skirt designer. She was also dripping in gold jewellery.

The smile vanished when Dean told her they'd come for the next collection on her payment to the Tallans. Carly found it hard to believe that this beautiful, together-looking woman was a drug addict whose dependency was sending her deeper and deeper into debt with the Tallans. She had no doubt this poor woman would soon lose her lovely business, as well as her looks. The thought made her sad.

'Are you okay?' Dean asked Carly once they were outside on the pavement after successfully collecting the debt. 'You were really quiet in there.'

'Aye. I felt sorry for her.'

'Don't. She got herself into the mess she's in. No one forced her to take the drugs.'

'I know but sometimes I feel shitty about what we're doing.'

'I get what you mean but the way I see it is we've got to look out for ourselves. Our family's rising in the world and that's the only thing that matters. We are not responsible for other people and their actions.'

'True but still...' She trailed off, unsure how to put her feelings into words.

'We've got enough going on without worrying about all the marks too.'

'You're right, of course. I just don't want to turn into someone I don't like.'

'You won't, you've got too much heart and your family will keep you steady.'

Carly smiled and nodded.

They both stared at each other when they got the same feeling at the same time.

'Someone's watching us,' she said.

'Don't look. Let's just get back in the car.'

She followed him to the car, Dean unlocking it before they reached it. He peered through the windows before they got in.

Once they were inside, Dean locked the doors while Carly clung onto the bag of money, determined not to disappoint the Tallans again.

'This is getting freaky now,' said Carly.

'Have you ever felt it in Haghill?'

'No, only when we're out on jobs.'

'Me too, meaning if we're not imagining it, someone knows our routine.'

'And we're back to David. He's the only one who knows where we're going.'

'Why would he follow us?'

'To make sure we're not cocking things up.'

'Maybe, but if that is what's going on then he'd be more likely to send someone else rather than follow us himself.'

'Do you remember what Eric Martin said about Reggy, who runs the Tallans' gym? What if he's the one following us?'

'Why would he?' shrugged Dean.

'Because either David's asked him to – but then again why bother sending someone employed to run the gym – or he's bugged the office where we always talk so he knows where we'll be visiting and when.'

'I wouldn't put that past him. We could do with looking more into this Reggy but I don't want to tip off David or the Tallans. They won't like it because it'll reflect badly on their judgement.'

'How do we go poking about their gym without them finding out?'

'We become members. They wouldnae think anything strange about that.'

'I hate gyms. They're full of posers.'

'I go to the gym and I'm no' a poser. Anyway, it wouldn't be for long, just until we can figure out what's going on.'

'I suppose it could work. We might even get a discount.'

'Let's mention it to David when we take the money back.'

They returned to the gym and met David in his office where they handed over the money and were paid for the job.

'You do remember what day it is?' he asked them.

Dean nodded. 'Time to pay our twenty grand.'

'Have you got it?'

'Aye.'

'Both of you?' he said, glancing at Carly.

'Yes, both of us,' she replied.

'Hand it over then.'

Dean produced the wads of money from the backpack slung over his shoulder and placed it on the desk.

'You look disappointed,' said Carly when David stared down at it.

'Why would I be?' he replied.

'Because you think we deserve a good kneecapping.'

'No, I don't. You're lairy sods but you don't deserve that. Neil and Rod will be pleased and I hope this is a lesson to always make sure you have some savings.'

'Lesson noted.'

'Good. You've got another job the day after tomorrow. I'll message you the details. Was there anything else?' he added when they stood there staring at him.

'We want to join the gym,' Dean told him.

'I'm not stopping you.'

'Do we get a staff discount?'

'No, you bloody don't. You're paid more than enough to cover gym fees, you cheeky bastard.'

'Great,' Dean replied, not at all phased by David's bad mood. 'We'll go and sign up then.'

'Wonderful,' he said flatly. 'Just as long as you don't think you can swan in here whenever you like.'

'We wouldn't dream of it.'

Dean and Carly exited the room, leaving David to shake his head.

'Fucking kids,' he sighed.

Carly and Dean signed up to join the gym, paying their first month's membership. They had hoped to meet the mysterious Reggy during the tour they were given of the facilities but he was nowhere to be seen. Carly didn't like the way one pretty blonde on a treadmill smiled at Dean as they passed by. She liked the way he smiled back at the woman even less.

She shoved the feelings of jealousy down. No way could she act on them but she had to admit, it was getting harder to ignore them.

Outside the gym, they paused.

'I don't feel like anyone's watching us now,' said Dean.

'Me neither,' replied Carly. 'Maybe we imagined it?'

'Somehow I doubt it.' He took out his phone when it beeped. 'Da's sent a message. He wants us to go straight to his place.'

'Sounds ominous.'

Dean drove them back to Haghill and they arrived at the house Eddie and Harry shared to see the two men already waiting with Jane.

'Who's watching over Da' and Rose?' Carly asked them.

'Peanut's with them,' said Eddie. 'He was having a good blether with Alec, they always did get on well. There's been another disappearance. This time it's a woman called Tina Hackett from Laurieston.'

'That's only three miles from here.'

'Aye,' replied Eddie, looking troubled. 'She's known for being a low-level dealer and a vicious bitch. Really handy with her fists too. A lot of men are feared of her because she's a loon who will go for anyone with a knife. Everyone calls her Twitchy Tina because when she gets angry her left eye twitches. She vanished yesterday morning, which isnae like her because her disabled maw lives with her and she loves her old maw. She wouldnae just waltz off into the sunset and leave her behind.'

'Any sign of where she went?'

'Naw. No one's any idea. Just like the others, she said she was being followed for a few days before it happened, only she wasnae scared like they were. She showed her pals the knife she always carried and said if anyone tried making her disappear, she'd stick it right up their arse. It seems she failed.'

'This is getting really scary now,' said Carly. She glanced at Dean before continuing, wondering if she should mention what they'd noticed. She didn't want to worry her family.

'What is it?' demanded Jane, spotting the look that passed between them.

'We think someone was watching us again today,' she replied.

'You're sure?' said Eddie.

Dean nodded. 'Aye.'

'Oh, God,' said Jane, dragging her hands down her face.

'We only notice it when we're collecting, never in Haghill.'

'Well, that's something at least,' replied her sister, not sounding in the least bit reassured.

Carly glanced at Dean again, wondering if she should tell them about Reggy and the gym but he shook his head.

'You said before that all the people who went missing were followed about their local neighbourhood,' Harry told his father.

'Aye, I did,' replied Eddie.

'Then this is something different. If it was the same, they'd have noticed it here too.'

'Good point,' said Jane. 'This could well be someone else, perhaps whoever tried to drag Carly out of a moving car. We still haven't identified those bastards yet.'

Dean caught a glint in his father's eye. Did he know who'd attacked them that day? He would ask him when they were alone.

'Have you asked the Tallans about these disappearances?' Jane asked Eddie.

'Aye, I have and they said they know nothing about it. They didn't seem to be very concerned but then again, they probably consider themselves too powerful to be affected by it.'

'Or they're the ones doing it,' said Carly.

'I've nae idea,' sighed Eddie.

'Did Twitchy Tina know the two men who disappeared?'

'No. From what I've heard, she never interacted with them and they lived in different neighbourhoods.'

'Something must connect them. If we find what that is, we'll find out who's behind it all.'

'Detective Savage.' Harry grinned.

'There's always the risk that we'll draw attention to ourselves if we start poking our noses in,' said Jane.

'You never said a truer word,' Eddie told her. 'So I think it's best if we keep out of it, for now.'

'And what about whoever's following us?' said Dean.

'Tell David. If someone is targeting you, he's the one who needs to know. When's your next job?'

'The day after tomorrow.'

'Tell him then. In the meantime, keep an eye out and let me know if you think anyone's watching you here.'

Dean and Carly nodded.

'Away you go then. The fitba's about to start.'

Dean, Carly and Jane all made a hasty exit while Harry, who shared his father's love of the game, stayed with him to watch it.

'So you've never seen anyone when you've felt you're being watched?' Jane asked Carly and Dean as they walked down the street together.

'No,' replied Dean. 'But the feeling's unmistakeable.'

'Is it a coincidence this starts not long before Jack Alexander arrives in Haghill?'

'Maybe not. I guess we're gonnae find out.'

* * *

Carly decided to go to the Tallans' gym the following day. She didn't tell Dean about her plans. He was going to Clydebank to meet up with friends he hadn't seen in a while, and she knew he'd only insist on accompanying her when she didn't want to disrupt his day. Carly told Jane she'd signed up to the gym because she wanted to get fit and her cheerful encouragement made Carly feel guilty for lying about her real reasons for going. Nevertheless, she stuffed some clothes and a bottle of shower gel into a carrier bag and caught the bus there. She really must get her driving licence. Cole had given her a few lessons when they were dating and she'd been quite good but it would be wise to get her licence now while she had the money.

After changing into leggings, trainers and a T-shirt – she had no gym clothes – Carly wandered into the main room and looked around, feeling lost. She spotted the treadmill and decided to have a go on that. She didn't even know what some of the equipment was for. On signing up, she and Dean had been told a member of staff would show them how to use everything on their first visit but she wanted to be alone to do a little spying.

After just five minutes of jogging, she was already bored and looked around for something else to do. Only a few machines were free but they looked complicated and she had no idea how to work them.

'Need a hand?' said a voice in her ear.

She jumped and whirled around to see Jack Alexander standing there. He wore a tight black gym vest, black shorts and black trainers. His exposed arms were covered in tattoos. On the left arm was a full-length sleeve of a Viking berserker warrior wrapped in a bear skin, the shadow of a bear rearing up on its hind legs behind the figure. On the left arm was another sleeve of a Spartan warrior complete with helmet and sword. It was stunning and very precise work and she couldn't help but be impressed. The ink only pronounced the muscles in his arms. There was also another tattoo on his chest but she couldn't make out what it was because of the vest. All she could see were wisps of what looked to be flames.

'You like my ink?' he asked as her eyes danced over the tattoos.

Carly dragged her eyes off his body and onto his face. 'What are you doing here?'

'What the hell do you think? It's a gym.'

'And you just happen to be here at the same time as me.'

'Yeah. Funny that, eh?' he said with a sly grin. 'Now it's your turn to tell me what you're doing here because it's certainly not to use the equipment. It's obvious you haven't a bloody clue what you're doing.'

'You're right, I don't. I just thought it was time I got myself in shape.'

'You look to be in great shape to me,' he said, eyes sliding up and down her body. 'Although you'd be much better off in proper gym clothes. Really tight, clingy ones.'

'You perv,' she said with a curl of the lip.

'I've been locked up for years, I can't help it.'

'You've been out for six months. Surely you've...' Carly trailed off and coloured.

'Taken care of that need? Yeah, but I have a very high sex drive. It requires constant satisfaction.'

His voice turned even deeper and was filled with suggestion. She was ashamed when she found it rather sexy. 'I bet the other men ran away from you in prison when you walked into the showers,' she retorted, tilting back her head.

Jack's chuckle was deep and dark. 'You've got a sense of humour. That's one of my favourite traits in a woman.'

'Great,' she said flatly. 'Well, I was just going...'

'I can show you how to use the machines,' he told her, taking her arm and escorting her over to a weight machine.

Carly was about to make her excuses and leave, when she wondered if this was the perfect opportunity to find out what the Alexander family was up to.

'Why would you do that?' she asked him. 'You hate our family.'

'I don't even know your family, so how can I hate you?'

'Because your cousin and her weans have no doubt been telling you how horrible we are.'

'Jess's kids are pains in the arse. Although I admit I quite like Cole. There's a cold ruthlessness about him that I can get behind but Dominic's weak and Ross is an arsehole.'

'And Brian?'

'Don't get me started on that wanker. He's as limp as a lettuce leaf. Jess was always fiery, right from being a little kid. I don't know why she married him. Maybe she enjoys regularly wiping her feet on the pathetic doormat.'

'She crushed the poor bastard over the years.'

'She's one tough cookie.'

'You sound like you admire her?'

'I always have. We're two peas in a pod really.'

'Why, has she sliced someone's stomach open too?'

'No, but she's capable of much worse than I am. I did that in self-defence but Jess enjoys trampling all over people. She'll stand on anyone if it gets her what she wants.'

'Does that include her own weans?'

'Yes.'

He frowned at a large, bald, muscular man who was staring at them. 'What the fuck do you want?' he demanded, black eyes flaring.

'I want to use the fucking leg press, if that's all the same to you,' snarled back the man.

Jack's lips drew back over his teeth. 'If you don't get out of my fucking face, I'll jam your head in it.'

'Take it easy, Jack,' Carly told him. 'You don't want to get sent back to prison.'

The bald man suddenly looked uncertain of himself. 'Prison?'

'Aye,' said Carly. 'He was inside for attempted murder.'

'And I swore that next time I'd do the job properly,' Jack growled at him.

The bald man held up his hands. 'Calm down, pal. I'll go and use another machine.'

'Good.' Jack smiled with satisfaction as the bald man retreated, clearly enjoying the fear he inspired. He turned back to Carly. 'I'm hungry. Do you want to get something to eat?'

'What?'

'I'm asking you out on a date.'

'A date? But... you can't.'

'Why not?'

'Because our families hate each other.'

He shrugged. 'So? I don't hate you. Quite the opposite actually.'

'But I'm Cole's ex.'

'Who gives a shit?'

'I...' Carly was thrown. What should she do? Seize this chance to get information out of him or leave? She didn't think having a meal with such a violent individual would be very wise; she could just imagine what her family would say and he was ten years older than her but wasn't this a golden opportunity to learn something that could help them? 'Okay then.'

'Great, let's go. I know a nice place in the west end.'

'Err, no.'

'What do you mean no?' He scowled.

'I mean I am not getting in a car with you. There's a café here at the gym. That will do.'

'I don't want to eat in some crappy greasy spoon.'

'It's not a greasy spoon. It has really healthy food and you're very fussy for someone who was recently eating slop in a jail cell.'

Carly expected anger, but Jack grinned. 'You're a feisty one, aren't you? Good. I can't stand meek little women. I like a lady with a bit of fire in her belly.'

'Well, aren't I the lucky one,' she said sarcastically. 'I'll go and get changed and meet you in the café.'

'It's a date.'

This man was so confusing to Carly that she just gave him a puzzled look before heading towards the door. Looking back over her shoulder, she saw those dark eyes of his were riveted on her. She was ashamed of herself when a tingle of excitement ran through her. There was something so alluring about that dangerous gaze of his.

'Don't forget he sliced someone's stomach open,' she told herself.

A passing woman heard this comment and frowned at her. Carly gave her an awkward smile before hurrying in the direction of the women's changing rooms.

19

Carly's thoughts spun wildly through her head as she showered before getting changed in the tiny cubicle. Should she ditch Jack and go home? But she'd come here to try and get some answers and he might have them. If he didn't tell her anything useful then her family didn't need to know. The thought of concealing anything from them was painful to her but if it could help them then it was worth it.

Determined on a course of action, Carly hitched her bag over her shoulder and left the changing room, her long damp hair streaming down her back.

She got a shock when she discovered Jack was lurking outside the door.

'What are you doing here?' she demanded when she almost walked right into him.

'Waiting for you,' he replied. 'I thought you might try and slip away.'

'Hanging around outside a women's changing room will get you sent straight back to prison.'

'You worry too much,' he said. 'Come on, I'm starving.'

Carly slunk after him down the corridor, the window to their left looking in on the gym through which they could see people furiously working out.

They took a door to their right into the café, which was large and airy, the windows looking out onto the back of the building, which was nothing but a walled courtyard with a few flower baskets to add a spot of colour.

Carly ordered a potato and pepper frittata and a glass of orange juice. Jack ordered chicken with asparagus and broccoli, accompanied by a latte.

They took a seat at a table by the window to await their food and drinks.

'So,' opened Jack. 'Tell me about yourself.'

'No.'

He smiled. 'Well, this is going to be an awkward meal.'

'I'm no' telling you anything you can use against me.'

'Talk about paranoid. I just find you interesting.'

'Fine. I went out with Cole and stood by him when he went to prison, until he dumped me in the middle of the prison visits centre, completely humiliating me. He was then released and said he wanted me back, only it was a trick so his brothers could kidnap me. They failed, thanks to my cousins. Your family then made my life a misery, forced me to quit a job I loved, kidnapped me and Dean, only they failed at that too and we escaped. They then attacked me and my family, but we kicked their arses and they've kept their heads down ever since, until now. Is that enough information for you?'

Jack pondered over what she'd said. A young, spotty waiter brought them their drinks and Jack picked up his latte and took a sip, his gaze distant.

'Aren't you going to say something?' she demanded when the waiter had gone.

'I'm thinking,' replied Jack before taking another sip.

'What is there to think about?'

'The fact that I asked you to tell me about yourself and you automatically told me all about my family. It's like you associate yourself with them.'

'I do not,' she said, insulted. 'I just wanted you to hear my side of the story because no doubt they've filled your head with tales of how terrible I am.'

'You're right, they have.'

'They've got a bloody nerve. I was minding my own business, just trying to earn some money and look after my da' when Cole was released and brought a whole lot of chaos with him.'

'Because your family started working for the Tallans.'

'Me and my sisters didn't even know about that deal back then. When Cole was released, my family was estranged from my uncle and cousins. We hadn't seen them in years. Cole and his brothers targeted us to lure my uncle back to Haghill. They bloody started it.'

'I see your point.'

'Then you're more reasonable than the rest of your sodding family. Ross and Dominic, I'm not really bothered about. It's in their nature to be pricks. It's Cole and Jess who really hurt me because I cared about them and I thought they cared about me but all the time they were just using me.'

Jack shrugged. 'That's my family for you.'

'Have they ever treated you badly?'

'Not badly. Brian's always been shit scared of me. Jess is a cold woman. She's been that way since she was little.'

'She always seemed so warm and maternal to me, which was what I needed after my maw died.'

'She would have spotted that in you and decided to use it. Jess is the queen of manipulation.'

Carly winced and looked down at her hands.

'Don't waste your time feeling bad about it. Believe me, she doesn't.'

'You're right, I suppose. And what would she say if she knew you were here having a meal with me?'

'She'd say *get all the information you can out of her*. She's convinced you have lots of secrets that she needs to know.'

'But I don't.'

'Course you do. Everyone has secrets.'

'And what are your secrets?'

His smile was dark. 'Now that would be telling. So, are you going to tell me why you really came here today?'

Carly took a sip of orange juice before replying, 'Are you?'

'I think you're here to find something out.'

'Like what?'

'The Tallans own this place, so it must be something to do with them.'

'I came here to work out. It's time I got fit.'

'You hate gyms, that was obvious just by looking at you. Why not go for a jog in the park? To you, anything would be better than coming here, which tells me you really are desperate to know something.'

Carly decided to take a chance. It might well pay off. 'Have you heard about the disappearances lately?'

'Disappearances?'

'Three people vanished after saying they were being followed. One of them was called Twitchy Tina.'

'Oh, those disappearances. Why are you bothering about that? You're not a copper.'

'Because I want to know what's going on.'

'And you think it could be connected to the Tallans?' Jack rested his elbows on the table and leaned forward in his seat. 'I knew talking to you would prove to be fruitful.'

Carly decided a change of tack was in order. 'Why did you try to cut that guy's stomach open?'

Jack sighed and leaned back in his chair. 'Like I said, it was self-defence.'

'You're trying to wheedle my secrets out of me, so you have to expect a dose of your own medicine. What happened?'

'It was a drug deal.'

'Were you buying or selling?'

'Selling,' he snapped. 'I'd never take that shit. It makes you weak.'

'My apologies,' she replied, finding it amusing that he considered taking drugs to be terrible but dealing them okay.

'The wanker I got sent down for was called Tommy. He decided he didn't want to pay and he was going to steal my stash, so he pulled a knife on me. But he was a pathetic druggie. I easily took it off him and slashed him with it to get him to back off. The blade went in deeper than I intended and it ripped open his belly. The fact that I ran off and left him on the pavement was what did for me in court, even though the arsehole had a history of assault and was known to the local police for carrying a knife.'

'So that's why you didn't get longer.'

'Yep. It also went in my favour that the knife was his and that his injuries didn't result in a lifelong dependency. But I did get done for excessive self-defence; the fucking judge hated me on sight, the bastard. Two years after Tommy attacked me, he stabbed an innocent woman to death in the street when he was off his head on meth. He got life for that. If he'd been put away instead of me that woman would be alive now.'

Carly nodded, not about to take his word for anything. It could all be lies to win her over. Cole and Jess had both lulled her into a false sense of security in order to use her and she refused to allow another member of the Alexander family to do the same.

'So, I'm not all that bad,' he added.

'You said you scared the monsters in prison.'

'And so I fucking should. A lot of them are paedos and kiddie murderers. They should spend the rest of their lives afraid, give them a taste of what their victims went through.'

'Why are you telling me all this? I don't get it.'

'Because I want us to be friends.'

'Your family wouldn't like that and neither would mine.'

'I could tell you a lot about what my family's up to.'

'Now why would you do that?'

'Because I think your family is going to be the most successful and I want to get on board with that.'

Carly laughed.

'What's so funny?' He frowned.

'Do you expect me to believe that? I may be young but I'm no' stupid. Don't treat me like I'm an idiot.'

'I'm not. The only two people in my family with brains – other than myself – are Cole and Jess and they are not capable of beating your family, despite what they think. It's yours that's on the up and I want in.'

'Even if you are telling the truth, how could we ever trust someone who can stab his own family in the back so easily, a family who gave you a roof over your head when you needed it the most?'

'Jess didn't give me a place to stay out of the goodness of her heart. She did it so I'd help her fight you lot. Don't forget, she doesn't have a heart.'

The drippy waiter brought them their food and they paused the conversation until he'd left them to it.

'I know that about her, now,' Carly told Jack, picking up her knife and fork. 'I wish I'd realised it sooner. She told me she called the polis the night Cole was arrested. She wanted him to get lifted because she knew it would break us up. The bitch didn't want me putting him on the straight and narrow.'

'That doesn't surprise me. Jess would put Lady Macbeth to shame. She's only using me like she used him. It's why I don't have that much loyalty to her. One day, that trait of hers will backfire.'

'I told Cole she was the one who got him sent to prison but he wouldn't believe me.'

'He adores his mum,' he said with an amused smile. 'They're always plotting together in corners. Ross is getting pissed off with it because he thinks Cole is usurping his place, like they're fucking heirs to the royal throne or something.'

'How does Dominic feel about it?'

'He just does as he's told.'

'And if Cole and Ross turned on each other, who would he back?'

The corner of Jack's mouth lifted into a smile. 'You're quite the tactician.'

'I don't think so. I just know a chance when I see one.'

'Dominic will back whoever he thinks will win.'

'Which will be Cole.'

'How can you be so certain?'

'He's smarter and more ruthless. Ross is too hot-headed and lets his temper get the better of him. Cole used to be like that but prison changed him. I remember who he used to be. His mother moulded him into what she wanted him to be.'

'You can't put it all on Jess. Cole has to shoulder some of the blame. He enjoys the person he is now.'

'What do you know?' she snapped. 'You haven't seen him in years.'

'I don't need to. It's obvious when he's plotting with his mum.

He thrives on it and he won't stop until he's got what your family has.'

'Our deal with the Tallans,' she sighed. 'Aye, I know. He's already made that very clear after the number of times his family's attacked mine.'

'They want to take it from you before you get any stronger.'

Carly, her appetite gone, put down her knife and fork. 'What makes them think the Tallans would even want them?' She frowned when knowing filled Jack's eyes. 'They've already spoken to Neil and Rod, haven't they?'

'Now that I couldn't tell you,' he replied before stabbing a piece of asparagus with his fork and taking a bite.

Carly thought furiously. The Alexanders were the Tallans' back-up plan in case her family failed. And she had already pissed off Neil and Rod, made her family look like amateurs, like a bloody idiot. 'What did they discuss?'

'Like I said, I couldn't tell you. Jess plays her cards close to her chest.'

'Would she even consider that you'd tell me all this?'

'Perhaps. Loyalty means a lot more to your family than it does mine.'

'What if you join us then the Tallans hand everything over to the Alexanders? You'd be on the losing side then.'

'Life's a gamble and I enjoy a flutter. It's the risk I get off on. But my presence on your side could tip the balance in your favour.'

'Or it could capsize us. What am I supposed to do with all this information? Tell the rest of my family?'

'Yes, because you've no choice. You know you can't keep it to yourself.'

'And what if it gets back to your family?'

He shrugged. 'Then it does.'

'They'd batter the shite out of you, at least.'

'They can try.'

Her eyes narrowed. 'You're the one who got Cole the gun, aren't you?'

Jack smiled. 'You really are a smart woman.'

'I knew he wasn't capable of getting one himself. There's much more to you than you're saying, isn't there?'

'Isn't there to everyone?'

Carly looked up when she heard someone call, 'Reggy.'

It was the woman serving behind the counter. She was holding out some food in a polystyrene tray to a man who was walking towards her across the room. He stood at six foot and was slim and trim in his light blue polo shirt and dark blue jogging bottoms. Reggy looked to be in his late thirties but his slicked-back black hair was very obviously dyed. He was handsome in a slimy, superficial sort of way. Carly watched him accept the tray of food and give the woman a charming smile before they launched into a bit of flirtatious banter.

'So that's why you're here,' said Jack.

Carly turned back to face him. 'What are you on about now?'

'I knew you were here for a reason other than working out. You're interested in him, aren't you?'

'No. Why would I be? I don't even know him.'

'He works for the Tallans.'

'Of course he does. He manages this gym and they own it.'

'He does a lot more for them than that. He's up to his neck in their dodgy deals.'

'Look, I haven't a clue who that... what's his name, Robert, did she call him?'

Jack's eyes narrowed. 'Nice try. He's called Reggy, as you well know.'

'Funny, he doesn't look like a Reggy.' She had expected some small, seedy-looking individual in a cardigan and corduroy trousers.

'Stop trying to change the subject.' Jack slammed down his knife and fork, gaze darkening as he leaned forward in his seat. 'What do you know about him?'

Carly leaned forward in response, spots of colour appearing in each cheek as her anger flared. 'Nothing, for God's sake. Stop fucking banging on, it's getting on my nerves.'

'You're lying to me.'

'And what are you going to do about it if I am, slice my belly open?'

Jack's eyes flared with rage and he gritted his teeth. They glared at each other across the table. Carly felt all that anger suddenly turn into something else and it set her heart pounding in a different way. There was something about Jack's eyes that drew her in. They were like nets. Once they caught you, they never let go. Just gazing into them told her how dangerous he was but that only drew her to him even more.

There was a crash from the back of the room and Carly physically jumped, released from the spell. The drippy waiter had dropped a tray of cutlery.

'Fucking wanker,' Jack growled under his breath while he glared at the waiter.

Carly shot to her feet. 'I've got to go. Sorry... I've just remembered an appointment.'

Before he could say another word, Carly had snatched up her bag and jacket and rushed towards the exit. She paused at the door to look back at Jack, who was giving her another of his suggestive dark-eyed stares.

Determinedly, she tore her gaze from his and left. What the hell was she doing? She'd been a second away from kissing him, an Alexander of all people. Thank God for the clumsy waiter. What was it with her and men she couldn't have? First her cousin and now a member of her family's closest rivals and not only that but a man who had recently been released from prison for attempted murder. She was terrified of getting hurt again, so maybe the fact that he was off limits was what she found attractive about him. If she wasn't careful, she was going to get herself into a lot of trouble.

Whatever the reason, her conversation with Jack had left her feeling disturbed. For all she knew he'd been sent by Jessica to try and gain her trust. But Jessica must know she would never trust an Alexander. No, Jack must have approached her off his own bat. That begged the question – had he been telling the truth or working on behalf of his family?

This question nagged at Carly all the way back to Haghill. She got off the bus a couple of streets from her home and walked the rest of the way. She had hoped her uncle would be at the flat but there was only Jane, who was helping their father eat his dinner in his room.

'What are you on today, Da'?' Carly asked him cheerfully.

'Mary made him some chicken noodle soup,' replied Jane.

'Mmm, smells great,' said Carly, her stomach rumbling. Now she wished she'd finished her frittata.

'Jane said… you went to the gym,' murmured Alec.

'Aye. I'm not sure I'll go back though.'

'Why? It's good for you,' he added, struggling to get the words out.

'I know but it's full of show-offs. I think I'll go swimming next time. I might not feel so uncomfortable then.'

'At least you tried,' he said before taking another spoonful of chicken noodle soup from Jane.

Alec managed half the soup in the bowl before indicating to Jane that he'd had enough. She placed the bowl on the table.

'Girls,' he began, 'I'm going to look at that care home tomorrow.'

'We'll support you in whatever you want to do,' Jane told him gently.

'I want you two to come with me, so you can see...' He paused to press the handkerchief to his face with a shaking hand. '...that it's a good place,' he ended.

'We will,' said Jane while Carly folded her arms across her chest. 'What time do you want to go?'

'Three o'clock. Eddie's driving me.'

'And what does he think about this?' said Carly.

'He doesnae want me to go but he understands I have to do it. He'd want the same if he was in my position.'

'Rose will be devastated.'

'Aye, I know,' he said sadly. 'But she'll adapt. You're all so busy now you can't be looking after me.'

'Then I'll pack in my job and look after you full time. That would be better than you leaving.'

'No,' he said firmly. 'That would be stealing your life from you and you need to start living it. This is the best thing for us all.'

Carly bit her lip and looked down at the floor.

'It's settled,' he murmured, leaning back into the pillows. 'Need to sleep.'

'We'll leave you to get some rest,' said Jane.

She kissed his forehead, picked up the bowl and left the room with her sister.

'Don't,' she told Carly once they were back in the kitchen.

'Don't what?' she replied.

'Don't make this even more difficult. It's what Da' wants.'

'I know but it doesn't mean I have to be happy about it.'

'None of us are but it's up to us to make this transition as easy as possible for him and Rose. If she sees how devastated we are about it then it'll only make it worse for her.'

'There's going to be no softening the blow. This is what she's been dreading.'

'It's what we've all been dreading. He won't be far, so we can visit regularly. To be honest, I think it's the best thing. It means he'll be safe from any retaliation from the Alexanders.'

'I hadn't thought of that. Speaking of Alexanders, I had an interesting conversation at the gym.'

'Oh, aye?' Jane smiled. 'Some hot guy chatted you up, did he?'

'Aye, but not in the way you think.'

Carly related her conversation with Jack, skimming over the intense moment they'd shared.

'Well,' said Jane when she'd finished. 'That *is* a surprise. What did you make of it?"

'I've absolutely no idea. If he was telling the truth then he's given us a big advantage but if he was lying then he's a typical fucking Alexander,' she said, glowering. 'What?' she said when Jane studied her closely.

'Jack's a very good-looking man.'

'Who enjoys cutting people's stomachs open, although he said it was self-defence. What is it now?' sighed Carly when her sister stared at her.

'You're defending him.'

'I am not. I'm just giving him the benefit of the doubt. Plus the guy he stabbed went on to murder someone. I looked it up online and that bit was true.'

'Whether he was telling the truth or not is irrelevant. I think the safest thing for us all is to stay away from Jack Alexander.'

'You're probably right but if the Alexanders are in talks with the Tallans, that could go very badly for us.'

20

Eddie and his sons took the news of Carly's conversation with Jack badly.

'The fucking snake,' spat her uncle. 'He only did it to get inside your heid. Don't let him,' he told his niece.

'Keep your voice down,' she retorted. 'Don't forget Da's asleep.'

'Sorry. Jeezo, I cannae believe he did that. How the hell did he know you were there?'

'He must have followed you from Haghill,' Dean told her.

Carly's gaze met his. He knew exactly why she'd been at that gym. Fortunately, he was keeping it to himself. 'The thought had already occurred to me and it gi'es me the creeps.'

'You didn't notice anyone following you?' said Eddie.

'Naw, and I was on a bus. I definitely would have noticed if he'd got on.'

'He could have been following in a car.'

'We'll never know what really happened. When he talks it's hard to know what's true and what's false.'

'The way I see it,' said Jane. 'We have two major worries from Carly's conversation with Jack – the fact that the Alexanders could have been in talks with the Tallans and that Jack can get hold of a gun.'

'I wouldnae worry too much about the second one,' said Eddie. 'Any idiot can get one if they go to the right people. It's the first that's our concern. If the Alexanders impress the Tallans enough, then they will hire them instead and God only knows where that will leave us.'

'Right up shit creek,' said Harry. 'That's where it'll leave us. Can you imagine the hell we'd be in if the Tallans booted us oot and got in the Alexanders?'

'Yes, Harry, we all can,' said Dean dourly.

'We don't even know that the Tallans have spoken to them,' said Carly. 'Jack could have just been trying to wind me up. In fact, I'm certain of it.'

'But the Alexanders have got a lot cockier lately,' said Jane. 'Maybe that's why?'

They all looked at each other, no one sure what to say. It was Eddie who broke the silence.

'I want you to do something Carly, hen,' he said. 'Feel free to say no because it's a big ask.'

'What is it?' she replied.

'I want you to get closer to Jack Alexander.'

'What?' Jane and Dean exclaimed in unison.

Eddie ignored them and continued to address Carly. 'I saw the way he looked at you in the pub. He could have chosen to approach you because he fancies you and you can play on that.'

'No way,' said Jane. 'He tried to murder someone, for Christ's sake.'

'Like I said, it's a big ask but it's all I can think of. We need to find out what his family's up to and my contacts have got nothing. Whatever's going on, the Alexanders are playing it very close to their chests and we know no other member of that family will tell you. But he might. I'm banking on him being honest about wanting to switch sides.'

'If his family is in negotiation with the Tallans,' said Carly. 'Then no way would he want to do that.'

'Aye, which makes everything he told you very suspicious. We need to get at the truth and you're our best way of doing that.'

'It's a ridiculous idea,' said Jane. 'Especially after everything that family has already done to her.'

'You come up with something then because it's all I've got,' retorted Eddie.

Jane sighed and looked down at the floor.

When it became apparent that she didn't have a better idea, Eddie turned his attention to his sons. 'What about you two? Can you think of anything?'

'Why don't we just grab one of the Alexanders and torture them, like we did Brian?' said Harry.

'I might have known. Your fondness for violence is getting a little worrying.'

'I think it's a good idea,' said Dean, eyes glittering. He was desperate to come up with anything that would stop Carly from having to get close to Jack Alexander. Not only was he worried about her safety, but he was jealous too. 'Only this time we grab Ross. The prick will soon talk once I start on the soles of his feet with a fucking soldering iron.'

Carly's gaze met Dean's and she saw the anger. 'I'm not sure that's a good idea,' she said.

'Course it is,' interjected Harry. 'It's the only way to get information out of that family. Ross is a coward; we all saw that when he attacked Uncle Alec.'

'That would be preferable than Carly having to get close to Jack,' said Jane.

'You think it's better we torture someone than talk to someone?' said Carly. 'Is that the path we want our family to go down?'

'Yes,' said Dean darkly.

Once again, a thrill ran down Carly's spine. It was just striking her how much she liked dangerous men. 'I'll talk to Jack,' she said.

'I really don't think—' began Jane.

'It's the best option,' interrupted Carly. 'I can control the situation and you lot can make sure I'm safe. It's better than torturing someone, even if that person is Ross Alexander. If we keep on that way God knows where it'll lead,' she added with a pointed look Dean's way.

Eddie nodded. 'We'll make sure you're safe.'

'And you're no' exactly helpless,' Harry told Carly.

'Thank you, Harry. I'm glad someone has faith in me,' she replied while looking from Jane to Dean.

'I do too, hen,' said Eddie. 'You can easily handle this. Now, we know he goes to the Tallans' gym, so you need to keep going until he turns up again.'

'The gym?' said Carly, crestfallen.

'I could go too,' said Dean. 'Keep an eye out.'

'He won't open up if you're there,' Eddie told him. 'The gym is a safe place, busy, full of people. Jack won't be able to do anything to her there.'

'He could outside the gym. He might wait for her and abduct her.'

'I'm sure I can manage to get on a bus without getting kidnapped,' said Carly flatly. 'Besides, it could take ages to bump into him at the gym and by then it might be too late. He's here in Haghill, so it makes sense to approach him here.' She looked to Jane. 'Do any of the Bitches live near the Alexanders' house who can keep an eye out for Jack coming and going?'

'Donna lives two streets away and she said she's seen him going to the bookies,' replied her sister.

'Makes sense. He told me he enjoys a flutter.'

'Anita's maw owns the hairdresser's across the road from the bookies and she lives in the flat above. You could keep watch from the flat and just accidentally bump into him in the street as he's going in.'

'No,' said Eddie. 'Make that when he's coming out. If he's keen to put a bet on he might not want to stop and chat.'

'Okay, sounds good,' said Carly. She would much rather hang around a flat than a gym.

'Try and get more information out of him about his family and the Tallans. We have to confirm whether or not they really have been in talks.'

'I'll do my best,' she replied, wondering how the hell she'd get information like that out of a man who couldn't be relied on to say a single truthful word.

Carly stared out of the window at the street below. Anita's mother's flat was very nice. It was only a small two bedroomed apartment, but it was elegantly decorated and smelled of vanilla. It also had a very comfortable armchair beside the window from which she could keep watch. It was eleven o'clock in the morning and she'd already been there for two hours. Anita's mother, Christine, had no problem letting her sit in her home all day while she worked in the salon below. Jane had been a friend of Anita's since they were at primary school, so the two families were well acquainted.

Carly had wanted to bring a book but her uncle had said she had to keep an eye out at all times. At first, she'd found watching people coming and going rather entertaining. There had been a couple bickering as they walked down the street. The man had grabbed the woman by her hair and yanked back her head but he'd soon been felled by her knee in his groin. She'd then punched him in the face, knocking him out before taking his wallet and rushing off down the street. A dog had then wandered up to the unconscious man, sniffed him and pissed on his head. That had woken the man up, who'd shrieked hysterically at the dog, which had run off yelping. Then the cabaret had ended and there had only been boring passers-by strolling down the road ever since.

'I hope I don't have to sit here all day,' she sighed.

Carly sat up straighter in her seat when a figure wearing black jeans and a black jacket appeared at the top of the street. Jack casually strolled along while talking into his mobile phone. The window was open a crack but it wasn't enough to hear what he was saying. It was tempting to push it open wider but it might draw his attention to her, so she left it as it was. There was a man walking a distance behind Jack, head down, hands stuffed into his jeans pockets.

Carly watched Jack enter the bookies, the man behind him carrying on down the street. Once Jack was inside, she called Eddie.

'He's here,' she said when her uncle answered.

'Finally. We're on our way.'

Carly hung up and turned her attention back to the window. Half an hour later she saw Jack pull open the door of the bookies while chatting to another man. She leapt to her feet and hurried downstairs, emerging in the salon, which was busy, all five chairs occupied. Christine, looking smart in her white blouse and cream-coloured trousers, curly light blonde hair bobbing about her shoulders, smiled at Carly as she passed, scissors and comb in hand.

Carly peered through the window and saw Jack just leaving the bookies. He turned and headed back the way he'd come.

Just as she reached for the door handle, Carly noticed the man who'd been behind him earlier coming back up the street, his eyes riveted to Jack's back.

Bloody hell, she thought. *He's following Jack.*

Carly scrabbled for her phone in her pocket, took it out and snapped a photo of the mysterious man as he passed by. He was about six foot with a slender build, and he wore blue jeans, a grey jacket, white trainers and a baseball cap pulled down low to obscure his face. She didn't recognise him but hopefully someone would.

Pulling up the hood of her jacket, Carly followed at a safe distance. It soon became apparent that Jack was wending his way back to the Alexander home. She didn't want to get too close but she also wanted to see if the man would follow Jack all the way or would even attack him. Jack for his part seemed oblivious, his attention solely focused on his phone. A man like him must have realised what was going on. Carly kept expecting him to turn round and confront his stalker but she was continually disappointed.

When she reached the bottom of the street where the Alexanders lived, she hung back at the corner, waiting to see if anything would happen but Jack went inside and the man following him carried on his way. When he was almost at the bottom of the street however the man stopped and turned. Carly ducked behind a car to watch him but he didn't spot her, too busy peering back at the Alexanders' house. He took out his phone and made a call before walking away, still talking into his handset.

She whipped round at the sound of footsteps behind her to see Jack Alexander.

'Where the hell did you come from?' she demanded.

'I saw you from the window watching the house,' he said with a smug smile. 'So I left by the back door. What the hell do you think you're doing? If Cole or Ross had seen you anything could have happened.'

'Are they in?'

'No, but that's not the point.'

Over Jack's shoulder she saw Harry and Dean further down the street. They stopped but they didn't retreat.

'You knew I was there but not the man who was following you,' Carly told Jack.

'Who was following me?' he replied.

'This man,' she said, taking out her phone and showing him the photo. 'I saw you leave the bookies and he followed you all the way back here and you didn't have a clue.' She didn't add that she saw the man follow him to the bookies as well because that would have told him she had been waiting for him.

Jack tilted his head and threw back his shoulders. 'I knew he was there all along.'

'No you didn't,' she replied with an amused smile. 'You didnae have a clue. You were too busy looking at your phone. I would have thought a man like you would be much more alert to his surroundings.'

With an annoyed grunt he snatched the phone off her to study the screen. Dean and Harry tensed but Carly took the opportunity while Jack was distracted to wave them back. They stayed put.

'Do you recognise him?' she asked Jack.

'It's impossible to tell who it is, he's so blurry. Unless he always looks like that.' He frowned when she sniggered.

'You remember what I said about the recent disappearances?'

Jack nodded.

'Every person who disappeared said they were being followed in the days before they vanished. And now you're being followed.'

'I'm taking it everyone who vanished was well known in the local area?' he said, handing her back her phone.

'Aye.'

'I've only just got here.'

'True, but your arrival has created ripples. There will be plenty of people who resent your presence here.'

'Like your family?' he said, eyes darkening.

'Aye, but hiring men with blurry faces to follow you isn't our style.'

The darkness vanished and he laughed. 'You're funny.'

'Thanks,' she said sarcastically.

'If you are worried that I'm being followed and will shortly disappear, why warn me? Why not just let whoever it is do me in?'

'I don't know. It just seemed like the right thing to do.'

At that moment, his phone made a noise. He took it out of his pocket to glance at the screen.

'I know that sound,' said Carly. 'It's a game, but which one?' A smile split her face.

'What?' He frowned.

'Are you playing Pokémon?' She grabbed his hand and pulled it toward her so she could see the screen. 'You are. Oh, that's just priceless. All the while you were being followed, you were looking for a Weedle.'

Rage sparked inside him like a flame, his eyes lighting up with it as he snatched his phone away from her. 'No, I fucking wasn't.'

'Yes, you were. Do yourself a favour and ditch the game while you're walking about before something bad happens to you.'

'What the fuck do you care what happens to me?'

'I don't. Call it a friendly warning in return for the one you gave me.'

'And what warning was that?' he said, shoving the phone back into his pocket.

'The one about your family's negotiations with the Tallans. I wonder what they'd say if they found out you'd told me that?'

His eyes narrowed. 'You wouldn't.'

'Why not?'

'Because you can't be sure whether I told you that off my own bat or if they put me up to it.'

'There's only one way to find out. I'll tell Ross. His reaction will tell me immediately which it is, he's so incapable of hiding his emotions.'

'You little bitch,' he snarled, squaring up to her.

'What are you going to do, Jack?' she said, gaze mocking. 'Attack me in the middle of the street? You'd be sent straight back to Monster Mansion.'

His right hand curled into a fist and he gritted his teeth. 'Go on then, tell him. See where that gets you.' He forced his scowl into a smile. 'He'd probably just tear you apart with his bare hands.'

'If he couldn't beat my wee sister then he'd have no chance against me.'

Jack tutted and glowered down at the ground, as though wrestling with himself. To Carly's surprise, when he raised his head he was smiling.

'You're a little firecracker, aren't you?' he said.

'You have no idea, so I don't recommend pissing me off or I will tell Ross what you said.'

Jack pointed to the Alexander home. 'Jess and Brian are in. Why don't you go in and tell them? They'll make sure to pass it on to their sons.'

'Fine, I will.' Carly hesitated, knowing her cousins would stop her before she got through the front door. She couldn't see Harry and Dean any more but she knew they were watching. She also suspected Jack was trying to lure her into the house.

'Aren't you going then?' Jack asked her.

'No. I don't need to talk to them. Everything you've told me is bollocks. If you are what you say you are, you would have spotted the man following you but you didn't, which tells me you're all mouth. You were practically a wean when you went into prison after you got in over your head. You didn't scare the monsters, Jack. They scared you.'

'You haven't a fucking clue what you're talking about,' he hissed at her.

'I know everything I need to know. It was nice talking to you,' she said before walking past him and down the street.

Carly didn't need to turn around to see if he was watching her. She could feel his eyes boring into her back. She pondered on the wisdom of winding him up. If he had been genuine about wanting to join their side then she'd probably ruined that but she'd stirred up a hornet's nest and she was intrigued to see what would happen next.

At the bottom of the street, two large forms leapt out at her.

'Jesus,' she breathed.

'Sorry for scaring you,' said Harry. 'What happened? We were watching but we couldnae hear anything.'

Before replying, Carly looked back up the street just in time to see Jack enter the Alexander home and close the door behind him.

'I just wound him right up. He didn't realise he was being followed because he was too busy playing Pokémon.'

Harry laughed while Dean smiled.

'No' such the big man after all,' commented Dean.

'Exactly. I told him he wasn't all he was making himself out to be and he didn't like that. I also said I'd let Ross know that he told me about their negotiations with the Tallans.'

'Why Ross?' said Dean curiously.

'Because he cannae control his temper. His reaction would tell me a lot more than Jess's or Cole's, who are better at controlling themselves.'

Dean nodded at the wisdom of this statement. 'What did he say to that?'

'He told me to go for it and said I should go into the house right then.'

'I'm very glad you didn't.'

'Who was following him?' said Harry.

'No idea. I managed to get a photo though,' she replied, producing her phone.

Both men studied the screen.

'I've never seen him before,' said Dean.

'Me neither,' replied Harry. 'But then the photo is a wee bit blurred. Well, if Jack does disappear then all the better for us.'

'And who will be next?' said Carly. 'It might be one of our family. We're better off finding out who this man is before that can happen,' she added, pointing to the image on the screen.

'You're right,' said Dean. 'We have to take this seriously.'

'Maybe the mystery man's still close by?' said Carly. 'He went this way,' she added before shooting off in that direction.

'Carly, wait,' called Dean as he and Harry hurried after her.

As they passed the Alexander home, they all turned to see Jack staring out of the living room window. His eyes flared when he saw them but he made no other move.

The three of them rushed down the street.

'He went left,' said Carly before turning the corner.

To her disappointment, they saw no one but they continued on regardless.

'There's the corner shop,' said Harry. 'Maybe he went in there?'

Dean and Carly waited outside while Harry went into the shop. He emerged a minute later with a triumphant smile.

'The prick was just in there buying ciggies. Apparently he turned right when he left the shop.'

They raced off in that direction, looking up and down every

side street and studying the occupants of each car that passed them by but there was no sign of their mystery man.

'Bugger,' sighed Carly. 'For all we know he could have got into a car and driven off.'

'Look,' said Dean, pointing down the street.

Carly and Harry turned to look.

'What?' said Harry. 'No one's there.'

'That bit of plastic on the ground.'

'Aye, shocking,' replied Harry. 'He cannae stand littering,' he told Carly while nodding at Dean.

'I don't mean that,' said Dean, rushing over to it and nudging it with the toe of his shoe. 'It's the wrapping off a pack of cigarettes.'

'Outside the pub the Alexanders frequent,' said Carly.

The three of them stared up at the frontage of The Wheatsheaf, which was a dark, squat, mean-looking building that gave the impression it was scowling at everyone who passed it by. Its windows were covered in mesh and its door was made of steel, like a high security prison.

'If we go in there, trouble will kick off,' said Harry. His face cracked into a grin. 'Let's do it.'

'Yeah.' Carly smiled. 'Great idea.'

Before Dean could urge either of them to caution, they'd walked inside. 'Great,' he sighed before following them in.

21

It took their eyes a moment to adjust to the gloom. The roof was so low the atmosphere was oppressive. The pub was pretty quiet because of the time of day. The landlord, who was called Lonny and was Derek's biggest rival, was standing behind the bar reading a newspaper. Casually, he glanced up to see who the new arrivals were and did a double take.

'What the hell are you lot doing in here?' he demanded, tossing the newspaper onto the top of the bar.

They ignored him as they looked around for the man who'd followed Jack.

'Oy, are you deaf?' he exclaimed.

Carly hurried over to him, taking out her phone. 'Have you seen this man?'

'Why? What the fuck is this, *Crimewatch*?'

'Just answer the question.'

'I'm answering nothing. Now bugger off out of it, you're no' welcome here.'

'Useless as always, Lonny,' she replied.

'That's it,' he said, charging out from behind the bar and

storming over to her. Before he could reach Carly, her cousins placed themselves in his way and his bravado wilted.

'Answer her,' Harry growled at him.

'No, I havenae seen him. Now piss off,' yelled Lonny.

'He must be telling the truth,' said Carly. 'He's not here.'

A door at the back of the room opened and out walked Cole and Ross. 'Why are you shouting now, Lonny?' demanded the latter. His eyes settled on the three Savages. 'What the fuck are you lot doing here?'

'Why shouldn't we come here?' said Carly. 'You're always popping into The Horseshoe where you're not wanted.'

'They were wantin' to know if someone had come in here,' Lonny told the Alexanders.

'Who?' Ross frowned.

At that moment, the mystery man in the baseball cap appeared behind Cole and Ross.

'Him,' said Lonny.

'Why do you want to know about him?' Ross asked the Savages.

'Because he just waved his willy at a group of young girls outside the corner shop,' said Carly.

Dean and Harry glanced at each other in surprise but said nothing, respecting her quick thinking.

'No, I didn't,' exclaimed the mystery man. 'I'd never do anything like that.'

'Aye, ya would, ya dirty bastard,' said Carly. 'Those lassies were only twelve years old at the most.'

'I didn't,' he cried when everyone in the pub turned to regard him with disgust, except Ross and Cole.

'Course you didn't,' said Ross. 'She's lying to make you look bad.'

'Why would I want to make him look bad?' said Carly. 'I don't even know him. We just happened to stop at the shop and the lassies were there, crying. We said we'd sort out the bastard for them,' she added with a glower at the mystery man.

'Paedos aren't allowed in my pub,' Lonny told the Alexanders.

'I'm no' a paedo,' cried the man. 'There weren't even any weans outside the shop. I went in, bought some ciggies and came straight here. Why don't you go and ask the woman working in the shop? She'll tell you.'

'How would she know?' said Carly. 'It all happened outside the shop.'

'We know you didnae do anything,' Cole told the man while keeping his gaze riveted on Carly. 'They're trying to damage our reputation. If it got about that we hang around with paedos no one would ever do business with us.'

'They won't anyway,' said Carly. 'Not after you lost against us so spectacularly.'

'That shows what you know, you stupid bitch,' Ross spat at her.

Cole's jaw set and he put a hand on his brother's arm, urging him to curb his tongue. Ross nodded, eyes flashing.

'Enlighten me then,' Carly told Ross. 'What don't I know?'

She noted Cole's grip on Ross's arm tightened, using so much pressure his fingers turned white.

'We're no' telling you,' said Ross. 'Just know that it will smash your family to bits.'

'That's enough,' Cole told him.

Cole might have been the younger brother but it seemed he had some sway over Ross, who went quiet.

'You're just lying to make yourself sound like the big man,' Carly told Ross, hoping to provoke him into another outburst. 'Our family humiliated yours and you cannae stand it, especially after my wee sister nearly tore your baws off. If she manages to get hold of them again, she said she'll turn them into a really tiny pair of earrings.'

There was a snigger across the room. A furious Ross whipped round but was unable to spot the offender. He turned back to face Carly, eyes full of rage.

'You know fuck all. Well let me tell you that when we've sealed our deal, you'll be the ones being humiliated, all of you. By the time my family's done with yours, there'll only be scraps of you left for the birds to peck at.'

'Shut up,' Cole hissed at his brother.

'There is no deal,' pressed Carly. 'You're utterly pathetic, do you know that, Ross? But then again, you always did live in a fantasy world. Now you're stuck here in this shitey pub...'

'Hey.' Lonny frowned.

'...coming up with lies to tell people to make yourself feel better while socialising with paedophiles. You're a disgrace, even to the name Alexander, and that is not an easy thing to achieve.'

When Ross charged at Carly, Dean and Harry placed themselves before her, their demeanour aggressive.

'Bring it on, big man,' said Harry, pleased it looked like he was finally going to get a good fight.

Cole grabbed his brother by the shoulder and spun him round to face him. 'She's just trying to wind you up to get you to spill the beans,' he told him. 'Don't let her get to you.'

Ross threw Carly a black look before taking a deep breath and raking his hands through his hair.

'Nice try,' Cole told her. 'But it didn't work.'

'He'll let your secrets slip one day. He's incapable of keeping anything to himself for long.'

'This pair cannae guard you all the time,' yelled Ross, pointing at her cousins. 'And I will get to you and make you regret that big fucking mouth of yours.'

'Is that supposed to scare me after my baby sister put you in hospital?'

Ross's temper erupted out of him and, not daring to tackle the brothers together, he kicked over a chair, breaking it.

'Oy, careful,' exclaimed Lonny.

'Wait outside,' Cole told Ross. 'I'll handle this.'

With one last glare, Ross left, kicking open the door as he went. It swung shut behind him with a loud bang.

Cole looked to Carly. 'You shouldnae wind him up like that.'

'Like that prick worries me. Whatever you're scheming, it will fail.'

'If you say so.'

Carly knew she wouldn't be able to rile Cole like she had Ross, so she didn't even try. 'Does this scheme of yours involve paedos?' she said, nodding at the mystery man.

'He's no' a paedo, as you well know. You're clever, Carly, you always have been but you need to be careful. Accusing people of things like that isn't good for your health.'

'Don't you fucking threaten her,' yelled Dean.

'So you do still fancy her then? You're a bunch of inbred twats.'

'Dean's my cousin,' said Carly. 'You're the twisted one thinking things like that.'

Inwardly Dean winced as she destroyed the last of his hopes.

'I suggest you leave and keep your noses out of my family's business,' said Cole. 'I'd hate to see you get hurt, Carly.'

'Let's go,' said Harry, realising staying would be fruitless. Not only would they not get the information they wanted, but it looked like he wasn't going to get his fight either.

'Aye, okay,' said Carly. 'It's a crap pub anyway.'

'Hey you,' said Lonny. 'It's way better than that toilet Derek runs.'

'Time to go,' said Dean when the customers started to look surly at this affront to their watering hole.

The three of them left. Just before going through the door,

Carly glanced over her shoulder at Cole, who was staring back at her. Once she'd been able to read every emotion in his beautiful green eyes but now he was a closed book to her.

She followed her cousins out, the three of them coming to a halt when they were confronted by a gang of six men, a smirking Ross at their head.

'Not so fucking smug now, are you, bitch?' he told Carly.

The pub door opened and Cole emerged with the man in the baseball cap, as well as three of the customers, all big, hefty men.

'You need teaching a lesson no' to come onto our territory,' said Ross.

'The whole of Haghill is our territory,' said Harry.

'Sounds like you're the one living in a fantasy world. You go where you're no' wanted, you pay the price.'

'Bring it on,' said Harry with glee.

'Stay behind us,' Dean told Carly.

'Bugger that,' she said, producing the baton from inside her jacket.

Just as Ross and his men were preparing to charge at the three of them, someone shouted, 'Oy.'

They all turned to see the Bitches storming down the road towards them, Jane at their head.

'Oh, Christ, it's that lot,' said one of Ross's men.

'So what?' he replied. 'They're just a bunch of women.'

'They're no' women, they're Valkyries.'

'Don't be a fucking coward. We can take them.'

From the opposite direction came Eddie and Peanut.

'Do the sensible thing and get lost,' Carly told Ross. 'While you're still able to walk.'

Ross grunted with rage before running off with the rest of his men, the Bitches chasing after them. Although the men had a good head start on them, they managed to catch up with one of their number and took him down like a pack of hyenas on a gazelle.

When Carly, Harry and Dean rounded on them, the customers from the pub and the man in the baseball cap rushed back inside. Only Cole remained.

'Are you wantin' your heid kicking in?' said Harry.

Cole regarded him disinterestedly before looking back at Carly. 'Do yourself a favour,' he told her. 'Take Rose and your da' and get out of Haghill. Things are about to get tough around here for your family and I don't want to see you get involved.'

'Don't tell me you still care?' she said sarcastically.

'Actually, I dae. I always have.'

Carly just stared at him in puzzlement as he returned inside the pub, closing the door behind him.

'Now he's the one trying to get into people's heids,' said Dean, not liking the look in Carly's eyes.

'You're right,' she replied, although her voice sounded faraway.

Jane jogged up to them. 'You all okay?' she said.

'Aye, fine,' replied Harry. 'Where did this lot come from?' he asked her, gesturing to the Bitches. They were all gathered around the unfortunate man who'd been brought down and were pulling off his clothes. They had big grins on their faces and were taunting the man's physical appearance. The man begged for mercy and the only concession they made was that they allowed him to keep on his underwear, although the hilarity only increased when they saw he was wearing a hot pink thong. Eddie and Peanut were watching, doubled over with laughter.

'I thought just you and Jennifer were in on this?' Dean asked Jane.

'I wasn't taking any chances,' she replied. 'So I got all the girls together. They deserve a treat.'

They all turned to look. The man had by now been stripped

entirely naked and he was running off down the street, hands cupping his genitals while four of the women pursued him, whipping his bare backside with his own clothes. They chased him halfway down the road before returning to their friends, chatting and laughing and tossing his clothes into the gutter.

'Nice one,' Carly told them.

'I agree,' said Harry, putting on his most charming smile. 'Beautiful work by beautiful ladies.'

'I don't see any fucking ladies,' said Stacey, a tall twenty-year-old woman with jaw-length light brown hair. She had sparkling blue eyes and a ring through her lower lip.

The women laughed but Harry wasn't fazed. 'You're all ladies,' he told them. 'And you should be dripping in silks and diamonds.'

The women all curled their lips before breaking into mocking laughter.

'I was only trying to be nice,' muttered Harry.

'You still don't understand that the Bitches are all about breaking social norms and stereotypes,' said Jane. 'We are not like those empty-headed morons on reality TV.'

'The Housewives of Haghill,' exclaimed Leonie.

The laughter increased, to Harry's chagrin.

'You smooth operator, you.' Carly grinned at him. She spotted Cole peering out at her from one of The Wheatsheaf's windows.

'Let's get out of here,' said Dean, who was keen to get her away from Cole.

The Bitches walked with them all the way to Eddie's house, Eddie and Peanut tagging along with them and talking quietly. Carly glanced back over her shoulder, wondering what they could be discussing. The way they hung back from the rest of the group indicated they didn't want anyone overhearing their conversation and she had a strong feeling that they were purposefully keeping something from her.

Dean walked alongside Carly and kept intermittently glancing at her.

'What?' she said, frowning.

'You didn't let Cole get into your head, did you?' he replied.

'Course not. Jeezo, you must really think I'm an idiot. Even if he meant it, I'd never go there again.'

Dean was relieved. 'Good,' he replied. 'I wouldnae be surprised if his cow of a mother told him to say that just to mess with you.'

The six of them entered Eddie and Harry's house to find dirty plates on the coffee table and even dirtier socks on the floor.

'You always were a slobby bastard, Eddie,' said Peanut.

'Hey, don't blame me for that travesty,' he replied, pointing to the socks. 'They're Harry's. I would have moved them but I was afraid they'd bite me. You've never seen feet like his before.'

'Da',' exclaimed an outraged Harry.

'Sorry, son.' Eddie smiled, not looking in the least bit apologetic. 'So, are you ready to tell us what was going on back there?'

Carly related the tale and when she'd finished, Peanut whistled.

'Wow,' said Peanut. 'The Alexanders were having Jack followed. They don't trust him.'

'So it seems,' she replied.

'And Jack didnae even notice he was being followed,' said Harry. 'Which tells us he's no such the big man.'

'Maybe, maybe not,' said Eddie. 'We all have our off days. The one thing it's safe to assume though is that man, whatever he was doing, was doing it on behalf of Cole and Ross.'

'What if the Alexanders are the ones who've been making people disappear?' said Dean.

They all turned to look at him.

'You can't be serious?' said Harry. 'That group of fannies?'

'Why not?'

'Because they're no' up to the job.'

'They're violent and ruthless, so why shouldn't they be able to make people disappear?'

'They haven't got the brains.'

'Cole and Jess have,' said Carly. 'And so does Jack. I find it strange that people started vanishing just as he arrives in the area. What if he's the one who made those people disappear and now his own family's afraid he's going to do the same to them, so they're having him watched? They must know about his Pokémon obsession and that he'd be distracted while out walking, giving the man in the baseball cap the chance to follow him and see what he's up to.'

'That is an excellent theory,' said Jane.

'Aye,' said Eddie. 'Impressive stuff, hen,' he told Carly. 'And I reckon you might be right.'

'There's one way to prove it,' said Peanut. 'If Carly is right then there's something linking the three people who vanished to the Alexanders. We need to find it. Hopefully, that would also confirm what they're up to and whether they really have been having talks with the Tallans.'

'We could talk to the friends and relatives of the missing people,' said Dean.

'Will they be willing to talk to us?' said Harry.

'The friends and loved ones of missing people always want to talk about it in case it helps find them, but it'll require subtlety. We don't want to offend anyone and we don't want it getting back to the Alexanders either.'

'That's Harry out then,' said Eddie with a pointed look his older son's way. 'He's as subtle as a kick in the goolies.'

'I cannae argue with that.' Harry grinned.

'I propose me and Jane go,' added Dean.

'Hey,' said Carly. 'Why are you keeping me out of it?'

'Because you have a history of losing your rag,' he told her.

'Dean's right,' said Eddie. 'Him and Jane are the best ones to handle it. Leave it to them.'

'Fine,' Carly said, holding up her hands. 'I won't argue.'

'That'll be a first,' said her uncle wryly.

'Do you have the addresses we need?' Dean asked his father.

'Aye, nae bother. Peanut, would you mind going with them? You don't need to go in with them, you could just wait in the car in case there's trouble.'

'Course, whatever you need.'

Eddie patted his shoulder. 'Cheers, pal. But it can wait until tomorrow. This afternoon we're taking Alec to look at that care home.'

They all nodded sombrely.

'What can we be doing while they're talking to the families of the missing people?' Carly asked her uncle, pointing from herself to Harry, wanting to change the subject.

'Stay out of trouble, that's what you two can do,' he replied sternly. 'I'll go and get those addresses you need, I jotted them down somewhere because I was thinking of questioning the families myself.'

When Dean saw his father head upstairs, he followed him into his bedroom.

'What are you doing?' Eddie frowned at him.

Dean closed the door behind him, ignoring the dirty clothes strewn about the room. 'I need to talk to you.'

'About what?'

'You know who attacked me and Carly that day on the motorbikes, don't you?'

'How the hell do you know that?'

'I can read you pretty well, Da'. So, who was it?'

Eddie sighed. 'Fine, but don't mention it to the others, especially Carly. God only knows what she'd do if she found out.'

'Go on,' said Dean, refusing to commit before he had all the facts.

'I went to the nearest hospital to where you were attacked. It was easy enough finding the men responsible.'

'You spoke to them?'

'I didnae need to. I recognised them. They were the Tallans' men.'

'What?' said Dean, eyebrows shooting up his head. 'But why?'

'They were testing you. Neil and Rod have been known to do that but no' so harshly. I reckon these men went a bit overboard.'

'Why test me and Carly and not Harry and Jane?'

'The Tallans must have seen you as the weakest links.'

'Charming.'

'Don't take it as an insult. It's only because you're the younger two. The fact that they then put you onto the blackmail operation tells me you impressed them.'

Dean sighed and shook his head as he processed this information. 'Now I understand why you don't want Carly to know. She'd kick off holy hell.'

'Exactly, so you can never tell her.'

'I promise I won't. Not telling her is protecting her. Well, at least the mystery is solved and those men won't come back for a second try.'

'They certainly won't but there are others who might try and take the money you collect from you. That will always be a very real danger, so don't sit back on your laurels.'

'We won't. I'm glad I know though. It's a weight off.'

'Good. I've told no one else, no' even Peanut, so let's keep it that way.'

22

Carly sat in the back of Eddie's car with Jane, their feet sitting in the rubbish that always filled the footwells of their uncle's car, the two sisters silent and sullen. Alec sat up front with his brother, who was driving. Carly was glad that Eddie had gone to the trouble of removing the pop cans and chocolate bar wrappers from the footwell of the front passenger seat so her father could get in easily. It had been quite a while since Alec had left the flat and then it had only been for hospital appointments, so he was rather enjoying this outing.

The care home was situated in Mount Vernon, just three and a half miles from Haghill. They were greeted on arrival by the manager of the home, as well as a nurse with a wheelchair for Alec to climb into. Jane and Carly were both surprised to see he was giving the women his best smile and his eyes were sparkling. They glanced at each other before following the others inside.

The sisters had to admit the home was impressive. It was a luxury care home with excellent food, a hairdresser's, library, communal computer room, a bar and even a cinema. The staff were all very friendly and seemed to really care about their patients. Alec was told he could even have a pet if he wanted to.

They were shown what would be his room if he chose to stay. It was a one bedroomed studio apartment, completely private with his own bathroom. The room was already fully equipped for his needs and he would have round-the-clock nursing care. Carly felt herself warming towards the idea, despite how desperate she was to keep her father at home. Here he would have the dignity he so desired as well as access to a lot more facilities. He would actually be able to enjoy himself rather than just be stuck in one room, like he was at home, and the way his eyes were alight with happiness finally brought her round to the idea. He hadn't looked so animated in weeks.

After the tour, the manager escorted them outside and left them to take a walk in the grounds before they returned to the car.

'You see, girls,' Alec told his daughters. 'It's a good place.'

'It is, Da',' said Jane. 'It's a fantastic place.'

'Did you see the grub?' said Eddie. 'It looked amazing. I think I'll sign up too.' He grinned.

Alec's smile faltered. 'It's a lot of money though. Are you sure we can afford it?'

'Absolutely,' said Jane. 'It'll be no problem and Uncle Eddie's going to help pay too. It won't just be on us.'

'Too right I am,' said Eddie. 'Don't worry about the cost, Alec. We've got it covered.'

'But it's four grand a month.'

'Stop worrying. It's a great place and if it makes you happy then it's worth every penny.'

The sisters beamed at their uncle.

'Okay,' said Alec. 'Then I'll move in.' He looked to his daughters and fought to hold out his shaking hands. Carly and Jane stepped forward to take one of his hands each. 'I don't want to leave you, girls, but this is the right thing for us all. And you'll be free.'

'You're not a burden to us, Da',' said Carly, blinking away tears.

'I am and I won't be any more. I want you to really live.'

Carly didn't know if she was being paranoid but she felt his gaze stayed on her longer than it did Jane. Once again she got the feeling he knew more about her than she thought.

* * *

Alec was exhausted after his outing, so they put him straight to bed when they returned to the flat.

'That went well,' said Jane as she made the three of them a cup of tea. 'I think Da' will be really happy there.'

'Course he will, surrounded by all those pretty wee nurses.' Eddie smiled. 'When I'm old and doddery, that's the place I'm going to.' He looked to Carly. 'You all right, hen?'

She nodded. 'Yeah. I see now this is the right thing to do.'

'It is. He'll have a much better quality of life.'

'I couldn't get over that cinema,' said Jane. 'It was so plush. I'd no idea care homes could be like that. And that piano bar was so lavish.'

'Aye, even the Tallans would love to drink there and we know what snobby gits they are.'

'The bar,' murmured Jane, her eyes widening.

'What is it?' said Carly.

'Bar... the bar.'

'Aye, it was a bar,' said Eddie. 'You having some sort of fit, doll?'

'In the paperwork I took from the garage where Cole works there was a receipt for a place called Death Loves Company. I didn't think anything of it when I saw it, I just thought it had got bundled up in the paperwork by accident, which wouldn't be surprising because the office was such a tip. It was for a pint of lager and a Bacardi and coke.'

'Those are Cole's and Jess's drinks,' said Carly.

'To be fair,' said Eddie. 'They're a lot of other people's too.' He looked back at Jane. 'What's so special about this bar?'

'It only opened a month ago near the Botanic Gardens. I remember reading about it in the papers. It's owned by some ex-reality TV celebrity. The Tallans were in the photos of the opening.'

'Are you saying Cole and Jess went to this bar to talk with Rod and Neil?'

'I don't know, maybe not. It is a bit of a stretch.'

'Worth checking out though.'

'How do we do that without the Tallans finding out?'

'There would be nothing unusual about you two checking out a hot new local bar, would there?'

'I suppose not.'

'Tell you what – take a couple of men along with you so it looks like a double date. That'll be a good cover.'

'You mean Dean and Harry?' said Carly.

'No, I don't mean your own cousins, I mean real men. You know what I mean,' he added when Jane chuckled.

'Well, okay,' said Carly, not really sure about this plan. 'We could take Liam and Graham,' she told Jane.

'Who are they?' said Eddie.

'We went to school with them and we're still friends. They're really nice guys, although I am a bit worried about dragging them into something that could turn dangerous.'

'All you're doing is going for a drink. You can scope out the bar but that's it, you won't be questioning people or getting into fights.'

'I suppose that would be okay,' said Jane.

'Good. Talk to this Liam and Graham then. Hopefully you can go tonight. Don't look so miserable,' he told Carly. 'You're going to a great bar with a couple of good-looking men. I take it they're good-looking?'

Carly and Jane nodded.

'Great, so what's the problem?'

'Nothing,' said Carly. 'I was just hoping for a quiet night in.'

'A quiet night in? You're only twenty. You should be out partying every night and waking up with a hangover.'

Carly knew he was right – that was what her friends did – but it wasn't for her. For too long she'd been at home caring for her father and working and she'd gone past all that childish stuff. It didn't interest her, but she wasn't averse to the odd night out.

Eddie for his part hoped Carly took to either Liam or Graham. Fingers crossed one of them would take her mind off Dean.

* * *

Carly and Jane entered Death Loves Company and paused to look around. The place was moody and gothic, the furniture all black, candelabras perched on the tables. The only illumination was from the orange wall lights. Images of skulls, ghosts and gravestones were dotted around the room in the form of pictures or resin replicas. The walls were black and the floor a dark grey. Some of the customers were dressed all in black with dramatic black and white make-up while others were just casual. There was a comfortable mingling of the two styles, which cast a pleasant, welcoming atmosphere.

'This is pretty awesome,' said Liam.

'Aye, it is,' replied Carly.

'Have you been here before?'

'No, but we've heard it's a good bar, so we thought we'd try it out.'

'Thanks for inviting us,' said Liam coyly.

Carly smiled at him. She thought he was a nice man. He was pretty easy on the eye too, although not in the same league as Dean or Jack Alexander. Liam stood at six foot one with the build of a rugby player, mainly because he enjoyed the sport. He had a mop of dark brown hair, soft light brown eyes and olive skin. They'd shared a kiss a few times and he'd asked her out on a date just last month but she'd turned him down. Although she did like him, she didn't think it would be fair to get his hopes up when her heart lay elsewhere. She was starting to wonder if she'd made an error inviting him out with them because he might read more into it than there was. His good friend Graham was tall and lanky with a button nose and sticky out ears but the overall effect was cute and he was good fun with a great sense of humour. Graham was always an asset to any night out.

They approached the bar behind which stood a tall figure dressed as a plague doctor with a long raven beak mask, a black hat and black cloak.

'What can I get you?' said a voice from within the mask.

'Hey, look at these cocktails,' said Liam, picking up the menu off the bar. 'Ectoplasm Ecstasy, Graveyard Gin Sling, The Blood Countess's Brew...'

Carly inwardly smiled as she was reminded of Mark Fowler and his dog.

Deciding to indulge in the spirit of the place, they ordered a cocktail each.

'Can you see in that mask?' Jane asked the barman when he reached for a glass to prepare their order and knocked it over.

'No' very well,' he muttered.

At that moment, from a back room emerged a woman dressed as Elvira. She wore a tight black dress that had a slit up one side to the top of her thigh, a long black wig and her bust pushed up to her chin.

'Hey, Gail,' called the plague doctor. 'Will you mix these cocktails for me? It'll be carnage if I try.'

'Nae bother,' she replied. 'We don't want smashed glass all over the floor again.'

'I'll go on my break; I need to take this mask off for a few minutes.'

The plague doctor vanished through a door behind the bar and Elvira smiled at them, painted red lips curling wickedly.

'I'm so glad he got lumbered with that costume and not me,' she told them. 'The poor sod sweats to death every shift.'

'I'll bet,' replied Jane. 'This is a great place, by the way.'

'Thanks, we're really proud of it.'

'Do you own it?'

'I wish. No, I'm the manager. The owner rarely comes in.'

'I bet it's always busy?'

'Most nights, although Tuesday does tend to be quiet. I'm no' sure why.'

'I heard someone famous owns it?'

'Aye, well, quite famous. They were in some reality TV show. I admit, I'm not into those.'

'Do you get a lot of celebrities?'

'We get a couple of footballers and some of the cast of *River City* are regulars.'

'Great,' said Carly, although she had hoped she'd mention the Tallans. They were well known in the local underworld but they certainly weren't the Kray brothers.

Elvira prepared their drinks quickly and Jane led them all to a table at the back of the room from where they could keep an eye on what was going on.

'Great drink,' said Liam who had ordered The Blood Countess's Brew. The thick ruby liquid did indeed resemble blood. 'How's your Graveyard Gin Sling?' he asked Carly.

'It's nice,' she replied before taking another sip of the green drink.

'I'm pretty sure my Ectoplasm Ecstasy is just a tequila sunrise,' said a disappointed Graham.

'What did you expect, real ectoplasm?' Liam grinned.

Jane had ordered the same drink as Carly, but the non-alcoholic version, wanting to keep a clear head.

Liam began to chat to Carly and she eagerly replied, while keeping an eye on what was going on. This left Jane to chat with Graham and, although she thought he was nice, she didn't find him attractive and she had to push his hand off her knee at one point. She quickly became concerned about Carly. Not only had she gone pale but her eyes were full of sadness and it looked like she could start crying at any moment.

'Carly, are you okay?' Jane asked her.

Her sister's lower lip trembled. As she shook her head a tear spilled down her cheek.

'What did you say to her?' Jane demanded of Liam.

'Nothing,' he exclaimed. 'I was just talking about a film I went to see at the cinema and she looked really upset.'

'It wasnae that really boring spy film we went to see, was it?' said Graham. 'There was no action or guns or anything exciting, just boring people in brown suits going around being smug. I nearly cried myself just watching it.'

'It's not the film,' Liam told him irritably before looking back at Carly.

'You don't really like me,' she told him.

'What?'

'You're just here out of sympathy. You think I'm ugly,' she sobbed.

'No, I don't,' said Liam, looking stricken. He placed a hand on her arm but she shrugged him off.

'Don't touch me,' she rasped. 'I'll make you ugly too.'

'Has she lost her bloody mind?' said Graham. He caught the fury in Jane's eyes and swallowed hard. 'Nae offence.'

'Hang on,' said Jane. 'Is that the cocktail with gin in it?'

'Aye,' said Liam. 'Why?'

'Well that explains it. A pal of mine reacts like this to gin. It can make some people depressed and Carly's never had it before.'

Relief filled Liam's eyes. 'Then I didn't make her cry?'

'No, you didn't. It's the alcohol.'

'Thank Christ for that.' He looked back at Carly, who was now sobbing into her hands. 'Err, what do we do?'

'Get her some water.'

'I'll go,' said Graham, eager to leave the table.

Jane swapped seats with Liam and began to quietly talk to her sister, telling her it was just the drink making her feel this way but Carly insisted it was because she was so hideously ugly. Their assurances that she was in fact the opposite did nothing to make Carly feel better and she cried harder. Neither did the glass of water Graham got her have any effect.

Elvira came bustling up to them, the way her bosom wobbled momentarily hypnotising the two men.

'Can I help?' she said, heavily made-up eyes full of concern.

'She's never had gin before,' said Jane.

'Oh, I see. It's no' the first time we've had this happen. It just takes some people the wrong way.'

'She finished it quite quickly. At least she enjoyed the taste,' said Jane with a weak smile.

'That's something at least,' said Elvira kindly.

'I guess that means we're heading home then.'

'Already?' said a crestfallen Liam.

'What do you suggest? We can't stay with her in this state.'

'Stop talking about me like I'm no' here,' said Carly, briefly lifting her face from her hands. Her make-up had run and streaked her cheeks with black mascara and grey eyeshadow.

'I think it's time we went home, sweetheart,' Jane told her gently.

'Good. I want to be with my da'. I don't want him to go into a care home,' she rasped.

'Oh no,' said Liam. 'I'm so sorry, Carly.'

'Would you like me to call you a taxi?' asked Elvira.

'Yes please,' said Jane. 'And thanks, you've been really good. We will come back because this place is great but we'll make sure she stays away from the gin.'

'You're very welcome.' She smiled before returning to the bar to use the phone, barely able to move her legs because her dress was so tight.

Elvira returned a couple of minutes later to tell them the taxi would only be five minutes and she even gave them flyers for a two-for-one offer on drinks. By this time Carly was starting to calm down and was feeling rather ridiculous, although her spirits were still low.

As they took her outside to get some fresh air, Carly noticed the plague doctor was back behind the bar. He briefly raised the mask to take in some air and wipe his face on a serviette before replacing it. Carly's eyes widened. It was the hairy man from the Tallans' gym. His eyes locked with hers and he hastily replaced the mask. Then she was led out the door and into the fresh air.

* * *

'I feel like such an idiot,' Carly told her sister as they got out of the taxi outside their flat. It was just the two of them. Liam and Graham had decided to go on to a club after seeing them both safely into the taxi.

'There's no need. Like Elvira said, they've seen it happen before.'

'I was sat there blubbing like a baby and in front of Liam too. He'll think I'm such an arsehole.'

'He didn't, he was really concerned. Don't worry about what other people think, it doesn't matter. All that matters is what you think.'

'I think I'm an arsehole,' she muttered.

'Do you still feel depressed?'

'No, but I've got a headache. And just thinking about that green drink makes me want to throw up.'

'I think you have a gin allergy. Just avoid it in future and it'll be fine.'

'Something useful did come out of tonight though.'

'Oh aye?'

'The plague doctor behind the bar. I saw him take off his mask. He was the hairy guy me and Dean saw talking with David at the Tallans' gym.'

Jane paused fumbling in her jacket pocket for her key. 'Really?'

'Aye.'

'I think we need to find out who he is and fast. Me and Dean have another collection tomorrow. Hopefully he'll be at the gym.'

23

Carly filled in Dean the next morning about what had happened at Death Loves Company as he drove them to the gym to meet David, leaving out her histrionics.

'A plague doctor?' he said. 'This bar sounds awesome.'

'It is but that's not the point. Liam said—'

'Liam?' He frowned. 'Is that the name of the plague doctor guy?'

'No. Liam's an old friend. He and his best pal Graham came with me and Jane to the bar.'

'So it was a double date?' he muttered, changing gear aggressively.

'Yeah, but only so we could check out the bar.'

'Why did you need to take men with you? Why couldn't just you and Jane go?'

'Because we thought we'd stand out more on our own. Does it really matter?'

'I suppose not. Are you seeing this Liam again?' he added, unable to help himself.

'Not like that. I've known him since primary school, so we're friends. Why are you giving me the third degree? Surely the important thing is that we have a lead to follow.'

Dean smiled reluctantly. 'You sound like a polis again.'

'What do you think we should do if the plague doctor is at the gym?'

He paused to consider before replying. 'We could try and get who he is out of David?'

'He won't tell us anything. He'll just look at us with his nippy sweetie face. I think we need to ask someone else. That dumb receptionist with the blonde curls fancies you. If you ask her, she'll tell you who he is.'

'She does?'

'Aye. Why are men always so clueless? Every time you speak to her, she does that annoying giggle that makes her sound like she's three years old and starts twirling her hair around her finger.' Carly decided to stop talking. She sounded like she was jealous.

'Well, I'll do my best,' was his reply.

On arrival at the gym, sure enough the annoying receptionist was there but there was no sign of the hairy man.

'Hi Dean.' She smiled, giving him a little wave.

'All right Naomi, doll?' he called back.

'All the better for seeing you, handsome,' she giggled.

'Oh please,' sighed Carly, rolling her eyes. She still had a slight headache after the previous evening and she was not in the mood for shite like this.

They entered the office to find David wasn't there.

'Well, that's never happened before,' commented Carly. 'David's so anally precise I didn't think he would ever be late for anything.' Her eyes skipped around the room, wondering if now was the right time to have a rummage and see what she could find.

'Don't,' Dean told her. 'I know what you're thinking and it won't help. You'll only get us into trouble.'

'You're probably right,' she replied, deciding he was speaking sense, although her eyes did dart about the room, attempting to spot something out of place, but there was just a desk on which was only a pot of pens. The only other piece of furniture was a filing cabinet in the corner.

'No, Carly,' said Dean firmly when her eyes settled on the filing cabinet.

'Fine,' she sighed, folding her arms across her chest.

The door opened and in walked David. He stopped and regarded them suspiciously. 'I hope you haven't touched anything?' he demanded, looking from one to the other.

'Dean's touched a nerve, if that counts?' said Carly.

She was surprised when David laughed. 'Everyone gets on your nerves, sweetheart,' he told her, closing the door behind him and taking a seat behind the desk. 'Despite your success with Melanie, I'm putting you on a normal debt collecting job today. Jane and Harry will handle the blackmail stuff. We're gonnae alternate you, so you'll divide the operation between yourselves. Neil and Rod think it's the way to go.'

'Sounds a good idea,' said Dean.

'They'll be delighted to hear they have your approval,' replied David acerbically. 'You've got an easy collection today. I thought it would only be fair after Mad Melanie went at you with a knife and a gun. It's some old git called Lester. He owes twenty-five grand. Because he's so old we cut him a special deal, so you're only picking up two grand from him.'

'Like a special OAP rate?' said Carly.

David's eyes narrowed. 'Don't get smart with me, lassie.'

After he'd told them the address, he dismissed them.

Dean and Carly left the office and meandered back towards the main doors. They were taking their time in case the hairy man was about but there was no sign of him and they left disappointed.

'This collection should be a nice change of pace,' said Carly as Dean drove them to their job.

'It's only a two grand collection though, meaning we'll get paid less. The higher the debt, the more cash we get.'

'Crap, I didn't think of that. I could do with more cash. Paying the Tallans that ten grand wiped me out. I like to have some savings behind me. I can't stand the thought of going back to being skint.'

Lester's house wasn't big and grand like Melanie's or Alan Harper's. It wasn't even in the same league as Spider's. It was a grotty basement flat underneath a dilapidated three-storey red sandstone house on a street where the majority of the houses had already been boarded up.

Dean and Carly stood at the top of the steps leading down to the front door of the basement flat, which was hidden in the gloom, even though it was a sunny day.

'I really don't want to go down there,' said Carly.

'Me neither but we've no choice.'

Neither of them moved, continuing to stare down at it uncertainly.

'It's creepy,' said Carly.

'I know but David won't be impressed if we go back and tell him we couldnae collect because we got creeped out.'

'We'd definitely end up in intensive care then.'

'Aye, so we'd better get moving. I'll go first.'

Usually Carly would object but she decided to make an exception in this case.

Dean went down the uneven steps first and she followed. The front door had been painted white and was peeling. There were a couple of planters containing nothing but dead brown plants, which had most likely given up because they'd been starved of light down in this grim place.

Dean knocked on the door and more paint flaked off with the

vibration. They both took a step back as they waited for the knock to be answered, unsure what was going to greet them.

The door was pulled open with a loud creak. A small, wizened old man blinked up at them, rheumy eyes enormous behind thick jam jar glasses.

'Wit ya wantin'?' he demanded.

'Are you Lester?' said Dean.

'Aye,' he slowly replied.

'We've been sent by the Tallans to collect,' replied Dean.

Lester nodded. 'Oh, right. Come away in then.'

Carly and Dean followed Lester inside, Carly closing the door behind them. She looked to see how it locked and if there was a key in the door. There was no key, just a Yale lock that you turned to open.

They'd both expected the flat to be dismal and grotty but, even though the light struggled to get in because of the low windows, it was clean, tidy and the scent of lemon furniture polish hung in the air. The furniture was old, some of it possibly antique, but it had been looked after.

'Do you want a cup of tea and a biscuit?' said Lester, blinking up at them in the middle of the living room.

'No, thank you,' Dean politely replied. 'We'll just take the money and get out of your way.'

'Fine, if that's what you want. I'll just get it.'

They watched Lester shuffle into the kitchen and he closed the door behind him.

'What if he's making a getaway?' Carly smiled at Dean.

'Then we'll easily catch him up.' He smiled back. 'Look at that Queen Anne style chair,' said Dean, pointing to a leather armchair in the corner.

'Which queen? Anne Boleyn?' Her lips pursed at Dean's patronising smile.

'No, not Anne Boleyn. Queen Anne of England who reigned from 1702 to 1714.'

'Never heard of her,' she retorted. 'How the hell do you know about Queen Anne's furniture anyway?'

'Not Queen Anne's; it didn't all belong to her. It's just Queen Anne. It's named after a certain style.'

Carly's eyes narrowed. Clearly Dean enjoyed dispensing his wisdom as much as his father did. 'Whatever.'

'I used to work for an antique dealer.'

'Doing what? Patronising the customers?'

'Funny. No, I just did some odd jobs about the place and ran errands but I learnt a lot. What?' he added when she frowned.

'I've not heard anything from the kitchen for a while.'

They turned to look at the door Lester had gone through.

'Let's check it out,' said Dean.

Carly nodded and they both crept up to the door, pausing to listen outside it before pushing it open. The room was small, nothing more than a galley kitchen. Like the living room, it was neat and clean but outdated. To their right was a door that led outside.

More importantly, the room was also empty.

'He must have done a runner out the back door,' said Carly.

'If he has then he can't have gone far,' said Dean, tugging at the back door, which opened to his touch to reveal Cole, Ross and Dominic Alexander.

'Christ,' exclaimed Dean, slamming the door shut.

They turned and ran back into the living room and down the hall towards the front door, which burst open and in stormed Jack Alexander along with two of his family's cronies, both large, handy men.

Carly and Dean were forced to retreat back into the living room but Cole and his brothers had entered through the back door.

They were trapped.

* * *

'What the fuck is going on?' demanded Carly.

The six men surrounded them, ensuring they couldn't escape.

'Lester went for a walk,' said Cole, standing before her.

'How did you know we were here?'

'That's something you don't need to know,' he replied.

'Err, actually, it's something we really do need to know and you're gonnae tell us.'

'He's telling you nothing,' Ross spat at her. 'Finally, you're gonnae get your comeuppance you mouthy bitch.'

Ross's eyes bulged out of his head when she waved an impatient hand in his direction, indicating for him to shut up.

'So what happens now, Cole?' she said. 'Are you going to beat us up, or worse?'

'He's gonnae get a kicking,' he replied, nodding at Dean. 'But you're coming with us.'

'You're not taking her,' snarled Dean, gently pushing Carly aside and thrusting his face into Cole's.

Cole's smile was mocking. 'You really have no choice. You're lucky you're only gonnae get a kicking. Ross and Dominic wanted to do much worse to you after you tortured our da' but we decided you're no' important enough to waste our time on when we have so much to do.'

'And what's that?' demanded Carly.

'There's a lot going on that you really have no idea about, despite Eddie asking around all his contacts. We've been too good at keeping it quiet but it's all coming out now. You're coming with us to ensure the rest of your family behaves, especially Jane.'

'The Bitches will tear the lot of you apart.'

Cole's smile at this made her insides squirm. Had he somehow got to the Bitches as well?

'If you insist,' was all he said. 'Now hands up. I need to take those weapons you're known to carry.'

Carly shrugged and raised her hands while he began checking her jacket pockets. She turned to glance at Dean, who was standing slightly behind her and gave him a knowing look. His response was a nod.

'Get the fuck off her,' he said, stepping forward and shoving Cole in the chest with one hand, sending him staggering back a few paces, causing him to trip over the coffee table.

While they were all distracted, Dean's other hand slid into the back of Carly's jeans where she'd hidden the taser.

'Ya fucking dick,' yelled Ross, lunging for him.

Dean produced the taser, aimed and fired. The barbs struck Ross in the chest, the shock they gave him knocking him off his feet.

While Carly smashed her baton into the face of the man standing to Jack's left, Dean grabbed Dominic and hurled him into Jack and the man standing on his other side and the three of them went crashing to the floor.

'Run,' cried Carly when she saw a furious Cole reaching into his inner jacket pocket.

The two of them raced into the kitchen and out the back door into a tiny back yard. Carly yelped when there was a bang followed by the smashing of glass. Glancing over her shoulder, she saw Cole standing at the living room window clutching a pistol.

'Keep moving,' cried Dean, grabbing her hand and dragging her through the back gate, which stood ajar.

Still holding hands, they raced down the back street.

'We can't go back to the car,' Dean told Carly when she tried to turn in that direction at the end of the street. 'They will have sabotaged it.'

Instead, they went the opposite way and ran until their lungs burned and they had no idea where they were.

'I think we've lost them,' gasped Dean, doubling over to catch his breath.

'Me... too,' panted Carly, who was covered in a fine sheen of sweat. She felt a little lightheaded too. Perhaps she should go to the gym more often? Once her heart rate had slowed a little and she didn't feel like she was going to faint, she said, 'Cole had his gun. He shot at us.'

'He wasn't aiming at us though,' replied Dean. 'It was a warning shot. Either that or he's really shite with it.'

'What the fuck is he playing at? The sound of the shot could have made someone call the polis.'

'No' in this neighbourhood,' replied Dean.

'No more fucking about. We're going straight back to David and demanding to know what the hell is going on.'

24

Carly called an Uber and Dean called his father to warn him in case the Alexanders returned to Haghill to take their frustrations out on the rest of the family. The taxi dropped them off outside the gym and they stormed inside.

They burst into David's office to find him sitting at his desk reading the newspaper.

'Come in, why don't you?' he said sarcastically, folding up the newspaper and placing it on the desk.

'Oh, we do apologise,' said Carly caustically. 'Did we forget our manners? That's easily done after you've been shot at.'

David frowned. 'Shot? Don't tell me Lester had a gun?'

'No' that wee fanny. I'm talking about the fucking Alexanders and a couple of their pals.'

'Wait, what? Calm yer jets and tell me the story from the beginning.'

Carly waved an impatient hand at Dean, indicating she wanted him to tell it because she was still gripped by anger.

Dean managed to relay the saga in a calm tone but his eyes flashed with rage.

'I see,' said David thoughtfully when he'd finished explaining.

Carly opened her mouth to yell at him but one look from Dean was enough to make her think again. Her anger hadn't helped them in the past.

David opened a drawer in the desk, produced a small black box and got to his feet.

'What's that?' said Carly.

'It's a device to check for bugs and I don't mean the type with six legs. They must have planted a tracking device on you.'

'No they didn't. Hey,' she added when he ran it up and down her front.

'Just let him get on with it, Carly,' said Dean.

'Fine,' she sighed, holding out her arms.

After checking her over and finding nothing, David checked Dean. Still nothing.

'It must have been planted on your car,' said David with a puzzled frown.

'They didn't find us that way,' replied Dean. 'They were already at Lester's waiting for us. He was in on it. Someone told them in advance where we would be.'

'That's impossible. Only the three of us knew.' His face creased with anger when they stared straight at him. 'I'm no' a fucking grass,' he bellowed.

'We're not saying that but when did you last check this room?'

'Well, it must have been...' He trailed off, lips pinching into a line.

'Well?' said Carly.

'I'm thinking,' he snarled at her.

Without another word, he began going around the room with the device. The camera he'd installed so the Tallans could watch his meeting with Carly and Dean had already been removed.

'Nothing,' he told them smugly after five minutes of searching.

'You didn't check the light fitting,' retorted Dean.

With a tut of annoyance, David climbed onto the desk and held up the device, which started to beep immediately. Reaching up, he unscrewed the cover of one of the lights to reveal a tiny camera.

'Oh shit,' he said, frowning at the device in his hand.

'That explains why only mine and Carly's collections were affected,' said Dean. 'You gave Jane and Harry their orders at the pub.'

'Who the fuck did this?' yelled David.

'You need to grab Reggy right now,' said Carly.

'Reggy, the manager?' David frowned at her.

'Aye.'

'Why him?'

'I'll tell you after. You need to get him before he discovers you found the camera.'

'Fine,' he said, jumping down off the desk. 'You two, with me.'

David yanked open the office door and stormed out, face like thunder. Carly and Dean followed him down the hall and into the café. Reggy wasn't there so they continued down the corridor and into the gym itself. As always, every machine was in use with people there to either seriously work out or pose. It was easy to spot the difference.

David stormed through the gym, through a door on the other side and down a quieter, narrower corridor Carly and Dean had never been down before. He shoved open the fire exit at the bottom and they found themselves at the rear of the building where there was a small car park.

'There he is, the twat,' growled David when he saw Reggy hurrying over to a dark blue BMW.

Reggy glanced over his shoulder and his eyes widened with fear. He broke into a run, yanking the car keys from his pocket as he went.

'Sic him,' said David.

Dean and Carly tore after Reggy, who aimed the key fob at the car and unlocked it. He'd just grabbed the handle of the driver's door when Dean tackled him. Reggy attempted to fight but Dean ducked, grabbed his arm and twisted it up his back before slamming him face down on the bonnet of his own car. When Reggy struggled, Carly punched him in the kidneys, making him cry out with pain and go limp.

David sauntered up to them, expression furious as he regarded Reggy. 'I found your camera. What the fuck did you do that for?'

'Things are changing,' replied Reggy breathlessly. 'The Tallans won't be where they are for much longer. I was taking care of myself.'

'That's bollocks; they're stronger than ever.'

'The smart people are getting in with the new order.'

'The Alexanders?'

Reggy snorted. 'They're just the attack dogs.'

'Who then?'

'I'm telling you nothing else. Argh,' he cried when Dean twisted his arm up his back.

'All right, go easy on him,' said David. 'We're not savages. No pun intended,' he told Carly and Dean. 'We'll discuss this like civilised people. Take him to the office.'

'Come on, you,' said Dean, dragging Reggy upright.

Dean couldn't frogmarch Reggy to the office through the gym without attracting a lot of attention, so he was forced to release him. Instead, he walked right behind him while David walked on ahead and Carly by his side.

'If you try to do a runner,' she told Reggy, producing the taser from her pocket and holding it down by her side so no one would see it. 'I'll shock you right in the baws.'

He sighed resignedly and nodded.

David opened the office door and Dean shoved Reggy through it; he stumbled and ended up sprawled across the desk. Dean then grabbed him by the back of the shirt and yanked him upright. Reggy attempted to push Dean away but as he lacked Dean's bulk, his efforts were in vain. Dean smiled maliciously and pushed him in the chest with one hand. Reggy fell back against the filing cabinet with a pained cry.

'All right, that's enough,' said David, taking the seat behind the desk. He gestured to the chair opposite him. 'Sit down, Reggy.'

Reggy nodded and took a seat. He was sweating and his hair was in disarray. He ran a hand through it, slicking it back off his head, attempting to recover his composure.

'Who are you working for?' opened David.

'I can't tell you,' replied Reggy. 'Sorry, pal, I like you and all that but I've made a sweet deal and I refuse to let anything fuck it up for me.'

'You do realise who you're speaking to, don't you?'

'Aye I dae but sorry, I have to put myself first.'

'Make him talk,' said David.

Dean nodded and drew back his fist. Reggy cringed and held out his hands to ward him off.

'Wait,' said David. 'Let the lassie have a go.'

Dean lowered his fist and stepped aside so Carly could approach Reggy. David watched with interest, curious to see what she would do.

Deciding to take a leaf out of Rose's book, Carly grabbed Reggy's crotch and twisted. His eyes bulged out of his head. When he started to scream, Dean clamped a hand down over his mouth to stifle the sound.

Carly relinquished him and David said, 'You ready to talk now?'

Dean moved his hand from their prisoner's mouth.

Reggy sagged back in his seat, panting, skin ashen.

'Well?' said David. 'We're waiting.'

Reggy gritted his jaw and shook his head.

'Carly.'

Reggy regarded her with wide, uncertain eyes as she looked down at the desk. When she spotted the large stapler sitting there, she smiled wickedly.

'Pull his pants down, Dean,' she said, picking up the stapler. 'I'm going to pierce his bell end.' She grinned and clacked the stapler in Reggy's face.

'It's Rod,' he exclaimed. 'He's gonnae kill his brother and take over everything. He's also gonnae kill you,' he told David.

The three of them stared at him in surprise.

An enraged David leapt to his feet. 'That's shite. Who told you? Was this Rod himself?'

'Naw, he's keeping himself apart from it all. Eric Martin told me.'

'Eric Martin...' Carly frowned. 'Mark Fowler's friend?'

'Hang on,' said David. 'Mark Fowler, the man you collected the money from?'

'Aye, the same. He thought he didn't have to cough up because he said the Tallans were on their way out. He said his friend Eric Martin told him. We went to speak to Eric who told us Reggy gave him the information.'

David's face turned purple. 'And why the fuck are you only just telling me about it?'

'Because we thought it was all exaggerated bollocks – no way could any of those fools beat the Tallans – and because we were already in your bad books after failing to collect from Mark. We were doing our own digging, seeing if we could come up with anything concrete before approaching you with it.'

'That's why you both wanted to join the gym?'

Carly and Dean nodded.

'I am really pissed off at you both for not coming to me sooner with this but we'll discuss that later. Right now, we need to get to Neil.'

'You're too late,' said Reggy with what could only be described as glee. 'Rod was gonnae make his move at eleven and it's already five to. You cannae get to him in time.'

They all glanced at the clock on the wall with dismay.

'We've only your word for that,' said David. 'I'll call him.' He took out his phone and dialled, foot tapping impatiently. 'He's not answering,' he said before hanging up.

'Because he's probably already deid,' said Reggy.

'The bollocks he is. We're gonnae stop it and you're coming with us.'

'You can't interfere,' said Reggy, eyes lighting up with panic. 'Rod will know I grassed.'

'Tough titty,' David replied as Dean hauled Reggy to his feet by the back of his T-shirt.

Reggy found it difficult to walk properly thanks to his aching genitals and Dean had to help him along, practically dragging him. They got a couple of funny looks from staff members who passed them by but David ensured they took the route that avoided the public areas.

'Reggy, are you okay?' asked one of the personal trainers, a pretty brunette with large dark eyes.

'No, I'm not,' he called before he was dragged out the door leading into the staff car park.

David produced the key for his black Audi and unlocked it.

'Sit in the back with him and watch him,' David told Carly and Dean.

Carly got into the back first, Dean shoving Reggy in before climbing in and pulling the door closed. David got into the driver's seat, gunned the engine and sped out of the car park.

He called Neil through the car's Bluetooth but it just rang out.

'Shit,' he said. 'That's not good. Neil always answers his phone. I'll keep trying.'

'Do you know where he is?' said Carly.

'He's going for brunch at a favourite bistro of his.'

'Surely nothing can happen to him in a public place?' said Dean.

'I wouldn't be so sure. Rod loves *The Godfather* films, he sees himself as Michael Corleone, and we all know what he did in the first film.'

Carly looked to Dean. 'I've not seen it. What did he do?'

'He shot two people dead in a restaurant,' he replied. 'But this isn't 1940s New York. Surely Rod wouldn't be so rash?'

'Neil's kept him down for years,' continued David, 'forced him to do things his way. If Rod's rebelling, he'll do everything he's been dreaming about for years, the stupid stuff Neil always ensured he never went through with.'

'But they're brothers,' said Carly.

'I always thought that meant more to Neil than it did Rod.'

'God, this is insane.'

'Tell me about it,' said David, calling Neil again but still there was no answer.

'Shall I call the rest of the family and let them know what's happening?'

'Not yet. Let's check our facts first. Reggy could be lying to us.'

'You'd love that, wouldn't you?' sneered Reggy. 'Then your narrow little world will still keep turning but it's about to explode apart. You're dead, all of you...'

He shrieked when Carly twisted his crotch again.

'Who else has Rod got on his side?' she hissed.

Reggy rhymed off a list of names that meant nothing to her but that Dean and David clearly recognised.

'Are these bad people?' said Carly.

'Very bad,' said Dean grimly. 'Think of the worst of Barlinnie all gathered together.'

'Hold on – some of those men who sided with the Alexanders the last time we fought them were from Barlinnie. Did Rod set those men to working with them? Was all this in play six months ago?'

She looked to Reggy for confirmation, who frantically nodded when her grip on his crotch tightened.

'The bastard,' she murmured before releasing him. 'I always knew there was something odd about him; he didn't seem right in the head.'

David tried calling Neil again but still there was no reply. In response, he pressed down harder on the accelerator.

They drove into the west end and turned onto a vibrant, trendy street with lots of pavement cafés and bars.

'Oh Christ, that doesn't look good,' said David when they saw the ambulance and police cars further down the street, which had been cordoned off.

The traffic was getting detoured by the police down a side street.

Dean took out his phone and tapped at the screen. 'There was a shooting fifteen minutes ago,' he said. 'The victim hasn't been identified but they're dead.'

'Jesus. Rod, the mad bastard, did it,' exclaimed Reggy with glee. 'He pulled it off.'

'Shut that fucking dick up,' said David. 'The back windows are blacked out, so feel free to go to town on him.'

Dean drove his fist into Reggy's stomach, which silenced his cheers as David steered the car down the side street and away from the scene.

'What do we do now?' said Carly.

'We need to get back to Haghill,' said Dean. 'If Rod is taking out the competition, then he might go for our family.'

'There are bigger fish he'll want to fry,' said David. 'Business partners of Neil's.'

'Maybe but I'm no' taking the chance.'

'We need to get home,' said Carly, her heart lurching. 'The Alexanders might choose now to attack our family.'

'Fine,' said David. 'I'll drop you off then I'll rally the troops.'

'Is that a good idea? I mean, for all you know they've gone over to Rod's side. They might kill you too.'

David didn't reply but Carly noticed he gripped the steering wheel tighter, knuckles turning white.

'She's right,' said Dean. 'If anyone's gonnae be next on Rod's hit list, it's you.'

'We need to talk to Eric Martin,' said Carly. 'And we know where to find him but first we have to warn the family.'

'I'll call Da',' said Dean, already dialling.

25

'Holy crap, Dean was right,' said Harry as he scrolled through the latest local news on his phone. 'A shooting at some fancy bistro in the west end.'

'It doesnae mean it's Neil Tallan,' said Eddie. Sweat had broken out on his back during the call with Dean and inwardly he was panicking. What the hell had he got his family into? If Neil was dead, Rod would come for them all and he wasn't sure they had a hope in hell of standing up to him.

'That's true,' said Jane. 'Fingers crossed Dean's information is wrong. Carly kept telling us something more was going on but we didn't take it seriously enough.'

'Aye and I'll never forgive myself for it.'

They all looked at each other when the doorbell rang.

There was a beat of silence before Eddie said, 'You two wait here, I'll go.'

'No chance,' said Harry. 'We'll come with you.'

Jane nodded, so glad Rose was safely at school. However, her dad was in bed and she was terrified of how vulnerable he would be if they were attacked.

The three of them approached the door, prepared to fight, Eddie snatching up the baseball bat on his way. He nodded at Harry to unlock the front door. Harry obeyed and pulled it open. Eddie leapt forward, drawing back the bat, ready to swing.

'Eat this, you bastards,' he roared.

Neil and Rod Tallan stood on the doorstep in their smart suits, frowning at him.

'What on earth are you doing?' said Neil while Rod chuckled.

'You're no' deid,' replied Eddie, gaping at him while lowering the bat.

'What? Of course I'm not. What the hell are you talking about?'

Eddie peered out of the flat, looking up and down the street while the brothers glanced at each other in confusion.

'Have you lost the plot or are you drunk?' Neil demanded of him.

'Neither. Come away in and I'll explain.'

'I should think so too.'

Jane regarded the Tallans warily as they entered. She didn't want them here in her home so close to her father but she had little choice.

They all filed through to the kitchen, the brothers taking a seat at the table, their air of authority such that they made it feel like an official boardroom.

'Just what the hell is going on, Eddie?' said Neil. 'Why did you feel the need to answer the door wielding a baseball bat, or is that just par for the course around here?'

'Carly and Dean called to tell us that you'd been shot dead and that Rod was responsible.'

'What?' the brothers exclaimed in unison.

'You should know,' said Jane. 'My da's asleep down the hall, so if you don't want to be overheard you need to keep your voices down.'

'They got the story out of Reggy, who manages your gym,' Eddie explained.

'I kept telling you that sod was a wee snake,' Rod said to his brother. 'Far too greasy and he's always kissing your arse.'

'Aye, all right. Go on, Eddie.'

'He said Rod was making a power grab and wanted you out of the way,' he continued with an apologetic look Rod's way. 'He said he'd had you shot at your favourite bistro where you always go for brunch. David drove Carly, Reggy and Dean there and they saw the area had been cordoned off and there were armed polis.'

'There was a shooting but as you can see I wasnae the victim.' A dangerous look filled Neil's eye. 'David is the real brains behind all this. He's recruited people, including the Alexanders, to take down no' only me and Rod but your family too.'

'David?' said Harry. 'But he's always seemed so loyal to you.'

'He's in a car right now with Carly and Dean,' said Jane, eyes heavy with worry.

'You need to warn them,' replied Neil. 'The story David gave them was shite to lure them somewhere. He's gonnae use them against us.'

'Shit,' gasped Jane, taking out her phone.

At that moment, Eddie's phone rang. He scrambled to pull it from his pocket. He looked at the screen and his eyes widened. 'It's Dean.'

'Let's hope it's really him and no' someone who's got hold of his phone,' said Neil dourly.

'Dean, son,' said Eddie the moment he answered. He breathed a sigh of relief. 'Aye, aye, stop talking and listen. Neil's no' dead. Aye, I'm sure, he's sitting right in front of me with his brother. This is David's doing, he's tricked you. He's making a power grab. Where are you? Actually, don't answer that. I'll track you on the app.' Eddie had insisted they all install apps on their phones so the rest of the family could find them in a hurry if necessary. 'We're on our way. You need to warn Carly too.'

'I'll message her,' said Jane. She didn't want to call her sister in case it made David suspicious and forced him to do something drastic. Her fingers flew across the screen, her heart beating hard as she typed out a warning to her sister and pressed send.

'Where are the Bitches?' Neil asked Jane.

'Close,' she replied. 'I told them to stay in the area when we thought you'd been shot.'

'Don't trust them. It's possible they've been got at. They may not all be for you any more.'

'They wouldn't follow Emma Wilkinson, not after I twatted her and kicked out her closest supporters.'

'No' Emma. Jess Alexander.'

'But she's too old to lead a girl gang,' said Harry.

Neil and Rod's arched eyebrows said they thought that was a ridiculous statement.

'We know she's been in negotiations with some of the girls,' Neil told Jane. 'You cannae trust any of them. Send them home.'

'Okay,' said Jane slowly. 'I'll send them all a text message.'

Neil watched her sternly as she typed out her message before pressing send.

'All done,' she said.

'Good girl,' he replied in a patronising tone that made her narrow her eyes.

'Where are you going?' Rod asked Eddie when he shot to his feet.

'To help Dean and Carly,' he replied.

'They can handle it,' said Neil. 'You're much better remaining here.'

'But what if they cannae?' he exclaimed.

Neil's look was icy. 'We know more about this situation than you. You also have to consider that you have a sick brother in the next room who cannae even walk on his own. So, if you want to do the right thing for your family, you'll park your fucking arse and wait.'

Eddie looked helplessly at Rod, who shrugged.

'Sit down, Da',' said Harry. 'I think we should listen to him.'

'I'll stay but I won't be able to relax until Dean and Carly are back home safe.'

'Where does Jack Alexander fit into all this?' Jane asked Neil. 'And not just him but Jessica and Cole too. I know you met them for drinks at Death Loves Company.'

The corner of his mouth lifted into a smile. 'Clever girl.'

'I'm a woman, not a girl,' she replied, furious at being patronised twice in a row, her eyes like shards of ice.

'Do excuse me,' he said sarcastically before addressing the table. 'I found out David was meeting with the Alexanders in secret, so I approached them with a deal to see what they would say. When they turned me down, everything I'd suspected was confirmed. Jessica, Cole and Jack Alexander aren't thick, unlike the rest of their family. They've made this move because they know they've been rumbled.'

'Who was really shot?' said Harry. 'Because someone was.'

'That remains to be seen.'

Harry glanced at Jane in confusion, who shrugged, no more enlightened than he was.

* * *

Dean hung up and forced himself not to look at Carly. He was conscious of David watching him through the rear-view mirror.

'What did he say?' David asked him.

'He said he'd get onto his contacts and confirm exactly what happened at the bistro.'

'So he's no' heard anything yet?'

'No, nothing.' Dean wondered if David had a weapon in this car. No doubt he was the one who'd got Cole his gun, so there was a good chance he had one too. 'I really hope this is a case of crossed wires and Neil's fine.' No way was he going to let David know his plan had failed and Neil was still alive. Letting him think everything was going to plan would take away his advantage. He'd done such a good job covering his tracks that not even Reggy had a clue who was really behind it all.

'Let's hope,' replied David.

David gave him one more scrutinising look through the mirror before turning his attention back to the road. Only then did Dean dare to glance at Carly. He saw she had her phone in her hand and was staring at the screen with wide eyes. When she looked at him, Dean shook his head imperceptibly.

'What's up with you?' Reggy frowned at him.

He was knocked out by Dean's elbow in his face and he slumped forward in his seat, only held in place by the seatbelt.

'What happened back there?' said David.

'He was making a move, so I knocked him out,' replied Dean. In case his dad was right and this was some insidious plot, the fewer people they had to fight the better.

'Fair enough. He's a prick anyway.'

'You got that right,' replied Dean, doing his best to sound relaxed.

Panic gripped Dean when he saw David reach across to the glovebox, no doubt to draw a weapon. They had to make their move right now.

He saw they were coming up to a set of traffic lights, which were on red. He glanced at Carly and gave her a look, which he hoped she could interpret. They worked well together, so fingers crossed she would understand.

'Look,' exclaimed Dean, pointing across the car to the passenger side. 'Isn't that Rod Tallan?'

When David looked, Dean reached a hand along David's right side and hit the central locking to unlock the doors. Carly and Dean both shoved the doors open before he could lock them again and threw off their seatbelts.

'Where are you going?' exclaimed David.

The two of them leapt out of the car, Dean into the road and Carly onto the pavement.

'Carly, get down,' yelled Dean, assuming David was pulling a gun from the glove box.

She ducked behind the car, out of the line of fire. At that moment, the traffic lights turned to green and the cars behind David's started to honk their horns when he failed to move.

Left with no choice, he drove on. Dean rushed to join Carly on the pavement before he got run over and they watched David take the first left to come back round.

'We need to get out of here,' Carly told Dean.

He nodded and looked around for inspiration. They were outside a small row of shops – a newsagent's, barber's, florist's and a bookies. He wasn't even sure where they were, all he knew was they'd left the west end.

'I think we're in Laurieston,' said Carly.

'We need to get off the street,' he said, nodding at the newsagent's. Dean looked left and saw David's car coming back up the road. At least he couldn't open fire on them in such a public place. 'Da' said he was coming for us. We can wait in there.'

They hurried into the newsagent's, Carly giving the woman behind the counter a reassuring smile. She was glad to see that it was a busy shop with customers constantly going in and out.

'Do you know that Neil's still alive?' Dean asked her.

'Aye, Jane sent me a text message. I don't like him very much but I think it's better for us that he is alive.'

'True. I'll let Da' know what's happening.'

'Dean, thank Christ,' said Eddie as soon as he answered. 'Are you both okay?'

'Aye. We managed to get out of David's car and we're in a newsagent's in Laurieston. We think it's Laurieston anyway, we're no' entirely sure.'

'Reggy?'

'Unconscious in the back of David's car. I knocked him out.'

'That's my boy,' said Eddie with pride in his voice.

'Where shall we meet you?'

'Err, that's a wee bit awkward. Neil and Rod said we're no' to leave. They think the flat could be hit any minute by the Alexanders and we need to be here to look after Alec.'

'I see. And Rose?'

'At school. I've sent her a message telling her to go to her friend's house when she's finished.'

'Good. Don't worry about us, we'll get home safely.'

'What about David?'

'We can handle him.'

'He has more people following him than we know. He's been planning this for a while. Be careful.'

'Aye, we will. See you later.'

'Well?' said Carly when he'd hung up.

'Neil and Rod are at your flat. Neil told Da' and the others to stay there to protect Alec.'

Carly frowned. 'Why would he care about Da'?'

'I don't know but he wants them there.'

'Neil only cares about someone for what he can get out of them.

He wouldn't give a single shite about Da'.' She regarded him with wide eyes. 'What if we're wrong?'

'David locked us in the car and was going to pull a gun on us.'

'We didn't think anything like that until our family contacted us to tell us what Neil had said and we assumed David was reaching for a weapon on the back of what we'd been told. We never actually saw one.'

'Why would Neil lie?'

'I've no idea but it doesn't feel right.'

The door opened and in walked David, who regarded them with confusion.

'What the fuck are you playing at?' he demanded. 'Why did you jump out of my car in the middle of the road?'

'You've turned against the Tallans,' Dean told him, putting himself protectively before Carly.

'What are you talking about?'

'Neil's no' deid, he's alive and well and he and Rod are at Carly's flat right now. They told our family that you've turned against them.'

'I haven't,' he exclaimed. 'I'd never do that. I've been loyal to them for years.'

'No' according to them you're not. You've been recruiting people against them, including the Alexanders. You're a traitor.'

These words seemed to genuinely hurt David and his brow creased with pain. He jabbed a finger at Dean. 'Not once in my entire life have I ever betrayed them. All I've done is work for them, obeying every order loyally.'

'So they're making it up, are they?' sneered back Dean. He looked down at his left arm when a hand started slapping it.

'Will you move out of my way?' demanded Carly.

Dean side-stepped.

'Thank you,' she huffed before turning to David. 'I knew something felt all off about this. Uncle Eddie wanted to come and pick us up but the Tallans told him to stay at the flat because my da' might need protecting.'

'He's right,' he replied. 'If this is the same da' with Parkinson's disease?'

'It is but I know Neil couldn't give a solitary shite about him. Also, why have they turned up at my home? They've gone out of their way to avoid being seen with us in public and now they just show up at the flat for all to see? It doesn't make sense. So tell us David, what's really going on?'

'I don't know,' he exclaimed. 'For the first time in my life, I haven't a bloody clue when usually I know everything. It all started when my cousin vanished a couple of weeks ago.'

'Your cousin?'

'Aye, he disappeared, just like the others.'

'By others do you mean Twitchy Tina?'

'Yeah. You know about all that?'

'Uncle Eddie told us about it but we'd no idea one of them was your cousin. Are the Tallans behind it?'

'No, course not.' He hesitated before continuing, 'Although I was beginning to wonder.'

'Why?'

David bit his lip and shook his head.

'I know you're loyal but now is not the time to protect them.'

'Okay,' he sighed. 'Because all three who vanished did some work for them recently.'

'That confirms it. The Tallans are behind these disappearances.' She took out her phone and showed him the blurry photo of the mystery man. 'Do you know him?'

David squinted at the photo. 'Aye. I think so anyway. It looks like Dillon Manson. He works for Neil.'

'Not Rod too?'

'No. They don't get on. Dillon's been in the game for years, he does a lot of Neil's dirty work. How do you know him?'

'He was following Jack Alexander. Is it possible Dillon's been making people disappear?'

'Perhaps.' David's face hardened. 'If he did kill my cousin, I'll fucking bury him.'

The woman behind the counter looked up and frowned when she realised they'd been standing in the corner talking furtively for a while.

David caught that look. 'Let's discuss this outside,' he told his companions.

'Oh aye, so your minions can kidnap us or worse?' said Carly.

'What minions? I don't have any minions,' he exclaimed.

'We'll talk on the street,' said Dean. He looked to Carly. 'We'll be safe, I promise.'

She nodded and the three of them exited the shop.

'So that's why you jumped out of my car?' said David. 'You thought I was going to kill you?'

'Possibly,' replied Dean. 'Or use us as hostages to get our family to do what you want.'

'Like what?'

He and Carly glanced at each other before looking back at him. 'We don't know,' replied the latter.

'You were going for a weapon in your glovebox,' Dean told him.

'Actually, I was going for a CD.'

'Who has a CD player in their car any more?' Dean asked David.

'I do. I like CDs, I cannae stand all this streaming shite, I don't understand it. I know you'd love to think I've got a small arsenal in my glovebox but the most interesting thing in there is a packet of mints. The polis know I work for the Tallans and they stop me regularly just for the hell of it. I'd have to be a total cretin to drive around with a gun in my car and that is something I am not.'

'The man makes a good point,' Carly told Dean.

'Come with me to speak to Eric Martin, like we were going to,' said David. 'I really think he has important information we need to know.'

'If we are right about the Tallans then we'd be walking into the lion's den,' said Dean.

'And if you're wrong we'll never get the information we need and God only knows what will happen. Neil and Rod are up to something and they're with your family right now. So, what's it gonnae be?'

'Christ,' sighed Dean. He looked to Carly. 'What do you think?'

'I'm ready to take a chance,' she replied. 'Are you?'

'I suppose we've no choice.'

'And if it is a trap, we'll batter the shite out of the lot of them.'

He smiled at her. God, he loved this woman. 'Aye we will.'

'Great,' said David, producing the car keys from his pocket.

'But I'm driving,' said Dean, snatching the keys from him. 'The way I see it we're doing you a favour, so like it or lump it.'

'Fine, we don't have time for an argument. Let's just get moving.'

'Wait, I'm searching you for weapons first.'

David huffed with frustration but obediently raised his hands so Dean could search him.

'Nothing,' he said when he'd finished.

'Happy now?' David scowled. 'Can we finally get moving?'

Dean nodded and they jogged across the road to David's car. Dean and Carly got into the front and David got in the back with the still unconscious Reggy.

Just to be sure, Carly opened the glovebox and removed the

contents. 'CDs, a pair of gloves and mints,' she told Dean. 'He was telling the truth.'

Dean drove them to the pub where they'd met Eric Martin.

'Let's hope he's here,' said Carly as they all stared out of the windows at the depressing building. 'What about Reggy?'

All three of them looked to Reggy.

'We'll take him with us,' said David. 'Besides, I think he's faking it.'

He jabbed a finger into Reggy's ribs, who woke with a shriek, his nose red and swollen.

'Come on, Sleeping Beauty,' David told him. 'We're going to the pub.'

'Great,' he groaned. 'I need a bevvy.'

'I bet you do. Get out.'

The four of them climbed out of the car and regarded each other mistrustfully. Only Dean and Carly were united.

'I guess we're going in then,' said Dean.

'Looks like it,' replied David.

26

The four of them walked across the road to the pub, Dean keeping a firm grip on Reggy's arm. He didn't think he would try to run off as he was still limping, but Dean didn't want to take the chance.

'After you,' Carly told David, gesturing to the door.

Rolling his eyes, he shoved open the door and walked in. Dean entered next, pushing Reggy in before him. Carly kept her hand on her taser as she followed the men inside. Rather than the expected trap there were just a few people sitting at the tables or propping up the bar. The two haggard women who had been there before were still present. Carly's stomach rolled over at the sight of their gin and tonics.

'There he is,' said Dean.

Sure enough, standing at the bar nursing a pint of lager and chatting to the landlord was Eric Martin. The landlord whispered something to Eric and nodded in their direction.

Eric turned to look and rolled his eyes. 'No' you again. What you wantin' this time?' His eyes widened when he saw David and a bruised and swollen Reggy. 'Shite.'

'Shite indeed,' said David dourly. 'We need to talk.'

Eric reluctantly joined them at a table in the corner.

'What's up with you?' he asked Reggy. 'Why are you limping?'

'She twisted my baws,' he muttered, pointing at Carly.

Eric's eyes lit up. 'Can I get some of that action too?' he asked her. 'How much do you charge?'

'Believe me, you don't want this done to you,' groaned Reggy. 'I still feel sick.'

'So what's this about?' said Eric.

'You know exactly what this is about,' said David.

'Actually, I don't have a clue.' Nervousness filled Eric's eyes. 'Unless it's about... the Tallans?'

'Bang on the money,' said David dourly.

'Great,' Eric mumbled. 'I knew this would come back to bite me on the arse.'

'You said Reggy told you that the Tallans were a spent force and that the Alexanders were taking over,' Dean told Eric.

Reggy's head snapped up. 'That's bollocks, Eric. You were the one who told me.'

'Shut it, you,' Eric growled at him.

'I won't shut up,' snapped Reggy. 'You told me because you knew I ran their gym and you thought I should know.'

'You're gonnae tell us the truth,' said Dean. 'Right now.'

'I cannae,' replied Eric, turning pale. 'Really, or he'll kill me.'

'Who?' demanded David, leaning forward in his seat.

'I... I cannae say. Please don't make me,' he said, eyes wide.

'Carly,' said David, eyes locked on Eric.

She reached under the table, grabbed Eric's crotch and twisted. The entire room looked round when he shrieked with agony. Carly released him and Eric sagged forward in his seat, hands cupping his crotch while trying not to throw up.

Everyone resumed their conversations as though nothing had happened, none of them bothering to come to his aid.

'If you don't tell us,' David said to Eric. 'Then she'll keep twisting until your baws come off.'

'It was Neil,' he wailed.

'Neil Tallan?'

'Aye, him. He ordered me to tell Reggy that Rod wanted to get rid of him when really it was the other way around. Neil thought Reggy would start spreading that rumour around because he's a massive gobshite but for once, he kept his enormous mouth shut,' said Eric with an accusing look at his friend. 'Neil wants everyone to think Rod was trying to kill him to give him an excuse to get rid of his brother. Rod has some dangerous contacts and Neil doesnae want them coming after him for revenge. He wants Rod out, he's sick of splitting everything down the middle. That's what he says anyway. He wants it all to himself; he's turned into a proper greedy bastard. He's trying to clinch a big deal but his new partners don't want Rod, they think he's an arsehole. They told Neil he has to get rid of his brother or the deal's off. Neil's got no choice. It's not personal, just business. He got me and a few others to spread the word that his own family was done. Rod set up the debt collecting side of the business. If people stopped coughing up, it would make Rod look like an idiot. Neil did that to make himself look better in the eyes of his new business partner.'

'Who's this new deal with?'

'Nae idea, he's been keeping that one very quiet but it's someone international with links to a cartel in Amsterdam. Neil's always wanted to break out of Scotland but Rod isn't as fussed, he doesn't have Neil's ambition but he's been willing to go along with it because it's what his brother wants.'

'Could his deal be with Toni McVay?'

'You must be joking. That coo doesnae like to share with anyone.'

David's eyes flashed. 'Neil's the one whose been making people disappear, isn't he?'

'Aye. They were people he brought in on his plan but he changed his mind when he realised they might betray him to Rod. A pal of his owns a factory and he let him dispose of their bodies in his industrial incinerator.'

David leaned forward in his seat. 'Who killed them?'

'Dillon Manson. He followed them around for a bit first, got to know their routines before snatching them and killing them.'

'One of them was a relative of mine,' thundered David.

Eric looked sheepish. 'Sorry, pal,' he muttered.

Carly took out her phone and showed Eric the image of the man who'd followed Jack. 'Is that Dillon?'

'Naw, no way. Dillon's got long hair and he's bulkier than that skinny prick. That guy looks like Wilson Parnell who works for Neil.'

'Why was he following Jack?' Carly frowned at Dean.

'Neil was probably trying to work out if he could trust him,' replied her cousin. 'Jack's still an unknown quantity.'

'So the Alexanders are working for Neil then?'

'Course they are.'

'What will Neil do now?' David asked Eric.

'He doesnae want to get sent down for Rod's death, so he's gonnae force some family called the Savages to kill him and take the fall for his murder too.'

'Do you know the Savage family?' said David while Carly and Dean gaped at him.

'Naw, I never heard of them.'

'Two of them are sitting right in front of you.'

Eric stared at Carly and Dean. 'This pair?'

'Aye.'

'Holy fuck,' breathed Dean. He slammed his fist on the table.

'This information would have been handy the first time we spoke to you.'

'Sorry,' said Eric with a wry smile. 'But Neil's way scarier than you.'

'I'll fucking rip you a new one,' yelled Dean, lunging across the table at him.

'Calm down,' Carly told her cousin firmly. 'We don't have all the information we need yet.'

Dean nodded and retook his seat while glaring at Eric.

'Why put the blame on us?' Carly asked Eric. 'Out of the two brothers, I much prefer Neil. We would have probably backed him if he'd asked.'

'Which goes to show how naïve you are,' David told her. 'Rod's been the one protecting your family, stopping Neil when he wanted to punish you more severely, convincing his brother to give you another chance. If it hadn't been for Rod, you and Dean may well have ended up with broken kneecaps after botching that collection.'

'Oh,' said Carly. 'I'd no idea.'

'Neil has been getting increasingly impatient with his brother for a while now, but I'm still surprised he's gone this far.'

'Who got shot at the bistro Neil goes to?' David asked Eric.

'A good friend of Neil's. He's trying to frame Rod for the shooting to give him an excuse to get rid of him.'

Carly turned to Eric, barely managing to restrain her panic. 'Rod and Neil are at my home right now with my family. Why are they there?'

A knowing dawned in Eric's eyes that none of them liked.

'You two are Carly and Dean, aren't you?' he said.

They both nodded.

'Neil was gonnae arrange to have you two kidnapped by the

Alexanders to force the rest of your family to kill Rod. Judging by the fact that you're both here it failed.'

'What will he do now?'

'I don't know but Neil always has a back-up plan.' He leaned forward in his seat, gaze boring into Carly. 'Always.'

She glanced at an equally stunned Dean before tearing her phone out of her pocket and calling Jane.

* * *

All was quiet and tense in the Savage flat. Jane, Harry and Eddie sat on one side of the kitchen table, Rod and Neil on the other. No one spoke, although Rod had tried to a couple of times but he'd been silenced by a warning look from his brother. For the first time, the Savages clearly saw that this was no equal partnership. Neil was definitely the dominant one.

The sound of Jane's mobile phone ringing was a little shocking and she hurried to answer it before Neil could tell her not to because, judging by the look on his face, he wasn't happy about her receiving a call.

'Who is it?' he demanded.

'Carly,' she replied, pressing the answer button and putting the phone to her ear before he could object. 'Are you okay?'

'Fine,' replied her sister's voice. 'Are you?'

'Aye. It's all quiet here.'

'Thank God. Listen, you can't react to what I'm about to say. Just make out like everything's normal, okay?'

'Understood,' Jane replied calmly.

Jane had to admit to herself that it was a struggle not to react to what her sister told her. It was even more of an effort not to glance Neil's way.

'You have to get out,' said Carly. 'Don't listen to Neil. We're on our way.'

'Okay, no problem,' Jane replied casually. 'See you soon.'

Jane hung up and took a breath before regarding the table, attempting to form what she had to say clearly in her mind. 'Thankfully, they're fine,' she said. 'David chased them for a bit but they managed to escape. They flagged down a passing taxi and are on their way here but they're taking the long way round just to make sure they're not followed.'

'That's a relief,' breathed Harry. 'I've been so worried about them.'

'Me too. I'll just go and check on Da', he's been quiet for a while.'

Jane glanced at her uncle and cousin and tried to convey to them that something was wrong but she wasn't sure the message had been received.

Jane was very conscious of Neil watching her as she left. She wandered down the hallway and knocked on Alec's door. 'Are you awake, Da'?'

She pushed the door open wider, walked inside and closed it behind her. Her father was asleep on the bed. Thankfully she hadn't disturbed him. How she wished he was already in the care home and wasn't caught up in this mess. What the hell were they going to do? They couldn't run away and leave him here. The only option was to get the Tallans out.

Jane took out her phone and started typing a text message to Jennifer. She hadn't told the Bitches to go home as Neil had ordered her to, thank God. What he'd said hadn't felt right, so she'd told them to stay close instead. Perhaps Jessica had got to a couple of the girls but she knew the majority couldn't stand the woman, so no way would they allow her to lead them. What she and her family needed was some of the usual mayhem her girls were great at causing.

After typing out her order, she pressed send knowing it would be followed to the letter. Now all she had to do was wait.

She looked to her father and smiled, finding the sight of him sleeping so peacefully reassuring.

'They won't lay a finger on you, Da',' she whispered. 'I promise.'

To her surprise, his eyes fluttered open. 'What's going on?' he said more clearly than she'd heard him speak in weeks.

'Nothing,' she replied, finding it difficult to lie because he'd surprised her so much.

'Don't... lie,' he breathed, producing his handkerchief from under the pillow and pressing it to his mouth.

'It's all okay,' she said. 'You don't need to worry.'

He had to swallow before continuing. 'Who... is here?'

Jane knew she couldn't deny they had visitors. Obviously he'd heard their voices. 'The Tallan brothers,' she whispered.

Alec sighed heavily. 'You're working for them...' He grunted with frustration when he had to dab his lips and swallow again. 'Aren't you?'

Jane nodded.

His gaze hardened. 'Eddie did this.'

'Don't blame him, Da'. We knew what we were getting into.'

'Are you in danger?'

'Neil is gonnae kill his brother and set us up for it. We have to leave.'

'Who else is here?'

'Just Eddie and Harry. Rose is at school and she's been told to go to her friend's house after. Carly and Dean are out.'

'Leave me.'

'No way.'

'I'll be fine. They're no' interested in me.'

'It's not an option. Besides, the Bitches are helping us.' Her father already knew she was back running the Bitches. At least she hadn't lied to him about that. 'Rod and Neil will be the ones leaving.'

'Neil has people working for him and they will come here. Just get out.'

'No.'

He huffed with frustration. 'So stubborn.'

'Because I take after you. We're going nowhere without you.'

'Fine, then take me and leave me somewhere. Just go. Please.'

Jane smiled at the sound of grinding metal from outside. 'No need. The girls have things in hand. Back in a minute, Da'.'

She got to her feet, hurried out of the room, down the hall and into her own bedroom that looked out over the front street. Sure enough, there were seven of the Bitches, led by Jennifer, attacking the Tallans' black Mercedes. They were actually prying off some of the bodywork with crowbars. They'd left the windows and tyres alone, as she'd instructed. After all, how could they leave in their car if they couldn't drive it?

Jane pushed open the window and the girls turned to give her a cheery wave. She waved back then raised her thumb, indicating they'd done their work and could go but to stay close.

The women nodded and raced off. Once they were out of sight, Jane closed the window and hurried back into the kitchen.

'I heard a noise and saw some kids vandalising your car,' she told the brothers. 'They've made a hell of a mess.'

'Wee bastards,' exclaimed Rod, leaping to his feet and rushing out of the room.

'How bad is the damage?' Neil asked her.

'Pretty bad. You're better taking a look for yourself.'

Neil gave her another of his scrutinising looks before following his brother out.

'Listen,' she whispered to Harry and Eddie when they'd gone. 'Carly told me that Neil's going to kill Rod in order to seal a brand-new deal he's making and he's going to force us to do it by kidnapping Dean and Carly and using them as hostages. We have to get out.'

They gaped at her in astonishment.

'Oh, and Da's awake and knows that we're working for the Tallans.'

'Holy shite,' exclaimed Eddie. 'First of all, let's lock the bastards out.'

'What about Rod?' said Jane.

'Who cares?'

'He's the only one capable of sorting out his brother. We need him. We can't let Neil win.'

'Aye, all right,' he said reluctantly.

'Who are you calling?' Harry asked him when he produced his phone.

'Peanut. Aye, all right, pal,' he said when his friend answered. 'Get round here, pronto. The shite just hit the fan. Oh, bugger. Just do your best, okay?' He hung up and looked to his son and niece. 'Peanut's visiting his maw, who lives in Gourock, so it'll take him a bit of time to get here. Right, you two, follow my lead.'

The three of them rushed down the hall to the front door, which was standing open. Rod and Neil were studying the mangled car, the latter swearing loudly and gesturing to it.

'Harry, with me,' said Eddie. 'Jane, wait here. The moment we're back inside, lock the door behind us.'

They nodded in understanding.

Eddie strode outside and up to the brothers, followed by his son.

'Hey, what's that?' he exclaimed, pointing down the street.

When the brothers turned to look, Eddie grabbed Rod and began dragging him back down the path with Harry's help.

'What the hell are you doing?' demanded Rod, struggling to free himself but Eddie and Harry held him too tightly.

'Saving your life,' Eddie told him. 'Trust us.'

'Get the fuck off me,' he yelled.

'Let my brother go,' exclaimed Neil, charging towards them.

Eddie and Harry hauled Rod inside and Jane closed and locked the door.

'Rod,' yelled Neil, banging on the door.

'Get the fuck off me,' snarled Rod, tearing himself free of their grip. 'You're both dead, do you know that? No one treats me like this.'

'Shut up and listen,' Eddie told him. 'Neil's gonnae kill you.'

'Don't be ridiculous.'

'It's true,' said Jane. 'Your brother's made a new deal with someone but they don't want you. If he doesn't kill you, then he doesn't get his deal.'

'I don't believe it. Neil would never do that to me.'

They all looked to the door when the hammering increased in noise and vigour.

'Rod, are you okay in there?' called Neil.

'I'm fine,' he yelled before looking back at the Savages. 'Who is his deal with?'

'We don't have that information.'

'Have you got any proof?'

'This is what Eric Martin told Carly and Dean.'

'Eric Martin? You cannae trust a word that prick says.'

'I think the best idea is to get out of here and then decide what we're gonnae do,' said Eddie. 'We can go out the back.'

'Wait,' exclaimed Rod, holding up his hands. 'Just let me think.'

They all regarded him expectantly as he began to pace the

hallway and run his hand frantically through his hair. 'You've only the word of a known liar for any of this.'

'Your brother made a deal with the Alexanders. They're to kidnap Carly and Dean and use them to force us to kill you.'

When Rod reached into his inner jacket pocket, Harry grabbed his arm and held it, allowing his father to snatch the gun secreted there.

'Why are you carrying this?' demanded Eddie.

'For protection with all the people going missing.'

'And if you'd got stopped by the polis?'

'Me and Neil don't get stopped by the polis any more.'

Eddie stared at the gun. He held in his hand the means to kill Rod and get on Neil's good side. If they performed this service for him, they'd be in and the Alexanders would be out.

'Da,' said Harry with warning in his voice. He knew exactly what he was thinking.

Eddie recalled Carly's words: *Is that the path we want our family to go down?* Not even he, despite his huge ambition, could murder a man in cold blood in front of his son and niece with his sick brother just down the hall. Besides, he would end up implicating his entire family. He'd already got them into this mess and he refused to get them in even deeper.

Instead, he pocketed the gun. 'We need to get out of here. Jane, get Alec ready to move.'

She nodded and rushed into her father's room.

'What are you going to do?' Rod asked him suspiciously.

'We're gonnae save your life.'

27

'We need to get back to Haghill,' said Dean as he and Carly shot to their feet.

'I'll come with you,' said David, rising too.

'What about this pair?' said Carly, gesturing to Eric and Reggy.

'Leave them. They're no more use.'

They left the table and rushed through the pub towards the door, which opened and in walked the three Alexander brothers with Jack and another three men.

'Not you lot again,' sighed Carly. 'You're really annoying, do you know that?'

'This time, you really are coming with us,' growled Cole, pointing a finger at her.

'We escaped before, we'll escape again.'

'You didn't escape last time. We let you think you had knowing you'd run straight to David. We want him too but couldn't snatch him from the gym, so we let you bring him out. Thanks for doing that for us by the way.' He smirked.

'Oh, fuck off out of our way; we've got to get back to Haghill.'

'You're coming with us. There's a lot going on that you don't know about...'

'We know everything, like Neil trying to kill Rod to seal his new deal.'

The Alexanders gaped at her.

'Now, we're leaving to get back to our family,' she continued. 'And God help you if you get in our way.'

'Grab them,' said Cole in a bored tone. 'We'll take David too; he could be useful.'

'You can fucking try,' he growled, slipping on some knuckle dusters.

The customers scrambled to get out of the way of the fight that was clearly about to start, although the two women remained at their table, drinking their gin and tonics, expectant smiles on their faces.

Carly regarded Cole warily, wondering if he was going to produce his gun but he didn't in such a public place.

'At last,' breathed Ross with a triumphant smile. 'Revenge.'

Carly had expected him to go for her and punish her for her big mouth, as he'd threatened to, but instead he ran at Dean and the two men clashed. To her surprise, Dominic was the one who lunged at her. She dodged, drew the taser and fired. Dominic moved and the electrodes went flying past him and hit the wall.

'You missed, bitch,' he yelled.

As he drew back his fist to punch her, she jammed the taser into his stomach and pressed the button.

'It has stun gun electrodes too, dickhead,' she said with relish as he dropped.

She glanced at Cole, who merely regarded his twitching brother with disdain. She wondered if he would attack her now but he remained where he was.

Carly cried out and staggered forward, dropping the stun gun as something slammed into her from behind. It was the man David had just punched in the face with his knuckle dusters.

'Sorry,' David called to her.

She picked herself up and had to duck as Ross was sent flying by Dean. He hit a table, which was upended, catapulting the half-finished drinks it held across the room. The two men sitting at the table grabbed Ross, blaming him for the loss of their lager and began punching him. Ross warded off the blows, headbutting one man and smashing a dropped beer bottle over the head of the other with a bellow of rage.

A hand fisted into Carly's hair from behind and she was yanked backwards so hard she was bent double. She found herself staring up into Eric Martin's face.

'This is for my baws,' he growled, drawing back his fist.

Carly tore the baton from her jacket and slammed it into the side of his face. Blood spurted from his mouth and he released her to press his hands to his bleeding face. Carly fell to the floor, landing on her back. She leapt to her feet, snatched an empty glass off a table and smashed it over Eric's head, who dropped.

She looked to Dean, who was dodging the blows of a baseball bat wielded by one of the mechanics Cole worked with. He managed to grab the man's arm, snatched the weapon from him and swung it into his right hip. The man screamed and went down. David was also doing a good job of slamming his knuckle dusters into another man's face. She looked to Cole and Jack, who were just standing there with Ross, who was dusting himself off and muttering angrily to himself. Dominic was attempting to get to his feet, recovering from being shocked. Why weren't they attacking? She didn't understand.

Frantically she looked around for the taser and spotted it under some debris from the upended table.

Cole leapt forward and grabbed it before she could. Carly

regarded him warily, expecting him to use it on her but he didn't. He just stood there, glowering.

'What are you waiting for?' she told him, wielding the baton.

When he rushed at her, she side-stepped and attempted to hit him in the arm with the baton but he dodged and she missed. They turned to face each other again, stalking one another while chaos raged around them. To her surprise, Jack, Dominic and Ross left the pub. From the corner of her eye, Carly saw Dean banging a man's head repeatedly off the bar before hurling him over it where he smashed into the optics, earning himself a mouthful from the cowering landlord.

'What's wrong, Cole?' she said. 'Don't you want to hurt me?'

Something hit Carly in the back of the head. She saw white light and attempted to cling onto consciousness, but she collapsed to the floor out cold, the baton falling from her hand.

'Nice one, Maw,' Cole told Jessica, who was standing there with a cosh.

'Get her in the car. Forget Dean. We have what we need.'

Cole nodded and slung Carly over his shoulder before rushing out. David, who had seen what was happening, attempted to make chase but Ross burst through the door and punched him in the side of the head.

David reeled backwards, eyes wide as everything swam out of focus. He staggered back a couple of paces before his legs went out from under him and he fell onto his backside.

'Dean,' he called. 'They've got Carly.'

Dean snatched up the baseball bat and tore out of the pub just in time to see Carly being dumped in the back of a car.

Before the driver could even start the engine, he'd raced up to the car and begun battering the windscreen with the bat.

'Start the car,' Dominic yelled at the driver.

His friend nodded and pressed the ignition button, all the while

Dean was dealing tremendous blows to the glass, which cracked before smashing.

'Go,' bellowed Dominic.

But Dean had leapt onto the car bonnet. The two men in the front seats covered their faces with their hands as he kicked in what remained of the windscreen. Dean reached in, grabbed the driver by the front of his jacket – he had failed to put on his seat belt in his panic – and dragged him out of the car. While bellowing like an angry bear, Dean bashed his head twice off the metal, knocking him out. All an astonished Dominic could do was gape at Dean in amazement.

While all this had been going on, Cole and Jack between them had hauled Carly out of the back of the car and were carrying her over to a second one waiting at the kerb with the engine running. Ross was behind the wheel. They shoved her in and threw out her mobile phone.

Dean leapt off the car and ran after them. He managed to put a dent in the rear passenger door but the vehicle sped off.

'Carly,' he roared, but the car was moving too rapidly for him to catch up.

There was a crack of plastic. Looking down, he saw he'd trodden on her phone, which he scooped up. They must have thrown it out so she couldn't be tracked.

'Dean,' called a voice.

He looked around, panting, to see David in the driver's seat of his car, engine running.

'Get in,' he told him. 'We can still catch them.'

Dean raced across the road and jumped into the passenger seat, David setting off the moment he was inside.

'Do you think they'll take her back to Haghill?' he asked David. Dean was verging on frenzy, panic and rage rising inside him. He couldn't believe they'd got hold of Carly but he swore to God he would get her back and inflict as much pain and misery on the entire Alexander family as he could.

'I don't know,' replied David, who had recovered from being punched by Ross. 'It will be where they'll feel most comfortable but the presence of your family and the Bitches might put them off. Impressive display back there, by the way. I don't think they expected you to smash in the windscreen like that and batter in their driver's head.'

Dean was grateful for how calm David sounded. For the first time, they felt like equals. 'I'll let the rest of the family know,' he said, taking out his phone.

He stared at the screen, trying to figure out how to phrase the bad news. Looking ahead, he saw the Alexanders' car sitting at the traffic lights. The traffic here was heavier, so they'd been forced to slow down. The lights changed to green and they turned left. David indicated to follow.

Dean dialled his father's number and put the phone to his ear.

'Da',' he said when he answered. 'Something terrible's happened.'

* * *

'Da's ready to move,' said Jane, exiting her father's bedroom to find her uncle and nephew still standing in the hall with Rod Tallan. Neil was no longer banging on the door demanding to be let in. He had at one point tried to break it down but had quickly given up when he'd realised it was made of metal. Since then, all had gone silent outside. Harry had peered out of the window. Although the car was still there, there was no sign of Neil.

Jane felt physically sick when she saw her uncle's face fall, his phone pressed to his ear.

'What is it?' she demanded as he hung up.

'That was Dean. He's fine but the Alexanders have Carly.'

'Shit,' she yelled, kicking the wall. 'Where have they taken her?'

'We don't know. Dean and David are following.'

'They'll come back to Haghill,' said Harry. 'Surely?'

'Maybe not, especially with us here,' Eddie told him.

'Well I'm not waiting to find out,' said Jane, pulling on her jacket.

'Where are you going?' Eddie asked her.

'To get Jessica Alexander. I'll make the bitch tell me where they're taking my sister.'

'What makes you think she's waiting at home like an idiot for us to storm around there and grab her?'

Jane turned on Rod. 'Where the fuck are they taking Carly?'

'How the hell should I know? If you hadn't noticed, I've been kept out of the loop more than anyone.'

Her eyes blazed with rage. 'Listen you, I don't care about the petty shite between you and your brother...'

'Petty? He's trying to kill me.'

'Whatever. His fucking minions have got my sister and they're going to use her to force us to kill you. So, I suggest that if you want to stay alive, you'll start fucking thinking before I get a bread knife from the kitchen and do the job for Neil right here, right now.'

'Take it easy, doll,' Eddie told her.

'No,' she retorted. 'All this is because of him and his brother,' she added, nodding at Rod. 'We've got caught up in their family's shite and I will not let Carly suffer for it.'

'Jane,' hissed Eddie, nodding at something over her shoulder.

'Carly?' rasped a voice.

She turned to see her father leaning on his Zimmer frame. The effort had taken so much out of him that his eyes were heavy with exhaustion and he swayed on his feet. Only sheer determination kept him upright.

'Jeezo, what are you doing, pal?' exclaimed Eddie, rushing to his side. 'You could have hurt yourself.'

Alec ignored the comment. 'Where's... Carly?' he murmured.

'It's okay, Da',' said Jane, regretting not keeping her voice down. 'She's fine.'

'Don't... lie to your father again.'

Jane looked to her uncle for inspiration.

'The Alexanders have snatched Carly,' Eddie told his brother sadly.

Alec sighed heavily and sagged so much that if Eddie hadn't been supporting him, he would have fallen.

'We have... to get her back,' Alec said, breathless with panic.

'And that's just what we're gonnae do.'

'Jennifer's on her way with a car,' said Jane. 'I called her while I was helping Da',' she told her uncle.

'Is that one of the Bitches?' Rod scowled. 'My brother said...'

'Fuck what your brother said. I think it's clear that we can't trust a word that comes out of his mouth.'

'It doesn't mean he was lying about that. Are you sure you can trust this Jennifer?'

'Absolutely.' Jane looked down at her phone when it bleeped in her hand. 'She's waiting for us out back. We need to go.'

'Let's get your coat on, pal,' Eddie gently told his brother. 'We'll discuss it more when we're on the move.'

Alec sighed and nodded.

'I'll just check what's going on out front,' said Harry before rushing into Alec's room to look out of the window.

'Can you see anything?' Eddie called to his son as he helped Jane get Alec's coat on.

'Naw, nothing and I don't like it,' he called back.

'My brother will undoubtedly be calling in the troops,' said

Rod. 'If you're wrong about this then the lot of you are dead. I hope you realise that?'

'No, it hadn't crossed our minds at all,' said Jane sarcastically.

Rod pointed a finger at her. 'Listen you—'

'Let's leave the telling off until later,' said Eddie. 'We need to get out of here.'

'Fine,' sighed Rod as he followed them all through the flat to the back door. 'But I've only your word that my brother is trying to kill me. God help you all if your information's bad.'

Eddie and Harry between them had to haul Alec along, who was panting rather alarmingly, his legs unable to bear his weight. Jane ran on ahead and peered over the wall, which she was just tall enough to see over. Sure enough, there was Jennifer in her mother's silver people carrier. Jennifer gave her a wave from the front seat and Jane smiled back. No one else was in sight.

'It's all clear,' she told the rest of the family. 'Let's go.'

She opened the back gate and looked up and down the street again just to make sure. She ran over to the back door and pulled it open so Eddie and Harry could manoeuvre Alec into the middle row of seats. They both got in with him and Jane slammed the door shut. She moved to get into the front with Jennifer but Rod had got there first. He smirked at her through the window, making her ball her hands into fists. Instead, she opened the rear door, jumped in and pulled it shut behind her.

'Go, Jennifer,' she called.

Her friend nodded, slammed the car into gear and stomped on the accelerator. Rod clung onto the handle above the door as he was thrown back in his seat.

Rather than turn left onto the road that ran down the front of the block of flats where the Savages lived, she turned right, heading away from there.

'So much for Neil and his minions,' said Harry. 'He didnae do anything.'

'You don't know my brother,' said Rod. 'If he's determined to do something, then he does it. That's why I have to kill him first. He won't bother chasing us, he'll think he's above that. He'll come up with something less obvious to get at us.'

'He doesn't need to chase us,' exclaimed Jane. 'His people have Carly. Please think – where will he tell the Alexanders to take her?'

'I have been thinking and I've no idea. Believe it or not, I do think a lot of your sister and I've no wish to see her get hurt but he'll have gone out of his way to keep wherever they've taken her a secret from me.'

Alec groaned with anguish and shook his head.

'I'm so sorry, pal,' said a stricken Eddie.

When he patted his brother's arm, Alec shrugged it off with a strength born of fear. Eddie was startled by the rage in his brother's eyes as he looked at him. He had no doubt that if anything happened to Carly, Alec would find a way to make him pay, brothers or not.

28

Carly found the gentle rocking motion rather soothing. She was slumped to the left, her head resting on something soft and warm. Had it not been for the horrible ache in her head, she would have felt comfortable and content.

'Is the bitch finally waking up?' said a voice.

Carly's body jumped when she realised the voice belonged to Ross Alexander.

Forcing her eyes open, Carly winced at the bright light that penetrated her brain. It took her several seconds to process the fact that she was in a car. Ross was staring round at her from the front seat with an intolerable look of triumph on his smug, gittish face. One of the mechanics from the garage where Cole worked was beside him, driving.

Hauling herself upright, she realised the warm shoulder she'd been resting on belonged to Cole. Sensing someone to her right, she slowly turned her head, wincing against the pounding this movement started up at the back of her skull. Jack Alexander glowered back at her.

'Oh, great,' she sighed. 'I'm stuck in here with you lot.'

'Headache?' said Cole when she pressed a hand to her forehead.

'Aye. A bad one.'

'Here,' he said, producing a pack of paracetamol from his jacket pocket. There was a bottle of Irn-Bru in the cup holder between the front seats. He grabbed it and handed the bottle to her.

'Hey,' said Ross. 'That's my bottle of ginger.'

'I don't want it if his nasty mouth has touched it,' Carly told Cole.

'You coo,' exclaimed Ross.

'It's unopened,' Cole told her, ignoring his brother. 'So you're good to go.'

Cole placed two tablets in her hand and she washed them down with the orange liquid. He took the bottle back from her and replaced it in the cup holder.

'I hope they don't take long to kick in,' she murmured, settling back into the seat and closing her eyes.

'They shouldn't. I'm sorry you were hit.'

'Don't apologise to her,' said Ross angrily. 'If anyone deserves a whack on the head, it's that bitch.'

'What about Dean?' said Carly.

Cole's eyes flashed. 'Why is it always about him?'

'I know you think there's something between us but there really isn't. He is my cousin though and I care about him, so where is he?'

'He got away, but it doesn't matter. You're the one we really need.'

'So you can force my family to kill Rod Tallan? Sorry, it won't work. We've already warned them.'

'It doesn't matter. They'll still do what we want, especially when we send them footage of you being tortured.'

Bile rose in the back of Carly's throat when Ross turned to look at her with sadism in his eyes. He hated her and would enjoy inflicting as much pain as possible on her. Cole wouldn't enjoy it, he didn't have the same callous streak as his brother but it wouldn't stop him, he had far too much ambition. She looked at Jack, wishing she hadn't made fun of his Pokémon addiction the last time they'd spoken, otherwise he might have convinced them to go easier on her. The hard look in his eyes as he stared back at her made her heart sink. She couldn't rely on any of these men to help her.

'My family will come for me,' said Carly. 'They won't just sit back and wait.'

'They can try but they won't find you,' replied Cole.

His confidence depressed Carly even more. She wondered if this could be her last day on this earth. Or would they inflict so much suffering on her she would be a cripple for the rest of her life? Perhaps she should fight? It wasn't in her nature to sit back meekly and do nothing but she didn't rate her chances against all these men while trapped in such a confined space. All she could do was pray her family reached her before she could be tortured.

'We're still being followed,' said the driver, glancing in the wing mirror.

'Well lose them then,' snapped Ross.

'It's Dean, isn't it?' said Carly. 'He's coming for me.' She turned to Cole. 'He's gonnae batter the lot of you.'

'If he tries, he'll get a bullet through his skull,' said Cole, patting his jacket pocket, telling her the gun was in there.

'You really have it in you to kill someone? You'll go back to prison if you get caught.'

'I'd kill myself first,' he said darkly.

'Then why do all this?' she exclaimed.

'Because I don't want an ordinary fucking life,' he yelled back. 'I'm sick of it. If I cannae have the money and the cars and all the good things, then I don't want to live.'

'You bloody idiot. There's so much more to life than all that shite.'

'No' to me there isn't.'

Tears filled her eyes. 'What happened to the man I loved?'

'He's dead,' he told her coldly. 'And good fucking riddance.'

'I don't believe that. He's still alive in there.'

'You're deluding yourself.'

'I guess we'll see when I'm being tortured.'

His gaze was so impassive, so without emotion, that Carly began to despair. But the thought that Dean was following nurtured a flame of hope in her heart and she smiled down at her hands.

* * *

'They're not trying to lose us,' said David as he drove.

'Meaning they want us to follow them,' replied Dean.

'Aye, so they can ambush us when we get there.'

'Da's keeping track of our movements through my phone. '

'It won't make a blind bit of difference. They have guns and we don't.'

'Then I'll tell them I'll kill Rod for them.'

'You can't,' exclaimed David.

'Why the fuck not?'

'Because he's the only one who will prevent your family from getting wiped out, which is what Neil will do if he wins. He can't let you all live, not after this. He'd kill me too.'

'I don't understand why he didn't bring you in on his plan?'

'I first began working for the Tallans through Rod. I was his friend, so Neil knows my loyalties will always lie with his brother if I were forced to choose. If Rod dies, then so do we. We have to keep him alive to protect ourselves.'

A police car passed them on the opposite side of the road and a wicked smile curled Dean's lips. 'I've got an idea,' he said, producing his phone.

'Who are you calling?'

'The polis.'

'I know this is a desperate situation but don't you dare fucking grass. You won't last five minutes.'

'I'm not grassing; credit me with a bit of sense. I just want to get their car stopped.'

He dialled 999 and reported the Alexanders' car for dangerous driving, saying he thought the driver was drunk and that they needed to be pulled over before they caused an accident. He also reported the make and model of the car, its licence plate number and location. The operator assured them it would be dealt with immediately.

'Let's hope your plan works,' said David, jaw tense with apprehension.

The police car that had passed them just a minute ago shot back up the road, siren blaring. Sure enough, it flagged down the Alexanders' car.

'Let's hope they search Cole and find his gun,' growled Dean. 'Then the wee bastard will be sent back to prison for years. Pull over,' he told David.

David nodded and managed to nab a spot just a hundred yards down the road from where the police car had pulled over the Alexanders.

Dean hopped out and began to jog up to them.

'Come on, Carly,' he murmured. 'You can do it.'

* * *

'Holy fuck,' exclaimed the driver. 'That polis car's flagging us down.'

'Dean, the twat,' muttered Cole. 'He called them on us.'

'The grassing bastard,' yelled Ross, banging his fist off the dashboard.

'Take it easy,' said Cole. 'Don't lose your rag with them. We can talk our way out of this. Guaranteed he won't have told them what's really going on because it would land his own family in it.'

'You're right,' said Ross, taking a deep breath while wrestling with his phenomenal temper.

'And you keep your mouth shut,' Cole growled at Carly.

She just smirked at him. What was he going to do, pull out his gun and shoot her in front of two police officers?

One of the officers knocked on the driver's window while his female colleague stood on the pavement, looking in at them sternly.

'Yes, Officer?' said the driver with a broad but nervous smile. 'Did I do something wrong?'

'Would you step out of the car please, sir? I need to perform a breathalyser test.'

'I can assure you I'm entirely sober.'

His creepy forced smile and the way he was sweating profusely caused doubt in the officer's mind. 'Please get out, sir.'

'Well, okay,' he reluctantly replied, removing his seat belt.

He climbed out and closed the door behind him.

'If he's had a drink,' muttered Ross. 'I'll do him myself.'

'He's not stupid,' said Jack.

Carly looked out of the window and her pleading gaze connected with the female officer's. Thankfully, she was alert and caught the look. She knocked on Ross's window and indicated for him to wind it down.

Ross, who was still fighting to contain his anger, gave the officer a bizarre, twisted smile.

'This is a treat,' he said. 'The most beautiful polis in Glasgow wants to talk to me.'

The officer just stared back at him, unmoved.

'Well, that was embarrassing,' said Jack quietly, making Carly snigger. When she glanced at him, she was surprised to see him wink back at her.

The police officer looked to Carly. 'Are you okay, miss?'

'I... I feel sick,' she replied. 'I need to get out.'

Cole turned to regard her with cold green eyes. 'If you feel sick then you're better waiting in the car.'

'I have to get out,' she told the officer.

The woman nodded and pulled open the door on Cole's side. 'Out you get then. You don't want to ruin the upholstery.' She tried to sound jovial but the look in her eyes told Carly she knew something was wrong.

Cole turned to look at Carly and the rage in his gaze almost took her breath away. For a moment, she thought he was going to draw the gun and shoot her there and then but he was more controlled than his brother and he got out instead so she could.

Carly glanced at Jack, wondering if he was going to stop her, but to her surprise, he just winked at her again and nodded encouragingly.

'Is that better?' the officer asked Carly once she was out of the car.

'Aye, thanks,' she replied, taking a few deep breaths.

'You do look very pale.'

Carly wasn't surprised. Not only had she been afraid but her head still ached.

'She's pregnant,' said Cole, taking her hand. 'That's why she feels sick.'

'And you're the father?' said the officer, looking sceptical. She hadn't missed Carly's surprise at this statement.

'Aye. We're very happy, aren't we, sweetheart?' he said, turning to her with a warning look.

'Deliriously,' she replied flatly.

'Carly,' called a voice.

They all looked round to see Dean jogging up to them.

'Who's he?' the officer asked her.

'My cousin,' she said. 'We're really close. Dean,' she said. 'I was hoping to bump into you.'

'You too,' he replied, gaze bouncing from Carly to Cole and then the police officer. 'What's going on?'

'Oh, something about a breathalyser test,' she replied with a dismissive wave. 'I had to get out of the car because I felt sick.'

'I see,' he slowly replied. 'I was gonnae get a coffee, if you'd like to grab one?'

'Sounds lovely.' She tugged her hand free of Cole's. 'You don't mind, do you darling?' she said, pronouncing the last word sarcastically.

'Actually, I dae. We're taking you for your first scan. You don't want to be a negligent mother, do you?'

Dean had no idea what they were talking about but decided not to say so in front of the police officer.

'That's next week, silly,' she said, slapping him on the arm a little harder than was playful. 'I'll see you later.' With that, she took Dean's arm.

'Carly...' Cole began.

'She can go for a coffee if she likes, sir,' said the police officer in a hard tone.

Carly glanced back over her shoulder at the woman as she hurried off with Dean and nodded. The officer nodded back, getting the strong feeling she'd performed her good deed for the day.

Cole was desperate to tear down the street after them but the last thing he wanted was for the police to search him with the gun in his pocket, so he got back into the car, resisting the urge to slam the door shut. He turned to look out of the back window and saw Carly and Dean get into David's car. It pulled into the flow of traffic, Carly giving him a cheery wave as they drove by, making him grit his teeth.

'It's okay,' Jack quietly told him. 'We've still another play to make.'

Cole just nodded. Although he hadn't relished the idea of torturing Carly, now he had absolutely no problem with it.

'Thank you,' Carly told Dean, hugging him. 'It was really clever of you to call the polis.'

'Did they hurt you?' Dean asked her.

'Apart from whacking me around the back of the head, no. I'm fine, although I have a headache.'

'Do you need a hospital?'

'Naw. We've more important things to sort out.'

'I'll call Da' and tell him we've got you back. The family will be so relieved.' Dean took out his phone with one hand, keeping the other around Carly, who was still nestled into him. He could see David giving them puzzled glances through the rear-view mirror but he didn't care, he was just delighted to have her back.

'Da',' he said jubilantly. 'We've got Carly. Aye, she's fine. They didn't lay a finger on her. Where shall we meet you? Okay. We'll be there soon.' He hung up. 'We've to meet them at a flooring shop across from the Barras Market.'

'Why there?' David frowned.

'Da's pal owns the place. It's somewhere to lay low and discuss what we're gonnae do.'

'Are they all okay?' Carly asked him.

'They're fine. They got Rod and Uncle Alec out.'

'Thank God,' she sighed with relief.

They had to drive through Polmadie to get there. They were just starting to relax when a motorbike shot out across the road in front of them. David was so caught up in trying not to hit it that he failed to see the black SUV coming at them from the left. It slammed into the passenger side of the vehicle. David wrestled with the wheel, the horrible shriek of metal as the SUV ground against the side of his car like something out of a nightmare. David was helpless to stop them from being shunted across the road. The car hit a wall with a sickening crunch and came to a rest, rocking from the impact.

David groaned and for the second time that day he fought against the blackness wanting to claim him as he saw figures swarming around the car. At first, he thought they were there to help, until he saw they were wearing balaclavas.

He flung off his seat belt and turned to look at Carly and Dean. To his dismay, they were both unconscious.

'Wake up,' he mumbled, tongue feeling thick in his mouth with shock.

The back doors were pulled open and Carly and Dean were dragged out. David was unable to help them, his own movements slow and lethargic.

The driver's door was opened by the rider of the motorbike, face hidden by the helmet. David managed to punch him in the crotch and he reeled backward with a cry. He shoved open the passenger door and practically fell out of the car just in time to see Dean and Carly being dumped inside a van.

'Finish him,' called the driver of the van through the open window while nodding at David.

As the van sped off, the driver of the motorbike produced a knife.

David scrabbled at his jacket pocket for his knuckle dusters. 'Come on,' he told his hands, which were still struggling to obey his commands.

The man lunged at him with the knife. David rolled and the blade struck the side of the car. He looked around for assistance but their attackers had chosen their ambush spot well. The large redbrick building to his right was closed and shuttered, a sign on the outside announcing Polmadie Car Boot Sale.

'I went to that car boot sale once,' he murmured to himself. 'I bought a radio. It didnae work.' David shook his head, wondering what the fuck he was thinking. The shock of the crash had affected him more than he'd realised.

David managed to slip one of the knuckle dusters onto his right hand, remaining in a crouch as the man in the helmet loomed over him with the knife. As his assailant drew back the weapon to strike, David slammed his fist into the side of the man's knee. There was a loud crack and the man threw back his head and howled with pain, the sound muffled by the helmet, before he collapsed to the ground.

David leapt on him and tore the knife from his hand before punching him twice in the belly. Fortunately for him the man's bike jacket didn't contain Kevlar, it was just leather, so the impact winded him.

David unfastened the strap around the man's chin and tore the helmet from his head. He recognised his attacker as one of the Tallans' heavies. They'd gone out together drinking several times. David had even been to his house and met his wife; he'd thought they were pals.

'Stevie, you feckless bastard,' David snarled at him before punching him again, knocking him out.

David staggered to his feet and pulled on the helmet. He mounted the bike, and was relieved to see the keys had been left in the ignition. He started the engine and shot off in the direction the van had gone but there was no sign of it.

Left with no choice, he decided to head over to the Barras to meet up with the rest of the Savage family. He just hoped they didn't blame him for this fuck up.

29

'I don't like it,' said Harry, who was keeping watch at the window. 'They should have been here by now.'

The six of them were gathered in the flooring shop, surrounded by rolled up carpets wrapped in plastic. It was closed for the day, so they had the run of the place. Rod had spent the time putting feelers out, trying to gauge who was with him and who was part of Neil's plan to have him killed. He'd cajoled, made promises and issued threats. The good news was, it seemed some people preferred him to Neil, whose pompousness had rubbed a few people up the wrong way, so Rod had some supporters.

'They could have got caught up in traffic,' said Eddie, who was sitting beside his brother at a small table. He was very concerned for Alec, who was shaking more than usual. He had hoped the news that Carly was safe would help but he was looking increasingly unwell.

'I'll try calling Carly,' said Jane.

'Try Dean instead,' Eddie told her. 'The Alexanders will have taken her phone from her.'

She tried but it rang out before going to voicemail. 'No answer.'

'I've got a bad feeling,' said Harry.

'Me too,' replied Jane grimly.

Harry glanced back at the window. 'Wait, someone's pulling up. Oh, it's just Peanut.'

'Let him in,' Eddie told his son.

Harry nodded and went to unlock the door for their friend before locking it again once he was inside.

'Any sign?' were Peanut's first words.

'No.'

They all rushed to the window at the roar of an engine, except Alec, who remained in the chair. They watched the vehicle pull up outside the flooring shop. The rider removed their helmet and practically slid off the bike to the ground.

'Jeezo,' said Eddie. 'That's David.'

'He looks injured,' said Jane.

'I'll get him inside,' said Peanut.

He opened the door and paused to look up and down the street before rushing across the pavement to help David to his feet. Slinging his arm around his neck, he dragged him into the shop.

'What happened?' Eddie demanded of David as Peanut helped him to a chair.

'They ran us off the road. Took Carly and Dean,' he murmured.

When David slumped as though he was about to pass out, Peanut slapped him, making him jump awake.

'Careful,' Jane told him. 'He's been in a car accident.'

'For all we know he was in on it and he set up Carly and Dean,' retorted Peanut.

'That's a good point, pal,' said Eddie, regarding David coldly.

This roused David and he regarded them with outrage. 'Hey,' he snapped. 'They were gonnae kill me. It's only thanks to my knuckle dusters that I'm even alive. Neil wants me gone because he knows my loyalty is to Rod.'

'That's true,' said Rod. 'David's always been my pal, no' Neil's.'

'I can't fucking believe what the greedy bastard's doing,' exclaimed David. 'This isnae like him at all, he's always been about being quiet and subtle, no' driving cars into people and abducting them in the middle of the street. It's fucking mental.'

'He's gone crazy with the greed,' said Rod. 'And I believe David. He isn't a traitor.'

'Thanks, Rod. I'm glad someone does,' he muttered while glowering at Peanut. 'Stevie Mack was gonnae stab me to death with a knife.'

'I never liked that wee fud.'

'I thought we were pals.' He slumped down in his seat. 'What a shitty day this has turned out to be.'

'Where have they taken Dean and Carly?' Eddie demanded.

'Nae idea. They didn't mention anything to Carly the first time they took her.'

Rod's phone bleeped. He took it out and smiled with satisfaction before replacing it in his jacket pocket. 'It's all in hand. Don't worry.'

Jane rounded on him. 'How can we possibly not worry?'

'Because a couple of my people have got hold of something precious to my brother and he won't dare hurt a hair on your sister's or cousin's heads.'

'Really?' she said, not trusting this information.

'Really. It'll be here in a few minutes, so you can see for yourself.'

'What is it?'

'I don't want to spoil the surprise.'

He looked so pleased with himself Jane could have slapped him.

'This will even up the odds considerably,' Rod told her. 'Just hang in there a bit longer.'

Jane wanted to cry with frustration but she kept it in. Seeing her distress, Jennifer went up to her and wrapped an arm around her shoulders. Jane gave her a sad smile before patting her hand. 'Da', are you holding up?'

'Don't worry about me,' Alec murmured weakly. 'Worry about Carly and Dean.'

The pain in his eyes distressed her. He should not be suffering this agony in his condition. Glancing at her uncle, she saw he was thinking the same thing, his eyes heavy with guilt. It would be easy to blame Eddie but they'd all known the dangers of working for the Tallans. The blame rested on all their shoulders, not just his.

* * *

Rose was worried. She'd done as her uncle had instructed and gone to her friend Tamara's house after her exam but now she couldn't get hold of any of her family. Carly, Dean, Jane and Harry weren't answering their phones. Although her uncle hadn't picked up when she'd called him, he'd sent her a text message saying everything was okay and he'd be in touch soon. She didn't like it. Her instincts were telling her that her family was in trouble and she wanted to help.

Rose had communicated her worries to Tamara, who came up with an excellent suggestion.

'Donna lives next door and she's one of the Bitches. She might know what's going on.'

'Okay, I'll go and ask her.'

'I'll come with you,' said Tamara, a pretty girl with long brown hair and mischievous green eyes. She was always up for an adventure and had caused her parents more than one sleepless night.

The two girls left the house and headed next door. Rose knocked and the door was pulled open by Donna herself.

'I can't get in touch with any of my family and I'm really worried about them,' said Rose before Donna could speak. 'Do you know what's going on?'

'Sorry, I've no idea,' she said kindly. 'Jane asked me and the rest of the girls to keep an eye out at your flat earlier but then she sent us away.' She didn't add that Jane had also asked them to vandalise a very pricey Mercedes as she didn't think it would help ease the girl's worries.

'They need help, I just know it but I've no idea where they are.'

'Me neither. Sorry, I can't help.'

'This is something to do with the Alexanders, they've started being pains in the arse again. I'm going to their house right now to find out what's going on.'

'You can't,' exclaimed Donna, grabbing her arm when she moved to storm down the path.

'I have to do something,' she retorted. 'You can come with me, or you can stay here.'

'Putting yourself in danger won't help your family.'

'My family are the ones in danger and I'm going to help them,' she yelled, tearing her arm free. 'The only way you can stop me is by locking me up.'

Donna sighed. She couldn't lock up Jane Savage's sister but neither could she let her go into the lion's den alone. 'Fine, I'll come with you,' she replied, making both Rose and Tamara beam. 'But let me round up more of the girls first.'

'Fine but please hurry.'

'I will,' said Donna, producing her phone from the pocket of her jogging bottoms.

Ten minutes later, another five Bitches had gathered at Donna's house and the eight of them stormed through Haghill towards the Alexander home. Rose walked at their head, enjoying the sense of power having six such capable women at her back created inside her. She could see why Jane enjoyed leading this gang.

Without hesitation, Rose stormed up to the front door of the Alexander home and banged on it. The door was pulled open by Brian. His eyes widened when he saw eight furious females on his doorstep.

When he tried to close the door on them, Donna and Leonie threw themselves against it and it whacked him in the face, sending him staggering back into the hallway. The women swarmed into the house, closing the door behind them.

'Where are your sons?' Donna demanded, looming over him as he stared up at them with blood trickling from one nostril.

'Out,' he shrieked back.

'Check the house,' she told the rest of the women. 'No' you two,' she added to Rose and Tamara. 'You can wait here with me.'

'Are we going to question him?' said Rose eagerly.

'Aye we are.'

'Can I do it?'

'Well,' she uncertainly replied. 'If you're sure?'

Brian's bowels shifted uncomfortably at the wickedness that filled Rose's eyes as she looked at him.

'I know exactly how to get him to talk.'

Brian was still sprawled on his back and he attempted to scoot away from her but Tamara stood on his right hand with a grin, halting him in his tracks.

Rose launched herself at Brian, landing before him and grabbing his crotch. His screams filled the house as she twisted.

'Now you know what your bastard son went through,' she hissed.

Brian could only stare up at this wild banshee that had burst into his home in astonishment, as well as agony, his mouth opening and closing like a goldfish's.

Leonie and the other four women returned and grinned at the scene.

'No one else is here,' she said.

Donna nodded in response.

'My family aren't answering my calls,' Rose snarled at Brian. 'And I think that's got something to do with your sons. Where are they?'

'I don't know, and that's the God's honest truth. They don't tell me anything any more. All I know is Jess is sleeping with Neil Tallan.'

'She never did have any taste,' commented Donna wryly.

'You're lying,' Rose told Brian before twisting his crotch again.

'I'm not, I swear,' he screamed. 'I'm leaving Haghill, I'm sick of the way they've treated me.'

'That could be true,' said Leonie. 'I found a packed suitcase in one of the bedrooms.'

'They think I'm weak, so they keep me out of everything,' said Brian sadly.

Rose sighed, released him and sank back on her haunches. 'I think he's telling the truth.'

'Me too,' said Donna. 'Now let's get out of here. If Jane finds out I let you anywhere near this house...'

'I'm not leaving until I find something to tell me where my family is.' She looked to Brian. 'I mean it.'

'Fine. There might be one thing. I installed an app on Jess's phone to follow her movements. She doesn't have a clue because she doesn't understand apps. I cannae say for certain that she is with my boys, but I reckon she might be.'

'Well don't just lie there,' exclaimed Rose. 'Tell me where the bitch is.'

Brian pulled his phone out of his pocket, brought up the relevant information and turned it round for them to see.

Leonie snatched the phone from Brian's hand. 'It's a street in Rutherglen.'

Rose sprang to her feet. 'Let's go.'

Brian sighed with relief when the women poured out of the house, taking his phone with him. Thanks to the pain in his groin, it was several minutes before he was able to stand. Once he was finally upright, he staggered upstairs, grabbed his suitcase and brought it back down with him. After pulling on his jacket and trainers, he was out the door, not even bothering to lock it. He hoped someone burgled the place, although he knew no one in Haghill would dare rob the Alexander home. He hopped into his car and drove off. He'd already emptied the joint bank account he shared with Jessica and had a few grand in his pocket but where should he go?

'Spain,' he said to himself, feeling better already.

He was leaving Haghill and he was never coming back. Brian just wished he could see his slag of a wife's face when she realised he'd taken all her money.

* * *

Carly groaned. The headache was back with a vengeance. She recalled the car hitting them, the horrifying sound of metal grinding on metal and then blackness. Where was Dean? He'd been in the car with her.

Desperate to know if he was okay, she opened her eyes and tried to sit up. Panic gripped her when she found she couldn't move. Looking down at herself, she saw she was lying on a wooden bench, her wrists and ankles tethered to the corners.

A blurry face peered down at her. Her vision cleared and she saw it was Dominic.

'She's awake,' he called to someone she couldn't see.

Furious, she spat in his face.

'You dirty bitch,' he said, drawing back his fist.

'No,' said a voice.

Dominic tutted and lowered his fist.

Cole appeared in her line of vision, looking down at her with dispassionate curiosity. 'How are you feeling?' he asked her.

'Oh, I'm just dandy,' she said sarcastically. 'Apart from the fact that I'm tied to a table.'

'It won't be for long, if your family cooperates.'

'Where's Dean?'

'He's over there,' he replied, nodding to the right.

Carly turned her head and saw her cousin was lying unconscious on the floor, chained to a radiator. He had a cut to the side of his head which fortunately seemed to have stopped bleeding.

'Dean,' she called.

He didn't stir.

'If I were you, doll,' said another voice, 'I'd worry more about myself than him.'

Neil Tallan came into view, spiking Carly's blood pressure. Two of his minions stood behind him.

'You total bastard,' she yelled.

Her head was snapped sideways by a hard slap to the face.

'I warned you to start controlling that mouth of yours,' he told her. 'But you haven't learnt.'

'And she never will,' said Ross, who she noticed standing off to one side with Jack. 'She's a slow learner.'

'Oh, fuck off, dickhead,' she told him.

'You see what I mean,' he told Neil with a knowing look.

'Never mind all that,' said Neil. 'Now, doll, we're going to have a wee chat with your family and if they do as I say, this lot here won't tear you into tiny wee pieces and believe me when I say that is something they are very keen on doing. You've pissed them all off one too many times.'

'Even you, Cole?' she said, looking to her ex. 'After all the times we said we loved each other?'

'Don't bother appealing to his good side, sweetheart,' said Neil. 'He doesn't have one any more. She made sure of that.'

'She?' Carly frowned. Her body jolted with anger when Jessica Alexander appeared in her line of sight.

Jessica's cruel painted lips curled into a smile. 'Oh dear, you do seem to be in a jam. Go on, beg me to stop them from hurting you.'

'You'd love that, wouldn't you, you old bag? I'm begging you for nothing.'

'Don't listen to her,' said Neil, wrapping an arm around Jessica's waist when her face fell at Carly's insult. 'She's just trying to get to you. You could be Cole's sister.'

'Sister?' laughed Carly. 'What the hell have you been smoking?'

Carly grimaced when her head was snapped sideways again, this time by a punch to the face from Jessica.

'Take it easy, sweetheart,' Neil told his paramour. 'There's plenty of time for that.'

As Carly lay there, dazed, she wondered if what Neil had said about controlling her mouth had been good advice.

'Does Brian know you and Neil are an item?' murmured Carly, deciding to choose her words carefully.

'He does,' replied Jessica. 'But there's nothing he can do. I've finally found a real man, so I'm divorcing that useless drip.'

'You're finally going to get the money, the big house and the cars you've always wanted.'

'I am,' Jessica replied, purring with satisfaction as Neil planted a kiss on her neck.

Carly glanced at Jessica's sons, wondering if they were going to object to their new daddy but none of them appeared bothered. All three held Brian in contempt.

'Right, time to call my feckless brother,' said Neil, taking out his phone. 'Get ready to speak to your family,' he told Carly.

She was tempted to tell him to go bugger himself but resisted the urge. She'd received enough blows to the head for one day.

As Neil made his call, bursting with self-congratulation, Carly looked to Dean again, who was still crumpled on the floor. She hoped his head injury wasn't a serious one.

'Rod.' Neil beamed, holding the phone out before him as he was making a video call. 'Good to see you, pal.'

'Don't you "pal" me you treacherous, two-faced twat,' thundered back his brother. 'I can't believe you were going to have me killed.'

'Sorry, it's just business.'

'We swore that the fact we were brothers would always come first. How fucking dare you?' Rod bellowed so loudly the speaker in the phone buzzed.

'All right, all right. I know it's not the ideal situation but this really is the deal of a lifetime and I know you wouldn't have hesitated to top me if you were in my shoes.'

'That shows how little you understand me.'

'This deal will put me on the international map. It means I can finally break out of Glasgow and if you hadn't managed to piss off so many people you could have been in on it too, but you will go around getting people's backs up and sleeping with the wives of dangerous people. You've no one to blame but yourself. You need to get some self-control, which is what I was just telling Carly here. Turn your phone round so her family can see her,' Neil told his brother.

Rod sighed and turned the phone around. Carly saw her family's appalled faces at the sight of her tethered to a table.

'Ross,' said Neil.

Ross loomed over her with a battery pack. He applied the prongs to her arm and her body arched and she shrieked as the agony tore right through her.

'I'm going to kill the lot of you, you bastards,' Jane screamed at the phone. 'You're all fucking cowards.'

'Where's my son?' boomed Eddie.

The phone was swung round to reveal Dean still unconscious on the floor.

'What have you done to him?' snarled Eddie.

'Nothing much,' said Neil. 'He was knocked out during the abduction and he hasn't woken up. That's not a good sign, he probably needs a hospital.'

'You fucking cunt,' thundered Eddie.

'Not a wise name to call the man who has your son and niece at his mercy.' The phone was swung back round on Carly. 'Punish him, Ross, for calling me that dreadful name.'

Ross grinned as he applied the prong to Carly again, only this time he'd rolled up her top and was attacking her bare stomach. Her hands snapped into fists and her body spasmed beneath the force of the shock running through her.

'Stop it,' screamed Jane's voice through the phone.

Ross obeyed but in response to Neil's command, not hers.

Neil turned the phone back round to face himself. 'Only you can save your loved ones. Kill my brother and you have my word they won't be hurt again. You've got twenty minutes. I'll call you back for your decision.' He ended the call and smiled with satisfaction. 'That went well.' He looked to Carly when she screamed in pain again to see Ross shocking her once more with glee in his eyes.

'Take it easy,' said Jack, pulling him away.

'Are you wantin' some of the same, big man?' demanded Ross, rounding on him with the prongs.

'Carry on like that and you'll end up killing her. A dead hostage is no use to us.'

'He's right,' said Jessica. 'I know you want revenge, son, but that can wait. The Savages are naïve if they think we'd ever give her back to them, intact anyway.'

Ross nodded and placed the device on a workbench. Jack stood by Carly's side and was relieved to see she was still breathing, tiny burn marks dotting the bare skin of her stomach and arms. Jack rolled her top back down to protect her modesty, trying not to think about how lovely and smooth her pale skin was. He glanced at Cole, wondering if he was going to object to his older brother's treatment of Carly, but he didn't look in the slightest bit bothered.

'You okay?' Jack asked her when her eyes slowly rolled open.

Carly's gaze was hazy and it took her a few seconds to focus on him. Her answer was unintelligible as she hadn't yet recovered the power of speech.

'Sorry?' he said.

'Go... find a Weedle,' she muttered.

When Jack chuckled, Cole's and Jessica's gazes both snapped onto him.

'Leave her be,' Jessica told him.

He held up his hands and retreated a few paces, joining Ross at the side of the room, Jessica's eyes studying him coldly. She hadn't liked his concern for Carly at all.

30

When Neil ended the call, Jane finally gave in to her tears, letting them silently roll down her face. Jennifer embraced her and Jane clung onto her.

'Jesus, I'm sorry,' said Peanut, who looked stricken on behalf of his friends.

'Mystery solved as to why Neil's suddenly turned into a greedy bastard.' Harry glowered. 'Did you notice Jessica Alexander in the background? I bet the bitch encouraged him to take the deal and top his own brother in the process. She's probably shagging him.'

'You're right,' said Jane, releasing Jennifer and wiping her eyes with the backs of her hands. 'She's manipulated him like she has her sons. We have to do something before they hurt Carly again and it looked like Dean really needs a hospital.'

They all turned to look at Rod, who held up his hands. 'You can't give in to my brother's demands. You know he'll kill you all if you kill me. He won't let Carly and Dean go either. He'll slit their throats and dump them in the Clyde.'

Alec groaned in anguish.

'He's right,' said David. 'Rod's the only one who can protect you and them.'

'So far he hasn't done a very good job,' replied Harry with a dark look.

'Just wait until my people arrive,' said Rod reasonably. 'It will be worth it, I promise.'

'You're just making it up to save your own hide. No one's coming, are they, Rod?' demanded Harry, advancing on him. The look in his eyes said that if killing this man would save his brother and cousin then he was more than willing to do it.

Rod produced a small, snub-nosed revolver that was strapped to his ankle and aimed it at him. 'Stay where you are. All of you, keep back.'

'Rod, this isn't the way,' said David. 'Threatening them won't help you.'

'I'm only protecting myself. That's better,' he said when Harry went still. 'Now, we're going to play this my way—'

His words were cut off when Alec kicked a chair into his right leg. Rod's knee crumpled and he dropped the gun. Alec managed to catch it in one shaky hand and aimed it at him.

'Jeezo, pal, I'd nae idea you had it in you,' said Eddie proudly.

'Careful with that, Da',' said Jane, rushing to his side. 'You might hurt yourself.'

'Killing you will save my baby,' Alec told Rod. His voice was a quiet murmur but his eyes burned with a ferocious fire.

'This isn't the way,' said Rod, slowly raising his hands. 'Now put that down; you don't even know how to use it.' His face fell when Alec managed to cock the weapon, even though his fingers were shaking and palsied. 'Oh, I see you do.'

'Da',' said Jane slowly. 'Carly once said that she didn't want to take our family down a dark path and this will put us on the darkest path possible.'

'Not you,' he replied, gaze locked on Rod. 'Just me.'

'It won't solve anything. Let's see what his men are bringing.'

If Alec heard his daughter, he didn't show it. He glared at Rod, finger wrapped around the trigger. When the shaking became more pronounced, he supported the weight with both hands.

'Come on, Alec,' said Peanut in a lighter tone. 'With the way you're holding it you're just as likely to hit one of us. Put it down and let's talk.'

Once again, it appeared as though Alec hadn't even heard him. He just continued to glower at the man whose very existence put his daughter's life at risk.

'I did some research on you,' Rod told Alec. 'I heard you were a ruthless bastard. Your only weakness was your wife and weans.'

'Too right,' said Eddie. 'So you might want to stop talking, it's no' helping.'

'A car's pulled up outside,' said Peanut, who was keeping watch at the window.

'That should be my men,' replied Rod, while staring straight back at Alec.

'We need him to confirm that it really is them, pal,' Eddie told his brother.

Alec nodded and Rod rushed over to the window, giving Alec the chance to lower the gun. Keeping it aimed at Rod had taken the last of his strength, so he allowed the weapon to fall into his lap.

'Why don't I take that?' said Eddie, reaching for it.

Alec's head snapped up to regard him, eyes bloodshot with rage and full of accusation.

'I'm so sorry,' said Eddie, hanging his head. 'I just wanted to make life easier for you and your girls.'

Alec's look told him they would discuss it later.

'Here is my surprise,' announced Rod with a pleased smile. 'And just in time too.'

Eddie looked back at his brother. 'We don't know if his surprise is to wipe us all out so he can escape.' He gestured to the gun. 'Please.'

Alec nodded once and Eddie scooped up the gun and handed it to Harry, who held it down by his side, ready to use if necessary. Eddie produced the pistol he'd taken from Rod back at the flat. Peanut looked to him and when Eddie nodded, he unlocked the door and pulled it open. Three men entered, the two elder ones frog-marching in the third, who appeared to be in his early twenties.

'Who's this?' said Harry, nodding at the young man, who was obviously a prisoner.

'This is Gavin. Neil's son,' announced Rod with a pleased smile. 'His bastard son to be precise. His mother used to be a stripper. Neil's gone out of his way to keep his real parentage a secret. The snobby bastard likes to be associated with higher class women than Gavin's haggard maw.'

Gavin glowered at him but didn't speak.

'You're using him as a hostage,' said Jane. 'If he hurts Carly and Dean, then we hurt Gavin.'

'Yes and Neil loves his son. He won't risk hurting a hair on his head.'

'Or you'll panic him into doing even worse to them,' said Harry.

'That won't happen. No one knows my brother better than me. This will work.'

Jane looked to her uncle. 'What do you think?'

'It's the only advantage we've got,' replied Eddie. 'We have to use it.'

Eddie didn't need to ask his brother if he was on board with this plan, he knew he'd be willing to sacrifice anyone to help one of his daughters. Rod had been right when he'd said Alec had a ruthless streak. If his body hadn't let him down, he would have already tracked down Neil and his little band and torn them apart for what they'd done. Eddie felt ashamed that he hadn't managed to do the same.

* * *

Leonie and Donna both had their own cars, so the women hopped in the vehicles and drove off, heading to the street in Rutherglen where Jessica Alexander was, or at least where her phone was. Donna had tried to persuade Rose to stay behind but the girl had a will as fierce as either of her sisters, but she had sent a disappointed Tamara home. Jane had told Donna that Cole carried a gun and the thought of Rose being exposed to that was frightening. The Bitches were all very fond of the three Savage sisters but the girl simply wouldn't listen to reason. Short of tying her up and tossing her into the boot, there was very little they could do, so Donna had allowed her to come along on the proviso that she do as she was told at all times. Rose's eyes were bright with excitement as she sat beside Donna in the passenger seat, telling her the youngest sister had just as much mayhem in her blood as the rest of her family.

The app on Brian's phone brought them to a large storage unit on a quiet street, the walls clad in profiled metal sheeting. It was ringed with a fence but the gate was ajar.

The two cars drove past the unit and parked further down the street.

'What do we do now?' Rose asked Donna eagerly as she switched off the engine.

'Now we check it out but just me and Leonie will go. You wait here with the rest of the girls. I mean it, Rose,' she said, voice heavy with warning when the girl rolled her eyes. 'Jane will probably kill me for bringing you with us.'

Rose looked contrite. 'I'm sorry, I don't want to get you into trouble but I'm just so worried.'

'I understand, but if we all go, then we'll be noticed and that could put your family in danger. Rein it in for them as much as yourself.'

Rose nodded seriously. 'I will. Promise.'

Donna smiled fondly. 'Good. Back soon.'

Rose and the other two Bitches in the back of the car watched Leonie and Donna climb out of their respective cars and hurry down the street together. Five minutes later, they were back.

'Well?' Rose demanded as Donna jumped back into the car.

'We saw through a side window. The Alexanders are in there.'

'And my family? Donna, please,' she pressed when the older woman sighed.

'They've got Carly and Dean. No,' she said forcefully, hitting the central locking when Rose attempted to open the door.

'We have to get them out of there,' she cried. 'The Alexanders hate them.'

'From what we saw, they're fine,' lied Donna. Dean had been out cold on the floor and Carly was tied to a bench but Rose didn't need to know that. 'I'm calling Jane. She will decide.'

Donna spoke so firmly, Rose nodded. 'Aye, you're right.'

* * *

'Ah,' said Rod with a satisfied smile when his phone rang. 'That'll be my loving brother,' he added sarcastically.

Sure enough, Neil's face popped up on the screen.

'Rod,' said Neil jovially. 'I can see the Savages wussed out. Too bad for Carly.'

'Just hold your horses,' Rod replied. 'Before you do anything drastic, you should know that I've got something of yours.'

Rod smiled with satisfaction at the panic that filled his brother's eyes.

'What?' demanded Neil.

Rod turned the camera so it was facing Gavin. 'Say hi to your da'.'

Gavin just stared at the phone with a hangdog expression.

Neil turned his customary purple before bellowing, 'Let him go, you fucker.'

'I don't think so,' said Rod, turning the phone back on himself. 'Now, here's what *you're* going to do. First of all, you'll release Carly and Dean unharmed.'

'Fuck off.'

Rod continued as though he hadn't spoken. 'Secondly, you and I are going to sit down and discuss this ridiculous situation you've got us both into.'

'Piss off. I'm discussing nothing with you. You'll only try to kill me.'

'Oh dear, does that hurt your feelings?' said Rod sarcastically. 'It's either that or your precious boy gets his throat cut.'

'Ross,' Neil bellowed furiously. 'Shock the bitch again.'

Rod produced a knife so quickly it shocked them all and he pressed it to Gavin's throat. Gavin went white and inhaled sharply but he didn't speak.

'I wouldn't recommend it,' said Rod. 'You know how fond I am of Carly and I don't want her harmed. The same goes for Dean. Any injury inflicted on them will be done tenfold on your son. You know what I'm capable of. I'm far more imaginative than you and your wee band of incompetents.'

'Ross, back off,' Neil roared at him before turning back to face the camera. 'I was going to give you a quick death seeing how we're blood but that's gone out the window now—' He went abruptly silent when Rod nicked the side of Gavin's neck with the knife and blood trickled from the wound. Gavin winced but once again remained silent.

Jane felt sorry for the boy who'd been dragged into this nightmare only because he was the son of the wrong person. It wasn't his fault but she knew she wouldn't hesitate to sacrifice him if it saved her sister. She was just realising that she'd inherited her ruthless streak from her father. Glancing at him, she saw Alec was watching proceedings grimly. All he cared about was getting Carly and Dean back.

'Fine,' growled Neil through a gritted jaw. 'We'll meet at the warehouse on Anderson Street. You know the one.'

'I do.'

'See you there in an hour,' said Neil before ending the call.

'Well played, Rod,' said David.

'Thank you,' he replied in a way that indicated he'd known all along that his plan would work.

'Can we trust him not to take his anger out on Carly and Dean?' demanded Jane.

'Absolutely. He won't risk the son and heir,' said Rod, clapping Gavin on the shoulder. 'Clean up his neck,' he told one of his men.

The man nodded, produced a tissue from his pocket and held it out to Gavin, who snatched it from him with a glower and pressed it to the shallow cut.

Jennifer's phone rang and she answered it. 'All right, Donna? Aye, she's here.' She held the phone out to Jane. 'It's Donna. She's said been trying to call you, but you've not been picking up.'

'My battery's died,' she replied.

'She's got something urgent to tell you.'

With a frown, Jane took the phone from her. 'Hi Donna,' she said into the handset. She went rigid. 'How the bloody hell do you know that? You know what, it doesn't matter. We're on our way.' She looked to the rest of the room with triumph. 'The Bitches have found Carly and Dean.'

'How?' exclaimed Eddie.

'No time to explain. We need to get over there,' she said, already rushing for the door.

'This is excellent,' Rod told his men. 'We can surprise my brother.'

'No, pal. You're staying here,' Eddie told Alec when he moved to rise. 'You'll only be a liability and you know it.'

Alec nodded and remained where he was, just the effort of trying to move exhausting him.

'Peanut, wait with him, will you?' said Eddie, nodding at his brother.

'No,' grunted Alec. 'I'll be fine.' He looked to Peanut. 'Go and help my baby.'

'If you're sure?' replied Peanut.

Alec nodded, his hands shaking even more than usual.

'The next thing you know you'll have all your girls back home safe,' Peanut told him.

His words did nothing to erase the immense pain from Alec's eyes.

31

'I don't fucking believe it,' bellowed Neil, slamming his fist against the wall. 'I should have known he'd pull a trick like that. Why didn't I send Gavin away?'

Jessica took his face between her hands. 'Look at me,' she said.

Neil's gaze connected with hers.

'Keep it together and think what to do. Losing your temper and shouting isn't going to help Gavin.'

Neil took a deep breath and nodded. 'You're right, babe. I have to meet him for that chat.'

'You can't. He'll try to kill you.'

'No' if I get there first.' Neil glowered.

'We've still got Carly and Dean,' Ross told him. 'They're our big advantage and we need to use them.' He produced a large knife. 'Let's cut off some of her fingers, that'll get them dancing to our tune.'

'That might make her family back off but not Rod,' an exasperated Neil told him.

'Aye, it will. It's the best thing we can do.'

'Shut your face, you thick cunt,' Neil roared at him.

'What did you call me?' snarled Ross. 'Get off,' he told Cole when he put a restraining hand on his arm.

'Take it easy,' said Cole.

'Oh, piss off. I'm sick of you telling me what to do. I'm the older brother, I should be the one giving orders.'

'I wouldn't trust you to give an order at McDonalds,' Neil told Ross.

'That's fucking it,' spat Ross.

When he tried to storm up to him, Neil's heavies placed themselves in his way.

'Move before you get hurt,' Ross told them with a manic glare.

'Will you catch a grip of yourself?' Jessica told him. 'We've got a crisis here and you're not helping.'

This admonishment from his mother was enough to make Ross quiet.

They all looked round at a laugh from Carly's direction.

'What's so fucking funny?' Ross demanded of her.

'Your bickering,' she chuckled. 'You sound like proper amateurs.'

'And you're Reggie fucking Kray, I suppose,' he barked, stomping up to her.

'Compared to you, aye, I am.'

'Back off, Ross,' said Jack.

'You're protecting her again. Don't tell me you've got a thing for her too?'

'Actually, I'm thinking of protecting Neil's son, if you'd forgotten about him?'

Jack's dark stare was so potent not even Ross would challenge it. 'All right, what's your fucking plan then?' he demanded. He was full of pent-up rage and was itching to take it out on someone.

Jack paused to consider his words before speaking. 'Your son's safe, for now anyway,' he told Neil. 'None of us can use our hostages. What you have to decide is who we need to get rid of. Only then will we be able to work out a plan.'

'Just so we're clear,' said Dominic. 'By get rid of you mean...'

'Kill,' replied Jack steadily.

'Oh,' said Dominic, who also flinched from that hard stare.

'Well Rod definitely,' said Neil. 'The man's a wild animal; I should have put him down years ago. David too. He's always been Rod's creature.'

'And the Savages?' pressed Jack.

'I've never been a fan of mass carnage but I see little choice.'

'They'll never forgive you for what you've done here today,' said Jessica.

'But they're not killers.'

'They may not have blood on their hands but all of them are very capable of taking a life should they deem it necessary. Do you really want to worry about them coming for you?'

'You're right, but I don't like big messes.'

'You've already made three people vanish without a trace. I'm sure you can do it again with the help of your friend with the incinerator.'

'An entire family going missing will raise a lot of questions.'

'It won't be the entire family. There's no need to hurt Alec and Rose but the rest have to go.'

'Aye, I suppose you're right,' he sighed. 'I knew hiring that family would cause me trouble. They couldn't just sit back and be convenient scapegoats, could they? Oh no, they had to fight back.'

Jessica sauntered up to Carly and peered down at her. 'You're very quiet given we're talking about the annihilation of your entire family.'

'Because you'll fail,' she replied. 'Your family fails at everything.'

Jack grabbed Ross's arm and kept a firm hold when he moved to strike her again.

Jessica leaned in closer to Carly. 'I saw your da' in the background of that call.' She smiled at the way the younger woman's eyes filled with emotion. 'It's sad seeing him so wasted. Alec was always so tall and strong. I remember him at school. Every girl had a crush on him. I did too but he never looked at me. Then your mother came along and he had no time for any other woman. It was always Margaret, until she got ill. Alec was such a vital man back then with needs, and sadly she could no longer fulfil them. That's when he finally looked at me.'

It took a few seconds for the meaning of Jessica's words to sink in. 'What the fuck are you saying?' said Carly, lips curling into a snarl.

'Didn't he tell you?' Jessica said innocently. 'We had an affair while your maw was ill.'

'You lying slag,' yelled Carly. 'He wouldn't touch you with a ten-foot pole.'

'Actually, he would. Repeatedly,' she replied with a malicious smile. 'He loved it too. I have very fond memories of our time together. If it's any consolation, your father is a very talented lover.' Her smile broadened as Carly glared up at her furiously.

'Why the hell would that be a consolation, you stupid bitch?'

Jessica's laugh made every muscle in Carly's body clench with anger.

'Everyone in Haghill knew, except you, your sisters and your daft maw.'

'Don't talk about my maw like that. She was ten times the woman you are,' bellowed Carly.

'That's not what your father said.' Jessica smirked.

It was the way Carly's upper lip curled back over her teeth that warned Jessica of what was to come. She just managed to move before Carly could headbutt her. So furious was Carly that she threw back her head and screamed with rage, frantically tugging at the chains binding her.

'You see, Ross,' Jessica told him with a smile. 'I've caused her far more pain than you ever could with your fists.'

He grinned. 'Nice one, Maw.'

Carly was tempted to think that Jessica was making it all up to hurt her, until she recalled Jim in the pub a few months ago telling her that Jessica had had lots of affairs. When she'd asked who with, his eyes had widened and he'd made up some crap excuse about leaving the iron on before running out of the pub. He'd known and so had everyone else. Only she and her sisters had been clueless and she felt so stupid and betrayed. All the while her beautiful mother had been dying, her father had been shagging this evil witch. The pain was overwhelming and tears rolled down her face.

'Hopefully now you'll realise that your father isn't who you thought he was,' said Jessica coldly.

Carly turned to look at Neil. 'You see what sort of amoral slag you're sleeping with?' she told him. 'She'll make a fool of you just like she did Brian.'

'That's ridiculous,' Jessica told Neil, sashaying up to him and sliding her arms around his neck. 'I cheated on Brian because he was weak and useless. He made me so unhappy. I was desperately trying to find a real man and now I finally have after searching for so long.'

She kissed him and Neil yanked her even closer and moaned into her mouth, making her sons' lips curl with disgust.

'What we've got is special,' Neil told his lover. 'I won't let any mouthy wee coo tell me different.'

'Then you're an idiot,' said Carly.

Neil released Jessica and stormed up to her, drawing back his fist. 'I'm so sick of your fucking gob.'

'Have you forgotten about your son?' she told him.

Neil grunted and lowered his fist.

'What I've just told her will torture her for the rest of her life,' said Jessica with satisfaction. 'If she manages to live beyond the next few hours that is. It will fester into a wound that will tear her family apart. That is a much better punishment than a punch to the face.'

She looked to her sons and Jack. 'Do not mention this to any other member of the family. That way, the rot can really set in inside Carly's mind. One day, that hate will be their downfall. Call it a back-up plan, just in case.'

Carly gave her a disgusted look before turning her attention to the ceiling as she mulled over what Jessica had told her. It didn't mean it was true but in her heart she knew it was. She recalled her father coming home late a few evenings when her mother had been ill in hospital. At the time she'd assumed he'd just been tired and stressed but now she thought she'd seen guilt in his eyes. If he'd had to have an affair, why did it have to be with Jessica Alexander, of all people? Had that been the reason why her father and uncle had become estranged? No, it couldn't have been, because that had happened before her mother had become ill. But she'd never believed the brothers had fallen out just because Eddie had owed her father money. Idly she wondered if it was anything to do with those nasty scars on her uncle's belly? Anything to stop her thinking about her father with Jessica Alexander.

When Jessica and Neil began to bill and coo over one another, Carly tilted her head away from them, the sight making her feel sick. She saw Cole with Jack, the two of them staring at her. Cole's eyes were cold and hard. Clearly the torment she was in meant nothing to him. Dean had been right. He'd only told her he still cared about her to mess with her head. Jack's gaze though, to her surprise, was softer. He wasn't enjoying her pain. Perhaps he wasn't the sadist she'd thought him?

'What do we do now?' said Ross with his usual impatience.

'We need to get ready to meet my brother,' said Neil dourly. 'It's important you all remain alert because he will have prepared a surprise for us. He's a slippery bastard.'

Dominic wandered up to Dean and nudged his leg with the toe of his boot. 'What about him? He's still out for the count.'

'Is he alive?'

Carly turned her head to face her cousin, her heart pounding with fear that he might have slipped away and no one had even noticed.

As Dominic bent down to take his pulse, Carly prayed for Dean's eyes to open, for him to grab the prick and snap his neck but he remained limp and unresponsive.

'Aye, he's alive,' said Dominic, straightening up.

'Thank God,' Carly whispered to herself.

'We'll take him with us,' said Neil. 'The more hostages we have the better. Leave him till last. Even if he does come round, he cannae do anything because he's chained up.'

'I want to come to this meeting too,' said Jessica.

'I'm not sure that's a good idea,' Neil told her. 'Me, my men and your boys can handle it.'

'You said I could help you in your business,' she said with a pout that would have looked more at home on a woman twenty years her junior.

'And you can but I don't want to put you at risk. You're too precious to me. Just a sec.' He turned to the men. 'Check what weapons we've got,' he told them. 'We cannae just walk into this meeting with our pricks in our hands.'

With that he returned to trying to convince Jessica to stay while the men began chatting and pulling various weapons out of their pockets. Therefore, only Carly noticed Dean suddenly rise up behind a clueless Dominic, who was too busy checking his phone. She smiled to herself. He looked absolutely lethal, especially with the blood staining one side of his face. His hazel eyes had turned dark with wrath.

Dean wrapped the chain around Dominic's neck and pulled, causing him to stagger backwards with a strangled cry, eyes bulging out of his head. He dropped his phone and frantically began clawing at the chain but his efforts to free himself were in vain. Dean looked so strong and steady Carly knew he'd been faking unconsciousness the entire time, waiting for the right moment to strike.

'Let Carly go,' said Dean. 'Or I'll strangle this fucking fanny to death.'

'He's no' got the guts to kill someone,' said Ross.

In response, Dean tightened the chain around Dominic's neck with such force his tongue stuck rigidly out of his mouth. His bulging eyes were full of panic and he was making alarming choking noises.

'Untie her,' bellowed Dean, his voice bouncing around the room.

Carly looked to Jessica, who was regarding her stricken son with cool disdain. There wasn't any fear in her eyes for Dominic's well-being, only contempt that he'd allowed himself to be taken hostage.

'He's serious,' said Neil. 'Untie her, Jack.'

He nodded and held his hand out to Ross, who tutted and dumped a key in his palm. Jack continually glanced at Carly as he moved around the bench unlocking each padlock attached to the chains that were tying her down, wondering if she was going to make a move.

'Does that key unlock this padlock?' Dean asked him, nodding to the one attached to his own chain.

Jack nodded.

'Slide it over here and if you try anything, I'll break his arm.'

Jack glanced at Neil, who nodded. He then slid the key across the floor to Dean.

'Back off,' Dean told Jack.

He retreated a few steps to stand beside Ross, who was so angry his hair was standing on end.

Dean found himself in a quandary. He couldn't unlock the padlock without releasing Dominic and losing his advantage.

Carly dragged herself up to a sitting position with a loud groan, the muscles in her back protesting after lying on that hard wooden bench for so long.

'I'll get it,' she said, sliding off the bench and staggering over to her cousin. She practically fell to the floor at his feet, picked up the key and fumbled with the padlock, her hands refusing to cooperate. It was like her body didn't want to escape.

The padlock finally clicked open and she tossed it aside before unwinding the chain from around Dean's right ankle.

'We're leaving now,' Dean told the room. 'If anyone tries to stop us, I'll make him pay,' he said, nodding at Dominic, who he held before him, aware that at least one of these people carried a gun.

'You're a fucking prick, Dom,' yelled Ross. 'Only you could get taken prisoner by our prisoner.'

His brother's response was an outraged gurgle.

'Someone stop them,' shrieked Jessica, more concerned with the loss of their hostages than the danger her son was in.

'Let them go,' said Neil, waving at his men to stand down.

'We can't let them go,' she yelled at him.

Neil took her hand. 'Trust me.'

It was then she saw he had a plan. All she could do was hope that he wouldn't let her down like her useless bastard of a husband had their entire married life.

'Carly, stay behind me,' said Dean when Cole produced his gun.

She hastily obeyed, although Cole didn't raise the weapon, he just held it down by his side. The three of them backed up to the door, Dominic's body shielding them from danger.

Carly opened the door in the main shutter and paused to look outside before Dean followed her, dragging Dominic with him. Dean pulled the door closed and slackened the chain slightly, allowing Dominic to fall to his knees and drag in lungfuls of air.

'Thank God you're okay,' said Carly, flinging her arms around her cousin's neck.

He kissed her cheek. 'Right back at you. Now let's get out of here.'

They rushed for the main gate, which still stood open, hauling Dominic, whose legs appeared to have turned to jelly, along with them. Before they reached the gate, six men strolled through it.

The three of them skidded to a halt.

'Shit,' said Dean. 'They're Neil's men.'

'That's why he let us go,' said Carly. 'He knew they were out here.'

'Back off,' said Dean, tightening the chain around Dominic again. 'Or I'll kill him.'

One of the men shrugged. 'So what? He's nothing to do with us. And he's a walloper. Now do the sensible thing and go back inside.'

Dean was forced to release Dominic so he could fight. The men continued to advance on them, so smug and confident they failed to notice the eight women converging on them from behind, Jane in the middle. Carly and Dean smiled as the women rushed up behind the men, moving silently in their trainers, and launched themselves at them.

Jane grabbed the man who'd spoken by the back of the jacket

and dragged him backwards while kicking his right leg out from under him. As he fell, she leapt on him, grabbed his head and banged it off the tarmac until he was unconscious. The rest of the men were similarly felled, with only the largest of them refusing to go down without a fight. It took four of the women to finally subdue him with a baseball bat to the head.

Carly raced up to Jane and the sisters embraced.

'How did you find us?' demanded Carly.

'Later,' said Jane, glancing back at the storage unit. 'Let's get you out of here first.'

Rod Tallan strode through the gates with Eddie, Harry, Peanut and David, the latter looking a little the worse for wear after his car had been rammed. There were also three men she'd never seen before, one with blood on his neck.

'Is my brother in there?' Rod asked Dean.

'Aye he is, with two of his men and all the Alexander family, except Brian.'

'Perfect,' he said, eyes shining with malice. 'Let's go and put them out of their misery then.'

Carly looked around for Dominic but saw he'd slipped away while they'd been distracted. Whether he'd gone back inside or escaped entirely, she had no idea.

'Come on, boys,' said Rod. 'Let's tidy up this mess.'

There was the screech of tyres and two cars came racing from around the back of the storage unit. A grinning Ross was in the driving seat of the lead car and he steered right at them, causing them all to run for cover. Only one of Neil's men who'd been felled by the Bitches was too slow in rolling out of the way and the car drove over his legs, making him scream.

'Da',' yelled Gavin, but Rod grabbed him.

'You need to get it into your skull that he only cares about himself,' Rod told his nephew. 'He was even willing to kill me, his own brother, just to close a deal. He'd throw you to the wolves the first chance he got if it served his purpose.'

'You're lying, you're just trying to come between us,' yelled back Gavin. 'My da' loves me.'

'Maybe but he loves himself more.'

Gavin's shoulders slumped with despair and he hung his head.

'What now?' said Eddie.

'Let's go back to Haghill,' said Rod. He clamped a hand down on Gavin's shoulder. 'We'll take our advantage with us.'

They all hastily left the storage unit before anyone noticed them, piling into four different vehicles.

Carly was reunited with both her sisters in the back of Donna's car.

'What are you doing here?' she demanded of Rose.

'She's the reason we found this place,' said Jane. 'She twisted Brian Alexander's baws until he told her he had an app to track Jessica's phone because of her affairs.' She gave Carly a questioning frown when her eyes flickered but her sister shook her head.

'Did they hurt you?' Rose anxiously asked Carly.

'Naw,' she replied, hugging her little sister. 'They're no' tough enough.'

'You're right, they're not.' Rose beamed, delighted to have her sister back safely. 'Is Dean okay?'

'He's fine too. Can we go home now?'

'We can,' said Jane. 'We just need to pick up Da' on the way.' She was puzzled by the look that came into her sister's eyes. She'd expected Carly to be happy about being reunited with their father but she just looked apprehensive. What the hell had happened back there?

32

Jane directed Donna to the flooring shop and they rushed inside, only Carly slinking in after them to find their father in the chair, shaking. He was even paler and looked to be struggling to remain upright. Animation returned to his eyes when he saw his daughters.

'Carly,' he murmured. 'You're safe. Thank God.'

No one was more puzzled than Alec when she didn't fly at him and hug him with her usual enthusiasm.

'Aren't you going to say something to him, Carly?' Rose asked her.

Carly shook herself out of it. 'Aye, course. Sorry, it's been a crappy day.'

She walked over to her father and bent over to hug him.

'I'm so happy you're back, sweetheart,' he said. 'Are you okay?'

'Aye, fine,' she replied, releasing him.

'Great,' he said, eyes shining with tears. 'I've been so worried.'

She forced a smile, unable to meet his eye. 'Shall we go home?'

'Yes please,' he said, giving her hand a gentle squeeze. When she just gazed down at him coldly, a creeping sensation slithered up Alec's spine. Something was very wrong.

'Come on, Da',' said Jane. 'Donna, could you give me a hand getting him into the car? Carly's tired.'

Between them, Jane and Donna managed to get Alec outside and into the front passenger seat of the vehicle.

The sisters got back in the car and Carly turned her attention to the window, losing herself in her thoughts. Donna and Rose put her sullenness down to what she'd just been through but Jane and Alec knew more was going on than she was saying.

* * *

They returned to Haghill to find a line of cars parked outside the block of flats where the Savages lived. The Bitches were once again on high alert, standing guard outside. Eddie and Harry rushed out to help Alec inside and into his bed. He was exhausted and could barely keep his head raised but he kept trying to look over his shoulder at Carly, who stared back at him stonily.

'I'll sit with Da',' Rose told her sisters. 'Make sure he's all right.'

Carly found a smile for her sister. 'Thanks, sweetheart.'

Everyone else gathered in the kitchen to discuss their next move. Carly was depressed to see Rod Tallan sitting at her dining table as though he owned the place. Gavin was seated to his right, curled in on himself, the essence of misery. David sat on Gavin's other side, looking a little more alert. Rod's men were gathered in a line behind his back like bodyguards.

On the bright side, Dean was there, standing off to one side with Peanut. His gaze immediately sought Carly out. She smiled at him and he smiled back. After what they'd been through together, she felt even closer to him. It was something warm for her to cling to in the light of the revelation Jessica had made. Had Dean heard that or had he really been unconscious some of the time?

'We need to find my brother as soon as possible,' announced Rod when Eddie and Harry had returned from settling Alec down. 'We can't allow him to make alliances and strengthen his position.'

'How do we do that?' Eddie asked him.

'Make those alliances first. It's already in hand, you don't need to worry about it. Neil's not the only one who's been making plans. I planted the seeds over a year ago and now it's time to make them grow.'

'You've been planning a takeover just as much as Neil has,' said Jane.

'Of course. Neil thinks he's the big man but there are a lot of people who would rather do business with me because I haven't got a massive pole up my arse.'

'He's shagging Jessica Alexander,' said Carly.

'Because he has no taste, despite the airs he gives himself. She's a despicable creature.'

Carly nodded heartily in agreement.

'What can we do?' said Peanut, gesturing from himself to his friends.

'Take down the Alexanders while I deal with my brother.'

'I don't understand why he's using them when he has men of his own,' said Carly.

'If he's sleeping with Jessica then he'll have taken them under his wing on her say-so. This is their induction and they'll be determined to prove themselves.'

They all looked at each other when there was the sound of screaming and shouting from outside.

Rose burst into the room. 'Jane, the Bitches are fighting each other,' she exclaimed.

'It seems my brother was telling the truth about some of them betraying you,' Rod told Jane.

'Christ,' she yelled before tearing down the hall towards the front door, followed by the rest of the Savages and Peanut.

* * *

Jane burst out of the front door to find the Bitches fighting.

'What the actual fuck?' she yelled, astonished by what she was seeing. Shaking herself out of it, she waded in, grabbed a woman called Helen, who was fighting with Jennifer, and rammed her fist into her stomach. Furious, she forced Helen up against one of the cars by her throat.

'Is this down to Jessica Alexander?' she demanded of her.

'Yes,' rasped Helen as Jane's grip on her neck tightened. 'And Emma Wilkinson.'

'I knew we should have battered that bitch,' exclaimed Rose.

'Get back inside, you,' Carly told her.

'No chance,' Rose retorted before running at another Bitch who was fighting Donna. With her trademark banshee shriek, she hurled herself at the woman, who fell and landed on her back. Rose landed on top of her and began slamming her fists into her face.

'The lassie's still got it.' Eddie grinned.

Carly threw herself into the fray too and the sisters and those loyal to Jane soon had the turncoats under control. Five of them had turned against her with the other eight remaining true. As four of the Bitches were absent, Jane knew more of them could be traitors.

'How did you ever think you'd win this fight?' Jane demanded of Helen. She'd forced the woman to her knees and had twisted one arm painfully up her back. 'You know you're outnumbered.'

'We're... just the distraction,' she gasped, eyes screwed shut with pain, terrified Jane would break her arm. She'd seen her do it to someone before.

'Distraction from what?'

'I don't know, they wouldn't tell me in case I told you. I'm sorry, I didn't want to do it but they threatened my gran.'

Jane released Helen, who slumped to the ground. 'Watch them,' she told the loyal Bitches while indicating the Judases.

'You got it,' said Jennifer before kicking Helen in the face, knocking her onto her back.

They raced back inside to find everyone as they'd left them in the kitchen and Alec was sleeping soundly in his bed.

'I take it you have the situation under control?' said Rod.

'Aye, the lassies sorted it no problem,' replied Eddie. 'One of the traitors said they were the distraction but they didn't know from what.'

'Check out the back,' Rod told his men.

The four of them nodded and left by the rear door.

'Not you,' he told David when he tried to haul himself to his feet. 'You look fit to drop.'

David nodded and retook his seat.

Rod's men soon returned.

'All quiet out there,' one of them told his boss.

'The distraction was meant to keep us here,' said Dean. 'Whatever's happening will happen somewhere else.'

'Wherever and whatever my brother's surprise is,' said Rod. 'It will be designed to draw me out of hiding, or to leave me alone with no protection.'

'What now?' sighed Carly when her phone started to ring.

'Carly, hen,' exclaimed Derek's voice. 'There's a load of lassies coming onto the estate led by Jessica Alexander and Emma Wilkinson and they're here for trouble.'

'Oh Christ. How many of them are there?'

'About twenty.'

'Is the rest of the Alexander family with them?'

'No.'

'Whereabouts are they exactly?'

'They've just gone past The Wheatsheaf and they're on their way here. Jim just ran in to warn me.'

'We're on our way,' she said before hanging up.

They all listened in grim silence as Carly related what Derek had told her.

'This is my brother,' said Rod. 'He's taking away some of my support.'

'Shall we stay?' Jane asked him.

His expression was as patronising as Eddie's could be. 'I don't think I need protecting by a bunch of women.'

The sisters scowled at one of Rod's men when he chuckled.

'Fine,' retorted Jane. 'Good luck,' she snapped before storming to the door. 'I've got a plan,' she told Carly as she followed her. 'But we need to meet them at The Horseshoe Bar.'

Carly nodded in response, imagining everything she would do to Jessica Alexander when she got her hands on her.

'Not you,' Jane told Rose when she realised she was following her sisters.

'You're going to need all the help you can get,' she exclaimed.

'Oh, fine. We don't have time for an argument.'

'Let them handle it,' Rod told Dean and Harry when they moved to follow.

'They can't take on all those women alone,' said Harry.

'They've got the loyal Bitches too. Remember, this is Neil trying to divide our forces. Don't let him win. The main attack is yet to come.'

'He's right,' Eddie told his sons. 'They'll be all right.'

'We hope,' said Dean, throwing Rod a dark look, wondering who the real enemy was here.

* * *

'So, what's the plan?' Carly asked Jane breathlessly as they ran towards The Horseshoe Bar followed by the loyal Bitches.

'Alcohol,' she replied. 'Lots and lots of it.'

'Getting pished is no' the answer.'

'That's not what I've got in mind. You'll see.'

They reached The Horseshoe Bar before Jessica, Emma and their women. Derek was at the door, watching out for them.

'I'm so glad you're here,' he breathed, his brow creased with concern. 'There's only eleven of you and you're a wean,' he added, pointing at Rose.

'Hey.' She frowned. 'I'm just as tough as my sisters.'

'We need your hardest spirits, Derek,' said Jane. 'Vodka, tequila, that sort of thing. We're going to set a trap.'

'Okay,' he replied before rushing back inside.

'Do you think this will work?' Carly asked her.

'I hope so, otherwise we're gonnae get battered.'

* * *

Rod smiled with satisfaction when his phone rang. 'That will be Neil.' He put the phone to his ear. 'Hello, dear brother.' He winced when Neil bellowed in his ear. 'Are you trying to make me deaf? Stop fretting, he's absolutely fine.' He held the phone out to Gavin. 'Say hello to your da'.'

'Hi, Da',' Gavin muttered miserably.

'Tell him how well I've been treating you.'

'I'm okay, Da'. Although Rod cut my neck with a knife.'

Neil's angry voice blared out loud and clear for all to hear as he heaped insults upon his younger brother.

'It's fine, don't worry,' Gavin hastened to reassure him. 'It's just a nick.'

Rod put the phone back to his ear. 'Satisfied? Aye, I can. One hour. See you then.' He hung up and regarded the room. 'We've to meet Neil at Death Loves Company.'

'Is that wise?' said Eddie.

'I know what I'm doing,' snapped Rod. 'You and your sons are coming with us.' He looked to David. 'And you.'

'Course,' replied David. 'You know I've always got your back, Rod.'

'What about Alec?' Peanut asked Eddie.

'Oh shite, we cannae leave him here alone.'

'Do you want me to stay with him?'

'Aye, that would be great. Thanks, pal.'

'Is that bar the best location for this meeting?' Dean asked Rod. 'Your family doesn't own it.'

'No, but we financed it. The prick who does own it is in deep with us.'

'So it's possible Neil will have got it to close for the evening just for this confrontation.'

'That's exactly what he will have done. We won't walk in there and find it full of happy customers drinking disgusting green cocktails.'

'And we're just going to walk into his trap?'

'Aye we are. Fortunately, I'm well in with the manager, the lovely Elvira,' he said before dialling. 'I'll arrange my own little surprise for my brother before he even gets there.'

'Excellent.' Harry smiled. Rod might be a smug git but his respect for him was increasing.

33

Darkness had descended. The only light came from the watery street lights and from the pub windows. The faces of the customers inside were pressed up against the glass to watch the show.

Carly, Jane and Rose stood alone in the middle of the road, watching the gang of women tramp up the street, led by Jessica and Emma. The women all carried weapons, including cricket bats and golf clubs.

'Emma's nose is still a mess after you smashed it,' Carly told Jane.

Emma Wilkinson was a beautiful woman but she'd been left with a very large lump on the bridge of her nose.

'I heard she's saving up for plastic surgery,' said Rose. 'The NHS won't cover it because it doesn't cause her any medical problems. Maybe she's here because she wants you to break it again for her so it can be reset?' she added, eyes twinkling as she looked at Jane.

'There's still time for you to go home, Rose,' she replied. 'I don't like it that you're here.'

'I'll be fine. Besides, I brought this,' she added, producing something from the back of her jeans.

'Is that Gran's rolling pin?' said Carly.

'Yeah.'

'She used that to bake with. She wouldn't have liked it to be used as a weapon.'

'Aye she would, she was as big a scrapper as any of us in her younger days. Da' told me all about her. She was known as The Terror of Townhead when she was a teenager.'

'So that's where we all get it from,' said Jane.

'Makes you proud, doesn't it?' Rose beamed.

'It does but for God's sake don't hit anyone in the head with it because it could kill them.'

'I'll be careful,' she casually replied.

'I recognise some of those faces,' said Carly, who had turned her attention back to the women marching up the street. 'They're from Parkhead and Cranhill.'

'You're right,' replied Jane. 'Only three of them are from Haghill and they've always been Emma's cronies.'

'It seems the Bitches haven't turned against you after all. They were forced to do it, as Helen said.'

'Perhaps,' said Jane, who already knew she was going to kick out the Judases if she was still leader of the Bitches by the end of the night.

The sisters spotted Karen, Fay and Meg, who had tried to help Emma in her fight against Jane for control of the girl gang a few months ago. They'd failed, thanks to Carly and Rose's assistance. Karen wore her traditional tight blue jeans, cropped top, lumberjack shirt and baseball cap and was giving them the finger with both hands.

Jessica and Emma came to a halt just twenty yards from the sisters, forcing their followers to do the same.

'Have the Bitches abandoned you already?' called Emma. 'They wouldn't have dared do the same to me.'

'It seems like someone got to them,' replied Jane.

'Oh dear, so sad. I'm here to take them back.'

'You can try.'

'Let's get this over with, shall we?' called Rose. 'The streetlights are reflecting off your massive nose and it's blinding.'

'You'll be the first to get battered, you stupid wee coo,' yelled Emma, pointing the golf club she held in her direction.

Rose's response was a belligerent snort.

While this exchange was taking place, Carly and Jessica had been glaring at each other. Carly was terrified the older woman would mention her affair with her father in front of everyone, so she spoke before Jessica could.

'Where are your sons?' she demanded.

'Still pining after Cole?' replied Jessica. 'Pathetic.'

'I stopped pining after that walloper when he set me up to be kidnapped. Where are they?'

'They've other, more interesting business to take care of.'

'Let me guess – sticking vegetables up their bottoms?'

Jessica's smirk fell. 'I see you haven't taken on Neil's advice about controlling your mouth.'

'It's hard to take seriously the advice of a dead man.'

'Neil was always the smartest and most organised brother. He will win and your family will be crushed,' Jessica sniffed.

'You do Rod an injustice. He's a lot smarter than you think.'

'Enough of this,' yelled Emma. She pointed at the sisters. 'I want revenge.'

'What for, your nose?' said Rose, making her sisters laugh.

'That's fucking it,' shrieked Emma. 'Get 'em.'

The sisters didn't move as the women charged at them as one. When they were just a few feet away, Jane produced a lighter from her pocket and ignited it. Jessica's eyes widened when she saw the dancing flame and the dark look in Jane's gaze. She let the lighter drop and a wall of fire erupted between the two groups of women running the width of the street, the interlopers screaming and shouting in surprise.

'Go,' Jane told her sisters.

The three of them turned and ran into the pub, dashing through the building to the back door, cheered on by Derek and his customers. They burst onto the back street where they met up with the rest of the loyal Bitches, who were waiting around the corner.

'We're still outnumbered,' said Carly as they turned left back onto the main road.

'That won't help them,' replied Jane with steel in her eyes, making her sisters grin.

The interlopers were so concerned with the wall of fire that they failed to realise they were being attacked from behind until Jane and her followers were tearing into them. The women at the back were hauled away from their friends and subdued before the rest of them had even noticed.

Rose whacked one woman in the back with the rolling pin, making her cry out and drop the golf club she carried. Rose snatched it up and used it to hook another woman's leg out from under her, causing her to fall into Jane's fist.

'This is great fun,' breathed Rose, brandishing the club in one hand and the rolling pin in the other, her eyes wild.

'We've got your backs, girls,' cried a voice.

Brenda and her three friends, along with Derek and Jim, rushed around the corner armed with weapons such as empty beer bottles and drip trays.

'Yes,' cried Rose.

When one woman ran at Jim, he punched her, snapping her head sideways. She turned back to glower at him, a trickle of blood dripping from the corner of her mouth.

'Bastard,' she yelled, drawing back the baseball bat she held.

'Oh Christ,' he cried, staggering backwards. 'Help.'

'Oh no you don't,' said Brenda, tearing the weapon from her hand and punching her in the face. This time the woman was felled. 'You okay, Jim?' Brenda asked him.

'Aye, thanks to you,' he said, a soppy, adoring look in his eyes. 'My hero.'

'Go back inside, you don't know what you're doing,' she told him before throwing herself back into the fray.

Carly tore through the women, using her taser and baton to great effect. She still hadn't reloaded the projectile barbs but she was using the stun gun electrodes. She was determined to get her hands on Jessica and make her pay for everything she'd done.

But when she finally reached the spot where she'd last seen her, Jessica was nowhere to be found. The cowardly bitch had run off.

'Dammit,' she grunted.

An idea occurred to Carly. She'd taken Brian's phone from Rose and she opened up the app, pausing to shock one woman between the shoulder blades who was locked in a furious battle with Leonie.

'Thanks,' panted Leonie, who had cut knuckles.

'You're welcome,' she casually replied. Carly smiled evilly when she saw Jessica was at the top of the road.

'Jane,' she yelled. 'I'm going after Jess.'

'Aye, all right,' she called back while battling Karen.

Carly was about to assist her sister, until she saw Jane grab the hem of Karen's long, flapping lumberjack shirt and yank it over her head, bending her double and trapping her arms. Jane brought her knee up into Karen's face, knocking her backwards before throwing herself on her and punching her several times. Rose was also fighting with gusto, swinging the golf club around her head, keeping any would-be attackers at bay.

When Jane joined Rose and the sisters began to fight back-to-back, Carly raced off in pursuit of Jessica.

It was a lot quieter and darker at the top of the street and she paused to peer around the corner. Jessica was up ahead. She'd stopped to catch her breath, leaning against the wall of a house. Keeping low, Carly silently approached, using the cars parked at the kerb as cover. The lighting wasn't so good here, just a couple of streetlights throwing weak orange puddles onto the ground, so she was able to remain in the shadows.

She ducked down behind a silver SUV to listen as Jessica took out her phone.

'Cole, it's me,' she gasped. 'We're losing the fight. The majority of the Bitches are still with Jane and some of the customers from Derek's pub are helping them too. I'm fine, I've left them to it. I'm coming to the bar.'

Jessica put her phone away and pulled a car key from her pocket. She pressed the fob and the lights on her BMW flashed. The cowardly slag had left her car here in case she needed to make a quick getaway.

Carly rushed down the pavement, her trainers masking the sound of her approach. As Jessica climbed into the driver's seat, Carly opened the passenger door and leapt in. The fear in Jessica's eyes was very satisfying. When the older woman tried to strike her, Carly brought up her left arm, deflecting the blow, and drove her own fist into her face. She then grabbed a dazed Jessica by her hair and slammed her face twice into the steering wheel. This caused the horn to honk but she knew no one would bother to find out what was going on.

'What's Neil planning?' she demanded.

Jessica was too stunned to reply.

'Answer me,' yelled Carly, making her jump.

'Trap... Death Loves Company,' she mumbled. The nasal tone to her voice indicated her nose had been broken.

'What sort of trap?'

'I don't know.'

'That's bollocks and if you don't tell me, I'll smash your face into the steering wheel until it's just pulp. Neil won't fancy you then,' she bellowed, her voice deafening in the confines of the car as all the rage about what this woman had done with her father came pouring out of her.

Jessica was smart enough to recognise that Carly was on the edge, so she said, 'He's going to set fire to the building with Rod and his supporters inside.'

'Are my family there?'

'Yes,' she breathed.

'Oh my God,' said Carly, taking out her phone and calling her uncle.

Eddie sat in his car with his sons and David outside Death Loves Company. Sure enough, the bar was closed, even though the road outside it teemed with life.

'If this is a trap,' said Harry, 'it's a bloody conspicuous place to pull it.'

'It is a trap,' replied David, who was sitting in the front passenger seat. 'Have no doubt about that.'

Rod, Gavin and the other three men were in the car in front of them, parked at the kerb.

'This must be hard for you, pal,' said Eddie, who was in the driver's seat. 'Years of loyal service to Neil and then he tries to kill you.'

'Oh no, I'm fucking delighted about it,' David replied sarcastically. He sighed. 'Sorry, I'm just pissed off. It's frightening how easily someone you've known for years can just one day turn around and try to murder you.'

'Aye, but that's the nature of the game we're in.'

'Suppose.'

When Eddie's phone rang, it connected straight to the car's Bluetooth, so everyone could hear Carly's voice.

'How are you getting on, doll?' he said.

'Oh fine. We're winning.'

'I knew you would,' he said, grinning.

'That's no' why I'm ringing. I've got Jess with me and she says Neil intends to set fire to Death Loves Company with you all inside.'

'Thanks for the heads up, sweetheart. You needin' any help back there?'

'No, we're good. Just mopping up the leftovers.'

'Nice one,' he replied before ending the call.

'That's disappointing,' said David. 'I had thought Neil would come up with something more original.'

'He must be desperate,' said Harry.

'I'll let Rod know,' said David.

He called his friend and listened to what he had to say.

'What?' exclaimed David. 'But...' He stared at his phone in dismay. 'He's hung up and he's said we've to go inside.'

'What?' said Harry and Dean in unison.

'He says to trust him.'

'No,' retorted Harry.

'You two wait here,' Eddie told his boys. 'Me and David will check it out. We'll call you if we need you.'

David didn't look too happy about this but as the order had come from Rod, he had no choice but to go in.

They got out of the car and met Rod and his people on the pavement. Gavin was with them, Rod keeping a firm hand on his shoulder.

'Why are your boys still in the car?' Rod asked Eddie.

'They're keeping an eye open out here. We don't want anyone sneaking up and locking us in a burning building.'

'Good point,' said Rod. 'Let's move.'

Eddie had to admire the way Rod approached the door into the bar fearlessly. He reached out and tugged at the handle and it opened beneath his touch. After pausing to peer inside, he shoved Gavin inside first before following.

Inside it was gloomy, so Rod hit the lights. The bar was empty, everything neatly put away. There was no cloying smell of petrol or anything that might indicate they'd stepped into a powder keg.

Rod grabbed Gavin by the back of the neck and held him firmly. 'Neil,' he called. 'I've got your son here.'

They all waited expectantly but there was no response and the place appeared empty.

'Billy,' Rod told one of his men.

Billy nodded, climbed up onto a particular table and held his lighter up to the smoke alarm.

'I suggest you all brace yourselves,' said Rod.

They were all doused with ice cold water as the sprinkler system burst into life.

'Just in case.' He smiled, dark hair plastered to his head.

'Bloody hell, I wish I'd put a jacket on,' said Eddie, who was only in a T-shirt, wrapping his arms around himself.

'Why isn't the alarm going off?' said David.

'I told Diana to deactivate all the alarms,' said Rod. 'She's the manager by the way.'

'Is that the surprise you got her to set?'

'Yes. I also told her to override the system so the sprinkler would come on immediately.' Rod didn't add that he thought his brother might use fire against him, given how it was his one and only fear thanks to an accident when he was a kid.

The sprinkler shut off, causing a shivering Eddie to sigh with relief. Everything was saturated and dripping wet.

'That should put paid to any fire,' said Rod. 'Neil,' he yelled, producing a knife and pressing it to Gavin's throat. 'I know you can hear me. Come out before I start stabbing the shit out of your son.' Movement behind the bar made him smile. 'There you are, you fucking worm.'

34

Carly shoved Jessica out of her own car, closed the door, climbed into the driver's seat and pulled on the seat belt. She took a moment to study the controls and recall what Cole had taught her. Thankfully it was an automatic with a button to start the engine, and she smiled when it purred into life. The car was facing the opposite way to the one she wanted to go and she didn't want to risk trying to turn around, so she put it into drive and set off, leaving Jessica slumped on the pavement.

At the bottom of the street, she turned left then left again, not daring to drive above twenty miles an hour in case she crashed into something. When she pulled up outside the pub, she saw the fight was still going strong, although Jane and her supporters definitely had the upper hand. Her sisters were both okay.

The moment Carly jumped out of the car, a hand clamped down over her mouth and an arm snaked around her waist. She tried to fight and scream but her abductor was too strong, so powerful they lifted her clean off the ground and she was carried around the corner.

Carly was pressed back against the wall and found herself staring into Jack Alexander's face.

'I'm not going to hurt you,' he told her. 'I just need to tell you something important.'

She yelled into his hand, attempting to tear her face free but he was immovable.

'I'm going to move my hand now. Please don't scream and just hear me out.'

The expression in his eyes wasn't angry or threatening. On the contrary, it was beseeching.

'Thank you,' he said when she nodded. He removed his hand and was relieved when she didn't cry out. 'You need to get home to your da',' he told her. 'Neil wants his son back and he's going to use Alec to make sure it happens. He knows he's been left alone with Peanut.'

'How the hell does he...' She trailed off as the horrific thought that Peanut had turned traitor occurred to her.

'One of Rod's men is feeding Neil information. Neil knows Alec's only got one person with him for protection.'

'Jesus,' cried Carly. She hesitated. 'Why are you telling me this? It's a trick, isn't it?'

'No, it's not. I have my reasons for keeping you safe.'

'Bollocks. You want me and my sisters to run back to the flat so your family can kidnap us for Neil. I expected something smarter from you.'

'It's no trick, you have to believe me,' he said, dark eyes boring into her. 'If you don't go home then Neil will kill your father. He's panicking, especially as his son's in danger and he can't get hold of Jess.'

'That's because I smashed her face into her own steering wheel and stole her car.'

His lips twitched with amusement. 'Good for you.'

'Aren't you angry?'

'No. All this chaos is down to her.'

Carly studied him closely before her face creased with anger. 'You're trying to distract me and my sisters. It's just another Alexander trick.'

'No, it's not. It's because I'm on the losing side. I just watched Jess and Emma get their arses handed to them, despite all their planning and scheming. I only back winners and that will be your family.'

'You're being very disloyal to your own.'

'They're not my family. Jess disowned me and my parents years ago. I've already got my own spy in the Tallans' camp. It's a man who works at their gym and Death Loves Company.'

'The hairy man?' she said.

'Yeah, him. You know him?'

'No, but I've seen him about and I thought he was suss.'

His gaze turned dangerous. 'You picked up on that but the Tallans never have. They're not such fucking big men after all.'

'You knew this was coming, didn't you?'

'Not this exactly but I knew something was going to happen.'

'Why tell me about your spy? Information like that could get you killed.'

'Which is why I know you'll keep it to yourself. You won't want a death on your conscience. At least, that's what I'm banking on. Now you have to get to your dad before Neil's people do.'

Carly stared at him mistrustfully before racing off down the street back towards the scene of the battle. She tore around the corner to see that it was over. Jane had Emma Wilkinson in a head-lock, Emma's arms flailing while Rose looked on laughing with Derek, Jim, Brenda and the Bitches.

'Jane, Rose,' cried Carly. 'We've got to get to Da'. Neil's going after him.'

'Jesus,' cried Derek. 'I'll come with you. My car's around the back.'

'No time. We can take this,' she said, gesturing to Jessica's BMW.

'Where did that come from?' said Jane. 'You know what, it doesn't matter.'

Jack watched with a satisfied smile from the bottom of the street as the Savage sisters, along with one of the Bitches, jumped into Jess's BMW, the pub landlord getting into the driver's seat, and the car sped off.

* * *

'Can I get you anything, pal?' Peanut asked Alec.

'No thanks,' he mumbled. 'I just need to sleep.'

'I'm no' surprised. I'll just settle myself here,' he said, gesturing to the armchair in the corner.

'If you want to watch TV, won't disturb me,' murmured Alec, eyes already closing.

'No way. Eddie asked me to keep an eye on you and I'm taking that literally. I've got a book to read.' He smiled, producing a dog-eared copy of *Jaws* from the back pocket of his jeans. 'My favourite.'

The corner of Alec's mouth lifted into a smile as his eyes finally closed. They snapped open again when there was the sound of breaking glass from the back of the flat.

'A bird's probably flown into the window,' said Peanut, leaping to his feet. 'No need to worry.'

Alec's response was a stony stare telling him not to be patronising.

'Sorry,' mumbled Peanut. 'I'll go and check it out.'

He left the room and, after retrieving the baseball bat from the umbrella stand, he cautiously made his way down the hall towards the kitchen. Peanut entered the room, almost colliding with the man standing there, face hidden by a black balaclava. They regarded each other with surprise before the man drew back his fist to punch Peanut. Acting on instinct, Peanut dropped the bat, blocked the blow and powered his own fist into his face. The man's eyes rolled up to the ceiling, his jaw falling open as he staggered back a couple of paces, stunned by the enormous power in the blow before toppling over like a felled tree.

When Peanut saw two more men entering through the broken kitchen window, also sporting balaclavas, Peanut retrieved the bat and ran at them. The man in the lead, who was stuck climbing inside, got the baseball bat full in the face and he collapsed forward, sliding downwards off the unit onto the kitchen floor, landing with his face on the linoleum, his legs still up on the unit, blocking the third man, who was trying to climb in behind him.

'Do you want some of the same?' Peanut roared at him.

Peanut was a pleasant, amiable man but when he was seized by the frenzy of battle he could be truly terrifying. His eyes turned bloodshot and bulged out of his head, as did the veins in his neck and forehead. All his muscles popped out of his body, making him appear even bigger, and he ground his teeth together.

The third man took one look at this enraged leviathan and scrambled backwards out of the window, landing on the grass below on his back like a beetle.

Peanut was about to leap outside after him and batter him with the baseball bat, until he heard the smash of glass from the front of the flat.

He raced back into Alec's bedroom to find his friend in bed, attempting to push away the man looming over him with a knife.

'Get the fuck off him,' roared Peanut, spittle flying from his lips as he smashed the bat against the wall.

'Drop it before I cut his fucking throat,' yelled the intruder, who was a lot calmer than his friends, his gaze ferocious through the balaclava.

Peanut took in a deep, heaving breath, his chest shuddering with rage as he realised he had no choice. He couldn't risk Alec's life, so he let the bat drop.

'Put your hands up,' the man told him.

Peanut raised them while glowering at the man, imagining tearing him limb from limb.

'We're taking him now,' the intruder told Peanut. 'Do the smart thing and stay where you are. We've got orders not to kill him but the boss never mentioned maiming him.'

'You cowardly fuck,' growled Peanut. 'And you do realise he cannae even stand on his own?'

'I know, which is why I brought my pals with me,' he retorted as though Peanut was stupid. 'Come and give me a hand,' he called over his shoulder.

When no one appeared in response to his call, he looked to the window. 'Oy, Damo, Norrie, where are you?'

Still no response.

'Maybe they've fallen asleep?' said Peanut.

'Shut the fuck up,' the man snarled at him. He turned his attention to Alec. 'Right you, get up.'

'He cannae get up, for Christ's sake,' exclaimed Peanut. 'He's practically bedridden.'

'Then you're gonnae help me and if you don't then he's fucking dead.'

Peanut liked those odds. The intruder would need both hands to help get Alec up, meaning Peanut would have plenty of chances to take him out.

He spied movement from the corner of his eye and saw Jane climbing in through the window. As the intruder had his back to the window, he failed to see her.

The intruder roughly grabbed Alec's right arm and hauled it around his own neck, making Alec groan.

'Don't be so rough,' barked Peanut. 'You're hurting him.'

'If he doesnae start cooperating, I'll break his fucking arm.'

'You're a real piece of shit, do you know that?'

'Call me one more name and he'll suffer for it,' snarled back the man while nodding at Alec.

'Fuck you,' grunted Alec before shoving one of his fingers into the man's right eye.

The man threw back his head and howled with pain. At the same time, Jane dropped down into the room. She jammed Carly's taser into his back, using the stun gun electrodes, and he dropped.

'Nice one, doll,' Peanut breathed with relief. 'He said he had a couple of pals...'

'They're unconscious outside on the pavement,' she said with a dark smile.

'Thank Christ for that.'

He snatched up the baseball bat at the sound of the front door opening.

'Da'?' called a voice.

Peanut lowered it again when he realised it was Carly. She tore into the room followed by Rose, Jennifer and Derek.

'Are you okay?' she demanded, racing up to her father.

'He's fine,' said Peanut as he and Jane helped settle him back into bed. 'There's another two in the kitchen. While I was dealing with them, this idiot came in through the front.'

'I'll check it out,' said Jennifer.

'Go with her,' Jane called to the others.

Carly, Rose and Derek nodded and followed her into the kitchen.

'Peanut certainly did a number on these pricks,' chuckled

Derek when he saw the man still sprawled practically upside down on his face.

'What shall we do with them?' said Jennifer.

'Let's just get them out of here,' replied Carly. 'It's the only thing we can do.'

Derek filled a jug of cold water at the sink and poured it over the face of the man Peanut had tackled first. He jumped awake with a startled cry.

'Hey, you,' Derek told him. 'Your cowardly wee plan failed. Take your pal and fuck off out of it before we smash your heid in.'

The man dragged himself to his feet and stood there, swaying. They all took a step back when it looked like he might fall over but he managed to stay upright and staggered to the back door, which Rose had opened for him. His friend was similarly roused and they were both ejected out the door, Rose kicking one of them up the arse as they went.

They returned to Alec's room.

'They've gone,' said Jennifer. 'Although I reckon they'll be seeing stars for a few days.'

'Good,' grunted Peanut. 'Cowardly fucks that they are.'

In her worry for her father, Carly had forgotten all about what Jessica had told her of her affair with him. Now, as she watched everyone crowd around his bed, it came rushing back and she was reluctant to approach him, thoughts of her lovely mother filling her head. Had she known of his betrayal? The prospect of her finding out something so devastating while she was dying was enough to break Carly's heart.

To distract herself, she called her uncle but he didn't answer, so she tried Dean instead. Just the sound of his voice made her feel better.

'Are you okay?' he asked her.

She smiled at the anxiety in his tone. 'Aye, we all are. We

battered Jessica and Emma and their people. Neil sent some men to kidnap Da' while we were all out but they got battered too. He was going to use Da' to force you to kill Rod. What's going on your end?'

'Not sure. My da' went into the bar with Rod and his men. They told me and Harry to keep watch outside. I'll let them know Neil's plan failed.'

Carly was very grateful that he and Harry weren't in the thick of it but she was also anxious for her uncle's safety. 'What can we do?'

'Stay put. The last thing we need is any of you being used by Neil. I'll call you when I can.'

'Okay.'

'Please be careful,' he said tenderly. 'I couldn't stand it if anything happened to you.'

'Right back at you,' she said equally tenderly before reluctantly hanging up.

She looked around and was startled to see her father staring right at her, ignoring everyone thronged around his bed. He knew something was wrong. She dreaded having that inevitable conversation with him because Carly didn't know how she could ever forgive him for what he'd done.

35

'My dear brother,' said Rod jovially when Neil emerged from behind the bar with five of his men, as well as the three Alexander brothers. 'How wonderful to see you again.'

'You're enjoying this, aren't you, you prick?'

'Immensely, especially as I have the son and heir,' he said, grabbing Gavin by the back of the neck so hard he made him wince.

Neil's smile was sly. 'If you hurt him, Eddie will kill you.'

'You must be joking,' retorted Eddie. 'I'm doing nothing for you after what you tried to do to my family.'

'Your nieces have been defeated. Jane no longer runs the Bitches and I also have something very precious to you – your brother.'

Eddie went rigid. 'You're fucking lying.'

'While you lot were here and your nieces were brawling in the street, my men went in and grabbed him.'

'Bollocks. Peanut was watching over him and no way could they get through that hard sod.'

'Your faith in someone named after a legume is rather naïve. He wasn't tough enough to beat six of my men.'

'I don't believe you. I want proof.'

'And you'll get it. They're on their way here as we speak. If you don't kill Rod right now, they'll kill your brother. It's time to choose.'

Rod turned to look at Eddie, his eyes full of threat, daring him to try it.

'Make a decision, Eddie,' pressed Neil. 'The clock's ticking on your brother's life.'

'I'm doing nothing until I know for sure. This could all be a bluff.'

'Fine. Call Norrie,' said Neil, waving a hand at one of his men.

His man produced his phone and dialled, glancing nervously at his boss when no one answered.

'He's no' picking up,' said the man.

'Well try one of the others then,' he snapped back.

Once again, his call went unanswered.

They all whipped round when the door burst open and Dean and Harry charged in.

'Da',' cried Harry. 'Neil tried to have Uncle Alec kidnapped but Peanut and the others battered his men's heids in. Jane beat Jessica too.'

Rod turned back to face his brother with a predatory smile. 'Then it looks like I hold all the cards. You really chose the wrong family,' he added, nodding at the Alexanders. 'It seems the Savages are far more efficient. You only chose that shower because you're shagging their maw. That's what thinking with your prick gets you.'

'You'd know all about that, wouldn't you?' Neil bellowed back, turning purple again with anger. 'Don't you dare stand there and lecture me.'

'Careful, Neil. You'll give yourself a heart attack.'

This comment only spiked his anger even more. 'Kill the fucker,' he told his men, who all produced guns.

'I don't think so,' said Rod, holding Gavin as a human shield as his own men pulled their guns and aimed them back at Neil's men. Even the three Alexander brothers were armed.

'This is mental,' exclaimed Dean. 'What are we gonnae do, shoot each other to death?'

'Looks like it,' said Neil, cocking his gun.

'And what will that achieve? Nothing.'

'Shut the fuck up,' Neil told Dean. 'You'll be singing "Kumbaya" next.'

'He's right though,' said Rod. 'How can we make money if we're all deid?'

'True,' replied Neil. 'But this new deal won't take off if—'

Cole turned and fired, shooting Neil through the back of the head. The sound was quiet, no louder than a pop, the weapon chosen specifically for this reason.

'Da',' cried Gavin as his father toppled facedown to the floor, the back of his head hanging open.

There was a moment of silence as they all stared at his dead body in shock. Eddie looked to Cole's brothers and noted they were the only ones who didn't appear surprised. They'd known that was going to happen.

Rod fired at one of Neil's men, who he knew to be a staunch supporter of his brother. He shot him in the head and the man dropped. Without pause, he shot the man standing beside him, striking him too with lethal accuracy.

The third man raised his hands when the weapon was turned on him.

'I know you weren't that loyal to my brother,' Rod told him. 'Join me or die.'

'I'll join you.'

'Excellent.'

Rod lowered the gun and the man breathed a sigh of relief.

'Good work,' Rod told Cole.

He nodded in response.

'What the fuck?' cried David. He looked to the Alexander brothers. 'You switched sides?'

'Aye. He was a prick,' replied Cole, nodding at Neil's prone form. 'We knew he was gonnae lose.'

'Killing him was my price for allowing them in,' said Rod, who didn't look at all cut up about his brother's death.

'And you think you can trust them?' David demanded of him.

'That remains to be seen. If they fail they will suffer the consequences, just like everyone who lets me down. But they could be assets to me.' Rod looked to Eddie. 'Your two families had better bury the hatchet and fast because I want you both working for me but that won't happen if you're too busy fighting each other.'

'I...' he replied before trailing off, still stunned by this turn of events.

'I mean it,' said Rod, voice heavy with warning. 'Shake hands right now or you're all fucking out. I will not have any infighting.'

'We're willing to do it,' Cole told Eddie. 'If you are.'

'You think it so easy after you tortured Carly?' demanded Dean.

Eddie waved a hand at him to be quiet.

'You got your own back for that after what you did to Dom,' replied Cole in that quiet, creepy voice.

'And can he be trusted to keep his cool and no' try to attack any of us?' said Harry, nodding at Ross. 'He's always losing his rag.'

Ross tilted back his head, the muscle at the base of his jaw pulsating, but he didn't reply, showing control for the first time in his life.

'He can,' said Cole. 'This is a chance for both our families to do well. Fighting each other will only ruin that for us all.' He extended his hand. 'Truce?' he asked Eddie.

Eddie considered for a moment before nodding. 'All right but put your guns down first. I'm no' shaking your hand while you're all holding them.'

Cole glanced at his brothers and all three of them slowly placed their weapons on the floor. Eddie looked to his sons, neither of whom appeared pleased by this turn of events but he was left with little choice, especially when Rod turned his death stare on him.

Eddie stepped forward to shake Cole's hand, his body tensing as he expected to get shot but Cole merely nodded.

'Thank you,' he told Eddie before releasing his hand.

'There,' said Rod. 'All friends again. Now *my* crew is stronger than ever. But I mean it,' he said, looking from the Alexanders to the Savages. 'Any fucking fighting with each other and I'll kick the lot of you out. I'll also make sure that no one else will hire you so, if you want to prosper, fucking get on, okay?' He bawled these last few words at them all and they nodded in response.

'Thank Christ for that,' said Rod, simmering down. 'It's like running a fucking nursery. Now, this is the new hierarchy – I'm in charge and David is my lieutenant. Cole, you'll lead your family, Eddie you'll lead yours and you'll be supported by Jane and her Bitches. I now realise what an asset those mad women are to me. Anyone got a problem with that?'

They all shook their heads but Dean noted the way Ross's eyes darkened and his right hand curled into a fist. He didn't like it that his younger brother was in charge. Interesting.

'Now piss off,' said Rod. 'I've got people who can clean up this mess. You'd best get used to this place because it will become important in our future operations. No more meetings at the gym, I don't trust it.'

When Gavin attempted to leave, Rod grabbed him by his throat and held him fast.

'If you breathe a word of this to anyone or think you can get revenge for your thick twat of a father, your pregnant girlfriend will pay the price. Understand?'

Gavin nodded, eyes bright with pain.

'Good. Now fuck off and I'd better never see you again.'

Gavin raced outside, the door slamming shut behind him.

The Alexander and Savage families also left and congregated awkwardly outside on the pavement.

'You really mean it about this truce?' Eddie asked Cole.

'Aye,' he replied. 'This is the chance we've been waiting for and we won't fuck it up with petty rivalries.'

'Petty?' growled Dean. 'You tortured Carly, a woman you used to love.'

'It was nothing personal, just business.'

'Is that all you've got to say?'

He shrugged. 'What do you want me to say?'

'How about fucking sorry?'

'Take it easy, son,' said Eddie, grabbing Dean's arm when he tried to square up to Cole. 'This truce benefits her too, so don't ruin it.'

'Aye, Da's right,' said Harry.

'Suppose,' muttered Dean, taking a step back. He looked to Ross and Dominic. 'What do you two think about this?'

'It's a great idea,' said Dominic, a thick purple stripe across his neck from where Dean had strangled him with the chain. 'I'm sick of all the fighting, I just want to earn some money.'

'Aye, me too,' said Ross.

Dean noted how his eyes flashed as he said this. The man wasn't happy, but it seemed he was willing to go along with things, for now anyway.

'None of us have any choice,' said Eddie reasonably. 'Not if we want to avoid being executed by Rod, because make no mistake, that's what he'll do if we piss him off. So let's make it work, eh, boys?'

The five younger men nodded.

'Good. What will your maw say about Neil's death?' he asked Cole.

'Nothing much. As long as we're earning, she's happy.'

'I'm shocked,' said Dean sarcastically.

'You fucking smug prick,' grunted Ross.

Cole put a restraining hand on his arm when he took a step toward Dean. 'No.'

Ross backed off, still not looking happy about taking an order from his little brother.

'I propose in Haghill we each stick to our side of the scheme,' Cole told the Savages. 'We'll go to The Wheatsheaf, you'll go to The Horseshoe Bar...'

'And never the twain shall meet,' ended Eddie.

'Precisely.'

'The shops are no man's land,' continued Cole. 'We all need to buy food and drink.'

'Fair enough,' said Eddie.

Cole extended his hand and Eddie shook it once again.

'It'll be interesting working with you,' said Cole.

'Right back at you.'

The three Alexander brothers strolled off down the street, Ross glancing back over his shoulder as if he expected the Savages to follow them.

'Well, that was... weird,' said Harry.

'We can never trust them,' said Dean. 'And I don't know how Rod can after how they turned against Neil so quickly.'

'He doesn't trust them,' said Eddie. 'He's no' stupid. He'll keep a very close eye on them but we've no choice but to get along, for now anyway.'

'Ross isn't happy.'

'Sod Ross, he's not the one to worry about. Cole's a stone-cold killer. He murdered Neil as easily as swatting a fly. That makes him one dangerous bastard. We must be very careful not to underestimate him.'

36

The Savage family was joyfully reunited at the flat, relieved to see each other alive and well. Derek and Jennifer stayed to join in the celebrations. Brenda and her two friends, along with Jim, had then turned up to make sure everyone was okay. When Mary and her husband had come in to see what all the noise was about, they too had been delighted to accept the glasses of wine that were thrust into their hands and the party was in full swing.

While everyone drank and laughed, Eddie headed into his brother's room to talk. The smashed window had been boarded up.

Alec regarded him stonily. 'I believe everything worked out.'

'Aye, it did.'

Alec fought against his failing speech, determined to not let his body get the better of him, for once. There were things that needed to be said. 'But it could so easily have gone wrong.'

'But it didnae, that's the important thing. We're all fine, as are your girls.'

Alec took a deep breath and dabbed at his lips with a tissue. 'And now they're working for Roderick Tallan.'

'They can handle it and they'll make more money than ever.'

'Money... isn't everything,' Alec growled.

'I know but it makes life a hell of a lot easier. Besides, we've no choice. Now the Alexanders are working for Rod, we have to do the same otherwise we'll lose his protection, weakening us and they will attack if that happens.' Eddie didn't like to add that they also needed to carry on working to pay for the pricey care home. He didn't want to heap that guilt on his brother.

Alec tutted, eyes flashing as he realised this was true.

'I'm so sorry, pal,' Eddie said, eyes full of sadness. 'I thought I was doing the right thing for your family. I was protecting them the only way I knew how.'

'By turning them into... criminals.'

'But they're so good at it. I know that's no' what you want to hear but it's true. They were born for more than an ordinary life.'

Alec knew this, he'd always known it. 'No' Rose. You keep her out of it. If not, I'll never forgive you.'

'I'll do my best but you know what a wee tornado she is.'

Alec grabbed his arm with surprising strength. 'Promise me.'

'Aye, all right, pal. I promise.'

Alec sighed with relief and released him, slumping back into the pillows.

'Do you forgive me?' said Eddie, eyes pleading. 'I'm so glad we're close again and I don't want to lose that.'

'Me too. I'm... pissed off at you. But I forgive you.'

'Thank you,' said a relieved Eddie.

'Now, I need to sleep.'

'Okay, I'll leave you to it. This will work out for our family, I swear.'

Alec just nodded, too tired to reply.

* * *

While everyone was partying and his father was in Alec's room, Dean approached Carly.

'Can I talk to you in private?' he whispered in her ear.

She nodded. They left the kitchen and sneaked into her bedroom.

'I'm glad you want a chat,' she said. 'Because I want to say thanks for saving my life back at that storage unit. If it hadn't been for you, I would have suffered a lot more.'

'Don't mention it. Are you okay after that?' he said, taking her hands, concern in his eyes.

'I'll be fine. Can you believe we're now working with the Alexanders?'

'No, and I don't like it. Anyway, that's not what I want to talk about.' He took a deep breath before continuing. He was still holding her hands and he gave them a gentle squeeze. 'I love you, I really do and all this has made me realise that we have to grab every chance we get to be happy because it can so easily be taken away. I don't care what anyone says, I want to be with you and—'

Before he could finish, she'd flung her arms around his neck and kissed him. Dean wrapped his arms around her waist and kissed her back hard.

'I love you too,' she said, beaming up at him. 'And I want to be with you.'

He grinned and took her face in his hands before kissing her again.

'I think we should keep it quiet for a wee bit,' she continued. 'The family's been through a lot. Let the dust settle and then we can spring it on them, but that doesn't mean we can't see each other in secret.'

'That's just what I was thinking.' He smiled, the fact that they were on the same wavelength only convincing him even more that this was right.

They fell back against the wall together as they kissed harder, the passion they harboured for each other threatening to overwhelm them.

'Will you stay over at my place tomorrow night?' breathed Dean.

'Too right I will,' she whispered, stifling the moan wanting to fall from her lips as he kissed her neck. 'I'll figure something out.'

'Good, because I can't wait to make love to you.'

The prospect caused her face to flush and her stomach to knot with desire. It was just what she would need as the next day her father was going into the care home. Although she was furious at him, she knew that by this time tomorrow, everything would have changed.

'Dean,' called a voice.

'For Christ's sake,' he tutted. 'That's Harry. If he finds us like this...'

'Go out my window,' she told him. 'Pretend you were taking some fresh air in the garden.'

He kissed her again before opening the window and jumping out, landing in the grass. Dean turned to kiss her once more before she closed the window.

'Carly,' called Harry. 'Are you in here?'

She just managed to close the window before he walked in, looking slightly drunk.

'Have you seen Dean?' he asked her.

'No, sorry,' she breezily replied. 'Maybe he's in the bathroom?'

'I already tried there.'

'Then I can't help you.'

A mischievous smile creased his lips. 'Is he under the bed?'

'Not unless he's been run over by a steamroller. It's a divan.'

'Oh, aye. The wardrobe then?'

She opened the door with a knowing smile. 'Do you want to check the drawers too?'

'Naw. I wonder where he is then?'

'Have you tried my da's room?'

'No. Good idea.'

He left and Carly returned to the kitchen with a smile just as Dean entered through the back door. Harry wandered in a few seconds later.

'There you are,' Harry said to his brother. 'Where the hell have you been?'

'In the back garden. I needed some fresh air. Why?'

'I just wondered. Here you go,' he said, thrusting a bottle of lager at his younger brother. 'And don't gi'e me any shite about not drinking. We're celebrating.'

'I wouldn't dream of it,' said Dean, accepting the bottle from him.

Soon Carly realised Jane was missing, so she popped into her father's room, but he was fast asleep, so she went to her sister's room instead.

She opened the door and her eyes widened. 'Oh, sorry,' she replied before hastily closing the door. Carly stood in the hallway, attempting to process what she'd just seen.

Jane rushed out of her room, pulling down her jumper. 'Carly, I...'

'It's okay, you don't need to explain to me.'

'But I do.'

Jennifer followed her out, her hair all over the place. 'I'm sorry you had to find out like that.'

'How long has it been going on?' said Carly.

'A couple of weeks,' replied Jane.

'And it's going well?'

'Aye,' she replied, smiling at Jennifer. 'Very.'

'Good, but, at risk of sounding an arsehole, I'd no idea you were gay.'

'I'm not. I do like men, but I like women too. I've known it for a while but I didn't know how to tell you.'

'I wouldn't have thought badly of you,' said Carly, giving her hand a gentle squeeze. 'I just want you to be happy. And it has to be said, Jennifer is gorgeous, even with the tongue piercing.'

Jane and Jennifer grinned.

'So, we have your blessing?'

'Course you do.' She smiled, hugging her sister and then Jennifer.

'Great,' said a relieved Jane. 'You're the only one who knows. We're keeping it quiet for now and seeing how it goes. Also, we don't know what the other Bitches will think of it.'

'They'll think whatever you tell them to think. It's safe to say you've got them well and truly under control, especially after booting out the traitors.'

'You're right but we don't want anyone judging us or talking about us, not until we're ready to go public.'

'I won't say a word.'

Eddie left his brother's room. 'Why are you lot lurking out here?' he asked them. 'Come and join in the celebrations.'

'Coming, Uncle Eddie,' called back Jane. She looked back at her sister and hugged her again. 'Thank you.'

'Nae worries.'

It seemed things were working out for everyone. Carly just hoped her older sister took the news of her relationship with Dean as well when they were ready to go public.

* * *

The next day involved transporting Alec and his things to the care home. Eddie drove his brother in his car, along with Jane and Rose, while Dean took Carly and Harry.

Dean and Carly found it difficult to keep their eyes off each other but Harry was nursing a bad hangover, so he didn't notice all the glances they gave each other.

The manager of the care home, as well as one of the nurses, were waiting to greet them on arrival and they all piled into Alec's new bedroom. They began placing his things where he directed them. Carly was glad for the activity because it meant she could avoid contact with him. Her father kept looking at her questioningly but she would always look away, the anger continually rising inside her.

It was only when he was settled in that he realised he'd forgotten a photograph of his parents. Eddie offered to drive back to the flat to collect it. Dean and Harry both had a debt collection to do, Harry offering to take Carly's place so she could be with her father on this important day. Jane took Rose for a tour around the facility as she hadn't seen it yet, leaving Carly alone with her father.

'There's no escape now,' Alec told her. 'Sit down.'

Realising she had no choice and that she needed to get this conversation out of the way before she drove herself crazy, she took the seat by his bedside.

'What's wrong?' he said. 'Please,' he added when she sighed and looked down at her hands.

Carly took a deep breath and forced herself to raise her head and meet his gaze. 'I know you had an affair with Jessica Alexander when Maw was ill.'

The look on his face told her everything she needed to know and her eyes filled with tears. 'So it is true. I'd hoped she was lying but somehow I knew she wasn't.'

'I'm so sorry,' he said, a tear sliding down his cheek. 'I didn't know what I was doing.'

Saliva gurgled in the back of his throat and he swallowed hard before continuing. 'I was so scared of losing your mother and raising you three alone. I was a mess.'

'And Jessica took advantage of that,' said Carly, eagerly leaping on this.

'She did but it was my fault too. She didn't force me. I hate myself for it.'

Alec had to pause again, not just because of his physical condition but because of the emotion threatening to overwhelm him. Carly fought against her impatience and waited for him to continue.

'Your maw needed me more than ever and I let her down,' he said.

'Did you love Jessica?'

'God, no. I hated her, I still do.'

The force of his words convinced Carly that this was true.

'She was always after me, right from high school, but I never wanted her. She's evil.'

'Aye, she is. And manipulative.'

'She saw I was vulnerable and scared and she played on that. But it was my fault too.' Alec slumped back into the pillows, the revelation of his secret exhausting him.

'Did Maw know?'

He shook his head. 'She was very ill by then... not always conscious.'

'How long did it go on for?'

'Just a couple of weeks. I stopped it a few days before she died.' Tears filled his eyes. 'If I could take it back...'

'But you can't,' she retorted. 'I'm just relieved Maw knew nothing about it.'

'That's why I'm ill now. Punishment.'

His face was filled with so much pain Carly's heart softened towards him a little. Nothing she could say would punish him more than he'd already punished himself. She knew he'd really loved her mother, she'd seen them often enough over the years talking and giggling together like teenagers. Her dad had looked at his wife with worship in his eyes; she'd been so lovely inside and out, unlike Jessica, who was just an attractive shell full of rottenness and evil.

'Have you told anyone?' he said.

Carly shook her head.

Alec breathed a sigh of relief.

'Does Uncle Eddie know?' she said.

'No. We'd been estranged for a while by then.'

'Why did you two really fall out? And don't say it was about money. That was certainly part of it, but there's more to the story. What happened?'

'Let sleeping dogs lie. It's the best thing.'

'If you don't tell me, I'll never forgive you for sleeping with Jessica.'

'Carly...'

'No, Da'. I saw the state you were in when Maw was dying and I absolutely believe Jessica saw her chance to get something she'd wanted for a long time and took it. The silly bitch probably imagined the two of you getting together after Maw had died but thank Christ you kicked her to the kerb. So I can find it in my heart to forgive you but not if you don't tell me the truth. If we've learnt anything recently, it's that family secrets can cause a lot of damage even years later. I won't allow that to happen to me and my sisters. If you don't tell me, I'll walk out of here and you'll never see me again.'

'Don't do that, my beautiful girl, please.'

Carly had to steel herself to be hard-hearted. She hated causing him distress and all she wanted to do was hug him, but she could not give in.

'Is it something to do with the scars on Uncle Eddie's belly?' she pressed.

Alec sighed and nodded. 'Eddie came to me saying he was in trouble.' He had to pause again as he wrestled with his violent emotions. 'Got on the wrong side of a drug dealer. I was afraid of being dragged into his world and it hurting my family. I told him no but he begged. I still refused. The dealer stabbed him and almost killed him. I felt so bad. The dealer was even threatening Harry and Dean... even though they were just weans back then.'

Carly leaned forward in her seat, eyes wide as she waited for him to catch his breath before continuing.

'I had to do something.'

'What did you do?' she pressed when he went silent.

Anguish filled his eyes. 'I killed the dealer,' he rasped.

Carly stared at him in shock. 'How?' she said when she eventually recovered her voice.

'We fought. He pulled the knife he'd used to stab my brother, so I took it off him and stabbed him in the heart. He died instantly.'

Alec hung his head and let the tears flow while Carly slumped back in her chair, feeling like she'd been punched.

'I didn't mean to,' he said. 'Accident, heat of the moment.'

'Did the polis ever come after you?'

He shook his head. 'The dealer caused them a lot of trouble. They were glad he was gone. Didn't investigate much.'

Alec slumped back into the pillows, breathing hard.

'Da', you okay?' said Carly.

'Aye,' he panted. 'Good to get it off my chest.'

'Did Maw know?'

He nodded.

'She forgave you?'

'She knew I was protecting our family.'

'Do Dean and Harry know?'

Another nod.

Carly decided not to be petulant and demand to know why they knew when she and her sisters didn't. The answer to that was obvious – he hadn't wanted his little girls to know he was a murderer.

'And that's why you and Eddie fell out?' she said.

'Aye. I'd warned him to avoid that man. His name was Murray but he wanted to make more money to support his boys with his wife gone. Wouldn't listen.'

'And you cut ties with him because he'd put you in that position?'

'Yes,' he said, voice growing weaker. 'I couldn't live with it. I nearly went to the polis so many times to hand myself in but your maw always convinced me not to, said you all needed me.'

'She was right.'

'Her love helped me get over it.' His face creased with tears. 'And I betrayed her with a woman I hate when she was dying. What sort of husband am I?'

To his astonishment and delight, Carly threw herself at him and hugged him like she always had.

'I don't blame you for what you did,' she said. 'You were protecting our family. I might not have been able to see it like that before but recent events have shown me how easily these things can happen. And I forgive you for Jessica. She manipulated you, just like she does everyone.'

'Thank you, sweetheart,' he said, embracing her. 'I love you so much.'

'I love you too, Da'.'

Alec kissed the top of her head, so relieved he hadn't lost his daughter.

As Carly clung onto him, she revelled in the memory of bashing Jessica's face off the steering wheel. The bitch had deserved it and more. But something was causing her even more pain and that was Dean.

The bastard had lied to her.

* * *

Carly stayed with her father for another hour to reassure him that she really did forgive him and she promised that she wouldn't tell her sisters. They would not be happy if they found out she'd kept something like that from them but she didn't want to tarnish the time they had left with their father.

Carly caught the bus back to Haghill and went straight to Dean's flat.

He smiled when he opened the door to her.

'Can I come in?' she said gravely.

'Always,' he replied, so happy to see her he failed to notice the wrath in her eyes. He wrapped his hands around her waist the moment he'd closed the door behind her. 'I've been thinking about you all day.'

When he moved to kiss her, she stepped away from him.

'What's wrong?' he said.

'You once told me our fathers became estranged over money.'

'Aye,' he said slowly, wondering where this was going. 'And it was true.'

'It was but that wasn't the whole story, was it? I just spoke to my da' and he told me everything about the drug dealer called Murray.'

'Oh,' said Dean sheepishly.

'You promised me hand on heart that there was nothing else. You lied to me,' she exclaimed.

'I know and I'm sorry but I didn't want to risk causing another rift. I'd only just found you and I couldn't stand to lose you.'

'After how Cole lied to me, I thought you of all people would understand that it would be a deal breaker.'

'Deal breaker?' he exclaimed. 'Surely you're not going to let this come between us now we've finally got together?'

'I can't trust you,' she rasped.

'For God's sake, Carly, you're overreacting,' he said, taking her hands.

'You blatantly lied to my face. I didn't think you would ever do that.'

'I admit I was wrong but I was afraid of losing you. I took the coward's way out.'

'And now you're going to pay for it,' she said before releasing his hands and turning for the door.

'Carly, please. I love you.'

'I love you too, but I can't be with you. I trust you to work with and as a cousin but I don't trust you not to hurt me as a boyfriend. I can't go through what Cole did to me again, I just can't,' she said, voice cracking.

'I won't, I swear,' he cried. 'I'll never lie to you again about anything.'

As he enveloped her in his arms, tears prickled her eyes. She wanted him so much but the fact that he'd lied about something so big was tearing her apart. It felt just as bad as when Cole had used her and Dean really seemed to have no idea of the magnitude of what he'd done, which to him had been nothing more than a white lie.

'It's too late. You've ruined everything,' she yelled.

'You're in shock. It's a lot to take on board but don't let it destroy us.'

'There is no us,' she retorted, shrugging herself free of his embrace before yanking open the door and storming out.

'Carly,' he yelled, chasing after her.

'Leave me alone,' she snarled with such vehemence he halted in his tracks.

All he could do was watch her retreat down the street, head down, hands shoved into her jacket pockets, long hair streaming out behind her.

He couldn't believe he'd lost her already.

37

That night in the pub, Carly drank more heavily than she normally would but, to her annoyance, it didn't seem to affect her. Despite wanting to obliterate recent events, they still swirled endlessly around in her head, the white wine doing nothing to dull them down. This should be a time for celebration. Their family had risen higher than they thought possible, they were earning even more money and finally they had negotiated a truce with the Alexanders, but she was unable to find the joy the rest of her family were obviously feeling. Eddie and Harry were already drunk and were laughing loudly, arms slung around each other's shoulders. In fact, most of the pub was drunk, Eddie having bought several rounds for everyone. Dean, for once, was enjoying the company of a woman in a short, tight dress that flashed plenty of thigh and cleavage, making Carly even more miserable. It was as though he'd forgotten her already.

Jane had realised that something was wrong. The woman Dean was all over was so opposite to his usual type that she couldn't understand why he was bothering with her, unless he was pished, but she knew he didn't like to get drunk.

'I wish Uncle Eddie would stop splashing the cash about,' Jane told her sister.

'Hmm,' was Carly's reply as she stared sadly into her glass.

'Still, it's good to see him enjoying himself after everything that's gone on recently.'

'Suppose.'

'That's it. You're telling me what's going on right now.'

Finally, she had her sister's attention.

'Nothing's going on,' said Carly, raising her head.

'You're bloody miserable. You haven't been yourself recently and I want to know why.'

'I miss Da'.'

'We all do,' she said more gently. 'And I get that but I know there's more to it.'

'No, there isn't. I'm just tired. How's it going with Jennifer?' said Carly, wanting to change the subject.

'Great.' She smiled. 'By the way, I'm staying at her place tonight and Rose is at her friend's, so you'll have the flat to yourself.'

'Oh,' said Carly, forcing a smile. 'Good.' She'd never once spent the night alone. Either her family members had been with her or she'd stayed with friends. The thought of being on her own rather unnerved her.

'Are you sure you'll be all right?' said Jane, seeing her expression. 'I don't have to stay at Jennifer's.'

'Course you do, she's your girlfriend and you need your privacy. I'll be fine.'

'But you haven't been yourself lately and I'm worried.' Jane was dismayed when the shutters came down again.

'I'm fine,' said Carly.

'But—'

'I need the loo.'

'Carly...'

Her sister rose and hurried into the ladies. Just what the hell was going on?

Jane turned to ask Dean if he knew what was wrong with her sister – after all, they were close – but she saw he had his tongue stuck down the tart's throat. It seemed he'd finally given up on Carly, which could only be a good thing. Was that what was wrong with her sister? Was she jealous?

Her question was answered when Carly emerged from the toilets a few minutes later and went rigid when she saw Dean kissing another woman. Her eyes filled with so much hurt it made Jane's heart ache.

She stormed back over to the table, snatched up her jacket and stormed out without a word. Jane didn't try to stop her; it would have been cruel when it was clear she was desperate to escape. Anger filled her as Dean continued to kiss the tart, who looked cheap and was nothing in comparison to Carly. She knew it wasn't fair of her to judge him, he was a single man and was entitled to kiss whoever he liked but he'd hurt her sister and she wouldn't let him get away with it.

'Oops,' she said, reaching across the table and knocking his pint into his lap, splattering the tart too. 'Sorry,' she added without the slightest apology in her tone.

This drew Harry's and Eddie's attention to the fact that he'd been kissing a woman. They both cheered and congratulated him while Derek approached with a bar towel, which he hurled at him. Jane hadn't been the only one who'd noticed how hurt Carly had been.

'Thanks.' Dean frowned, noting the anger in the older man's eyes.

'Wipe your face too,' Derek told him. 'You've got cheap lipstick all over your mouth.'

'Err, this isn't cheap lipstick,' said the tart in an irritating, high-pitched voice, the sort Dean usually hated. 'It cost six quid.'

'It looks like you've smeared spam all over your lips,' retorted Derek before returning to the bar.

She scowled at him before leaning into Dean to kiss his cheek. 'I'll just go and clean myself up, gorgeous.'

'Aye, all right,' he muttered, wiping his jeans with the towel. When she'd gone, he looked to Jane. 'You did that on purpose.'

'Aye, I did. You hurt my sister's feelings.'

'Good.'

Her eyes flared. 'What did you say?'

'She hurt me. She doesn't want me.'

'Of course she does. You didn't see her face when she saw you kissing the slag.'

'Candice is not a slag. She's a nice girl.'

'You don't usually lie, Dean,' she said, gaze hardening.

'Listen,' he said, lowering his voice. 'I havenae been with a woman for months because I've been waiting for Carly. Well, she's made it very clear that she doesn't want me, so I'm going to scratch an itch that's been annoying me for a very long time. Is that so bad?'

'If you sleep with Candice your itch won't just be metaphorical.' She got to her feet with a haughty look. 'I'm going to Jennifer's. Do what you like.'

Dean slumped back sulkily in his chair as Jane left, mulling over her words. He was almost tempted to run after Carly, until his brother and Eddie sat down on either side of him.

'Well done, son.' Eddie grinned, patting his shoulder. 'That Candice is a cracker.'

'You think so?' he replied.

'Aye,' said Harry. 'I've made a play for her before but she turned me down. It seems she prefers brains over looks.'

'You've done well, son,' said Eddie. 'Finally, you've found someone to take your mind off Carly. Just make sure it stays off her.'

'Aye, I will,' he mumbled, his father's words dampening the urge to chase after her.

As both Eddie and Harry were drunk, they failed to notice the misery in Dean's eyes.

'Here comes your lady,' said Eddie. 'We'll leave you to it.'

They retook their seats and Candice resumed her place by Dean's side.

'So.' She smiled at him. 'Do you want to come back to my place? My flatmate's staying over at her boyfriend's tonight, so we'll have it to ourselves.'

Dean took in Candice's false eyelashes that looked like spider's legs, her fake orange tan, the clingy dress and hair extensions. She was everything he didn't like in a woman but she was here, which was more than Carly was.

'Aye, all right.'

'Great,' she said.

He took her hand and led her to the door before he changed his mind.

'Thank God for that,' Eddie told Harry as they watched the couple leave. 'I was worried we'd have incest in the family but that lassie has taken his mind off Carly.'

'Aye, for tonight anyway,' replied Harry. 'But I doubt he'll fall in love with her.'

'He doesn't need to. She'll make him realise there are other women out there.'

Harry wasn't so sure; he knew his brother's feelings for Carly were strong but only time would tell. Anyway, he was determined not to worry about anything tonight. He smiled at a woman across the room who was giving him the eye. He had his own wild oats to sow.

* * *

Carly slunk home, refusing to give in to the tears wanting to fall. She knew she had no right to complain. She'd had her chance with Dean and she'd rejected him. He could sleep with whatever tacky slag he wanted to. But it still bloody hurt. She hadn't expected him to move on so quickly, not after how much he'd professed to love her.

The thought of returning to the empty flat was a depressing one, so she was tramping the darkening streets, pondering on whether to visit one of her friends, but most of them had kids and the last thing she wanted right then was to be surrounded by wailing weans. She could pick up a bottle of wine and a pizza and watch a tacky film to try and take her mind off Dean.

Just as she'd decided on this course of action, a voice called her name.

She looked round to see Jack Alexander jogging across the road towards her.

'Not you,' she tutted before carrying on her way.

He hurried after her. 'Can we talk?'

'We've nothing to say to each other.'

'I think we do,' he said, falling into step alongside her.

She stopped and rounded on him. 'Have you any idea of the awkward position you've put me in?'

'I know and I'm sorry but it's better you know.'

'It's bloody well not. I'll be in so much trouble if anyone finds out I know you worked against your family and that you have a spy in Rod's camp.'

'No one will find out. If they do, I'm fucking dead.'

'We shouldn't even be seen talking to each other; we're still on opposing sides, even though we've made a truce.'

'Sexy, isn't it?' he said with a mischievous grin.

'No, it's not.'

'Where are you going?'

'Home.'

'Where's the rest of your family?'

'In the pub. Why, are you going to run to your family and tell them I'm alone and vulnerable?' she snapped before continuing on her way. To her chagrin, he followed.

'You know I won't do that.'

'Actually, I don't. Leave me alone.'

'What's wrong? You look really upset.'

'Nothing's wrong. I'm just tired.'

'It doesn't look like it to me.'

'It's none of your business.'

'Fine, you're right. But you look like you could use someone to talk to.'

'I don't want to talk to anyone. I want to go home and get drunk.'

'Sounds like a plan. I'll come with you.'

Carly rolled her eyes. 'God, you're annoying.'

'So I've been told. I also really like you. It's why I told you my secret.'

'And if you piss me off I'll use it to destroy you.'

'No, you won't.'

'How can you be so sure?'

'Because I think you like me too. A bit anyway,' he added when she gave him a withering look. 'Dean's hurt you, hasn't he?'

Carly didn't speak, she didn't trust herself to.

'I know you have feelings for each other, that's pretty clear. What did he do, get off with someone else?'

'Yes,' she muttered through gritted teeth.

'Then he's an idiot. You're the best-looking woman in Haghill.'

'It's not helped me so far.'

'Just stop,' he said taking her hand.

'Get off,' she said, tugging it free.

'There's no need to be so angry, I don't want to hurt you.'

'I can't help being angry,' she retorted, furious tears stinging her eyes. 'My da's had to go into a home, my family was attacked and the man I love rejected me.'

'You love Dean?' he said gently.

She nodded, swallowing down the emotion wanting to pour out of her.

'I didn't realise.'

'And now I'm standing in the middle of a street at night talking to a man who tried to kill someone.'

'You think you've got it bad but at least people aren't constantly reminding you of the biggest mistake you ever made.'

'Because slicing someone's stomach open tends to stick in people's memory,' she snapped back.

'You're right, it does. I could have knocked out the twat but I didn't, I went too far but I was young, stupid and scared. I've never told anyone before that I was terrified during that attack. I really thought he was going to kill me, so I lashed out. It could have happened to anyone and I've got to spend the rest of my life with that bad decision hanging around my neck like a fucking ten tonne weight.'

Carly looked contrite. 'I'm sorry for that.'

'Yeah, well, I've only myself to blame. Then I got released and was given a second chance only for my evil bitch of a cousin to rope me into something that could send me back to prison or worse. Things were really shit, until I met this beautiful woman who knocked me off my fucking feet. That's you, by the way,' he added when she regarded him uncertainly.

'Oh.'

'Yeah, you're younger than me but I don't care. If Dean messed up his chance, then all the better for me. Now, I propose we get a bottle of wine from the shop and go back to your place. I want to take you to bed.'

She blinked at him in surprise. 'You don't beat around the bush, do you?'

'Life's too short.' He took her hand and raised it to his lips. 'So, what do you say?'

Carly was sorely tempted. 'I don't understand you. Sometimes you come across as really dangerous and sometimes really nice. You're like Jekyll and Hyde.'

'That's because I'm a bit of both.'

'And which one will I get?'

His gaze darkened. 'You'll have to wait and see.' He leaned into her, his eyes pinning her. 'Are you ready to take a chance?'

After what she'd been through recently, the darkness in that gaze spoke to her. He was so close they could have kissed. Excitement thrummed through her body. He smelled good too, his scent fresh but masculine.

'Aye, I am,' she breathed.

His lips curled into a smile.

'But we'll go back to my place just to talk and we'll take it from there. If you think you can just take what you want, you'll get your baws twisted.'

'I shall behave like a gentleman,' he said with a bow, making her smile.

Carly made Jack wait outside the shop while she went in to get a bottle of wine, not wanting anyone to see them together because it would undoubtedly get back to her family. As she browsed the shelves, she considered the wisdom of what she was doing. If her family knew they'd hit the roof, telling her she was putting herself in danger. For all she knew, Jack's family had told him to seduce her, but she was getting sick of organising her life around what other people thought she should do. It was up to her who she slept with, no one else and she did find Jack very attractive. She knew part of why she wanted to do this was revenge against Dean. No doubt he was having sex with that slag, so why shouldn't she do the same with a man she liked? She didn't feel like she would be using Jack; he was shrewd enough to know that would be part of it, it was why he'd decided to proposition her now. Bugger it, she was going for it and if it did turn out to be a mistake then at least it was *her* mistake, no one else's.

There was a question in Jack's eyes as he watched her exit the shop with a bottle of white wine in a carrier bag. It was the same look he'd given her when she'd come across him waiting for her outside the ladies' changing rooms at the gym.

'No, I won't do a runner,' she told him.

'I did wonder. Feel free, if you like, I'm not the type of bloke to force a woman into anything.' The naughtiness returned to his gaze. 'Although there's a good chance I would chase after you.'

Carly's cheeks flushed. She thought that sounded rather hot. 'And what would you do if you caught me?'

'I don't think I'd be able to keep my promise to be a gentleman.'

'I'm no' sure you can keep it anyway but I'm willing to give you a chance. Just so you know, you only get one chance with me.'

'So I've already heard.' He smiled.

They continued on their way to Carly's flat, and she braced herself as she unlocked the door and stepped inside, wondering if he would attack her or if this was another set-up by his family, but he followed her inside and waited while she closed and locked the door behind her.

'Alone at last,' he said with another dark smile.

Carly didn't reply as she removed her jacket, hung it up on one of the hooks by the door and removed her shoes. Jack followed her example and they entered the kitchen, Carly closing the blinds before switching on the light.

'I get the feeling you're ashamed of me,' he said.

'Not ashamed. I just don't want this getting back to my family.'

'What would they do if they knew?'

'First, they'd turn you into mush, then they'd tell me how stupid I am. What about yours?'

'Well, they'd turn me into mush too. Or they'd kill me. One or the other. They wouldn't even bother to talk.'

'Sounds just like the Alexander family,' she said, taking the bottle of wine out of the bag and unscrewing the lid.

She produced a couple of glasses and began to pour. Before she'd finished, Jack came up behind her, rested his hands on her hips and ran his lips down the side of her neck. The gesture was light and sensuous and made her tingle.

'You've spilt some,' he whispered in her ear when her hand shook and dripped wine onto the worktop.

'I don't care,' she breathed as his hands slid under her top and began lightly stroking her stomach while his lips continued their delightful work.

She dumped the bottle on the counter and leaned back against him as her body responded immediately to his touch. Carly had to admit that the illicitness of the situation only made it even more exciting. Part of her was saying that this was madness and it wasn't too late to back out but her body was telling her to disregard that whiny voice.

She tilted her head to kiss him and he moved his hands down to her jeans. Carly gasped when he slid his hand inside her panties.

'Someone's been neglected for too long,' he murmured into her mouth.

She turned in his arms to face him and kissed him hard, locking her arms around his neck. Grasping the hem of his jumper, she pulled it up, Jack raising his arms and she cast it aside. His body was as athletic as it had appeared at the gym, only now she could see the tattoo on his chest was of a laughing demon surrounded with flames. Even the bulging eyeballs contained fire and they felt to burn right into her.

'Do you like it?' he said.

Carly dragged her gaze off the tattoo and onto his face. Once again, his eyes had taken on that dark, dangerous look. She hadn't been wrong when she'd said he was like Jekyll and Hyde.

'It's very striking,' she replied.

'I had it done when I was released from prison. I have a friend in Bradford who's an amazing artist. He did my other tattoos.'

'He's very talented.'

'If you ever want one, I can get you a good rate.'

He rolled up her top slightly to expose her smooth midriff. 'Perhaps one along here,' he said, sliding his finger across her stomach, just under her belly button.

His touch made her tingle, but she was acutely aware of the fact that it was the exact place where he'd once cut someone open.

'Or perhaps here,' he continued, moving his hand around to her back and running his fingers up her spine. He smiled when her head fell back and she moaned.

He removed her jumper and it joined his own on the floor.

'So beautiful,' he whispered, reaching round to unfasten her bra.

That joined the growing pile of discarded clothing and he took a moment to admire her. She was so long and lithe, her smooth skin the colour of ivory.

Jack kissed her from her stomach all the way up her body, taking his time, enjoying teasing her. By the time he reached her mouth, her cheeks were flushed and she was covered in a fine sheen of sweat.

'Last chance to change your mind,' he whispered in her ear.

Even the feel of his breath on her skin was enough to make her gasp. Carly's eyes rolled open and were bright with determination as well as desire.

'I won't change my mind,' she replied.

Jack smiled and unfastened her jeans. He took her right there over the kitchen unit where her family made cups of tea and coffee. As the powerful sensations built to a crescendo, she threw her arms wide, knocking over a jar of coffee. A box of teabags was sent flying across the unit and the mug tree was knocked over, one mug rolling to the edge of the counter before falling off and shattering on the floor. As Carly came loudly, tossing back her head, Jack arched his spine and groaned, slamming his left palm down onto the counter, sending the spoon rest clattering onto the hob.

Neither of them spoke for a full minute, the only sound their frantic breathing as it gradually slowed.

'Well, that was a treat.' He grinned, kissing her neck.

'Aye it was,' she said. God, she felt good. That awful tension had finally gone from her body and every muscle was warm and relaxed. 'We've made a mess of the kitchen though.'

'Sod the mess,' he said, kissing her again.

He released her and straightened up, stretching. Carly did the same, wincing at the ache in her lower back, which had been pressed against the unit. No doubt she'd have bruises tomorrow.

'What?' he said when she regarded him curiously.

'It's my turn to wonder if you're going to run out on me.'

'You must be joking. Finally, I get Carly Savage right where I want her. No way am I going anywhere, unless you want me to?'

'No, you can stay, although you will have to leave early before my sisters get home. Sorry.'

'Don't be, I understand. Right, where's your bedroom?'

'Down the hall, first on the left.'

'Let's go then,' he said, picking up the glasses. 'You get the bottle.'

'Okay.' She smiled.

They curled up together in her bed, Carly glad she'd exchanged her single bed for a small double when she'd started earning more money.

After enjoying a couple of glasses of wine, during which they laughed and talked, avoiding the sensitive topic of their families, the Glaswegian underworld and Jack's time in prison, they had sex again before falling asleep. Carly was a little surprised when Jack wrapped her in his arms. She hadn't enjoyed the warmth of a man for so long she found herself smiling into his bare chest as his fingers gently stroked her back in that sensual way of his.

She was jolted from a deep, satisfying sleep by a knock at the door.

Carly sat bolt upright, instantly alert.

'Are you expecting anyone?' said Jack, sitting up with her.

'At two o'clock in the morning?' she retorted, glancing at the clock on her bedside cabinet.

They went silent when the knock came again.

'Carly,' called a voice. 'Are you in there?'

'It's Dean,' she said.

'Carly,' he repeated, louder.

'What are you going to do?' said Jack.

Carly didn't reply immediately as she considered her response. Did the fact that Dean was here mean he'd dumped that tart? Hope rose inside her, until the pain of not only his lying to her about something so serious but of him kissing that slag in the pub returned. Had he just come from that awful woman's bed thinking he could climb straight into hers?

Carly's face turned to stone. 'Nothing.'

They nestled back into bed together, Jack smiling slyly up at the ceiling as he held her in his arms.

The sound of shouting soon stopped, he surmised because Dean had given up and gone on his way.

You blew your chance, Dean, he thought to himself. *Now she's mine. This woman's a fucking powerhouse. She's not realised yet that she's the driving force behind her family, not her older sister or uncle. Together, we'll be stronger than both our families combined and we'll take everything from Rod Tallan.*

Jack held her tighter in his arms as he imagined a future where the whole city would be afraid of him. No one would dare mention his past again.

Carly drifted back off to sleep, blissfully unaware of Jack's dark plans for her future.

ABOUT THE AUTHOR

Heather Atkinson is the author of over fifty books - predominantly in the crime fiction genre. Although Lancashire born and bred she now lives with her family, including twin teenage daughters, on the beautiful west coast of Scotland.

Sign up to Heather Atkinson's mailing list here for news, competitions and updates on future books.

Visit Heather's website: https://www.heatheratkinsonbooks.com/

Follow Heather on social media:

 twitter.com/HeatherAtkinsoɪ

 instagram.com/heathercrimeauthor

 bookbub.com/authors/heather-atkinson

 facebook.com/booksofheatheratkinson

ALSO BY HEATHER ATKINSON

Wicked Girls

The Savage Sisters Series

Savage Sisters

A Savage Feud

The Gallowburn Series

Blood Brothers

Bad Blood

Blood Ties

Blood Pact

The Alardyce Series

The Missing Girls of Alardyce House

The Cursed Heir

His Fatal Legacy

Evil at Alardyce House

PEAKY READERS

GANG LOYALTIES. DARK SECRETS.
BLOODY REVENGE.

A READER COMMUNITY FOR
GANGLAND CRIME THRILLER FANS!

DISCOVER PAGE-TURNING NOVELS
FROM YOUR FAVOURITE AUTHORS
AND MEET NEW FRIENDS.

JOIN OUR BOOK CLUB
FACEBOOK GROUP

BIT.LY/PEAKYREADERSFB

SIGN UP TO OUR
NEWSLETTER

BIT.LY/PEAKYREADERSNEWS

Boldwood

Boldwood Books is an award-winning fiction publishing company seeking out the best stories from around the world.

Find out more at www.boldwoodbooks.com

Join our reader community for brilliant books, competitions and offers!

Follow us
@BoldwoodBooks
@TheBoldBookClub

Sign up to our weekly deals newsletter

https://bit.ly/BoldwoodBNewsletter

Printed in Great Britain
by Amazon

33415197R00228